gethsemane hall

gethsemane hall

by

David Annandale

DUNDURN
TORONTO

Editor: Allister Thompson
Design: Courtney Horner
Printer: Webcom

Library and Archives Canada Cataloguing in Publication

Annandale, David, 1967-
    Gethsemane Hall / David Annandale.

Issued also in electronic formats.
ISBN 978-1-4597-0225-7

    I. Title.

PS8551.N527G48 2012   C813'.6   C2011-906601-7

1   2   3   4   5   16   15   14   13   12

  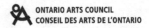

We acknowledge the support of the **Canada Council for the Arts** and the **Ontario Arts Council** for our publishing program. We also acknowledge the financial support of the **Government of Canada** through the **Canada Book Fund** and **Livres Canada Books**, and the **Government of Ontario** through the **Ontario Book Publishing Tax Credit** and the **Ontario Media Development Corporation**.

Care has been taken to trace the ownership of copyright material used in this book. The author and the publisher welcome any information enabling them to rectify any references or credits in subsequent editions.

J. Kirk Howard, President

Printed and bound in Canada.
www.dundurn.com

Visit us at
Dundurn.com
Definingcanada.ca
@dundurnpress
Facebook.com/dundurnpress

Dundurn
3 Church Street, Suite 500
Toronto, Ontario, Canada
M5E 1M2

Gazelle Book Services Limited
White Cross Mills
High Town, Lancaster, England
LA1 4XS

Dundurn
2250 Military Road
Tonawanda, NY
U.S.A. 14150

For Margaux, always.
And to the memory of Douglas Payne.

acknowledgements

This is a book whose existence owes more than these acknowledgements can express to the love and support of my family members in Canada and in England. My thanks, for putting me up (and putting up with me) as I traipsed around on my research trips, to Douglas and Hazel Payne; Joan Payne; and Stuart, Val, and Claire Payne. For always being there, thank you to my parents, Eric and Eleanor; to my sister, Michelle; and to my brother, Robert. For many shared hours of watching horror films, and for keeping me on my toes, and for the wonderful intangibles of family, my thanks to Kelan Young and Veronica Young. And for *everything* (and quite a bit more besides), thank you to my wife, Margaux Watt.

My thanks also to my agent, Robert Lecker, who is making so much come to pass for me.

Finally, special thanks to everyone at Dundurn and Snowbooks for making the dream of this book a reality, and to Allister Thompson and Anna Torborg for the superb editing. The story in these pages is dark, but the story behind them has been a joy.

chapter one

the lessons

The first lesson.

The night was a slick of oil. The darkness clung and smothered. Beneath it was a roil of sick colours. The slick was thinner in town, more diluted. A false comfort.

Pete Adams sat in The Leaping Stag. The Friday night carvery was in full swing. The night was blasting wind and squalls of rain, and the patio was closed. Adams sat next to the French windows. He would have preferred to sit in the centre of the pub, but the weather had called one and all to warmth and companionship. The Stag had been crowded since early afternoon. His plate was heaped high with beef, ham, turkey, and buffet vegetables, and he wouldn't leave until he'd eaten. That was the deal he had made with himself. He almost laughed. He was delaying the inevitable, and his tactics were pathetic. He poked his fork into a piece of turkey, turned it over, but didn't eat. He wasn't hungry. He sipped his Boddington's instead. He savoured the taste, already missing it.

Someone told a good joke two tables over. A birthday was happening, and there was a round dozen friends sitting together, their laughter rising over the collective, hearty roar of the pub. Adams soaked up the noise and loved it more desperately than the ale.

John Porter stopped by Adams's table. Outside, the wind gusted hard against the doors, rattling them. "You're in for a blustery walk home, Mr. Adams," the Stag's owner commented, then laughed, a deep baritone sound bouncing in the echo chamber of his chest. He always laughed as if his every statement, no matter how banal, were a punchline.

Adams's smile was pained, but he treasured the guffaw, held it close, a precious gift. "Oh, I think I'll manage," he said and kept the wince from his eyes.

The second lesson.

"Your daughter misses you," his wife said.

The line worked. Richard Gray felt the guilt of long absence, felt it as a sharp tooth in his lower chest. He couldn't tell from Lillian's tone if she were making a point or just stating a fact. He didn't know if she wanted him to feel the tooth. The difference hardly mattered; the tooth struck home. "I miss her," he replied, after clearing his throat. "I miss both of you."

"Then come home."

"I can't. Not now." He was calling from a makeshift office in the town of Abéché, in Chad. He still had the smell of the refugee camp in his nostrils, that blend of malnutrition, disease, desperation, death. He would be back there in the morning, doing what he could, which felt like nothing, and the next day he would be off again with Patrick Hudson, into the Darfur region of Sudan, where the stench was stronger, where the blend was hatred, rape, murder. Genocide. *Where is God?* he kept asking Hudson, his faith turning slippery. *We're here, aren't we?* Hudson answered, firm and sure even with his eyes wide open.

Gray envied him, needed his strength, and couldn't abandon him now. Not now.

Lillian sighed. "I understand, but ..." She paused. Her tone was kind, which only made things worse. She took a breath, and asked, "If not now, when? Do you really think things are going to improve?"

UN resolutions. International agreements. The Sudanese government making commitments. Intervals of lull and false-spring hope. And then the butcher machine revving up once more. How could he think the curtain would ever be brought down over the slaughter? *If not now, when?* He'd been here almost two years, home to England only for Christmas. Jill was fourteen now. He was seeing her grow through time-lapse photography. If he stayed away much longer, would he return to find his child gone, replaced by a distant woman? Right now, she missed him. Then his mind was flooded again with images of distended bellies and eyes weeping thick and milky tears. He couldn't leave now. Not now.

Before he spoke again, he listened to the sounds of home on the other end of the line. Lillian was on her cell, and he could hear traffic. "Where are you?" he asked.

"On our way back from Hammersmith. Jill was at a concert." They had a flat in Chelsea.

"Do you think you could swing by the office?"

"Richard, it's very late."

"I know. I'm sorry, but there are some papers we need faxed before we cross back into Sudan, and ... please?"

There was a moment of silence instead of a sigh. "All right."

"Thank you."

"Richard."

"Yes?"

"You aren't going to get yourself killed, are you?"

Time, gentleman.
  Yes.

Adams stood up. As he shouldered his way to the cash register, Roger Bellingham touched his elbow. Adams stopped, exchanged a long look with the old man. Bellingham's eighty-five-year-old eyes were sunken with the exhaustion of decades of resistance to the undertow. He searched Adams's face, and his lips pursed slightly, as if recognizing an unavoidable truth. "Do you want company?" he asked.

Adams couldn't answer at first, his throat closing at the magnitude of the offer. "Do you still have a choice?" he asked.

Bellingham hesitated, looking even more tired. With a struggle, he said, "Yes."

"Then stay here." Adams shook his head. "But thank you."

There was a parking spot on Chiltern Street, across from the building that housed Ties of Hope. Lillian pulled in. "Are you coming up?" she asked Jill. Jill shrugged but opened her door and climbed out of the car. Lillian almost spoke to her daughter's silence, but held back. Jill wasn't being sullen. That wasn't her style. She was upset. She shuffled across the street, playing with the lighter she had brought to the concert, flick flick flick. Lillian replayed her end of the phone call in her mind and bit her lip. She could hear now the underlying accusation in her tone, and realized her frightening choice of words. *You aren't going to get yourself killed, are you?* What a stupid thing to say. What a stupid way to end the call. No *I love you* to reassure Jill. Idiot. *She's still a child. Fine way to frighten her.*

Lillian got out of the car and followed Jill to the building, pulling her keys from her purse.

Adams paid for his untouched meal. "Have a good night, then," Melody Searwood said as she handed him his change.

"Good night," Adams said and lingered over her face an extra second. He focused on one lock of her long red hair. It curled against her cheek and stopped a mere tickle away from the corner of her mouth. He loved that detail and held it tight as he stepped out into wind.

Lillian squinted at the keys. Little of the streetlamp's light reached the shadows of the doorway. "Will Dad be okay?" Jill asked.

"You know he will be," Lillian answered, speaking a lie and a command. She found the right key and let them in.

The storm had no rain, but it had voice. It roared at Adams as he walked down Hawkesfield Road, away from the Stag. It pushed at him, flapped his clothes, and made his eyes tear. And somehow, he still left Roseminster behind faster than usual. The night thickened.

The brainchild of Patrick Hudson, nurtured by Richard, and blessed by the Anglican Church, Ties of Hope had grown out of the two men's missionary work. Hudson had the dream; Richard had financed it into being. They had both sweated it into something that clung tenaciously to the idea that it was changing reality for the better. When she wasn't worried for Richard or missing him, Lillian admired the dream. She loved and smiled at the sight of the two friends in full flight. Hudson was a head shorter than Richard and looked half his weight. It wasn't that Richard was overweight; it was that Hudson was so thin, he ran serious risks in a stiff breeze. Hudson's light brown hair was wild curls. It and his beard framed his face with a permanent explosion of surprise. Richard, darker, was clean-shaven and close-cut. His suits were conservative. Jill teased him for being a stuffed shirt. Richard responded that he liked his shirts stuffed. When he and Hudson were together and disappeared into the shared mental space of their projects, Jill would walk through their bubble and make pointed comments about Jeeves and the Hippie. Lillian couldn't fault her daughter's powers of observation.

Lillian sometimes joined in the teasing, but she didn't joke about Ties of Hope. Oxfam with a faith component: that was how Hudson had described his vision. World Vision without the coercion. Lillian knew he still wasn't wild about the name, but was making do. He had first come up with Clasping Hands, which Jill had immediately converted into Grasping Hands. Ties of Hope, though awkward, seemed immune from Jill. Once, Lillian had seen something lurking in Richard's eyes, and she had thought he was going to make a crack. He'd been back for Christmas, and things overseas had not been going well. The joke, Lillian had thought, was going to be bitter, but Richard had held it in.

She and Jill took the stairs to the third floor, turning lights on as they went.

Adams arrived on the grounds of Gethsemane Hall. He nodded in greeting and acceptance.

They reached the third floor. The call continued to plague Lillian. She was upset for her own sake, now. She wanted to speak to Richard again.

Adams looked at his piles of equipment, stacked up in the library. He was too resigned to feel contempt.

These things happen.

The building was an old one. So were its pipes. Metal gives. Gas leaks. The offices of Ties of Hope were full. Lillian opened the door. Her nose wrinkled at the smell. Jill played with her lighter.

Now he was on the roof of the gatehouse tower. One step, one step, one step, and he was at the parapet. He climbed up. The tips of his shoes hung over the drop. Adams looked out into the night. It was thick with the truth he had climbed up here to flee. He tried to think of the curl of Melody's hair. He failed. Time to lie to himself one last time. Time to treasure a dream of escape. He took another step.

Two hours after Adams applied his lesson, the phone rang, a bell summoning Richard Gray to a school of his own.

chapter two

homecoming

She had left Kansas a long time ago. Now she found that it really was true that there was no place like home. There wasn't a single place that felt like home. Not anymore, now that Langley was about to turn its back on her. Louise Meacham sat in the office of the secretary to Jim Korda, director of the CIA. She was waiting for her summons and her execution. No place like home.

Not that home itself had ever been where the heart was. Meacham had grown up in Brooklyn, trapped in a walk-up apartment, the walls of which had pulsed with the rhythms of her father's fists even when he wasn't actually using them on her mother. Meacham had prayed each night for flight, but her mother, more terrified of the uncertainties of loneliness than the certainties of her husband's brutality, had stayed. For Meacham, home was where the hurt was. At thirteen, her adolescent fury took the shape of a supreme hope, the longing for the One Good Thing that would make all things well: her mother dead and her father in jail. When it became clear that the One Good Thing was not going to happen, not before it was too late for the children, Meacham learned a lesson that, over the following decades, she grew to think of as the Next Best Thing: know that the world is shit and don't wait for it to transmute into gold.

At fifteen, she might as well have been forty. She fled, taking her three younger sisters and baby brother. She found work. She held the new unit together. Barely. Menial labour and premature adulthood wore her to the bone, but she applied the Next Best Thing and beat the world into submission. When baby Brad was old enough to look after himself, she finally started college, years late but with a determination that ate up the lost time. She forced the world to give her a life. Pummelled, the world gave in just that much. By the time she had her political science degree, her rage at her parents had transmuted to a cold understanding. But not forgiveness — that would never come. They had died within six months of each other. Meacham found out only when the estate lawyers wrote to her. She didn't grieve.

Her master's thesis in poli-sci was a defence of realpolitik so hard-headed it was almost brutal. It came to the attention of the right people. When she was twenty-five, she was recruited into the CIA, and she had thought, until now, that she had found a kind of home. It wasn't Kansas. It was more like Oz re-imagined by Sauron, but her work and her world-view were a good fit. She went in with no idealism, and so she suffered no disillusionment. She worked her way up, chipping through glass ceilings. By the time she made station chief in Geneva, she was the supreme weathercaster. She could sense shitstorms before they even formed and knew to take cover.

Her system worked to perfection for thirty years. But when it broke down, it broke down all at once. She still wasn't sure what had happened, but the body count was in the triple digits, and the embarrassment to Washington, which was what really mattered, was enormous. She had walked away, but not fast enough. Ducking the aftermath wasn't doing her any good. The message to meet with Korda had been waiting for her when she returned to the States.

Its wording was curt, its tone dismissive. The implication: she was a small annoyance in the big picture, one to be squashed when she fit into the calendar. She began to think that the one thing worse than *being* collateral damage was *knowing* that you were.

She'd been waiting now for forty-five minutes. Korda's secretary was a woman fifteen years her junior, but she had told Meacham to sit down as if she were a child summoned to the principal's office and hadn't looked at her since. Not a good sign. Meacham, knowing the kind of day this was going to be, had armoured herself for battle. She wore a grey pantsuit. Her eyes were grey. A decade ago, in her mid-forties, her hair had followed suit. She'd let it. The combination usually worked in her favour: grey lady equals iron equals formidable. She'd learned how to disembowel with a look. She'd need all her strength on this day, when she was beneath a peon's notice. Finally, the secretary's phone rang. The woman answered and looked at Meacham for the second time. "He'll see you now," she intoned.

Korda was tapping his finger on a report when she walked into his office. "Close the door," he said. He gave the cover one last rap and folded his hands. "So," he said. "What are we going to do with you?"

In Roseminster, Lord Richard Gray stood on the porch of St. Rose's church and shook hands. The last time he had accepted the good wishes of so many, meant in quite this personal way, had been on the same spot, at Jill's baptism. "Thank you," he muttered, again and again. The words were as meaningless a rote gesture as the handshakes. Through the suffocating clouds of numbness came lightning flashes of cold, bitter anger. Was he supposed to be receiving comfort from this dog-and-pony show? Did these people really think they were doing him the slightest bit of good? *This is for your benefit,* he thought. *Not mine.* They came, they shed their tears, and they returned to their lives, relieved that the tragedy was not theirs, that their grief was contained within the period of the funeral service.

The parade finally finished. Gray mumbled his empty thanks one more time, and the last of the mourners filed off. Gray watched him go and couldn't remember who the man was. One of Lillian's relatives? An old friend of his? He didn't care. There was no curiosity. The clouds in his head were dark as well as thick, and they worked to block any thought that wasn't part of the tangle of misery, loss, and guilt.

"Richard," Patrick Hudson said.

Gray turned his head. Hudson stood with the Reverend John Woodhead. The concern in Woodhead's eyes was genuine but professional. Hudson's grief came the closest to reflecting Gray's own. "Thank you for the service, Reverend," Gray said, still on autopilot.

"May God comfort you," Woodhead said.

The rage was sudden, surprising, enormous. It burned off the clouds and filled his mind with its clarity. *Comfort me? Comfort me? Would He enjoy that? Is that what pleasures His Divine Majesty? To destroy you so He can comfort you? No,* Gray thought. *No.* He would not accept comfort given on such sadistic terms. He held the anger inside, though, and nodded to Woodhead. But he felt the clarity grow sharper yet, approaching epiphany. He turned and walked away from the church.

Hudson joined him. "Where are you going?" he asked.

"Home."

"Here? I don't think the police will let you, not yet."

No, probably not. He'd forgotten about that. He had forgotten that death had come calling on him three times that night, not just two. The third death was hard to keep in mind because it was an irritation, not a wound. He'd never even met Pete Adams, had only spoken two him on the phone a couple of times. The bulk of their contact had been letters or email. He felt regret, but had no room for grief for a man he didn't know. Not now. "I want to see the place, anyway," he said.

"I'll drive you."

Gray shook his head. "I need the air."

Hudson fell into step beside him. Gray eyed the stone walls as they walked. It was the moss that drew his attention. It was the detail that drove home just how lush England was. During the endless months in Sudan and Chad, he'd grown used to the desiccation. He associated the desert with death. Here, life was an exaltation of green, the air a nectar of temperate humidity. He was home, but the abundance was almost an affront, not a comfort.

Hudson said, "You looked angry back there."

"Did I?" Gray answered, giving nothing.

"When John mentioned God's comfort." When Gray said nothing, Hudson continued. "I don't suppose this is something you care to hear right now —"

"You suppose correctly."

Hudson ploughed on. "Don't turn away. This is when you need your faith most of all."

Gray snorted. "And where was God when I needed Him most of all?"

"He's with you now." Hudson's voice was strong with gentle sincerity.

They walked for a minute in silence. Gray didn't snap back at Hudson. He was too tired, too numb, and coming from Hudson, the words didn't have the empty-tin ring of platitudes. They never did. Hudson was just enough of an iconoclast that he had always known the priesthood itself wasn't for him. He still would have made a good one, Gray had always thought. He did make a fine missionary. He was the man Gray had aspired to be, and over the years he had followed Hudson's example. He had also followed his friend's dreams. They had done good. They had built Ties of Hope into something real and effective. He had felt what he thought was the genuine warmth of faith. But now? Jean Paul Richter said it: *Every soul in this vast corpse-trench of the universe is utterly alone.*

They approached the drive to Gethsemane Hall. The police were still investigating. The barriers were still up. Home was barred to him. Gray didn't rage. The Hall was home only in the ancestral sense. He'd spent most of his life in the London holdings of the family, and much (too much) of his adult life abroad. But today the fact that he couldn't enter his own grounds was an echo of the larger barrenness of his return home. London was hardly any better. The flat was huge with the sounds of absences. He'd been staying in Roseminster, at the Nelson Inn, caught in limbo.

"Stay with me for a while," Hudson said. "I don't think you should be alone."

"I want to be." Gray stared through the gate. He couldn't see the Hall from here. He thought he could sense it, though, a huge weight that anchored the landscape.

"Do you realize," Korda asked, "what an embarrassment everyone who was in Geneva and is still alive represents? Do you?"

He hadn't invited her to sit. Meacham said nothing, stood with eyes forward and waited for the rhetorical questions to end. *Smug little bastard*, she thought. *You weren't there, and aren't you happy?* Korda was a fat, balding bureaucrat who snuggled securely in his corner of the political game. He wasn't an intelligence officer. He was a game-player. He was a lousy administrator, but he played the game like everybody else was blind and stupid. Meacham could almost admire him for that skill. He was playing even now. The situation should have been an easy read. Meacham was here to have her career sliced up and handed to her in a paper bag. But she couldn't tell if Korda's anger was genuine. She could sense angles being played. She risked a glance at Korda's face. His expression was doom and damnation, but his eyes were twinkling. Something was making him happy. *Figure it out*, she told herself. *Then work it.* She waited for Korda to speak again.

He opened the report's cover and pretended to read. "Tell me what you know," he told her.

What was he doing? Giving her the rope with which to hang herself? "About what?"

Mistake. He glared. "Don't be coy. Tell me what you knew before the media went berserk."

"The Deputy Director of Operations was running what I thought was an investigation into terrorist incidents at anti-globalization protests." *Incidents* was an understatement. A cluster of dirty bombs had gone off at Davos while it was hosting the World Economic Forum. Right in the middle of the protests. Explosions, bodies torn apart, panic, good times. Most of the resort town was now uninhabitable.

"You didn't know he was working with the people who actually were responsible for the bombs?" Joe Chapel, the DDO, had been cooperating with a Russian mob king. The story was that the damage had been part of a plan to cause a backlash of support for the World Trade Organization, beef up the WTO's powers, and bring the organization to heel. Craziness. Might even have worked, though: in the early aftermath, the words "protester" and "terrorist" had become synonyms. Then everything had gone south, and the partners had started killing each other. Chapel was in the hospital, the Russian was dead, and his Geneva corporate headquarters had become a slaughterhouse. Better yet, informed sources were claiming the collusion went all the way to the Oval Office. Unbelievable. So insanely stupid, it was probably all true.

"I didn't know," Meacham said. "Not until everything started exploding."

"Convince me."

"I walked away."

"From the damage? Of course you did."

"No, from Chapel. He wanted loose ends tied up."

"You mean cleaned."

"Yes."

"He was ordering black bag jobs how recently?"

"Up to the day I left."

"And you disobeyed a director's order?"

"I did."

"Why?"

"Because it was stupid."

Korda smiled. His face broke out in sunshine, and this, Meacham could see, was genuine. He wasn't pissed at all about Chapel's fiasco. He was overjoyed. Had he and Chapel been on the outs? If so, the rumours hadn't reached Meacham in Geneva. But Korda's pleasure had the kind of purity that only came with the defeat of an enemy. The right moves became clear.

Korda said, "That doesn't say much about your loyalty to a superior officer."

You testing me? Meacham thought. *Screw you.* "I'm not loyal to nonsense."

"Some might say you're lacking a certain quality of patriotism."

Meacham shrugged. "Then I hope they enjoy singing 'Nearer My God to Thee' when the ship goes down."

Korda was beaming bright. He was responding to a kindred spirit. *Nailed you*, Meacham thought. "Sit down, Lou," he said. When she did, he said, "I'll be honest. It was good that you walked away, but you didn't walk away soon enough. You're tainted. We've even had to field a couple of media calls about you. Those are really bad optics, because, as station chief, you shouldn't have any optics at all."

"Can we skip to the end?" she asked. "Do I still have a career?"

"Still want one?"

"It would be nice to come home."

Korda nodded. "I think you're someone I can work with. But don't get me wrong. If you're any kind of liability, or even just a perceptual one, you're toast. That's the kind of sweetheart I am. *Capisce?*" He leaned forward. "Two things, then. We need you out of the wrong spotlight. And you have to earn your redemption."

"Meaning what?"

"Did you know Pete Adams?" Now the twinkle in Korda's eye promised nothing good.

"Never heard of the man. Should I have?"

"Not really. Just curious. He was small fry in the Directorate of Science and Technology."

"Was?"

"Was. He was also, in his spare time, a ghost hunter. I ask you. That had better have been an interest that developed *after* he was recruited. Anyway, he was on vacation while Geneva was melting down, and what do you suppose he did for his holiday? I'll tell you what he did. He rented himself a haunted mansion in England, is what he did. Set up a whack of equipment, is what he did. Threw himself off the roof, is what he did. Generated a shitload of bad publicity and paperwork nightmares for me, is what he did."

Meacham was having difficulty processing. "Sounds like a fruitcake."

"But a public one. The British press is all over him. They love this stuff."

"How did they find out he was Agency?"

"His mother."

"His *mother*?"

Korda nodded, rolled his eyes. "She's blaming us. Cover-up, murder, secret ops, the usual thing."

"So?"

"So we defuse by going public. An investigation will be made into his death."

"By me."

"By you."

She shook her head. "How exactly is becoming tabloid fodder going to reduce my visibility? *Spook Hunts Spooks*. You know that's what will happen."

Korda was all happy Buddha. "Pretty much. Lots of entertainment, and if the investigation gets his mother to shut up, it will be harmless and the right kind of distraction. Try to keep the profile down, if you can. But even if you can't, you being mixed up with ghosts makes for a much sexier story than a tangential connection to Chapel. See where this is going?"

"An inoculation."

"Good for you." Korda lost his smile and turned serious. "I do want to know why he died. There have been enough bad scandals to last us a decade or three. If this wasn't just suicide, I want to know what kind of a missile is heading our way before it hits. Am I clear? Do this right, Lou. Screw up, and I feed you to the hounds."

Patrick Hudson watched Gray's face. He looked for a crack in the stone. Right now, he'd take just about any kind of animation, but he didn't want to see the anger again. It frightened him, because in it he saw more than the common rage of bereavement — he saw a core of hatred. That rattled him. It looked like a turning away. "This is the worst time for you to be alone," he insisted. "I'm going to deny your request."

Gray turned to him, his lips pressed into a razor line, the edged cousin to a smile. "I thought you said God was with me." Sarcasm. Anger. Hatred. "So I guess I'm not alone."

"That's not what I meant."

"Oh? You mean I *am* alone?"

Hudson took a step back. There had been plenty of nights in refugee camps, when they were exhausted from physical labour and the mental anguish, when he and Gray had played theological games. Gray, always more tentative in his faith, always needing reassurance, especially when surrounded by darkness and war, would try to catch Hudson out in contradictions and paradoxes. Hudson enjoyed the game. He knew Gray wasn't really trying to blast a hole through his beliefs. He was instead looking for answers, waiting for his objections to be shot down, hoping that Hudson would buttress his own convictions. Now, though, Gray's tone was different. Now, he was playing for keeps.

Hudson tried to come at him from the side. "Richard," he said, "we have just spent months and months and months with people who have lost every last one of their relatives, who have seen their wives and husbands and sons and daughters and parents raped and tortured and murdered. And do you know what was probably the single biggest thing that sustained me during that time?" He waited, but Gray didn't answer. He simply stared, and Hudson felt his words lose their strength, turn brittle and shallow. He forged on. "It was their faith," he said. "If anyone in the world had a right to give up, to be angry with God, or to give up even on the mere idea that there *is* a God, it was them. And they didn't. They kept going, thanks to that belief." He waited again.

Gray continued to stare back. He barely blinked. Gradually, the focus of his gaze shifted from Hudson to a point past his shoulder and a universe away. "Did I say I didn't believe anymore? I don't think I did."

"Do you?"

"I don't know. I may believe in a cruel God. That would make sense, wouldn't you say?"

Hudson wouldn't. The cold implacability of Gray's logic washed over him and sucked colour from the world.

Gray shrugged. He began to leave but then frowned. He looked back down the drive to the Hall. Hudson saw him concentrate, saw his face clear of grief for the first time since the news of his loss. In its place were puzzlement and something that looked like fascinated disgust. Then Gray shook his head. The grief and the resentment returned. He walked off. Hudson hesitated before following. He knew his duty was to stay with his friend. But now he didn't want to. He didn't want to hear what Gray might say. Along his fortifications that held doubt at bay, he had found a hairline crack.

"Stop it," he muttered and began to follow.

Then he felt it, too. Barely more than a thread, but beckoning as a dry finger, he felt the need to turn back towards the Hall. He stared, waiting for a revelation. None came, but the tickle, the pull remained. He couldn't see the Hall, but he felt its eyes on him. He snorted at the fancy. *Ridiculous*, he thought.

Ridiculous, the idea of an invisible entity watching him.

The thought was sour, the irony unwanted. He wrenched himself away from the gate and hurried to catch up with Gray.

chapter three

a scientific investigation

"What is it?" Anna Pertwee asked. She knew there was something as soon as she descended from the van. Edgar Corderman, parked behind her, had his cowering puppy look. *Don't hit me*, his face pleaded. She'd never hit him. She couldn't imagine anyone getting physical with his baby face and angel-thin frame. But he drove her crazy when he went into pre-emptive grovelling. Those were the moments when she thought even Mother Theresa might have considered raising a hand or a sandal.

"Sorry, Anna." Corderman winced at imaginary blows.

"Sorry for what? What did you do?"

"I forgot the film."

Don't close your eyes. Don't roll them. Take that breath. Hold it. One, two, three ... Ten. Let it out. When she spoke, her voice was calm, quiet, unthreatening, and she had her blood pressure under control. But the reprimand slipped out anyway. "I specifically asked you before we left —"

"I know, I know. I thought I had it, and what with packing all the equipment, I forgot to check, and ..."

Pertwee held up a hand. "It's all right. Better we realized this now than later. I'll go in and start setting up. You go down to the chemist's and pick up a dozen rolls. Do you have enough money?"

Hesitation. "It didn't even occur to me to —"

Breath. One, two, three ... Ten. Exhale. She fished her wallet out of her purse. "Here," she said. "And what speed are we buying?"

No hesitation. "Eight hundred. Or four hundred, if that's the best they have." Bright, quick answer, front-row student with the hand high in the air. And this was a man in the twilight of his twenties. Well. You worked with what you had. Corderman meant well and tried harder.

Pertwee gave him a smile. All is forgiven. "Off you go, then." She watched his Volvo drive down the hill toward central Bexley. *Was I that young once?* she wondered. She hoped not. But there were fewer than ten years between them.

She opened the van's side door and began to load up. Camcorder, tripod, and Electromagnetic Field Detector to start with. She adjusted the shoulder straps and looked at the house across the street. She didn't feel as hopeful as she had when speaking to the woman yesterday over the phone. Whenham Avenue was pleasant, well-tended, quiet, the ideal London commuter satellite. The house was semi-detached and modern. The atmosphere was comfortable, not numinous. Doubts crowded in, but she tried to banish them. *Keep the mind open,* she reminded herself. Negativity would kill whatever chance there might be for contact. The spirits would run from her. *Chin up,* she thought and crossed the street.

Winnifred Tillingate opened the door before Pertwee could ring. She was tiny, in her late sixties, and had the bounce of a lifelong sportswoman. Her hair was cumulus-white, fine as air, and held down under a paisley scarf. Her smile was enormous and genuine. Pertwee saw no trace of charlatan. She began to feel better.

"I'm *so* glad you've come." Winnifred beamed as she led Pertwee to the living room. "It is *so* nice to be taken seriously for once, especially by a member of the scientific community."

Scientific community. Yes, well, er. Pertwee had her dreams, but she could tell Winnifred a thing or two about not being taken seriously. There was a time when she might have been a member of the community. She had her bachelor's degree in astronomy. She'd begun her master's. Then things had changed. She'd deviated, her former professors and classmates would say. Epiphany was her version. "Is there a room where the manifestations are strongest?" she asked.

Winnifred nodded like a bird. "Right here," she said. "This very room."

"Oh, good." Pertwee looked around. Pictures of grandchildren in triptych frames. Old console TV. Lots of china collectibles. It was her mother's home from five years ago, before the cancer had taken her for the last six months to the palliative care clinic. Then Winnifred sat down, and the flashback was complete. She was sitting in a high-backed wooden chair with padded arms. Before her was a round table in the form of a Norman shield. Victoria Pertwee's table had been engraved with astrological signs, but it had been circular, and the chair was identical. It was what the elder Pertwee had always called a Medium Chair, and Anna felt a mix of melancholy and skepticism. Winnifred put her hands on the chair's arms and closed her eyes. "They're close," she murmured. "I can tell."

So could Mother, thought Pertwee. But she began to set up her equipment anyway. Victoria had been a fake. A real throwback to the spiritualism craze, knocking sounds, tinkling bells, rising table and all. Pertwee's father, Charles, had been the technician behind his wife's huckster. The act was old, but it drew in the nostalgic and the gullible, along with their money, by the boatload. The twist was that Victoria had actually *believed*. Not in her shows, but in her ability. As far as she was concerned, she really did speak with the dead, and Pertwee could remember real, private séances with her mother as far back as her toddler years.

She had spent her childhood with the reality of spirits as entrenched as that of Father Christmas. Both illusions had collapsed in adolescence. She had revolted against her mother's ethereal dreamworld and her father's fakery machine. Her cynicism propelled her through the sciences in school and university. She had run a mile from anything that smacked of spirituality. Then her parents had died, too soon, a year apart. Her father's death had had her searching for comfort. Her mother's had given it to her. Sitting by her bedside in the hospital, clutching her hands as they relaxed from the pain finally ended, Pertwee had seen, *seen,* a glow hover for three full seconds over Victoria's head. All the old loves and beliefs had come flooding back. Father Christmas was real again, and Pertwee was going to prove it.

She'd been at it for eight years. She had photographic evidence, visible and infrared. She had Electronic Voice Phenomena recorded on tape and stored on her hard drive. She had records of ectoplasm, cold spots, and automatic writing. She had everything she needed to be convinced that her mother's hopes were real, and that the comfort was real. But she had nothing that would make a skeptic listen to her. It was as if her five years of university had been wiped from history. Most of her friends from that period wouldn't return her calls. The ones who still saw her would glaze over when she tried to talk ghosts, their smiles becoming equal parts polite and pained. She knew she should give up on them, but she didn't. She had felt the touch. She had the evangelical calling. The science she used would be a tool of validation, not debunking.

"How long have you been sensitive?" she asked Winnifred.

"All my life, dear."

"And have you been aware of spirits everywhere you've lived?"

"Oh, my heavens no. Only this house and my grandmother's."

That was promising. Pertwee felt her confidence grow as she headed out to the van for the rest of the equipment. Thermal scanner. Digital and 35mm cameras. Tape and digital recorders. Motion detectors. She hauled them all inside, and while she set the tools up around the room, she opened herself to the space. She sought its rhythms and those of its inhabitants. *I'm friendly,* she told them. *Feel free to speak with me.* She took her time, triple-checking every calibration, but also breathing in the atmosphere. When she was set up, she continued to walk around the room, learning its corners, reaching out and touching the shelves and knick-knacks, making the space her home, making herself a known quantity and not a stranger. After a half-hour, she was ready. This was when she was used to loading the cameras. If only she had film.

"Is that your assistant?" Winnifred had left her chair to be out of the way during the set-up, and now she was standing at the living room window.

Pertwee followed her gaze. Corderman was back. He had one leg out of the car, but he wasn't making any further progress. He seemed engrossed by something on the passenger seat. Pertwee sighed. "I'm afraid it is," she said, and went outside. "What do you think you're doing?" she asked as she approached.

Corderman looked up. "Sorry. Just reading this." He passed her the newspaper. It was the *Sun,* and the article, halfway through the tabloid, was headlined "*Ghosts Murder Spy in Devon.*" She scanned the piece, and when she read the words "*Gethsemane Hall,*" she said, "Oh, no."

"That's what I said." Corderman nodded. "That's just not right. They shouldn't be writing things like that about that place."

"No," Pertwee agreed. "No, they shouldn't." She was growing angry, undoing all the good, calm work she'd done inside the house. She folded the paper and tossed it onto the back seat of the car. "We'll think about that later," she said. "Now is not the time. We have a job to do here. Focus, Edgar. Can you do that?"

"Yes."

"Are you?"

"Yes. Yes." He was emphatic, indignation forgotten. She could say this for Corderman: he switched gears quickly.

In the house, Winnifred was back in her chair. Pertwee made Corderman sit on his eagerness and walk around the room for a quarter of an hour. Then they loaded the cameras. Pertwee tied her hair back to keep it from straying into a lens. She opened her log book, noted time, temperature, and conditions. "Are you ready?" she asked Winnifred.

"I always am, dear. When the spirits call, I answer."

"All right, then." Pertwee fixed her eyes on a spot in the air halfway up to the ceiling. "To the spirits who are listening, I ask your permission to record your presence." She waited ten seconds. She didn't expect a positive response, but she wanted to leave room for a negative one. There was nothing. "Thank you," she said. She turned back to Winnifred. "Shall we begin?"

The older woman smiled. She relaxed in her chair, and her eyes lost focus. Pertwee watched. The camcorder was running. She had one of the 35mm cameras in hand. Corderman had a digital. Those were more idiot-proof. Pertwee waited.

And there. The temperature dropped. She felt it. She *felt* it.

Before they left, Pertwee thanked the spirits. It was the least she could do.

She had a darkroom set up in her row house in Coulsdon South. It was a former bedroom. The house was small, but she lived alone, so there was plenty of room for the equipment. She and Corderman poured over the prints. They had snapped off three hundred shots over the course of the day. The digital pictures were disappointing, every one of them stuck in the mundane. Three of the 35mm shots, though, were looking promising. All three had been from late in the session. The first, which Pertwee had shot around sunset, showed a vaguely oval red discolouration around Winnifred. The other two, taken after nightfall, had small, bright lights pinpointing the air above Winnifred's head.

"What do you think?" Corderman asked. "Ectoplasm?"

"These look more like spirit lights," Pertwee said, pointing to the night shots. "This one," tapping the red nimbus, "I'm not sure. An aura, maybe." Maybe, and yet she knew the comments to expect if she showed the photographs to a skeptical audience. Dust on the lens. Light on the film. Glare. Not to mention that whatever authority pictures might once have had lay in ruins, thanks to Photoshop. "Let's check the recordings," she said.

They listened late into the night, each with headphones. Corderman handled the tapes, Pertwee the digital material. Pertwee heard hours of nothing, cranked high and turned into static, punctuated by the sounds of clicking equipment, shifting seats, a cough here and a sneeze there. Hoping for a miracle, she checked the times of the promising pictures. "Fast forward," she told Corderman and read off the times. The search was easier on the computer. She scanned ahead, watching the display for spikes. Nothing clear stood out, but she turned the volume up still higher. She tried to shut down every sense but hearing.

There. In the midst of the white noise blizzard, she thought she heard a voice. "No," it said. She rewound, listened again. There it was. "No." She wasn't making it up. She was sure the word was real. She opened her eyes and turned to Corderman. "Anything?" she asked.

He was frowning. "I'm not sure." It was the sentence he used when he desperately wished he had something but didn't.

"Come listen to this," she said. He crossed the room, and they traded headphones. Pertwee played with the tape until she found the spot. Her digital recorder was more compact than it was hi-fi, and there was a lot less noise on the tape. The static was thinner. The voice should have been clearer. It wasn't. But she heard it at the right moment, a faint but articulate denial, breaking surface just before going down and drowning. *No.* "So?" she said.

Corderman shook his head. "My hearing must be worse than yours."

"Here." She unplugged the headphones, played the computer's recording back through the speakers. "You can hear someone say 'no.' Listen." Static wind, aural clouds forming and dissolving, hypnotic. "*There*," she said when the sound came. She stabbed a finger at the wave pattern. There was the smallest hiccup.

"Let me hear it again," Corderman said. He was excited now. He stared at the wave display during the playback, and this time his face lit up. "I heard it," he said in happy awe. "I heard it."

Pertwee isolated the clip and saved it to their archive of EVP. She was feeling pretty good, too. Audio and visual phenomena coming at the same time. Explain that as lens glare. She went over the temperature readings. No dip. That was disappointing, but not conclusive. Cold spots didn't always register except on the psychic level. She leaned back and judged the night well spent.

Corderman was dancing in his seat. "We have something. We really have something."

"Maybe," Pertwee qualified, even though she agreed.

"What maybe? This is definitive."

"There were no fluctuations on the EMF Detector."

"That doesn't mean we're wrong. Spirits don't *have* to disrupt the field."

"No, but consistency across the readings is always more impressive."

"To whom? To people who wouldn't believe even if you captured a spirit and put it in a bottle?"

Pertwee didn't answer. He was right, but she couldn't bring herself to let go of her fantasy of converting the skeptics. She wanted back into the community of science. She deserved it. She was rigorous in her work. She didn't make sensational claims. She was even careful to a fault with her image. No unicorns, Birkenstocks, and unkempt hair to keep her locked in the flake compound. She followed fashion trends like a hawk, navigated the trade winds to maintain a look that married professional with flair. She had good skin, good hair. She did a good media face when she had to. But the backs remained turned to her.

Corderman didn't push things. He was ready to move on. "What next?" he asked.

"Next you go home, and we both sleep." *We've earned the rest. We've done good work.*

"But is there anything else lined up?"

"Nothing definite." A couple of calls had come in that she wanted to follow up on, but nothing too exciting.

"Because I was wondering ..." Corderman pointed at the *Sun*, dropped on the floor beside the outside door.

Pertwee's mood took a dive. She stood, walked over to the paper, and picked it up, handling it like toxic waste. She read the article again, thoroughly this time. Her lips were pressed into a stone line.

"Is that steam coming out of your ears?" Corderman asked.

Not funny. She kept reading. Despair fought with anger. This was the sort of giggle-piece that helped confine her research to the outer darkness, that prevented her work from ever being taken seriously. But that wasn't the worst thing about the article. The worst was the slander of Gethsemane Hall. "Liars," she muttered.

Corderman looked uneasy. "I don't know, Anna. Do they really make up deaths?"

"I don't mean about that. I mean about why it happened." She understood why the reporter had run with the story the way he had. Ghost hunter visits haunted house, plunges from tower. Writes itself. Scary, killer ghosts were much sexier than the sometimes sad, sometimes happy, often melancholy souls she encountered. There had always been talk among ghost-hunters about angry or dangerous spirits. Pertwee had her doubts. She had never found any evidence of malevolence, and she put those beliefs down to the fears and perceptions of the observers. Ghost could be frightening, yes. That wasn't their fault.

But Gethsemane Hall. Of all the places to tar with a house-of-horrors brush. In the community, the house was legendary, and it was saintly, which was as it should be, given its original owner. The stories that had filtered out over the generations had turned the house into the Lourdes of ghost-hunting, and yet it had never been properly investigated. Pertwee was surprised that this Peter Adams had been given the go-ahead. In the past, the owners had always shot down any request. She had tried several times, then given up, especially since she had begun to acquire a media profile. It wasn't huge, and it wasn't lurid, or so she hoped, but it was there. It was a regular thing, now, for one of the tabs to call her up whenever they wanted a scientific-sounding gloss on a ghost piece they were doing. They were using her, and she knew it. She used them right back, the heightened visibility opening doors and bringing people and opportunities for investigation to her that she might never have had otherwise (though no doors to the science community, oh no, never there).

Just over three months ago, the payoff had been huge: a high-profile haunting underscored by her authentication of the event. She was officially a Quoted Expert. She couldn't deny she was pleased. The problem was if the owners of a house weren't big on the media. In the past, the Grays had been private to a fault. The dowager Lady Gloria had died five years ago, though. Perhaps the heir was more open. She should have checked, rather than assumed the new regime would have the same policy. And now some amateur had beaten the professionals to the punch and had gone and either tripped over his own clumsy feet or committed suicide on the premises. The Hall's name was public now and would be stained forever.

Unless you do something about it. Unless you dig up the spectacular, tabloid-worthy proof that there is nothing wrong and everything right with this place. Unless you risk everything, and go public for a cause that's bigger than you or your precious reputation. And is there really any of that to lose?

"We're going," she told Corderman.

"Where?"

"Devon."

"To the Hall?"

She nodded. "Tomorrow morning. We're taking all the gear. All of it. If you forget something vital, I'll break your neck." But she was smiling. *I'm coming to you*, she thought, picturing the Hall. *I'm coming to save you.*

chapter four
the cleaner

Gerald Fretwell looked amused. Meacham couldn't blame him. He glanced out his office window before leading her out and paused, gazing down at the cluster of reporters camped out in front of the Millbank entrance to the British Security Service's headquarters. Fretwell's already cheerful face broke into a wide grin. He was a small man. His grey hair had receded to a token statement on the top of his head and was buzz cut. His eyes bulged, giving an air of permanent, jaded surprise at the silliness of the world. "Are these yours?" he asked, pointing.

"Probably."

"Seen many?"

"At the airport. Outside my hotel. Here."

Fretwell laughed. "I'm sorry," he said. His smile was kind and old with experience. "Welcome to the world of leaks."

Meacham sighed. "No surprise. Korda wants us to be seen behaving well."

"You have my sympathy, dear heart." With that, he led the way from his office.

The MI-5 building had been refurbished and updated, but it was still old, still on historical registers, and its massive stolidity put the lie to the modern equipment. Meacham kept expecting to see manual typewriters and carbon paper instead of laptops and laser printers. Fretwell led her down to a large evidence room. The space was sterile, fluorescent-cold. Pete Adams's possessions were laid out on three large tables. "Thanks for doing this," Meacham said. "I'll try not to leave too big a footprint on local turf."

Fretwell waved her caution away. "Don't be silly. To be honest, we're happy to follow your lead."

Meacham raised an eyebrow. "What's the catch?" Since when did one agency defer to another so happily?

"Oh, don't misunderstand. Our Peter was indeed the subject of jurisdictional conflict. But ... what's the opposite of a tug of war? MI-6 said we could have the case. His dying here made this an internal matter, they said. Could well fall into counterterrorism or counterespionage, they said. Bastards. We said that as he was a member of a fellow foreign intelligence agency, they should take charge and liaise with your people." Fretwell shrugged. "We lost the coin toss."

"I see." Meacham did, her heart sinking still further. She sensed the chance of a reborn career shrink to nothing. She thought she could hear Korda laughing somewhere. Still, if she completed the mission, maybe she could at least hang on to her pension. She mentally rolled up her sleeves. Time to work. "Anything worth pointing out now?" she asked.

"That depends on your taste for the absurd," Fretwell said. "As you can see, there's plenty of electronic equipment." He gestured to the first two tables. "Some of it has potential espionage applications. Recording devices, low-light and zero-light cameras, that sort of thing. Nothing for transmitting, though, so douse your hopes for a good, clean double-agent story right now. Everything here is geared toward reception. And then there are these." He handed Meacham a stack of spiral-bound notebooks. She flipped through first one. Page after page of draftsman-crisp printing of recorded temperatures, times, weather conditions, types of experiments, and the results, which, at first glance, were negative across the board. She checked the dates. The oldest notebooks were from years ago. Adams had been riding his hobby horse for a long time and in far more places than Gethsemane Hall. "Completely obsessive and completely ridiculous," Fretwell observed. "If this is a cover, it's bloody brilliant."

"I wish." She picked up a MiniDV cassette and looked a question at Fretwell.

"Ah," he said, uncomfortable now. "Yes. That. You'll be wanting to take a look at that." He took her over to a workstation that had a monitor and every form of media player.

"You've seen it," she said as she slipped the cassette into a camcorder at least a decade old.

"I have."

"And ...?"

"It's one of the reasons we're happy to step aside. The tape is cued up to the relevant sequence."

The scene was grainy and green, a staircase shot in infrared. The camera was at the stop of the stairs, looking down. The image was too murky for detail, but the steps looked steep and old. The picture flickered steadily. "Time lapse?" Meacham asked.

"Yes. One second shots, every ten seconds. He could fit an entire night onto one tape."

Meacham watched. The flicker began to work on her head. She hadn't slept on the plane and was still on her feet after arriving at Heathrow at five in the morning. She struggled to keep her vision clear and hoped her pulse wouldn't pick up the rhythm of the picture and start throbbing. "I don't see anything," she said.

"You won't. Listen for it."

When it came, she jumped. She glared at Fretwell, but he wasn't laughing. He was still uncomfortable and a little green around the edges. The sound was a one-second slice from the centre of a scream. It was deafening, piercing, a siren that was redolent of rage and agony. When Meacham's heart steadied, she noticed that her throat was sore, as if in sympathy with the howl of vocal chords scraped by broken glass. The effect of the scream was made worse by its truncation. There was no origin, and no conclusion, only an *in media res* stab to the senses. Meacham waited until she felt composed again. She cleared her throat. "Okay," she said. "Is there more?"

"No." Fretwell sounded relieved.

"Okay," she said again. She stopped the playback anyway, eliminating any chance of another surprise. "Excuse me, but what the fuck was that?"

"We don't know. Neither, according to this," Fretwell held up a hardbound diary, "did Adams, though you can imagine what he speculated."

Meacham turned to look back at the table and the raft of recording units. "Does this sound turn up anywhere else?"

"We're still checking. He made hundreds of hours of audio. But we don't think so. His journal entries for this date express frustration at not having a recorder at the same location as the camcorder."

"Was there anyone else in the house?"

Fretwell shook his head. "The police gave the place a going over, and so did we. No one was there but Adams."

Meacham leaned against the work station. "Your take?"

"Without having seen his psych profile ..." Fretwell paused, giving Meacham the opening to offer the information. When she said nothing, he shrugged. "Our best guess is depression." His smile was wry. "One might say his interests were a bit on the morbid side."

Not morbid enough, though. There was nothing in his file to suggest instability. Adams was an odd duck, but seemed a pretty happy ducky. "And what about that scream?"

Fretwell's unease returned. "We're still working on that. How does an audio glitch sound? Some kind of electronic gremlin? These are the thoughts that are calming things down around the office."

"Good enough for government work."

"Precisely."

She flirted with the temptation. "*Ghost Hunting Spy Was Suicidal*" for the tabloids. A more bureaucratically worded version of the same in a report for Korda. No reason why this wouldn't work. The tabs didn't have the scream recording, after all. Ta-da, job done, home again by the end of the week. Oh, for life to be that simple. She sighed and resisted. The story might look neat and tidy. That didn't mean it actually was. The loose end of the scream was still dangling. There was always the possibility of a leak re-igniting media interest. The worst case scenario was a failure to follow Korda's injunction: *I want to know what kind of missile is heading our way before it hits.* Going with the tidy story might turn out to be as good a defence as closing eyes and plugging ears against the missile. She had to know definitively, one way or another. "I'm going to have to check into a few things," she said.

Fretwell grunted in sympathy. "Better you than me, dear, that's all I can say."

Meacham walked over to the equipment again. She riffled the pages of a notebook. "How much longer will you be going through this stuff?"

Fretwell gave her his sad smile. "You must have mortally angered the gods. Let me guess. If you need this unholy tech mess, you'll be wanting it down at Gethsemane Hall."

"I must look depressed."

"You do." Fretwell thought for a moment. "Will the end of the week be soon enough?"

"I'll call you from there, let you know. If I can muster the right troops, I won't need any of this."

"You should be so lucky. In the meantime ..." He pointed to the notebooks. "Feel free to abscond with those. We have all the copies we'll need."

"Thanks."

"No, thank you. You've just added to the downward slope. Now the shit can roll down past me." He smiled, one of the happiest people Meacham had seen all year.

That night, she sat in her hotel just off Charing Cross Road and ploughed through the notebooks. There was much she couldn't decipher. She was going to have to consult an expert, she realized, and shuddered at the implications. Her season in Hell was going to be long and hot. Exclamation and question marks were scattered like seasoning over the pages, becoming more and more frequent as the dates crept closer to Adams's leap. They were suggestive but told her squat. The diary was more detailed and interesting. She started with the date of the scream, and saw that Fretwell was right: Adams was amphetamine-excited about his recording. He was also crack-mad about not having caught more. No surprises there. What had her frowning was how surprised Adams was. Not that he'd recorded anything at all, but that the sound was a scream. *Isn't that what ghosts are supposed to do?* Meacham wondered. Not the ones at Gethsemane Hall, apparently.

Adams kept referencing the house's history and reputation, but never went into detail on either. Meacham gathered that the Hall was supposed to be a good place but couldn't piece together more than that. What was clear was how, from the moment of the scream onward, Adams had started unravelling. Meacham flipped back to the beginning for comparison purposes. His entries from his arrival at the Hall were enthusiastic and profuse, the work of a man happy with the time on his hands. By the end, his writing was terse, perfunctory, and cryptically paranoid.

The last entry was dated two days before he died. Meacham checked the notebooks again. These had notations as recently as his last morning. He had worked right to the end, it seemed, but he wasn't enjoying his work.

The final entry in the diary: *I wish I could leave.*

And this was why cleaning jobs were so dirty. She was going to have to bring in another party, someone sane but informed about craziness. Someone she might actually think was okay. Someone who didn't deserve to be pulled into the shit, in other words. But hey, that's why you get paid the big bucks.

Sometimes, life smiled. She was owed that, given how many frowns she'd been landing. Life smiled while she was eating a room-service breakfast. She had the radio on and was listening with half an ear as she flipped absently through the morning papers. Her antennae twitched, and, with a *click*, she was all ears. She heard the man she needed speak. She had a moment of sympathy for him. He didn't know what was heading his way. Then she put herself on the collision course.

They were almost packed and ready for Roseminster. Pertwee was acting in a spirit of relentless optimism. She and Corderman were going to descend on the town like Operation Overlord, and their sheer momentum would force Gray to let them investigate. There was still the little matter of tracking him down. There was no answer at Gethsemane Hall, which meant he was probably in London, and that would make it easier for him to say no. Pertwee wanted Corderman in place and ready to roll before she confronted Lord Gray. The closer they could come to presenting him with a *fait accompli*, the better.

Corderman had popped down the road for the morning papers. Pertwee wanted to be off, but Corderman needed his football scores. So he said. *He needs his Page 3 girl*, Pertwee thought. But when he stepped into the flat, he looked ashen. "What's wrong?" she asked, heart skipping. Gethsemane Hall in the news again? Corderman was turning into the bearer of bad news whenever he picked up his fix of Fleet Street yellow.

"It's Bromwell," Corderman said. His voice trembled on the verge of tears.

Bromwell. Pertwee's biggest triumph, the one that had made her the Quoted Expert, the one she wasn't sure whether it would help or hurt her with Gray. "What?" she asked again.

"Crawford's been there," Corderman whispered.

"Rubbish," she said in pointless denial. She reached for the paper.

"It's not in there," Corderman said, though he didn't resist when she snatched the *Sun*. She heard him but turned the pages frantically anyway, as if energy of action would summon help. "I heard him on the radio," Corderman went on. "He was being interviewed."

"When did he go?"

"Just after us."

Of course. The bastard was probably drawn by the publicity. She'd presented him with a huge, inviting target. He wouldn't rest until he brought down everyone's joy. She'd never met him, but she felt the prick of personal animosity in his choice of investigation site. "What did he say?" she asked.

"Guess."

She didn't have to. "He did another one of his surveys, didn't he?" When Corderman nodded, she asked, "How many participants?"

"I can't remember exactly. Over six hundred."

Crawford had all the resources of a university behind him. Kent believed in his work. It was respectable, but just sexy enough to be media-worthy. If she had that kind of backing, she'd be producing results that would show him where to go. "He talked about magnetic fields, didn't he?"

"He found some strong variances."

"He debunked Bromwell."

Corderman's eyes were shining. *Don't cry,* Pertwee thought. *Don't you dare cry. This isn't over. We're just getting going.*

Pertwee said, "Load up."

"But what are we going to —"

"We carry on. The new project is even more important now." She gave Corderman a punch on the arm. *Buck up, soldier.* "Crawford had better watch out. Gethsemane Hall is going to debunk *him.*"

Corderman's eyes still shone, but now with a warrior's hope.

chapter five
god's good plan

Meacham decided to hedge her bets. She felt good about the inspiration the radio had given her. One skeptic was good. Two would be better. She wasn't just going to clean the Adams fiasco. She was going to sterilize it. She found the other name she wanted in the background files. The face was in a picture taken at Adams's funeral.

In Paris, Kristine Sturghill was working the saw down to the bone. She was well down into the flesh and gristle. The sounds were a chuckling gurgle of wet snaps. The woman she was working on didn't twitch. She looked dead sexy, every pun intended. Blood flowed, poured, pooled. The floor was covered in a growing puddle that reflected the lights from its darkness. She cut through the last of the gristle, and there was the grind as the blade sank its teeth into bone.

The audience roared.

Sturghill was performing at La Bourgeoise Épatée. The theatre was a hole in the wall in the Rue Notre-Dame de Nazareth in the 3rd Arrondissement, spitting distance from the stolid respectability of the Arts et Métiers museum, only two blocks from the bustle of the Boulevard St. Martin, but far enough east to be removed from the sleaze factor of the peep shows and porno palaces that sprang up the closer the Grands Boulevards came to Pigalle. The building had been a theatre off and on for a hundred and fifty years, and was making its mark in its new incarnation by revelling in its own filth, while tapping into its age for class. The in-crowd was squirting with pleasure. La Bourgeoise Épatée put on shows that were unapologetically pornographic and cheerfully debased, but had an aura of hipness that meant the city guides carried the listings in the same sections as the grand dame of La Comédie Française, rather than relegating it to the sex-tour back pages with the likes of Chochotte and Sexodrome. The decor was restored neo-classical, the seats new and spacious. The lighting was excellent, and Sturghill had to admit that even the dressing rooms were not only clean (a bonus, given what she'd dealt with in the past) but comfortable. Actually comfortable.

The hall was packed, the box office fat, and she was making nice coin. So where was the love?

She leaned into the saw, and the sound of grating and snapping bone filled the space. Not a twitch, not a visible breath, from the woman. A huge crack, and she was through. There was an enthusiastic gout of blood. The offal stench was building. Sturghill had already severed the upper torso, and now she pulled the centre of the box out. More blood pooled. The butchered woman, motionless, sexy, dead, glowed in the spotlight. Sturghill stepped forward and grinned at the audience. She was wearing the full Dietrich: tux, fishnets, stilettos, blonde killer as sexy as her red-headed victim (have to match the blood, don't you know), dressed in just enough masculine garb for that extra piquance of double-edged homoeroticism. She raised the saw blade and licked some blood from it. God's thunder of applause. She doffed her top hat and bowed low. Fade to black on the scene of slaughter. That was the orgasm. Resurrection was old hat and unwanted.

Where was the love? She wondered that again back in the dressing room. Her feet were aching from the heels, but nothing new there. That wasn't enough to sour her on the gig. Maddy Tibbert had climbed out of the coffin and was towelling off the blood, in a hurry for her first post-show cigarette. "Went pretty well," she said.

"I thought so," Sturghill agreed, her voice flat.

"You sound chipper."

Where was the love? "The show's getting to me, I guess."

"Girl, this was your baby."

"I know. I know." The trick was so old it was cool again: the box painted with lengthwise stripes so the connecting sections between the removed middle and the head and legs looked thinner than they really were, leaving plenty of room for Tibbert to bend herself into position. The gimmick was the blood. Sturghill's inspiration had been an old Herschell Gordon Lewis movie, *The Wizard of Gore.* In the film, the gory illusions had turned out to be real. Sturghill ran with the idea, and pretended to mutilate her assistant. She'd loved Lewis's bloody tongue-in-cheek attitude, wanted shock and satire in her own act. The early shows in the goth clubs had been fun, the audience buying exactly what she was selling. She was pretty sure they were in on the joke. She hoped they were. Either way, word spread, the gigs improved, and then the call had come in from Paris. And here she and Tibbert were, gravy train at full throttle.

So where was the love? Not in the audience. That was the problem. They weren't buying the satire. They might claim to be. All the reviewers did. But Sturghill wasn't buying what *they* were selling. She knew what was going on. Rocks were being got off, far too many of them, over the sight of one woman carving up the other. Her fault for playing up the sex. *What happened to irony?* she wondered. She knew the answer: it had become a first-rate alibi for guilt-free indulgence. *I'm not a misogynist,* the audience said. *I don't really like seeing women pretend-butchered. I'm appreciating the social commentary. Now get me hard again, you bitch.*

The love had been leaking away for a while. The breaking point, the moment where the love had died and the freeze had set in, had been Pete Adams killing himself. The poor bastard had no family and was buried in England. At least that meant Sturghill had been able to attend the funeral. The event had been too depressing. Adams had been a smart guy, too smart to wind up believing his own bullshit, but there he was, another audience with no irony. Dead in his seat. They'd met in college, had hung out a fair bit before he'd joined the Agency, a decision that Sturghill still had trouble forgiving. She didn't want to believe that someone she liked, someone she respected, would work for that outfit. At least she was aware of the little bit of irony in her disappointment. She must have some faith after all, if someone could betray it.

They'd stayed in touch, though. Just enough so that the network of friends spread the word when he died. A few made it over from the States. A handful more sent wreaths and cards. Most were absent and silent.

Sturghill changed out of her fishnets. She balled them up and threw them on the chair.

"They do something to you?" Tibbert asked.

Sturghill made a face. "Isn't any of this bothering you?"

"I never bought your whole make-a-statement idea, you know that. So it's all good."

"There are guys creaming to see you bleed."

Tibbert shrugged. "Like this is news. At least they're paying for it. They don't touch us, and neither of us is naked. Things could be worse. Shit, Kristine, we're making coin, and we're living in Paris. I'm trying to see the problem here."

Sturghill didn't answer. *Look at what you're doing, girl,* she thought. *You were working on a humanities degree. You were going to change things. Look at what you're doing. Look at what you're wearing.*

André Curval poked his head in the dressing room. He ran La Bourgoise Épatée and was a happy, happy man. "Kristine," he said. "Phone."

She followed him to his office. His desk was an anal retentive's wet dream of order, pen and papers in perfect regimentation, nothing permitted off the perpendicular. The walls were a collage of old Moulin Rouge and Folies Bergères posters, overlapping and tangling with each other, as if Curval had heard somewhere that impresarios had to be messy, and this was his one concession. Framed behind his desk was his baby: an original poster for the Grand Guignol. Curval waved her to the desk and left her to it. When the woman on the other end of the line introduced herself as one of Adams's colleagues, she almost hung up. "Stay the hell away from me," she said. "You people have done enough damage."

"You're probably right," Meacham answered, hooking Sturghill's curiosity just enough to keep her listening. "I'm asking you to help undo some of it."

"How?"

"Let me ask you, how devoted are you to his memory?"

"What do you mean?"

"Are you worried about soiling his life's work?"

"For the Agency? Not likely."

"That's not what I meant. I think we both know the Agency was just a job for him."

Memories of his ghost obsessions in college. Her frustrations that a man so smart could be goddamn gullible. She had never understood why he'd needed so badly to believe. "Go on," she said.

"What did you think about his research?"

"It was nonsense."

"You're a skeptic."

"I'm a magician. You want ghosts, I'll give you ghosts. I'll give you the whole rotten parapsychological menu. It isn't hard. You going to tell me what you want?"

"I'm trying to clear up what happened to Pete."

Sturghill snorted. "Ohhhhh," she said with sarcastic revelation, "you want the truth."

"If it does what I need," Meacham said, and her cynical honesty disarmed Sturghill. "I'm more interested in shutting down publicity. Ghosts are really good attention-getters. Debunked ghosts, not so much."

"Why should I agree to be your debunker? There are plenty of other magicians around."

"I thought you might want to know how he really died."

"He killed himself. He snapped, probably under the weight of too much bullshit. Spiritual lies or your kind, I don't know, and I don't care. Same difference."

"Are you sure?"

Sturghill hesitated. "I'm under contract here," she said and realized she was setting the terms of her surrender.

"Don't worry about it," Meacham said, and Sturghill found she did believe in the woman's confidence.

In the dream, he was back at St. Rose's Church, going through the funeral again. He knew he was dreaming because he felt the pain of repetition, sensed the sadism of a force that would make him experience ritualized loss once again. Knowing he was dreaming didn't diminish the pain. The anguish pressed him down, a granite weight, as he tried to stand for the hymn. The injustice of the re-enactment was colossal and could only be for the benefit of a cruel deity's amusement. Something was laughing at him. He looked up. Standing above the altar was a large wooden crucifix, its Christ bigger than life. The Christ was laughing at him. Now he was looking at the face in close-up, was staring into its wide mouth, could see where the red paint of its throat had chipped, saw lips peeled back from tree-ringed teeth. He couldn't see Christ's eyes. He couldn't see anything but the laugh, the maw of red disappearing to black. The laugh itself was looking at him, the mouth so contorted with mirth that the very expression had become sentient. He tried to yell back at it, to give back his hatred, but the laugh was too huge, too strong, visible even when he closed his eyes. The laugh grew from howl to tsunami roar. Its register climbed hysteria's ladder from exultation to frenzy, and finally it was the scream of the heart of the universe.

Gray woke up. His room was pitch dark, the gloom a velvet blindfold on his eyes. Something was wrong. The space felt too big. His bed was an isolated island, the walls too far away. He wasn't where he should be, but the alien room also felt familiar. He pulled his arms out from under the sheets. Cotton rubbed against his skin, confirming that he was awake, but the room did not click back to itself.

He placed his arms at his sides. He splayed his hands against the bedspread and froze. His palms slicked. He shouldn't be touching a bedspread. His own bed had a comforter, not this. He moved his fingers, trying to chivvy his imagination out of its delusion. Instead, he traced contours of terrycloth material. He became aware of the musty smell of age. His throat dried. He knew where he was. As a child, on those rare occasions when he and his parents had gone to visit Aunt Gloria, he had stayed in this room in Gethsemane Hall. It had been decades since he had last slept there, but his body remembered the touch of the bed, the aloof distance of the walls. *I am not here,* he thought. He swallowed, hurting his throat, and the precision of pain shot down any last hope that he was still dreaming. He whispered, "No." His voice was hoarse, small in the big dark.

He sat up, strained his eyes, could still see nothing. A smothering claustrophobia mixed with his terror. He turned to his left. In his room at the Hall, there had been an oak bedside table here, with a table lamp. In the London flat, there was no table. Instead, the head of the bed had shelves. He reached above his head and didn't find the shelves. He touched oak instead, and when he moved his hand to the left, he touched one of the posters that belonged to the Hall's bed. He reached further, and there was the bedside table. And there was the brass of the lamp.

He had been holding his breath, and he let it out now in a moan. He moved his hand up the lamp, and his fingers found the switch. He hesitated, terrified that sight would be the final nail in reality's coffin. He waited three more breaths, giving sanity one last chance to reassert itself. Then he turned the switch.

Light. He was in his London bedroom, and its dimensions were generous for the city, but far from cavernous. A comforter covered the bed. There was no bedside table. Gray's heart downshifted from arrhythmia. Then he realized that the light that was on was the ceiling light. Its switch was on the wall, on the other side of the room from the bed.

They woke up.

In Roseminster, Anna Pertwee and Edgar Corderman were in separate rooms at the Nelson. Pertwee was gasping when she came to. The nightmare left no memory, but it did leave a trace: the sensation of being dragged down into a whirlpool. Corderman woke himself up with his whimpering. He didn't know why.

In London, Louise Meacham snapped her eyes open and leaped out of bed. She turned on the light and saw that there was no one in her room. This did not comfort her.

Patrick Hudson was yanked out of sleep by a stiletto-bladed sense of sudden, irrevocable loss.

In Paris, Kristine Sturghill's heart was giving the good pound. She had dreamed of the show, and this time, Tibbert's legs had fallen off. She wasn't ditching the gig any too soon. England called to her.

Ripples reached as far as Washington. Jim Korda stirred, uneasy, but went back to sleep.

James Crawford didn't wake up, because he wasn't asleep. He was pulling an all-nighter, finished up a damned article because he'd let the damned submission deadline creep up on him like a damned fool again. He was putting the references together when a premonition passed over him like an oil slick. He stopped typing, startled. The slick receded, and he went back to work, just that little bit rattled. Just a little.

Gray didn't go back to sleep. The mere thought was ice in his gut. He got up and moved through the flat, turning on all the lights. Then he sat in the living room, TV turned on to a broadcast of *Sink the Bismarck*. He waited for day, and for the first time since receiving the news of his family's death, his dominant emotion wasn't grief. It was fear, but, he thought, and almost smiled, a change was as good as a rest. Bit by bit, he came to believe that. He felt the first hint of relief.

He settled more comfortably into his chair. On the screen, Kenneth More was looking stern and enforcing discipline in the situation room. Gray thought about his hallucination. He put the experience down to that, dismissing the inconsistencies as sleep confusion. As the immediacy of the terror passed, he tasted something like nostalgia. As a child, he had never enjoyed the pilgrimages to see Aunt Gloria. But they were now so far on the other side of the barrier of his bereavement that the memories had an appealing glow. They had a pull. So did the Hall. The room he had thought he was in beckoned, untainted by adult memories. Adams's death didn't seem like a deterrent any longer, just an irritation.

The dream bothered him more. The laughter was what did it. Reason told him the vision was his own subconscious at work.

Emotion said otherwise. Emotion moved him to anger. And when a course of action presented itself, when he saw a petty but satisfying bit of retaliation, he smiled. He was so out of practice with the gesture that he didn't know, at first, what he was doing.

Everything was part of God's good plan. The trick was to remember that. Some days, the trick was harder than others. Hudson had sensed this was going to be one of those days the moment he'd woken during the night. His intuition was handed bad karma confirmation when he reached the office. Deborah Culberth, who ran admin for Ties of Hope, was wearing a kicked-puppy face when he walked in. Culberth was the queen of indomitable. The hit had to be a big one to rock her back on her heels.

"I'm sure I don't want to know," Hudson said as he sat down. Ties of Hope's new digs were temporary, and they felt it. The office was a single open room, devoid of furniture except for tables, chairs, and couple of phones. The space was a ridiculously expensive rental in Croydon, but it was the best they could do on short notice until they found something more permanent back in London. Its windows looked out onto a rail line and a construction yard big with industrial noise.

"I was just talking to Richard," said Culberth.

Now he was sure he didn't want to know. "And?"

"He's pulling his funding."

Hudson didn't answer right away. He was listening to a dream die. The sound was disappointingly banal: no clap of thunder, no ominous chord, not even a click, just the uncaring background growl of the machine grinding and grinding beyond the office window. A train rattled by, and the world moved on. Hudson tried to imagine a way of picking up the pieces of the dream. Couldn't be done. Gray was the financial foundation of Ties of Hope, and he'd just triggered a demolition charge. "Did he say why?" Hudson asked.

"He said he's shifting everything to Oxfam."

So he wasn't giving up on humanitarian efforts. Hudson saw some glowing embers of hope amid the ash. "Was he calling from home?"

"I think he was on his mobile."

Hudson picked up the phone and punched in the number.

Two rings, then Gray answered. "Hello, Patrick," he said. There was a lightness to his tone that surprised Hudson. He sounded almost cheerful, but the sun in his voice was still overlaid by steely bitterness. Hudson could hear a background static murmur of motorway traffic. He pictured Gray in his car, speeding into the distance, pulling further and further away from him. The image hit him with a sense of final loss and of efforts too little and too late.

"Why, Richard?" Too many questions, so he asked them all at once.

"Revenge."

"Against whom?"

"God, I suppose." Harshness in his voice. He wasn't supposing at all.

"Don't. You mustn't."

"Why not? The money's still doing its work. What's the problem? Too attached to your hobby horse?"

Hudson flinched at the truth, pushed it away. There were greater truths at issue. "That's unfair and unworthy of you."

"I'm not feeling very fair these days, for some reason."

"Please don't turn away from God. Now, more than ever, you need —"

"Haven't we already had this conversation? I think we have. Unless you have anything new to add?"

Hudson fumbled in the pause. Gray's hostility was so out of character, it was derailing his train of thought.

"I didn't think so," Gray continued.

"Please ..." Hudson heard himself plead, and he knew he had lost.

"I'm sorry," Gray said, and his tone became gentler. It bothered Hudson even more to hear his friend speaking now not out of anger, but in the firmness of mature thought. "I know I'm hurting your life's work." Another pause, as if he were struggling with a decision. "I'll do my best to find a replacement sponsor for you."

"Then why —"

"Because none of my money is going to help spread faith. And tapping a substitute is the last bit of help your god is going to have from me." He was still speaking calmly. "Anyway, if the money's there, what do you care?"

"That's not fair."

"No, you're right. Apologies again. But why does my faith matter so much? It doesn't affect yours." Long pause, during which Hudson couldn't answer. "Does it?"

"Of course it doesn't." His throat was thick with lies.

"Ciao, Patrick." Gray rang off.

Hudson stood with the phone to his ear, listening to nothing. He made himself replace the receiver in its cradle, made himself look around the room, made himself concentrate. Faces looking at him, expectant, nervous. "Don't worry," he told them. "He'll help us find someone else."

"And if he can't?" Culberth asked.

"He will." He picked up his coat and unopened briefcase.

"Where are you going?"

"To make sure," he said.

An hour later he was on the train to Roseminster, rushing to preserve his faith.

chapter six

the meet cute

James Crawford's office was the home of a busy man. The books on the shelves were in alphabetical order, each in its place. But the flat surfaces were stacked high with papers. Toppling piles merged in a cacophony of unfinished business crying for attention. Crawford had just enough clear space on his desk for his laptop and coffee mug. He was cradling the cup, though he'd finished his drink several minutes ago. He was in his mid-forties, thinning hair shaved to stubble dark as his perpetual five o'clock shadow. Bullet head, battleship jaw, meat-tenderizer hands, he looked like he would be more at home bashing immigrants in the street than ensconced as a physicist at the University of Kent. There was nothing of the yob in his voice, though. His tones were gentle, his speech a deep, comforting murmur with just enough inflection to keep the listener interested. Meacham thought he was the most convincing speaker she'd ever heard, and they'd only been discussing his work in the most general terms. His was the voice of reason personified. No wonder the true believers hated him. He could make them sound like psychotic cranks by saying no more than "Good morning."

Meacham was sitting in a chair facing Crawford. He needed new furniture. The chair squeaked whenever she moved. She tried to keep still.

Crawford said, "I appreciate your being candid about who you are. I am, therefore, very curious to know what possible interest my work could be to the CIA."

"Fair enough." Meacham laid it out for him: Gethsemane Hall, Adams, the clean-up mission.

After she was done, Crawford looked pensive. "My turn to be honest," he said at last. "I won't pretend that the CIA is my favourite organization."

Meacham shrugged. *Not mine, either*, she thought.

"In fact, I have serious ethical issues with just about everything you do."

She shrugged again. "We're not in it for the love. But what are you telling me? That you're not interested?"

"I didn't say that. Gethsemane Hall is pretty well known. I'd like the opportunity to investigate it."

"So?"

"So I want things to be clear between us. My investigation will be independent and will go where I see fit, and I will publish my findings regardless of whether they help or hinder your agenda."

"Have you ever found evidence of a genuine haunting?" Meacham asked.

"No. Never."

She smiled. "Then I don't think we're going to wind up working against each other."

"Right, then." Crawford's grin was small, but it was a good one. "Tell me something, though. No offense, but your outfit has never worried too much about being rigorously truthful. If you want to debunk the ghost angle, all you have to do is announce that you conducted an investigation, even if you didn't, and that there is no such thing as ghosts, even if there is. It isn't as if most people will have their minds changed about you, one way or another. Why bother with me?"

"You implied it yourself. When was the last time anybody believed what the Agency had to say?"

"I see. I'm your credibility."

There was more to it than that, though Crawford was right. "I want the investigation done properly. It's important to me."

Crawford gave her a searching look. "You do sincerity very well," he said, reluctant optimism in his voice.

"All in the training," Meacham said, and Crawford laughed. "Do you believe in ghosts at all?" she asked.

"Never seen a reason to, yet. Do you?"

"No."

Crawford must have seen that she wanted to say more. "But ...?" he prompted.

"I've read a few of your articles. This business about magnetic fields ..."

He nodded. "I know. That almost sounds like crackpottery itself, doesn't it?"

"I didn't say that."

"I did. The thing is, magnetic fields can be measured. And don't mistake me. I am *not* arguing that the fields are ley lines or any such rubbish. I think the case is fundamentally pretty simple and logical. In locations where there have been consistent reports of hauntings, there are also measurable magnetic field fluctuations. So which makes more sense: presences from beyond or the observers being affected by the fields?"

"That's a rhetorical question."

"It is." Crawford looked sly. "But I believe I detected a need for reassurance in the way you brought up the subject."

"I guess I find the idea that you don't have to believe in ghosts to experience something a bit disturbing."

"You mean the fact that *you* might is disturbing."

"Hard-core rationalists don't like thinking they could be susceptible."

"No, we don't," Crawford agreed.

"Have you ever experienced anything?"

"Not often, but yes, I have. I had a few creepy moments at Bromwell, I don't mind telling you. Knowing what the likely cause for the willies is does rather take the sting out of them, though."

"That's what I want to hear. I want to be able to trust my own investigation."

"Then I can reassure you. If you know what to expect, sensing presences won't be that big a deal. It will almost be a disappointment if you don't."

Meacham liked the logic. Finding out that Adams had his mental train derailed by something real but non-supernatural was the best scenario she could imagine. Debunking, plus the bonus that the CIA didn't necessarily employ unstable loons. Perfect. "How soon can you make it down there?" she asked.

Crawford swept his eyes over the post-nuke landscape of his desk. "The day after never. Or tomorrow." He sighed, dismissing deadline nightmares. "Shall we say tomorrow?" He was beginning to sound excited. Meacham had counted on his not being able to resist the biggest debunking target on the current scene. "I take it you have Lord Gray's permission to investigate the Hall?"

"Working on it." Her two brief phone conversations hadn't gone well. Bad timing, what with the funeral of his wife and daughter. He'd hung up before she'd made it past the preliminaries. She had all her other ducks lined up now, so time for direct measures. Gray was letting her in the house, like it or not.

Pertwee and Corderman left the Nelson, stopped at the Tesco to stock up on meat pies for the day, and then mounted their guard at the entrance to the grounds of Gethsemane Hall. Shortly after three, a silver Bristol approached the drive. Pertwee stepped into the middle of the road and waved. The car slowed to a stop. Corderman took Pertwee's place in the road, and she went to the driver's side. The tinted window did not descend. "Excuse me," Pertwee said.

After another few seconds, long enough to signal extreme reluctance, the window went down. Gray looked out at her, his gaze closed and bullshit-intolerant. "You're blocking my way," he pointed out.

He was handsome, Pertwee thought, and she very much wanted him not to be angry with her. He had the narrow, refined features that bespoke aristocracy, minus the inbreeding. His tan was deep weathering and experience, not a UV bed's cosmetic vanity, and the hollows of his eyes were hard grief and deep anger. Pertwee was having a romance-novel reaction, and she hated herself for it. Her knees weakened all the same. "I'm very sorry," she said. "And I really don't want to intrude during your time of loss." Damn it. Her speech had been prepared, revised in her head for hours, and that's exactly what it sounded like. She saw the clouds gather on his face and gave up on her spiel. It was dead as week-old fish. "Look," she said. "My name is Anna Pertwee, and I investigate ..." She stopped herself. Her confidence was flooding away the longer Gray looked at her. She tried again. "Your house is so important —"

He cut her off. "No," he said and started the car.

"You don't understand —"

"I think I do."

"The bad things people have been saying about your home. They're wrong. I can give your house its reputation back." Oops.

Gray leaned on the horn. Corderman jumped, rabbit-scared by the blast. He dashed to the side of the road. Gray pointed at Pertwee. "Piss off," he told her. He punched a remote clipped to his sun visor and the gate opened. He drove in, then stopped as the gate closed behind him. Pertwee only just restrained herself from dashing through while she had the chance. Gray climbed out of the car and stood, arms crossed, while the gate clanged to. "Another thing," he said. "If I see either of you again, I'm calling the police." He glanced at his watch. "And by 'again,' I mean if I can still see you thirty seconds from now. I said piss off, so hop to it."

No more romance novel thoughts as she and Corderman drove back into Roseminster. She wasn't thinking about the first tiff that leads to eternal passion. She was humiliated. She was taking Gray at his word: she was pissed off. She parked not far from the church and burned rage-holes into the dashboard with her stare. Corderman had been smart and had stayed quiet during the drive. Now he made a mistake and spoke. "So?" he asked. "What's the plan?"

"The plan," Pertwee repeated, flat.

"Yes. Plan B." He gave her a poke on the shoulder. "Hey, chin up. This was a setback, but we'll bounce back." When Pertwee said nothing, Corderman took the hint. "I'll ... ah ... I'll see you back at the rooms." He swallowed. "I'll try to come up with something."

"Yes, Edgar," she spat. "You do that."

"Right. Right." Chastened, he got out of the car.

Pertwee watched him go up the road. When he was out of sight, she climbed out of the car. She walked until she reached the church square. She stood beside the Victoria Jubilee monument at the intersection of Wake Street and Charmouth Road. The ground sloped gently down in every direction from here. She stood at the modest peak and heart of Roseminster, took in the town, and resented it. The town should have been perfect. Its potential for that perfection made its failure to meet her expectations a betrayal. With a population of 5,500, Roseminster was big enough to boast one stand-alone supermarket but small enough that it had avoided the plague of large malls. Most of its citizens still did their daily shopping at the stores that rubbed shoulders along Wake Street as it ran by St. Rose's Minster Church. Newsagent's, chemist's, grocer's, all present and correct, still the traditional high street. Roseminster had its own parish fair at the end of May. Its architecture was traditional, and there wasn't much to signal the second half of the twentieth century, let alone the beginning of the twenty-first, apart from the day-long crush of traffic down too-narrow and contorting streets.

Roseminster was proud of its history. Little plaques dotted the streets, playing up each cameo the town had played in the Norman conquest, the civil war, or the Second World War. If there were a town, Pertwee thought, that should take pride in its ghosts and protect them from calumny, this was it. She hadn't expected, on arriving, to be treated as a celebrity. She didn't rate herself with that much delusion. What she had expected was a certain support for her project, a sense that she and the town were on the same side. No such luck. She'd given up trying to enlist the locals as collaborators after the first half-dozen responded to her overtures with an evasive politeness that stayed just this side of actual coldness. She hadn't encountered hostility, and no one other than Gray had told her to piss off, but she had met an indifference so studied it amounted to a campaign. She couldn't understand it. It wasn't as though Roseminster had been shielded from the media's lurid gaze. The fuss was dying down a little, but the town had made the headlines in the tabs, and its name meant something now. It had a reputation. Pertwee couldn't believe the rep was one the residents were happy to let stand. She was here to help them remove the town's tarnish and restore its shine. They gave her no help. They gave her a brick wall. Well, no more, she thought. Not after today. She was going to force the issue.

She went back to the Nelson and spent the rest of the afternoon marshalling her arguments. Corderman poked his head in her room at one point, mumbled something incomprehensible when she gave him an impatient look, and ducked out. Evening rolled around, and she was ready. She went to find Corderman, and he seemed ready to flinch when he saw her. She had her equanimity back now, and felt guilty. "I've been a bitch, haven't I?" she said.

"Well ..." His tone was playful and relieved.

"Cast iron? Steel-plated?"

"And copper-bottomed."

"I'm sorry."

He shook his head. "You don't have to be. I understand how important this is."

"No reason to take it out on you. Anyway, all better now."

"We have a plan?"

"We have a plan. Part of which might involve my going all copper-bottomed again. If that happens, don't freak out, okay?"

"Roger."

"Let's do this, then."

There was a pub on the ground floor of the Nelson. Pertwee's initial thought had been to mount her campaign here. She changed her mind after looking around for a minute. Most of the patrons were having meals rather than simply drinking and were seated singly or in pairs. She was looking, she decided, mainly at visitors. Not enough locals for what she had in mind. Though she would keep this scene in her back pocket. Might come in handy later.

"So?" Corderman asked.

"Let's eat out."

The Leaping Stag was at the edge of town, just before the forest that separated Gethsemane Hall from Roseminster. Far from central, it was closer to the residential areas than the Nelson. Pertwee had stopped in briefly the day before, but the pub's obvious potential hadn't struck her until now. When she entered, she knew she'd hit paydirt. This was the local. This was where Roseminster came to relax and debrief. All the tables were taken, most by groups of four or more. The bar was packed. It occurred to her that if she wanted to make herself unpopular, this was the place for it. Swallowing was suddenly difficult. Corderman must have noticed. "Is this going to be okay?" he asked.

"I don't think things are going to become violent."

"Good." His posture relaxed.

What now, Genius? The grand gesture, seductive in the abstract daydreams of glory, lost its appeal now the moment had come. It shrivelled at reality's touch. She was going to address the pub, was that it? Was that what she was really planning to do? How? Climb up on the bar? Draw everyone's attention by doing a trick with ping pong balls? Was she insane?

"So?" Corderman asked, and this time she had no good answer for him. "What's the plan?" he prompted.

The plan was to grow up. "I had a stupid idea," she said. (If she had the nerve, though. Maybe. Maybe. Try something a bit more subtle first.) She approached the bar and ordered a pint of Kronenbourg. "Mind if I ask you something?" she asked the big man who served her.

"One minute, luv." He moved up and down the length of the bar, filling orders with the efficiency of a balletic automaton. He made a complete pass, then, caught up for the moment, he came back to her. "What can I do for you?" He laughed. Pertwee didn't get the joke, didn't even see it, but she caught the infection and joined in.

She held out her hand. "My name is Anna Pertwee, Mr. ..?"

"John Porter." His grip was made for hoisting tankards. "Yes, I know who you are." Still friendly, but a hair less jovial. His eyes gave away nothing.

So far, Pertwee had behaved. She knew she could trigger at least some small media dust-ups if she wanted. She hadn't in the past, that damned hope for credibility restraining her from making any overt alliances with the useful but dangerous tabloids. She hadn't spoken to any reporters in Roseminster, didn't think they even knew she was here. But the word of her presence was out, it seemed, at least on the local channels. "Do you know why I'm here?" she asked.

"For the Hall." That laugh again, but the eyes were wary.

"Yes, but not for the same reason as all the newspapers. I'm not about making life worse for people."

"Never said you were, miss."

"But you think I am. My impression is that most of you do."

Porter shook his head. "We really don't, you know."

"But you won't help me get into that house."

"A man's entitled to his privacy."

"What privacy? With every red-top in existence camped on his doorstep?"

"They aren't —"

"You know what I mean. I'm sure Lord Gray hasn't been able to answer the telephone in a normal fashion a single time since he returned from Africa. But to be honest, I'm thinking about the greater good. I'm thinking about all of you."

"Are you, now." No laughter. He was very quiet. For a moment, he was impassive enough to take up residence on Easter Island, then he shifted his attention to her right. "Excuse me," he said and did another lap of the bar. When he returned, he was still serious. "How, exactly, can I help you, miss?" Formal, almost stiff, that wall she'd run into so many times rising again.

"You don't seem to understand. I want to help *you*. All of you. The good name of Gethsemane Hall has been smeared, and so, through association, has Roseminster's. You don't want to become known as the British Amityville, do you?"

"Exactly." Corderman had come to stand at her elbow, and piped up now. Pertwee held up a hand to shush him. Porter ignored him.

"What are you proposing to do?" Porter asked.

"Investigate the Hall properly. Show people what it's really all about."

"And you think you know what it's about?"

"Of course! Don't you?"

Porter scratched the back of his neck, studied the bar surface as if he could see his reflection. "You'll really have to pardon me, miss. Duty calls." He swept away, and Pertwee heard him begin to laugh again as he took orders.

You bastard, Pertwee thought. *Just for that, I am going to make a scene.* Her outrage fuelled her courage. "Right," she muttered.

"Should I be brave?" Corderman asked, half-joking.

"I would say yes," she said. She grabbed an ashtray and rapped it against the bar. "Excuse me!" she called. The woman standing next to her barely glanced her way. "Excuse me!" Again, louder. Her voice disappeared into the conversational roar. "*Oi!*" A few more looks, some awkward shuffling of feet. She was on her way to being an embarrassment instead of a provocateur. She considered climbing on the bar after all, but it looked narrow. People were leaning over it. She pictured herself falling over and began to flush in the anticipation of humiliation. "Can you whistle?" she asked Corderman, raising her index fingers to her mouth to indicate the kind of ear pierce she wanted. He shook his head. She couldn't, either. Her shoulders slumped. Useless. She couldn't even make a nuisance of herself. "Let's go," she said.

As she headed for the exit, a man stepped forward to intercept her. He was very old. His back was as round as his shoulders, as if from a weight too heavy and carried too long. His eyes were the long plummet of fatigue. He touched his forehead with two fingers, tipping an imaginary cap. "Might I speak with you?" he asked. Pertwee nodded, and the man led them outside. He introduced himself as Roger Bellingham. "I do think you mean well," he began. "You would, however, be doing the town and yourselves a service by leaving the Hall alone."

"I'm sorry. But I don't think it's fair for you to keep the house to yourselves. It's too important."

His laugh was a short, bitter bark. "Oh, dear me, that isn't what we're trying to do."

"What, then? Are you afraid of it?"

He didn't answer. He poked at a stone on the pavement with his stick.

"Can't you feel it?" Pertwee pleaded. She spoke quietly.

Bellingham looked up, the movement sharp and quick. "Feel what?" A hint of alarm.

"It's hard to describe. Like a pull. When I looked down the drive toward the Hall, and knew I was so close, even if I couldn't actually see it, I felt drawn to it. Do you understand what I'm trying to say?"

"Perfectly."

"Then you do feel the same thing?"

"I have felt tugged toward that house every moment of every day of my life." He said this with a resignation and despair so profound, Pertwee's heart gave an unpleasant lurch.

"Then all the more reason," she began, "for you to help —"

Bellingham held up a hand. "Do you love the sea?" he asked.

Pertwee sputtered for a moment, trying to catch up. "Yes," she said, confused.

"But if you were swimming, and you encountered an undertow or a riptide, what would you do? Even if you love the sea, you don't want to approach it on its own terms."

Corderman asked, "Are you saying the house is bad?"

"It can't be," Pertwee answered, firm. "It was the home of a saint."

"You seem very sure," Bellingham commented.

"Am I wrong?"

"No. It was on that site that Saint Rose the Evangelist lived and died. You are right about that."

"And people have, for centuries, found spiritual renewal in that house."

Bellingham gave her a curious look. "Yes, those are the stories. Go on. What else do you know about the Hall?"

Corderman jumped in. "Some people believe the spirit of Saint Rose looks out for whoever stays there. More likely, she created a conduit to a higher plane, and that's what people are experiencing. Either way, it's the most transcendent residence in Britain."

"Is that a fact? My, my, how reassuring."

"I don't understand your sarcasm," Pertwee said.

"That's because you haven't lived here. You cannot, because we who know it best do not, understand the house."

"Maybe you need to be an outsider. How many Parisians visit the Eiffel Tower? I have made a study of such places as Gethsemane Hall, you know."

"I don't doubt it. But if you'd been thorough, then I doubt you'd be here. You would either dismiss the stories you've heard as fanciful and not bother with the place, or you would draw the correct conclusions and stay far away."

"That makes no sense. All the tales about Gethsemane Hall are positive ones. Except the most recent. That's why we can't let it colour the world's perception of the house."

"How reliable are those other stories? No, don't answer. I'll tell you. They're worthless. I have done some research, too, over the years. I wanted to understand this thing that was pulling at me. Do you know, every person who has ever written about what a wonderful oasis of peace and tranquillity and salvation and I don't know what other rubbish the house is, has never actually resided there?"

"But Edward Hardsmith's *The Lights of Gethsemane Hall* —"

"A fraud. I have seen the correspondence from the Gray family to their solicitors. Hardsmith was a fabulist. He never visited the Hall."

"But the details he gives of the town. Even allowing for the passage of a hundred and fifty years, they're extremely accurate."

"He stayed here. In town. That is far from being a guest of the Grays. The family itself has never spoken of the house, and their tenancy here has not been joyful. Take a good look at the sources that speak glowingly of the Hall. They are all based on hearsay, or on the experiences of those who visited Roseminster and felt the pull." Bellingham gave her a smile grim with knowledge. "One feels drawn to a place one is convinced is holy. The conclusion one arrives at is obvious."

"And what makes it wrong?" Pertwee demanded.

"Live here for a while, young lady. Not for a week or a month, but a year." His voice was fading, turning into the dry whispers of old pages rubbed together. "Then you'll know." He touched his forehead again and walked away. Pertwee thought he seemed to be leaning against a strong tide.

chapter seven

the first night home

It was as if he were chasing the jitters down.

He spent the day settling in. He went through the house, opening the windows to banish the stale air. He made lists of the supplies he would need to pick up tomorrow. He avoided one room. He killed the evening with the news and a bottle of Chardonnay, but he did not set foot in the room. He did wonder why he was delaying until nightfall. The answer he gave himself was that he was waiting for maximum silliness before he brought out the big guns of rationality. *Prove it*, he told himself. *Fine*, he responded. He took his pyjamas out of the master bedroom and tossed them onto the floor in front of the shut door. *There*, he said. *That's where I'm sleeping tonight.*

And now it was time to sleep. He went to confront the bedroom from his childhood and his dream (he called it that now, downgrading the experience from hallucination, whistling in the dark with semantics). The room was on the first floor, in the northeast corner of the Hall, the most remote of a suite. There were two entrances to it: from the west, through two other rooms; and from the south, through a bedroom that connected to the Old Chapel. During the visits here, his parents had taken the westernmost room of the suite, the one with the big windows and the most light. He thought back to those stiff Christmases and Easters with relatives he barely knew, all of them, it had seemed to him, old enough to remember the Crusades. He remembered his resentment and anxiety at his parents placing an empty room between himself and them. Their privacy, his quarantine. He had feared the space filled with absence on the other side of both doors.

There was absence everywhere now.

Gray stood in the bedroom, waiting for the jitters to drive him out. The mustiness was uncomfortable in its familiarity, the real world shaped in the perfect sensory mimic of his dream. He knew that he had causality reversed, that the room had always had this smell of old bed linen and older carpets, and that his dream had dredged up body memories from decades past. But the dream was recent, its impact more real and disturbing than his rift with Hudson. It laid claim to being first, creating a wake for the conscious world to follow.

Gray approached the bed. It was covered by the hideous terrycloth bedspread he had dreamed and remembered. It was the pale yellow of old, stained newspaper. It had crawled onto the bed sometime early in the last century, and no one had had the decency to throw it out. The room was used so rarely, it had been allowed to sink into its sullen bubble of stasis. Gray could see nothing that had changed since he had last slept here, over twenty years earlier. He could see nothing that differed from the dream. He stretched out a hand. His fingers tingled as they neared the bedspread. His shoulders were tense with anticipated shock. If the cloth dissolved into slime on contact, he might almost be relieved. Instead, the moment of touch was exactly what he had expected, exactly the dream. Of course it was, he told himself. What did he want terrycloth to feel like?

He was annoyed with himself. "Get *over* it." He spoke aloud, trying to break up the silence. Instead, the sound of his voice turned into a stagnant echo, nothing except a reminder that there was no one to answer. Angrier yet, he sat down hard on the bed. The mattress was old and soft. He sank into it like it was quicksand.

He snorted, at what he wasn't sure. He looked at the brass lamp on the bedside table. It remained aloof. He shook a finger at it. "You think you're smart, don't you? You're not. You're stupid and inert. You don't frighten me." The lamp said nothing. Gray returned its silence. He waited. The unease was not enough to make him run. It began to wither in the face of rationality's scorn. He began to stand but was so deep into the mattress that the leverage was difficult. The mattress began to feel less like a bog, more like an embrace. A bit of a nap, Gray thought, feeling more welcome in the Hall now that he had conquered the silliness. He was also tired. He kicked off his shoes and lay down. He sank into the middle of the bed. He was very comfortable. *I should turn off the light*, he thought, but he closed his eyes instead.

When he was four, when dreamland had too often been hostile, dangerous territory, he had spent many consecutive nights trying to catch the exact moment that sleep came for him. He had never succeeded. But now, without trying, without desire, he saw and knew the instant. He felt sleep arrive, and it was a juggernaut blow of darkness.

chapter eight

the league of concerned friends

The night was a memory tomb. Gray didn't wake until late morning. When he did, everything from his arrival until that present moment had vanished into the dark. He knew what he had done the evening before. The information of his activities was available to him. But this was data, not memories. He might as well have read about the last twenty-four hours in someone else's journal. The dream back in London had a concreteness that the real events did not. He sat on the edge of the bed, confused. He felt as if a chunk had been tugged from his mind, leaving only the hollow trace of what had been there.

He stood up, trying to shake the feeling, and the thought crossed his mind that he should leave. He shrugged it off. He hadn't been sleeping well in London. If his memories were dead and flat, he also felt refreshed. Even if there was a claw-scrape of unease in his chest, even if he had faced this room like a potential enemy last night, he felt at home. He had settled into Gethsemane Hall the way he had sunk into the mattress, surrendering to the soft pull. The house was giving him the first real embrace he had received and accepted since Lillian and Jill had died. He was in no hurry to flee it.

And yet he had to go into town today. There were groceries and household supplies to buy. He experienced sudden relief at the thought of going outside the grounds of the Hall. *Make up your mind,* he told himself. He didn't. Instead, he let his instinct hurry him. He shed the clothes he'd slept in, and showered. The bathroom was just off his parents' old bedroom. Lady Gloria had had newer fixtures installed, mixing with the old, and there was a plastic-and-chrome flex shower head coiled in the claw-footed tub. Afterwards, he went back into his room and eyed it up and down for a minute, wondering if would spend the night here again. He put off the decision and left through the south door, crossing the other bedroom into the Old Chapel. There were no longer any pews or altar, but the fourteenth-century stained glass window had never been removed. The space was narrow, the ceiling high and raftered. When the new chapel had been constructed in the eighteenth century, the old one had briefly been converted into yet another bedroom, then storage. Within Gray's memory, the space had always been empty, a limbo room to pass through to reach stairs to the ground floor, a pointlessness whose shape was the only memory of what it once had been. He was halfway down its length when he fell.

He fetal-curled against the sudden agony of loss, harsh and fresh as the moment of first news. He whimpered. The blows were physical. His wife and daughter were dying again, *right now*, in the IMAX surround of his mind's eye. He began to shiver. Absolute-zero sweat slicked his body. He couldn't move. His eyes were clenched shut, but another wave of chainsaw grief hit, and the pain snapped his lids open. He was staring at the window, looking up at the glass collage shaped into the Madonna and child. He flashed on his nightmare of the laughing crucifixion, and his rage was suddenly as big as his grief. "Ffffff," he whispered. "*Fffffffuuuck ... yyyyyyyou,*" he snarled, to the general and the specific.

And then he could move. He unlocked his arms, straightened his body and crawled forward. His body temperature rose. After a few feet, he was breathing again. He made it to his feet and stood, swaying. He wiped his forehead. The emotions receded, withdrawing waves sucking at sand. *What?* he thought. *What the hell?* He glanced at the window, felt nothing now but low-grade resentment. He ran from the chapel, thundered down the stairs. He kept running until he was outside and was drawing in air lush as the vegetation. He couldn't make it to his car fast enough.

His tires spun gravel all the way up the drive, but when he reached the gate, his foot eased off the accelerator. The urgency to flee the Hall was draining away, being replaced by a sense of foolishness and the resurgent pull of homing instinct. He was running from what, exactly? His own grief? Didn't he expect that there would be moments like the one he had just experienced? Of course there would be. Even as the rationalization dissipated the last of the terror, he distrusted it. He didn't like the way his emotions flattened out, as if a switch had been flicked. Then he saw what was waiting for him on the other side of the gate. He stopped the car.

It was a scrum. Reporters and photographers were so many pustules clustered at the entrance. They spread out to block the road as he approached. His hand hesitated over the gate's remote control. He counted maybe a dozen people. The options were bad. He could try to nose through with the car, but at the speed he would have to go to avoid injuring someone, they could stay with him indefinitely. If there were an accident, the Furies would pursue him to his grave and beyond. The other choice was to go it on foot, enter the quagmire without a protective metal shell. Ugly as slime. But at least the worst kind of stupid damage he could do would be with his fists.

Maybe I can deal with them, he kidded himself as he shut off the car's engine and climbed out. Maybe if he didn't run, gave the carrion hunters what they wanted, they would be satisfied and move on to the next carcass. He didn't even know what they were after, though he had an ugly suspicion at the back of his mind. Maybe he was wrong, though. Maybe this was just a last gasp of interest in him. Maybe all these things. *Maybe*, he thought, *pigs are performing at the Biggin Hill air show*. Still, he shaped his face into an expression he hoped was polite and pleasant. He stepped up to the gate to open it manually. "Good morning," he said.

The cacophony was instant. The reporters yelled questions that sounded like accusations. The photographers opened with a heavy barrage. Gray tried to convert the wave of sound into a white noise background. He almost managed it as he walked through the gate, but enough of the words shouted were the same and he understood them whether he wanted to or not. He heard *Lord Gray* and *haunted* and *refuse*. He thought, *Bloody hell*. The scrum closed in and jostled him as he locked the gate. He held on to his temper. "You know," he said, "I can't very well answer your questions if I can't make them out." He spoke at a conversational level. If they wanted to hear him, they could shut up. He smiled. There was a moment of relative silence, and he began to walk forward. It was like wading in neck-deep water.

"Lord Gray," someone began again. *Sun? Mirror? Mail?* Did it matter? "Will you be permitting a scientific investigation of the phenomena at Gethsemane Hall?"

"This is my home. For reasons that should be understandable, I am seeking a bit of seclusion these days." He thought that sounded all right. Then he made a mistake: "So, no."

Too abrupt. The gloves came off. "How can you block access to the most significant spiritual site in Britain?" "How do you justify one man's wishes standing in the way of a potential benefit for humanity?" "Are you trying to keep the house's powers to yourself?" "Have you been talking with the ghosts?" "Would you be open to a study if you were satisfied it was *scientific*?" "Are you cooperating with the CIA?"

The CIA? he thought. "Excuse me," he said and tried to push through.

The scrum pushed back. "Have you been speaking with your dead wife?"

He stopped walking. He glared at the reporter who'd asked the question. The man was six inches from his nose. Gray saw red but kept just enough restraint not to throw a punch. It barely mattered. Somewhere in the recesses of his fury, a tiny voice was telling him that they'd won, that they'd goaded him into just the sort of reactions that made sexy pictures. The voice drowned in the crimson anger. Gray spat in the reporter's face. Cameras buzzed and clicked like a swarm of cicadas. Frenzied by the scent of blood, the swarm descended. Gray's anger turned to claustrophobic panic. The scrum became a mob. As Gray descended into instinct and the shouts multiplied, the questions at last did turn into white noise. He fought to free himself. He pushed and shoved and lawsuits be damned. He moved forward by what felt like inches. He was yelling, but he didn't know what. He couldn't think, and he couldn't hear himself. He roared and thrust both hands out in front of him. He caught a reporter on the upper chest. The man stumbled back, lost his balance and fell over. He took three others down, domino crash. A gap opened. Gray leaped through it over the jumble of limbs and cameras. He landed awkwardly, and his left knee spasmed. He ignored the pain and ran. Behind him, the pack bayed and gave chase.

He tore up the road and gained a few seconds. He had months of staying alive in Africa to give him stamina. The wolves were slowed by equipment and the crush of numbers. Gray took the bend before town, and fifty yards ahead was The Leaping Stag. *Sanctuary.* Behind him, the pack realized the quarry might escape, and its own fury gave it speed. The howls drew closer. Gray saw the door open. People began to emerge, the lunch crowd drawn outside by the noise. One of them was John Porter. He gestured at Gray, egging him on. Gray pumped his legs faster, squeezing the stone for adrenaline even as he was reaching the wall of his sprint. Someone held the door open for him, and he barrelled through. He sagged against the bar, gasping, and looked back. There was a scuffle at the entrance. Porter and three other men were holding back the media tsunami. "*We're closed,*" Porter bellowed. Gray had often heard Porter raise his voice, but never in anger.

"Like shit you are," a reporter snarled and tried to barge past.

Porter was a man with no media fears. His fist smashed hammer and brick into the man's face. The reporter slumped. His screams were nasal from blood and shattered cartilage. The rest of the pack drew back, skittish at the sight of blood from one of their own. That wasn't a regulation play. "This is private property," Porter told them. His arms were folded, and he was the Colossus of Rhodes, back on the scene and right pissed off. A photographer made the mistake of finding the courage to get in his face. "The Management," Porter said. He smashed the camera from the man's hands. The lens shattered on the pavement. "Reserves the right." He grabbed the photographer's collar. "To refuse service." He threw the photographer. Gray had never seen that done before. The man was actually in the air for a good second. Porter stepped back in, shut the door, and locked it. He nodded once, as if agreeing with himself, and applause followed him back to his post.

His breath beginning to even out, Gray settled himself on a stool and his elbows on the counter top. "Thank you," he said to Porter.

Porter's laugh carried an extra dollop of satisfaction. "Thank *you.*" He opened and closed a fist. "Never thought a bit of violence could be so satisfying." He glanced out the window. "I think you'll be here a while. Get you anything?"

"Ploughman's and a pint of Guinness." He hadn't had breakfast. Now he felt ravenous.

"Nothing like exercise to work up the appetite, eh?" Porter asked, laughing.

"I'd say more the relief of escaping your enemies."

"Ah." No laugh. Porter lowered his voice. "They're not all on the outside," he said.

Gray looked around. "Is Patrick here?" He'd been expecting Hudson to turn up since their phone conversation. The campaign to hunt him down and drag him back to the fold would be protracted and heartfelt. Gray wondered how much bruising their friendship could take. He'd done most of the bruising himself. He felt a rush of guilt.

"Not yet today," Porter answered.

"But he is in town, I take it."

"Came in just before closing last night." He placed a glass by Gray's elbow.

"Let me guess. He left a message that I could find him at the Nelson." Porter nodded. Gray wondered if Hudson would give up and go home if Gray avoided him long enough. More guilt at the hope, more shame. *Coward*, he thought. He knew that Hudson would not go. His friendship ran too deep. *Not really worthy, are you? No. I'm not.* He shoved the remorse away to deal with later. "So who is my enemy here?" he asked Porter.

"Here she comes now." The barman pointed. "She's good. I don't know how she found out you were a regular, but she knows."

"Hardly a state secret," Gray said. He watched the woman approach. She was in her fifties and looked like one of those people who appeared athletic without ever actually engaging in sports. Her salt-and-pepper hair was swept back and cut short. Her features were narrow, and her eyes looked as though they had seen the best bullshit the world had to offer and had stopped being fooled by it decades ago.

She stopped in front of him. "Lord Gray," she said.

"Do I know you?"

"You've heard my voice on your answering machine, I'm sure. You're not easy to get hold of."

"That isn't accidental." He hoped she would take the hint.

She smiled tightly, indicating that she had caught his meaning and was going to ignore it. "Found you, anyway, and I'll lay money that you're going to wish we never met. Louise Meacham. Central Intelligence Agency."

Gray absorbed this. "Are you supposed to just come right out and admit that?" he asked finally.

"Not in the normal course of events." She shrugged. "But I seem to be doing that quite a bit lately."

"I don't suppose the normal course of events would bring you here."

"Correct. Did you know that Pete Adams worked for the Agency?"

He shook his head. "Not until the story was in the news."

"Guess why I'm here."

He sipped his Guinness. "I would really rather not. I have the horrible feeling I'd guess right."

"I want access to your house to conduct a full investigation."

"The police already did that."

"You're going to force me to say it, aren't you? A paranormal investigation."

"*Scientific*, no doubt." He gestured towards the window. "You put those bastards up to this?" His blood pressure rose.

"They track me. That's why they're back in force now. But by the time I'm done, every last rumour of a ghost will have been boxed, labelled, and shipped off to Guantanamo Bay. We want the place's reputation purged and boring. That should take the heat off you."

He thought about this. "What would your investigation involve?"

"Three of us, plus equipment, living in the house until we're done."

"Which would be when?"

"I'm not running the science. If it were up to me, we'd be in and out in an afternoon."

"I doubt that would satisfy the true believers."

Meacham snorted. "Nothing would. But we still need a solid counter-story out there."

"*You* do."

Her smile was cynical enough to be honest. "This is a clean-up job. My agreement, though, with the scientist who's going to debunk your house, is that we do this right."

"I didn't come out here to live in a circus," Gray told her. Meacham was beginning to sound as if he'd already given her the green light, and he wanted her to back off.

"I realize and appreciate that. This is a difficult time for you."

Gray knew a rote statement when he heard one. His hackles rose. "No, I don't think you do realize. Not at all." He held up a hand, warning Meacham not to interrupt and let the silence build to an uncomfortable length. Then he said, "I have no reason to allow either you or the crackpots into my home."

"I might be able to compel you to cooperate," Meacham said. Her tone was at odds with the words, as if she really did find what she was doing distasteful.

Gray didn't have the sympathy to spare. "I'll wait to hear from the Home Secretary. Meantime, leave me alone."

Meacham hooked her thumb in the direction of the window. "You think they will?"

"You think a CIA investigation into the paranormal won't draw them? And don't tell me that they wouldn't find out. You just laid out the exercise as a massive PR campaign. So I see no purpose in continuing this conversation until you have a police contingent to back you up."

Meacham nodded. "I'm sorry you feel that way. I'd prefer it if we could work together."

Gray raised his hands. "I'd prefer it if my wife and daughter hadn't died."

"Should you change your mind —"

"You'll be at the Nelson, along with the rest of my personal care contingent."

She placed a bill on the bar. "His drink is on me," she told Porter. "I'll see you later," she said to Gray.

"I'd rather you didn't."

"You won't have a choice." She gave him a wink as she left. Gray wasn't sure if that defused or backed up the threat.

He finished his drink and ate his lunch. He took his time, hoping the tab mob would move on. They were still outside when he'd finished. "I don't suppose they've forgotten about your back door," he said to Porter.

"Worth a look." He was back a minute later, shaking his head. "Not many, but still enough bring the wrath of God down on you." He started to laugh, thought better of it, went back to polishing a glass. "What were you planning to do today?" he asked Gray.

"I was hoping to pick up some groceries. Very subversive."

"Give me your list."

"Are you sure?"

"If my dear father could see me now, running errands for the aristocracy. He'd smack me upside the head, he would. He would be consumed with the righteous fury of a lifelong union man. Reason enough for me to make a stop at Tesco's for you, yes it is." His laugh was back in full force. "As for you," he went on, "are you comfortable on that seat?"

Gray considered the long day of forced asylum that stretched ahead. "I might move to a booth."

"When you're ready to go home, say the word. Someone will run you back."

"Thanks." Gray ordered another pint, then stood up to head for a booth in the corner. It looked like private enough place to kill the afternoon.

"Want me to tell anyone you're here?" Porter asked. He was serious, now, and sounding very significant.

Gray surrendered, as much because of Porter's concern as his own guilt. "All right, Mother. You can call Patrick."

Hudson showed up less than ten minutes later. He must have been camping out by his phone. He hesitated before sliding onto the bench opposite Gray. "May I join you?" he asked.

"Of course." *Have I been pushing him away that hard?* Gray wondered. *Yes, I have.* Withdrawing the funding was a solid slap in the face, but he didn't regret doing it. He was still drawing satisfaction from the act. He hoped Hudson understood the gesture wasn't aimed at him. He gave his friend the first smile he'd granted him since the funeral. "It's good to see you."

"Really?"

"I haven't been easy to know, recently. Sorry." He saw hope spread over Hudson's face, and he shook his head. "But no, I'm not going back on my decision."

"It isn't the money I'm most worried about."

Here we go, Gray thought. *How many times are we going to chase around this circle?* "I appreciate that," he said. He tried to steer the conversation into more neutral, less spiritual, waters. "I made the right decision to come down," he said. "Had a very good night." The morning had been weird, but never mind. He'd run from the Hall as fast as he could, but now he felt the need to get back. The pull was very strong. He was wanted at home.

"I'm glad." Hudson sounded genuine. "I don't mean to hound you, Richard."

"Though you chased me here," Gray bantered.

"Probably not the best way to bring back the lost sheep, is it?"

It was the first time they'd joked with each other since the explosion. Gray wanted to keep the tone light, but honesty won out. He didn't want Hudson living on false hopes. "I wish you'd accept that this sheep is well and truly lost. That would make life easier for both of us."

Hudson smiled. "I don't give up easily. I promise not to piss you off, though. I will say this. You would find what you're going through much easier if you would let go of your anger."

"There you're wrong. You're really, really wrong." He told Hudson about the paralyzing grief and the anger that had freed him. As he spoke, he saw his friend's brow furrow with concern.

"That doesn't sound good."

"Why not?" Gray asked.

"Because anger doesn't work that way. It imprisons. It doesn't liberate."

"Mine did."

"That's my point. Whatever it was you experienced, it wasn't healthy. It definitely wasn't normal."

"You should talk to this idiot woman who thinks the place is haunted." When he saw Hudson looking thoughtful, Gray added, "That was a joke."

"I know."

"You're not taking it as one."

Hudson didn't reply for a moment. Then he asked, "Is that the only strange thing you've experienced at the Hall?"

Gray hesitated, and that was enough.

"There's more, isn't there?" Hudson went on. "You should be really careful."

"I didn't think ghosts fit in with a properly understood Christianity."

"I'm not saying there are ghosts in the Hall. I'm saying that it sounds to me like there is *something* wrong with the place. I don't know what it is, only that it's wrong."

Gray buried his head in his hands. "Let me guess how the rest of this goes. You want to stay there with me and check this out."

"Couldn't hurt."

"You'll have to stand in line. Everybody but Greenpeace has been on my case to have access to the Hall."

"You might want to consider at least some of these requests."

"No. I want to be alone."

"Go back to London, then. Open the Hall up, and when everything's over, come back down. If the place turns out to be safe."

The thought of the leaving the Hall was acute and painful. His heart pinched. He wanted to be there now. Run away to London? Unimaginable. The strength and irrationality of his need worried him. There *was* something wrong. But his need to be back at the house was stronger. "I'm not going anywhere," he told Hudson.

"Will you at least think about letting me hang out a couple of days?"

"I'll sleep on it."

Most of the reporters were gone by late afternoon. There were other stories to chase, and deadlines to meet. Gray knew the reprieve would end the next morning, when he would begin his starring role in the papers. He could imagine the pictures and the accounts. He'd given them plenty to work with. He expected a wide-eyed, slavering gargoyle described as a selfish lunatic bought and paid for by the CIA. He tried to tell himself this would all be entertaining.

Porter drove him home and helped carry bags of groceries inside. The kitchen was the former butler's pantry, off the courtyard on the north-east side of the ground floor. The colours were lighter here than in much of the Hall, the wood and paintwork a weathered blond. The room wasn't big, but it was a perfect adaptation for a single person living in the Hall. It had been at least fifty years since there had been more than one permanent resident.

"Thanks," Gray said as he and Porter unloaded the last of the bags. "Can I offer you a drink?"

Porter shuffled his feet. He looked antsy, a man wrestling with conflicting discomforts. "I really should be off. The pub can't mind itself."

"Your staff seems pretty competent."

"That they are. They are. But no, must be going."

Curious, Gray asked, "Does the house make you uncomfortable?"

Porter began to protest. "Oh, it isn't that. I didn't mean to suggest —"

"It's all right," Gray reassured him. "I'm not offended. I'm just interested. I've heard enough wild stories about the Hall today, never mind what happened to Pete Adams. Do you dislike the house, John?"

"No, not exactly. It's just ..." He groped for the words. "The fact is, I would like to stay. I want to stay."

"Then why don't you?"

"Because I don't know *why* I want to stay. I just do." Porter looked at the floor. "Everyone in town does," he muttered.

Gray almost missed the last sentence. He was trying to fend off the ice water that flooded his heart at the mention of irrational desire for the Hall. *Run*, said an instinct. *Stay*, said a stronger need. "I see," he said, his voice as quiet as Porter's.

The other man looked up. They locked gazes. "I think you do, at that," Porter said. "You'll be staying, then." When Gray nodded, he held out his hand. "Be well, then."

Gray shook. "Thank you," he said, uncomfortable with the weight of meaning the exchange had taken on.

He saw Porter outside. The barkeep walked as though fighting against an undertow, as if each time he lifted a foot, he might start walking backwards. His brow was shining with effort by the time they reached the drive. He was unhappy to be leaving. And yet, when he started his car and drove off, Gray saw relief loosen his features.

Gray made himself an omelette for dinner. His evening was the same as the previous one, as if through repetition, he might make himself remember the experience, and not just the chronology, the next morning. He thought about moving to the master bedroom, but inertia called him back to his old room. He went to bed a little before midnight. This time he was able to change into pyjamas before he fell asleep.

He didn't sleep through the night. He sat up with a shout in total darkness. His eyes were wide against the nothing that surrounded him. His heart was a deafening kettle drum. He didn't know why he was awake. He couldn't remember dreaming, but he felt the aftermath of a jolting night terror. He reached out, still panicky-blind, fumbled with the bedside table, the table that felt like an unpleasant surprise in its familiarity since it had come to visit him in London before he had come to see it. He found the light and turned it on. The room looked back at him, poker-faced.

His heart was slowing down, tempering its volume. He was very, very awake. He got out of the bed. He was prodded by the feeling of having left something undone. He couldn't imagine what. He suspected the answer was nothing; he had forgotten nothing. He followed the discomfort out of the room, through the suite, back to the Old Chapel. He turned on the light and stood in the doorway. The nagging at the back of his mind had evaporated. *See*, he told himself, *there's nothing that needs doing now, for Christ's sake. Go back to bed.* He didn't. He eyed the chapel. The stained glass window was painted black by the night. The space was illuminated by a low-wattage chandelier hanging from the middle of the ceiling. The light was a dim amber. Shadows were gathered spectators around the periphery.

Gray eyed the centre of the room. His lips were dry, and when he tried to lick them, so was his tongue. *Go on*, he told himself. *Follow the scientific method. You know it's all bullshit, so prove it.* He walked forward. There was no mark on the floor where he had collapsed, but he knew the exact spot all the same, and he eyed it, rabbit to cobra, as he approached. *Humbug and bullshit*, he thought, *humbug and bullshit, mantra of reason*. He stopped when he was one step away. *Humbug*, he thought. *Grow up and get over this*. He took the step.

The grief slammed him to the floor again. It was so fierce it flooded out the terror that rose at its coming. Loss scourged him with barbed wire. He opened his mouth wide to howl his pain. Instead, he snarled. Lead grief transmuted into golden anger. The unfairness, the bloody-minded, capricious *perversity* of an all-loving god had him roaring and gave him strength. He didn't crawl this time. He wouldn't give the deity that satisfaction. He declared war and rose to his knees. Then he was on his feet, his hatred a molten, neon glow in his veins and behind his eyes. Crystalline revelation: revenge was the only worthwhile goal. He strode forward to begin his campaign. Within two steps, the emotions evaporated. For a moment he was a wrung sponge, exhausted. Then fear regained its usurped throne. Gray turned around to stare at where he'd fallen. He found he couldn't swallow. He tried to rationalize, came up with nothing better than dead-of-night terrors and psychological predisposition. He didn't buy it. He'd had confirmation of the tabs' wettest dream. Meacham would be terribly disappointed if he let her team in.

A sliver of hope, just then: maybe not. Maybe her pet scientist *could* debunk what had just happened.

He backed out of the chapel and took the stairs to the ground floor. He would spend the rest of the night in the library, he decided. He would sit in full illumination, try to read, maybe try to sleep, and above all try to reconnect with the rational world. The staircase creaked under his feet. The noise was huge and alarming. Gray winced as if he would wake something up. *Stop it*, he told himself. *Stop that* now. He couldn't allow himself to believe what he very much did. He began to grow angry again as the immediacy of terror receded. He was angry at himself. He expected better of his mind.

He reached the bottom of the stairs and stopped when he realized what room opened across a short hall from him. The crypt lay directly below the Old Chapel. He wished he didn't see a connection. As punishment, he made himself approach the doorway. He turned on the hall lights and looked inside. There were no fixtures in the crypt, and the illumination spilled a pale glow into a third of its depth. It had remained unchanged since the fourteenth century. The stone-ribbed vault was low, and the space looked like a small, sullen church. It had never been one, to Gray's knowledge. It was square, except for an odd recess in the southwest corner, invisible now without the daylight leaking in from the small window in the east wall. *Nothing*, Gray thought. The word was hollow, its meaning evacuated by the Old Chapel. *Go inside*, he said. *Prove something.*

He went inside, but only to cut across the width in the light from the hall. He stayed close to the wall, didn't look into the crypt's interior. He moved quickly, almost running, until he reached the other doorway. He wasn't grabbed. His heart didn't stop. He began to feel foolish and was relieved. *You're not off the hook yet,* he scolded, and went to the kitchen, where he found a flashlight in a drawer next to the sink. He headed back to the crypt and shone the beam into its depths. The stone was impassive. He looked at the ceiling and visualized the layout of the chapel above. He thought the chapel's danger zone coincided with the central keystone. *One more experiment*, he thought. He wondered why he was even contemplating this. He decided he could wait until morning, then realized that he was already walking forward. *Hang on*, he thought. He changed his mind. He told his feet to stop. They ignored him. He stood beneath the vault. The night made a fist and smashed his skull.

The dream came down on Roseminster. It took everyone. Citizen or visitor, investigator or media, they all went down. Anyone who had ever had a thought of Gethsemane Hall had the infection, and the symptoms clamped down hard. (In Washington, Jim Korda's wife wondered why her husband was gasping dread in his sleep and why she couldn't wake him up.) The dream had no images. It told no narrative. When at last they escaped it, the sufferers would not remember the dream, because there was nothing in it to remember. There was only the black, suffocating, strangling, immense and knowing. The dream said nothing, but it taught a lesson. It was the lesson whose pain and truth were so complete that it stabbed Roseminster awake. Every infected soul woke shrieking at the truth, unable ever to share the nightmare because of the lesson.

The lesson had three words: *you are alone.*

chapter . nine

jaws wide open

The experience of having the lies stripped away was like nothing else. Gray had thought he'd had the last of his delusions sandblasted by the death of his wife and daughter. He'd been wrong. He knew that, now. There was an infinite abyss of things he did not know, but he could see his old, comfortable ignorance for what it was.

He was sitting on the floor, curled against the northwest corner of the crypt. He'd been here since he woke, half an hour ago. He couldn't remember the night before, but he could feel its effects in the scoured, purged hollow of his psyche. He shivered, the stone cold against his back. He was sore. He was drained. He was frightened. He was angry. The night was a dividing line, his existence sliced by it into before and after, and he raged against the knowledge that, in a way he couldn't understand because he couldn't *remember* what had happened in the blackness, the event was bigger than the burning death of his family. The truth was so wrong, he began to weep.

The morning light was indifferent, cool. It turned the crypt grey. The vault leaned over Gray, brooding, keeping what it knew to itself. He wiped his eyes and climbed to his feet. He wobbled. His circulation was sluggish, his joints older and colder than the stone. He stuck close to the north wall of the crypt, away from the keystones, as he stumbled out. The grey stuck to his eyes, filming the world with limbo-ooze, reducing everything to something less than reality. Plato's shadows were revealed at last for what they were: magic lantern lies for the frightened and the childish. He moved through a global anaesthetic until he was standing in the courtyard.

The day was bright enough to blind saints. Gray blinked and squinted. His eyes took forever to adjust. When he could see, he took in the constricting embrace of the walls. He sensed their force when he took a few steps toward the exit. The Hall didn't want him to leave. He didn't mind. He didn't want to go. He *should* want to. There had been plenty of times in Africa when he had been afraid for his life, but this was the first time he had ever felt sweetwater-pure terror. But the need to stay was just as strong as it had been yesterday. He thought perhaps he knew why. Something had taken the lies away, but they hadn't yet been replaced with anything. He had to understand. If there was a truth that huge and terrible here, he had to know what it *was*. He hadn't fled Africa when he'd been frightened. He'd been there to do something, something important and meaningful. Absolute rubbish, he realized, but the belief had sustained him. Belief wouldn't hold him up here. But its lack might.

He kept walking. The walls let him pass, but with reluctance. *Come back soon*, they whispered. *I will*, he answered. He didn't bother with his car. The exercise was working heat back into his bones. He went up the drive, and the welcoming party was at the gate, as expected. There were more of them today. He wasn't surprised. He'd put on good entertainment yesterday morning. The clamour began as he reached the gate. He raised his voice, and the distinguished press quieted enough to listen. "Ladies," he said, nodding to the few he saw and thinking, *Whores*. He opened the gate. "Gentlemen," nodding again, thinking, *Bastards*. "I imagine you have the same questions as before, with a few new ones for good measure." He was smiling, and he could tell that was throwing the pack off its stride. His good humour didn't compute. "I must apologize for my bad temper yesterday. I hadn't slept well." The lie sounded odd when he spoke it, as if it were really the truth. "I promise you much greater satisfaction today."

The shouts began at once, but he held his hands up and said nothing until there was calm again. "I would like to beg a few hours of your patience, however." He checked his watch. "I have a few necessary preparations to make and some people to speak with. If you would grant me the time and the *privacy*," he gave his chuckle a knowing, hail-fellow edge, thinking, *You unmitigated shite*, "to get this done, I will meet you back here at six o'clock. I, not to mention several other parties, will be more than happy to answer all your questions then." They began asking them now. He lifted a hand again. "And," he said, "and, I think you'll really like the answers if you do me this service. Thank you for your understanding." *You miserable bags of vomit, I hope you choke on your own balls.*

Anna Pertwee watched Gray talk to the press. Her chest was constricting with guilt. She hadn't been able to bring herself to read the morning editions. The shots of Gray striking back had actually made two front pages. She'd walked into the newsagent's on Wake, two blocks from the Nelson, seen what was on display, and fled in shame. But she made herself come here, halfway down from the Stag, to see what she had wrought. A coward's guilt would have been even worse than what she was feeling. She'd left Corderman back at the hotel. She didn't want anyone else added to the list of those passing judgment on her.

She'd been here since just after eight. The discomfort in her chest kept her from being bored. After an hour, Gray had appeared. She'd braced herself for escalation. She'd been terrified about what form that would take. She didn't expect the calm that broke out. She couldn't hear what Gray was saying, but his voice wasn't raised. The reporters were listening. Some photographers were snapping, but the efforts seemed perfunctory. Then the impossible happened. The Red Sea parted, and Gray walked up the road. Alone. Pertwee's jaw sagged. She was so stunned she didn't think to retreat as Gray drew close. He spotted her, and she snapped out of her daze.

Gray didn't look angry. He was smiling. His expression struck her as a bit off. There was a sardonic intensity to it, as if his mind were endlessly repeating the same bitter joke. "Good morning," he said, his tone not at all hostile. "Ms. ... Pertwee, I believe it was?" When she nodded, he went on. "I guess we have to start again. The fates have spoken. I suppose the fact that you're still here, despite my threat of calling the police, means that you haven't given up on the idea of investigating my home."

"Yes. I'm sorry; I don't enjoy being a pest."

Gray's laugh was sour and short. "Yet here you are. Well, I'm glad. I was just going to go looking for you, as a matter of fact."

"Oh?" *To serve me a writ?* she wondered.

"Yes. I've reconsidered. You're welcome to the Hall." He didn't sound reluctant.

She was having trouble keeping up with the surprises. "I ... really?"

"I insist upon it. If you hadn't come to me yesterday, I would probably be trying to find you or someone else in your field today."

She had all the evidence she needed for the Hall's spiritual agency right in his conversion. If only he didn't look like he knew so much more than she did, like he was setting up a lethal practical joke. "That's wonderful," she said. "We can be there right away."

"Give me until six. There are a few other people I have to contact."

"Others?"

"You're not going to be the only team there." Pertwee knew her face fell, and Gray's smile became fierce. "You wanted the investigation. It's going to be *thorough*," he said, and when she flinched, he walked away.

Meacham had been about to put the wheels in motion when Gray knocked on her door at the Nelson. "I thought I was going to have to fight a lot harder than this," she said after he told her why he was there. "What changed your mind?"

"Let's say I was visited by three spirits." He gave her a speculative look. "How hard were you going to press me?"

"You have no idea." Meacham smiled, but she kept her expression grim. She wanted him to know life could have been hell. "If I had to, I would have brought the hammer down hard. I would have hated doing it."

"But not enough to hold back."

She shook her head. An empathetic ember flared up. Gray's face was pale, stretched with tension. The man looked as if he'd been through a week of zero sleep and waking nightmares. She decided to confide in him, at least far enough that he would know he'd made the right decision. "You know how it is with wounded animals," she said. "They'll fight tooth and claw for survival, and you're stupid to block their way."

"You're one of these animals?"

"Yeah. Sorry, but I value my survival over yours."

"I appreciate your honesty." He sounded genuinely amused, and his tone was the warmest Meacham had heard it yet.

"I appreciate your flexibility," she said. "I don't think you'll regret this. I wasn't lying when I said a debunking will help you out, too."

"You sound very sure about the results."

She cocked her head. "Aren't you?" She studied his face more closely. There was an odd shine in his eyes. She couldn't decide if she was seeing fear or excitement.

"I want your scientist to be rigorous."

"He will be. I'm debunking your house whether he does or not. That's what I have to do for my survival. But you'll get the straight goods, with no massaging."

"Where's your man?"

"In London, waiting for the word."

"He should be able to make it here by six, then."

"I'm not sure. I think he's more likely to arrive tomorrow. He has a fair bit of equipment to haul down."

"No," Gray was emphatic. "The equipment can follow along later. I want him here at six. That's one of the conditions of access."

"I hate to point it out, but you're not in a position to set conditions. I'm still holding a hammer."

"Humour me. Why make life hard on yourself?"

"Fine. What happens at six?"

Shark grin. He was thinking of something big-time hilarious. "How do you like the media?"

"I steer clear. Nature of the job. Why?"

"At six, we present ourselves to the ladies and gentlemen of the press."

Gray spoke to Hudson, then strolled up Wake. He was killing time now. He wasn't sure why he was playing up the theatre. Petty vengeance, yes, there was that. At least as far as Pertwee was concerned. There was more, though, and he couldn't give it a name. There was simply the necessity for an event. The press conference would be a ritual. It might be marking a beginning. He suspected that was how Pertwee would see it: the moment that the way to the redemption of Gethsemane Hall opened to her. It might be the beginning of something for him, too. He wanted the knowledge the investigations would give him. He wanted to know what the truth was that had scraped him so raw last night. There was something else he wanted, though he didn't know what it was.

It linked up to the truth, and to the conflicting truths Hudson, Meacham, and Pertwee were throwing at him. It was an action, but he couldn't see if he was its subject or object.

Houdini had begun his massive campaign of debunking spiritualists because he had been disappointed by their charlatanism when he first turned to them to try to contact his dead wife. The example was famous. If someone pointed out the parallels to his case, Gray wouldn't be surprised. *Have you been speaking with your dead wife?* the reporter had asked. No, he hadn't. He asked the next question: *Would you, if you could?* He wondered if he were walking that road, another of the bereaved looking for comforting platitudes from the beyond, Hallmark greetings from the lost. *Having a wonderful time, dear. Wish you were here.* The thought of hearing Lillian's voice again spread ice through his gut. The idea entangled itself with the after-effects of the night's truth and became toxic. He tried to avoid the next thought, but it came anyway: his daughter's whisper from the darkness. Terrified nausea swept over him. He stumbled, broke into a short run, trying to escape implications he couldn't even articulate.

This evening was not going to mark a beginning. Not, at least, of the sort that Hudson and his other friends would wish for him. There were no fresh starts about to dawn over the horizon. What rose might not even be the sun.

Endings, then. Oh, there were endings as saccharine and false as new beginnings. They were called *closure*. With such endings, he was supposed to *turn the page, close the chapter, move on.* Those endings were among the biggest lies in the Book of Wishful Thinking. He didn't feel one of those coming on. He sensed something far more worthy of the name.

He stopped in front of St. Rose's just as he understood the nature of the day. He realized he was looking at the town, at the world around him, as if he would not be seeing these things again. After he had spoken with Hudson, he had thought, with relief and satisfaction, that once the press conference was out of the way, he wouldn't have to leave the Hall again. Now he wondered if he was ever leaving. The cold spread though his body once more. *Don't be silly,* he tried to tell himself. He didn't listen. He was frightened. And still the need rose to be back at the Hall. The tug scared him even more, but remained undiluted by the fear.

St. Rose's stood on a small green that was elevated a man's height above the level of Wake, turning it into the summit of Roseminster. Gray climbed the steps to the green. Straight ahead was the stone column of the war memorial. Beyond it, where the square formed a point and Wake rose to its level, was a squatter, shorter pillar enclosing a fountain, a golden jubilee tribute to Victoria. The thirteenth-century tower of the church was square, stolid, crenelated at the top. It looked ready to fend off all besiegers. It didn't hold off Gray as he walked to the front door and went inside.

The interior was simple, despite being an amalgam of modifications and renovations over eight hundred years. The walls were white and unadorned. The austerity was broken by the glowing violet of the stained glass window, and by a carpet from nearby Axminster, its intricacy faded now by wear. Scaffolding rose in both aisles, and Gray's tongue caught the dry taste of fresh plaster dust. He sat down in a pew and looked across the expanse of the choir toward the altar and its small cross. The church wasn't a big one, but the altar seemed to Gray an enormous distance away, aloof and useless in the indifferent daylight.

His family had roots as deep as Roseminster's. The Domesday Book placed his ancestors here. When it had been decided that a church would rise in honour of St. Rose, the Grays had financed a large part of the original construction, and they had been involved in its growth and transformations all the way down the line to him, the terminus. Somewhere in the dusty, unvisited attic of his finances, he knew, there was an endowment that had made the scaffolding he saw possible. He was the church's lifeblood, but he felt disconnected enough to be its cancer. *Where were You?* he thought, eyes on the cross, so small and remote. *I believed in You. I worked for You. I loved You. What did I do that needed punishment? What did my wife and daughter do? I sent them on an errand to facilitate Your work, so we could help the starving and the persecuted and the bereaved and others who, by Your great love, have been left screaming on the rack. For that, they should be smashed and burned? Is that more of Your love? It passeth all understanding, all right, it bloody well goddamn does.*

The questions felt pointless, stones thrown in a hollow echo chamber. They were silly gestures, meaningless as a genuflection. The crucifix was an abstract widget on a mount. Gray tried to reach back to his anger and resentment at the funeral. There was nothing to grasp. Even his rage from the day before, when he had lain on the floor in the Old Chapel, seemed, if not ludicrous, misdirected. *Hello?* he thought. *Is there anybody there?*

No answer. He was on the verge of thinking that there never had been, that he had devoted a good chunk of his life and unintentionally sacrificed his family to Hudson's imaginary friend, but he hesitated. That wasn't right, either. Gethsemane Hall was a rebuke to rationalism. He had been brought low last night. He was being propelled down a road that did not lead to Damascus.

He tried to open himself up to the church. He could remember when that was easy, though the memories were remote and unclear. *Last chance*, he thought. *If You're there, help me.* He waited. The cold in his blood spread. He began to be afraid he might, after all, receive an answer. He stood up. There was nothing here. The place was empty. On his way out, he paused beside a table at the rear of the pews. He ran his eyes over the church literature and yellowing postcards. He flipped through the parish magazine, scanning White Elephant announcements, vague but spiritually unobjectionable editorials, calendars of church events, and Biblical crossword puzzles. He felt angry again. The rage had a bit more focus, now. He could identify a target. It wasn't a deity who was, at best, AWOL. It was faith itself, the belief in the benevolence of an absence or worse. He was pissed at blindness. He felt an almost evangelical need to make people see.

He left the church, fit to shake its foundations.

They caught the train to Roseminster at Waterloo. The trip would take the best part of three hours, and they were barely out of London when Kristine Sturghill fell asleep. James Crawford knew other people who responded to train travel like infants in cars, lulled to unconsciousness by the rhythm and motion within minutes. He used to be one of those, but that was years ago, when the trains still rattled and clanked and there was a pronounced, constant *ka-chunk-ka-chunk, ka-chunk-ka-chunk* lullaby. Over the last couple of decades, the trains had become too silent, the beat surfacing only every so often. If he tried to close his eyes, he would listen too hard, on the edge until the next iteration.

He spent the time sorting notes, trying to organize his thoughts. He'd left instructions for the shipping of his equipment. He expected it to arrive at Roseminster in the morning. Not much left to do in the meantime, really. He had his investigation procedures down to a routine, and the only variables would be site-specific, adaptations mandated by the geography of the house. He wouldn't know what those would be until he saw the location. He tried to find something productive to do, anyway. He was trying to keep his mind off the previous night.

No such luck. The screen of his laptop turned into a collection of blurry runes. He circled around the nightmare, trying to find solid ground on which to dismiss it. It wouldn't let him. It hag-rode him, digging up questions that he had thought buried for good and all a long time ago. They were rotting, but still potent. He had lost his faith over thirty years ago. He'd been raised nominally C of E, his family going to Easter services and the occasional carol ceremony. His religion had been a thing of background noise, unquestioned because he'd never thought about it. He'd been confirmed because it was the done thing, an exercise in trivia memorization that he had found enjoyable for the pomp but no more meaningful than a good television show. Still, there had been a certain comfort to his belief. It was part of life's solid bedrock. It would always be there. It didn't occur to him that the foundations might crack.

A year after his confirmation, the seismic tremors began. The distant early warning signs were some puzzling over the nature of Hell, logical inconsistencies in the Bible stories as he knew them, and a vague awareness of pretzel-form rationalizations. The catalyst was religion's great nemesis. From his first infatuation with dinosaurs at the age of four, he'd loved science, and he hadn't imagined a conflict between it and his taken-for-granted faith until the earthquake came during his fourth form. He'd been researching a science project on black holes. He couldn't even recall the name of the book he'd read. It was a general readership text, setting out an equation-free introduction to the subject. All very straightforward, except that in the first chapter, the author went off on a tangent, taking the concept of black holes as a jumping-off point to demonstrate the complete irrationality behind the mere concept of a deity. The questions he had asked on the rare occasions he had thought about God at all became fully formed doubts. Within a year, the doubts had become convictions.

By the time he started university, the nonsensicality of any form of spirituality was, to him, so transparently self-evident that he found any sort of belief that would not or could not subject itself to empirical testing to be frustrating, almost to the point of a personal affront. There had been a time, at the beginning of his twenties, when he thought that a sufficiently well-backed argument should be enough to purge people of their irrational tenets. When he looked back at that younger, activist self, he knew he'd been as naive as the ten-year-old believer. If anything, he'd been worse, possessed by the same fervour as the most dogmatic born-again Christian. He liked to think he had a more jaundiced view of himself and his activities now. He might have begun his debunking odyssey in an effort to show the faithful the errors of their ways. He didn't for a moment believe that he was rolling back superstition in the minds of the true believers anymore. If somewhere out there was a mind that was just questioning enough to be touched by his work, well and good, but he didn't look for that. He was still a creature of his convictions. He was old enough to know that, now. What interested him was not so much curing people of bizarre beliefs, but why they held the beliefs in the first place. He'd loved true ghost stories as a child. He still did. He found what was behind them even more fascinating. The thrill of discovering that stories of haunting were not just the products of overheated imaginations, but could be attributed to actual, physical, measurable phenomena, was evergreen. He hoped there was something at Gethsemane Hall. It would be too disappointing if the house's reputation was based entirely on hearsay.

One more effort at self-honesty, now. *Go just a little deeper. Aren't you going to derive just a little, eensy-weensy bit of satisfaction in publishing a complete demystification of the Hall? Aren't you imagining the faces of the place's most fervent and ill-informed propagandists? Well, yes. Just a bit. Just one small bit.*

The purity of his motives wasn't what was bothering him. It was that awful nightmare that had left no memory but much trouble of the spirit. *You are alone.* Of course they were. He hadn't woken with any new conviction. But it was as if a hammer had come and smashed the nail of his belief all the way home. He knew that there was no all-loving father watching over the world. He knew that dead is dead, and gone is gone, but now he felt those truths in a new way. They hurt. They made him uncomfortable. The full abyss of *gone* was yawning wide. The true coldness of the universe was reaching into him, just at an age when he thought he had long-since come to terms with the idea. He didn't appreciate what felt like fresh, visceral knowledge. His unwelcome reactions to it included a half-formed hope, shut down and demolished as soon as it appeared, that maybe he had been wrong for the last three decades.

He was going down paths that weren't productive. He gave up trying to channel his thoughts into something that passed for work. He shut down the word processor and opened a game of solitaire.

Sturghill woke up just after the train stopped at Yeovil Junction. Meacham had introduced him to the magician just before heading down to Roseminster. Crawford had been impressed by the breadth of her knowledge. "You know a lot more about science than I do about magic," he had told her.

"Don't worry, I won't pretend to tread on your turf," she had replied.

"Please, feel free to do so. Any extra insight will be a huge help. I'm not one of those scientists so arrogant he believes he can see through magic tricks just because he knows the laws of physics."

She'd grinned; they'd shaken hands and forged Reason's Alliance.

Now she yawned and stretched. "Sorry," she said. "Didn't get much sleep last night."

Crawford smiled. "Too excited?"

She shook her head. "Unbelievable nightmare."

Crawford's smile went rigid.

Six o'clock. The curtain rose.

Meacham wouldn't have put Gray down as having a flair for the theatrical. The brooding, hounded widower she had spoken to in the Stag had seemed a long way from irony and fun. The appearance had been misleading. He was getting his own back on all of them. She could see a twinkle, small but present, in his eyes, as if he were a man in the first stages of resurrection. She didn't blame him for his amusement. The scene was pretty damn funny. She was exhausted after the hell-suite of the night before, but she could still summon a chuckle or two.

They were standing with their backs to the gate, still closed, to the grounds of Gethsemane Hall. Gray was speaking to the reporters, chatting buddy-buddy with the people who'd chased him, swinging pitchforks and torches, into the Stag the day before. They were listening, polite as hell, not interrupting. Meacham and the others were standing behind him. He introduced each of them. Crawford and Pertwee were fun to watch when each realized who the other was. Crawford looked tired, too — they all did — but he was eyeing Pertwee with a humour that was dancing on the edge of contempt. Pertwee was giving him the cold-fish stare. Her sidekick, Edgar Corderman, looked like all he needed was the word from his mistress to leap at Crawford's throat.

Pertwee's face sank even further into unhappiness and hostility when Gray introduced Sturghill as a magician. Gray threw some mischief around by playing coy with a couple of the introductions. He left out Corderman completely, as if he hadn't even noticed he was there. He gave Meacham's name, but not her profession. There was one more omission. Meacham looked around and spotted Patrick Hudson hanging around just beyond the scrum, on the sidelines with the gathered curious of Roseminster. Meacham had met Hudson on the walk down to the gate. He had told her that he would be at the Hall too, and that he was a friend of Gray's. He had peeled off from the group as they reached the site of Gray's theatre. He didn't want to play, and it looked like Gray was respecting his wishes. The rest weren't Gray's friends. They were using him to reach the house. No special consideration for them. Just a little bit of vengeance.

Gray twisted the knife a bit further. "But I shouldn't presume to answer for the experts," he said. "I should do them the courtesy of letting them speak for themselves." And so he threw them to the wolves.

Pertwee jumped in first. She was the fish closest to being in water. She started to blather on about the spiritual fountainhead that the house was, yadda yadda yadda. Meacham found herself tuning out, realizing that she would now be hearing variations on this theme for days on end. The reporters were looking bored, too.

They knew the refrain by heart, it had no beat, and they couldn't dance to it. One of them threw a spanner into Pertwee's works. "But if you believe there are supernatural forces in this house, isn't it possible that they caused the death of Peter Adams?"

"*No.*" Pertwee quivered with the force of her denial. "It is simply not credible that the spirits could cause anyone harm."

"Why not?" another asked. "There are good people and bad people. Why not good and bad ghosts?"

"That isn't the way the spirit realm works," Pertwee began.

"What about Hell?"

Meacham realized the questions weren't serious. They were just giving Pertwee the gears.

Pertwee tried again. "That's a fundamental misunderstanding. As I hope to show here, the only danger is when people react badly and harm themselves."

Booooring. They were looking for new juice, not finding it. A couple of questions flew Crawford's way, but they were half-hearted, pure rote. Did he think Gethsemane Hall was haunted? "I have yet to encounter a single authentic instance of haunting," he answered. "But I will withhold judgement until I've completed my study."

A bright young thing, clearly pleased beyond measure with the way his shirt looked on him, turned to Meacham. "And is the CIA's position that the reports of ghosts here are —"

"Fucking horseshit," she said, and smiled sweetly. Christ, this was fun. To Gray she said, "Can we go in now?"

He must have had his finger on a remote. She still jumped a bit when the gate opened. Before her, the drive descended from the early evening light to a black tunnel of trees. The hollow of dark stared into her, expectant.

chapter ten

the grand tour

Meacham thought, *Here we go*. She heard the gate close behind her. The sound was a restrained latching of metal, but it felt like the hollow boom of a vault door. After twenty yards, the gravel drive's steep gradient dropped into the trees. The oaks reached across to each other, making a roof and blocking the sunlight. Meacham had thought *tunnel* just before they walked through the gate, but now, as they approached, she kept thinking *funnel*, and then, before she could stop herself, *throat*. *You*, she told herself, *have the willies*. When was the last time that had happened? The most recent memories were from childhood, too faded to carry emotional weight. The closest thing to fear in her adult life had been in Geneva, when everything had gone wrong in ways so inexplicable and surreal, and on a scale so colossal, the balls-up had seemed almost supernatural. This was different. This was the creeps. This was looking at dark woods and not really wanting to go in.

This was also idiotic. The dream was the culprit, she decided. It was still bothering her. Its insidious and nasty nothingness had her heart pinching. Her gut had been hollowed out by a visceral crash course in existentialism. She resented the merry havoc games of her subconscious. She knew what she believed, and that was already close enough to nothing for government work. She shouldn't be having sucker-punch aftereffects from a dream, for Chrissake. She put her overreaction down to a lack of sleep. The nightmare had finished her for the night. She was never at her best when sleep-deprived. No one was. Decisions were unreliable, responses irrational under those conditions. The history of the Agency was a testament to the effects of too much coffee and nerves, and not enough sleep and reflection.

They passed under the shadow of the oaks. The underbrush was night-thick. The trunks were fuzzy with moss. Meacham could hear the green. She looked to the right and left of the drive, but her view stopped a few yards into the mass of trees and ferns. Hardly unusual, she reminded herself. Typical English vegetation, which made up for its limited space by mightily concentrating its resources. She stared into the woods, armed with the knowledge of the mundane. The gloom stared back, and she blinked first. Crawford had told her: specific environmental factors could trigger unease or worse. She hung on to that fact. *(And you're tired — you're overtired.)* She walked a bit faster, stepping a bit harder than she had to, encouraging the real-world crunch of gravel under her heels.

She caught up to Hudson. *Do your job,* she told herself. *Be useful. Know these people. Gather the intel.* She'd read a file on Hudson. She had the breakdown on everyone she was going to be staying with at Gethsemane Hall. At one point she had considered using Hudson to approach Gray, but she had discarded the idea once word starting coming back that the two weren't working together anymore. She also doubted, given Hudson's causes, that he'd be open to collaboration. Knowing him now had a different importance. She knew what most of the agendas in the group were. She didn't have his filed away yet. "I noticed you didn't speak at the press conference," she said.

Hudson had been frowning at the woods. He looked at her now, as if relieved she had drawn his attention. "I don't have a public interest in the results of the investigations."

"How about a private one?"

He thought that one over. "I suppose so."

Meacham caught him looking at Gray. The lord of the manor was several paces ahead of the rest of the group and moving fast. *(Wee wee wee, all the way home.)* "You're worried about him," she guessed.

Hudson didn't seem concerned or surprised that she'd read him. "Yes," he said.

"About his health?"

"His spiritual health." He gave Meacham a wry smile. "I don't think that's uppermost on your mind."

"No," she admitted. "It isn't. But why are you worried?"

"There's something wrong with the house."

"You think the place is haunted?"

"No. If you accept the tenets of Christianity and really think them through, there isn't really room for the idea of homeless spirits."

"Then ..."

"A place doesn't need ghosts to be spiritually unhealthy. Take Abu Ghraib, for example." He paused, and Meacham caught a twinkle. "Even if the place were closed down and empty, I don't think anyone could spend time there without suffering some sort of damage."

"I didn't realize Gethsemane Hall had that kind of reputation." She glanced over her shoulder. Pertwee was out of earshot, thank God. She was bringing up the rear with Corderman, walking behind Crawford and Sturghill. The ghost hunter was talking with Corderman and still glaring death beams at Crawford's neck.

"It doesn't."

"What makes you think there's a problem, then?"

Hudson nodded towards Gray. His face was twisted for a moment by needle-sharp worry and hurt.

Meacham purged the levity from her tone. "You've been friends a long time?" She knew they had been, but better to let Hudson open up and tell her more than she could glean from dry analysis and summaries of dates.

"I was his best man."

"Have you spent a lot of time here?"

"Never. He hasn't been here for years. He came when he was younger, but I don't think he liked it much. Now he doesn't want to leave."

"People change." She spread her arms to take in the trees as they funnelled them down. Cool air rose like breath to meet them. "After what happened to him, if he wants to be alone, this is a good place."

"I know."

"So?"

He shrugged. "I'm not sure. He was shattered and bitter before he decided to come down. Now there's something off about him. I don't think his staying here alone is healthy."

"He won't be alone now."

Hudson nodded, looking relieved as well as worried.

But then the drive made a sharp bend, and they hit the transition between the untended woods and the gardens. The variety of tree species multiplied. Oak, elm, chestnut, willow, and pine lined the circumference of the grounds and protected the isolation of the Hall in its cleft. Then there were the yew trees. Meacham had never seen so many. They were the forward guard of the perimeter, a force of massive, twisted age. Their branches were a confusion of pythons, their trunks thick as history. Their roots were coiled high on the ground, ready to propel them forward if the need arose. They were England, and they were watching. At first, Meacham could only see fragments of the house through the branches, but the drive made its final descent free of the trees.

Gray paused on the elevation, waiting for everyone to catch up, the proud host presenting the first real view of his home.

Gethsemane Hall was an exercise in architectural stratification, arranged around a central courtyard. Authentic half-timbered Elizabethan gables with strangely placed mullioned windows became faux Elizabethan Victoriana whose timbers were too regular and clean. Bursting in between was medieval stonework that was built for defence, not aesthetics. The house showed the history of its renovations like tree rings. A massive gatehouse tower dominated the west front. It was one with the foundations, works that made everything more recent look like a temporary afterthought. The house was surrounded by a moat. To the right, the gardens spread out over two levels split in half by a fifteen-foot change in elevation. The half nearest the house was formal. Exuberant flower arrangements bordered the moat wall. On the other side of the drive, which followed the wall, was a lawn, wide open except for a huge scotch pine that twisted as if agonized by its own height. Its branches pushed against a phantom west wind.

The upper level of the gardens was a planned wilderness. The trees ran riot. Willows drooped over a lake, and a monkey puzzle burst, incongruous, between them. The lake fed a cascade nestled in the rise between the two halves of the grounds. The cascade spilled into a rectangular pond. From this distance, the pond seemed still. Meacham looked from it to the moat. She noticed that the moat's water wasn't stagnant at all and guessed that the pond must feed into it underground.

Pertwee had pushed ahead a couple of steps and was gazing at the Hall and its grounds with baby-wide eyes. Her breaths were deep and big, as if she could suck the scene into her lungs. "This is so beautiful," she said. Meacham agreed. "Can't you feel the peace?" Meacham differed. Pertwee wouldn't give it up. "Just like its namesake," she said.

Meacham saw Hudson stiffen. *Interesting,* she thought. The subject of religion came up, and Hudson, of all people, reacted as if an unforgivable social breach had been committed. Why was that? Then she saw the way he was watching Gray: wary, braced.

Gray didn't disappoint. "You mean the peace of the garden where Jesus asked God to let him off the hook? Where he was scared witless? Where he was quote *in agony,* unquote? Where his sweat was ..." Dramatic pause. He turned to Hudson. "How does it go, Patrick?"

Visible reluctance before the answer. "'His sweat was as it were great drops of blood falling down to the ground.'"

"As it were," Gray repeated, sour fun on his face. "And yes, where Judas delivered the kiss. Is that what you feel, Ms. Pertwee? The peace of betrayal?"

Pertwee reddened but held her ground. "None of what you said has turned the Garden of Gethsemane into an unholy place. It is still revered."

"That's sweet," Gray said. He spoke the words without irony, without condemnation. Because of that, even Meacham felt the burn. Pertwee swallowed hard and assembled a brave face. Meacham watched the joy return to her eyes as she gazed on the hall. The girl bounced back quickly. Her belief system was solid. She was going to be a headache.

"How old is the house?" Sturghill asked.

"The oldest sections are over six hundred and fifty years old," Gray said. "There have been additions and changes constantly. The most recent were commissioned by my aunt."

Meacham said, "Your gardens look very well-tended. I thought no one had been living here."

"There's a firm in Axminster. My family has dealt with them since the fifties. They look after things."

"No one local can do it?" She was surprised a gardening service hadn't set itself up nearby.

"It's not that they can't. There's a very good landscaping company here. They prefer not to work here."

"The locals don't like your house, I take it."

"It's more complicated than that. They don't want to spend time here because they really *do* want to spend time here."

"I don't understand."

"I do." His expression as he looked at the house was an indecipherable mix of love, longing, and fear.

"Then why do you stay?"

"Because I've given in," he answered, and started walking again.

He led them around to the gatehouse tower. A narrow stone bridge crossed the moat. They passed through the tower's arch and into the cobbled courtyard. A disused fountain stood in the centre. Against the south wall, Meacham saw an enormous dog house. It had half-timbered sides and an orange tiled roof. It looked like a chunk of gable that had been detached from the roof of the house. Meacham pointed to it. "For Cerberus?" she asked.

"It's from the 1870s," Gray answered. "Built for Falstaff."

"Who was?"

"A Saint-Bernard and Rottweiler cross."

"Must have been very effective at keeping the barbarians from the gate," Crawford commented.

"The house has never really had problems with attackers."

"Why not?" Meacham asked.

"Its location, mainly. It's very isolated."

"It isn't very far from town."

"True," said Gray, "but Hawkesfield Road is recent history, by the Hall's standards, and the drive even more so. The house is hidden by the forest, which is still pretty thick, so imagine it five or six centuries ago. There's at least one story of a raiding party that targeted the Hall but became lost in the woods."

A doorway in the courtyard led to the outer hall. "This used to be the buttery," Gray explained. "There was an entrance to the Great Hall from the courtyard, but that made for a very drafty eating experience. My family finally had the idea of walling up that doorway and using this as the way into the Great Hall. Only took them five hundred years to come up with that innovation." The room was very spare. There was a wooden bench in one corner, and beside it a Chinese vase with a few dead stalks of bamboo. A painting of George III hung on the wall opposite the entrance. It was going dark and waxy with sunlight and grit.

The Great Hall had a high, vaulted ceiling. The upper half of the space was light, wooden timbers arching over white walls. Very dark oak panelling sucked away light in the lower half. In the centre of the room, placed lengthwise, was an oak table, massive enough to pass for a dolmen. It looked small in a room that had been designed for several tables of its size. A heraldic frieze circled the room at the top of the panelling, just above Meacham's eye level. Coats of arms were surrounded by gryphons, lions, giant wolves, and dragons. Lots of dragons. There were two tapestries, one above the door as they entered, the other on the opposite wall. The nearest was the most badly faded of the two. A woman stood in the centre of a forest clearing, a Latin speech bubble emerging from her mouth. She was surrounded by a kneeling crowd. Meacham kept thinking there were other figures in the trees, but every time she looked more closely, she saw nothing but twining vines and hanging fruit. "Saint Rose the Evangelist," Hudson said. "The local patron saint."

"She lived on this site," Pertwee said.

"Or so the story goes," Gray said, deflating her.

"Are you saying she didn't?" Corderman demanded.

"I'm just waiting for something more definite than tradition to make the case," Gray answered.

Meacham had no difficulty identifying the subject of the other tapestry. She'd seen plenty of encounters between Saint George and the dragon. Much of this work had faded, too, but the reptile's colours and definition were still very strong. George and his horse were fading into nothing. The horse was rearing in front of the monster, and George's lance was pointing at the ground instead of at the dragon. The stance looked awkward, like an accident waiting to happen. The lady stood behind the dragon, gazing at George with what struck Meacham as complete disinterest. Then she noticed that the woman wasn't chained. The dragon, bigger than in most other representations she'd seen, was looming over George with a knowing look. The portrayal seemed to be coming from some parallel universe, where the knight was a patsy about to be roasted.

The northwest doorway brought them to the staircase hall and another change in style. The fireplace and panelling in the Great Hall, Gray explained, were Elizabethan. The staircase was Jacobean. A grotesque, snarling face stared back at Meacham from the newel post. Its features bore the anger of a defeated enemy. Gray started up the stairs. "I'll show you your rooms," he said.

"What's through there?" Corderman asked. He was standing by the hall's other doorway, peering into gloom.

"The crypt," Gray said. He didn't come back down the stairs.

"Can we check it out?" Corderman was shifting from foot to foot, drawn by Gothic stone, seduced even more by the evocative name of the room.

Gray hesitated, then shrugged. "Of course," he said. He followed as they entered the crypt, but Meacham saw him hang back by the entrance.

The room was ancient emptiness. Meacham couldn't see the interest beyond the obvious ghost story atmosphere. Then Pertwee squealed. "There's a cold spot!" she said, as if it were the bestest Christmas ever. She was standing beneath the central keystone, spreading her arms in ecstasy. She was also shivering. "Really strong," she murmured. Christmas and birthday combined. She shot an accusing look at Gray. "Didn't you know this was here?" Gray shrugged again. He was watching Pertwee intently, as if expecting her to combust. "Why didn't you tell us?" she demanded.

"I think," Crawford said, "that he's letting us gather our own first impressions of the Hall."

"Free of suggestion," Sturghill put in.

"I'm not imagining this," Pertwee said. She moved aside. "Go ahead, you try."

Crawford stepped forward. He froze, his eyes startled wide. Pertwee's smile was told-you-so. Christmas and birthday and summer vacation all in one. Crawford jumped back, stared at the spot he'd been standing. He reached forward. He snatched his hand back, bitten, then tried again. He kept his hand out this time. Meacham watched him work to reacquire his composure, recapture the scientist and tamp down the freaked-out caveman. "Very striking," he said.

"Well?" Pertwee asked. "Explain that away."

"I'm not drawing any conclusions until I've examined the phenomenon properly. You won't mind if I don't completely ditch the scientific method? Ta, darling."

Pertwee reddened, embarrassed and annoyed, eyes to the floor. Meacham thought the ghost hunter's anger was aimed as much at herself as at Crawford. *No shortcuts if you want to be taken seriously, honey*, she thought. Then she waded into the spot herself, while she was still feeling snarky.

It was like opening a door to January. There was no transition. The air around Meacham went from room temperature to numbing in an eye-blink switch. The cold sucked at her, trying to pull her down through the floor. Her heart stopped, then sprinted loud and hard. The rules of her universe were broken. She wanted to run. She made herself stay put. *Environmental conditions*, she reminded herself. *You don't know what's going on, so you want to howl and pray to the dragon not to eat the sun.* She was used to being out of the loop. Her years at the Agency had taught her this was a normal state of affairs. No matter how much you thought you knew, there was always a whole new realm of magical and incomprehensible manoeuvring going on above you. And the wizards were always just as stupid and venal and human as everybody else. They just had better intel and leverage. She fought down the urge to exclaim. She said, "Pretty weird," and that was good enough. She let someone else try the ride.

Gray was frowning. "You're all just experiencing cold?" he asked. Sturghill, checking things out, yelped and laughed and nodded. "Nothing else?"

Heads shaking. *What more was he expecting?* Meacham wondered.

"What did you experience?" Pertwee asked.

Gray didn't answer. He turned and headed back up the stairs again. They followed, and he brought them to the Old Chapel. "While you're at it," he said, and he gestured for them to enter. His face was unreadable.

Corderman scampered forward, first one in, no rotten egg. He stopped with a jerk and a yelp. He pumped his fist. "Found it!" he yelled, victor of the scavenger hunt.

Give the boy a balloon, Meacham thought. But he was right. There was another cold spot here. Even knowing what to expect, it was still a shock when she touched it. It didn't seem as cold as the one in the crypt. She said so.

"You're right," Pertwee said, too excited to worry about agreeing with the CIA bogeywoman. She looked around the room, measuring the spot's distance from the outside wall. "Isn't it directly above the one downstairs?" she asked. When Gray nodded, she said, "Have you explored any deeper?"

"There's a basement?" Meacham asked, surprised.

"No," said Gray.

"There are caverns," Pertwee declared.

Gray rolled his eyes. "That's folklore."

"What," Meacham demanded, "are you two talking about?"

"Saint Rose lived on this site," Pertwee explained, "but not in this house. It wasn't built yet. There was a grotto on the grounds, and it led to a network of caves big enough to live in. She worked and ate and slept there. The caves became a pilgrimage site. People would come —"

"— from miles around to hear her preach," Gray finished, adding a sing-song rhythm to the cliché. "The saintly hermit in a cave. Can you imagine anything more picturesque? I'm sorry to disappoint you, but there are no underground shrines here."

"You can't prove that," Pertwee said.

"I don't have to prove a negative. I think I would know if such a thing existed."

"Have you ever looked? Haven't you ever noticed any architectural anomalies?"

"No," Gray said, but Meacham thought he hesitated for a fraction of a second. "Now if you're done playing, I'll show you where you'll be sleeping."

There were four bedrooms linked to each other off the Old Chapel, and a fifth that had a door opening onto the staircase. Gray scooped up some clothing as they passed through the small corner room. "Someone else can stay here," he said. "I'll be on the other side of this floor." The two larger spaces, the one furthest from the chapel and the one off the staircase, were solar bedrooms, with much bigger windows, and had doors onto a shared bathroom. Pertwee and Corderman took the room near the stairs. It was, Gray said, called the Sunset Room. Its oriel window faced west. Hudson took the room beside the chapel, Crawford the corner, with Sturghill next to him. That gave Meacham the other solar bedroom. This was the Garden Room. Its north-facing window looked out over the grounds. "Luxury," Meacham said and meant it. But the real luxury was in that view. The furniture was old, valuable, and stiff as an upper lip. The couch was overstuffed, the chairs hardbacked and forbidding. There was the stale smell of disuse and old dust. The fabric was slightly oily to the touch. The room was a still life to the garden's exuberance of green. Standing at the window, Meacham saw Gray make his way up the drive. A few minutes later, he reappeared, followed by a small van. He'd sent for their luggage. *Well,* Meacham thought. *Here we are, and here we stay.*

Hudson had to cut through Meacham's room to reach the New Chapel. He knocked on her door, poked his head in, and smiled an apology as she waved him through. She was unpacking her suitcase. Hudson saw a profusion of papers already spreading out on the Victorian tables. She had a collection of utilitarian suits laid out on the bed. There weren't many, and they could mix and match with each other. She struck Hudson as someone who approached dressing with the same dispassionate efficiency she would bring to intelligence work. "Settling in all right?" he asked.

She skipped the pleasantry. "What did you think of the cold spot?"

"I don't know." He didn't.

"A bit disturbing, yes?"

"Yes."

"Still think there's no such thing as ghosts?"

"I don't understand the cold spot. That doesn't mean it's supernatural. I don't pretend to understand the internal combustion engine, either, but I don't think cars are powered by black magic."

"True." She went back to her unpacking.

Interesting, Hudson thought as he left the room. He'd been prepared to dislike Meacham. He'd had the occasional run-in with the CIA in Africa. The encounters had been brief, tangential to the agendas of both parties, and nothing he cared to repeat. He had been bothered not just by their means, but by their rock-of-ages commitment to an unquestioned end. Crossing paths with the agents was a clash of religions. At least, he told himself, he had the decency to wrestle with doubts now and then. Meacham was different. Maybe the few of her colleagues he'd met were exceptions, but there was no fervour in her. Her jaundiced openness about who she was and why she was here was refreshing. He even liked her sardonic fatalism. What impressed him the most was a more open mind than he had expected. She didn't hide that she was here as the force of debunking, and that Crawford was her big gun. But she was asking questions without, he felt, already knowing the answers. She was looking around with her eyes open. *So there,* he thought. *Proof that no one is beyond redemption.* There was comfort in that.

He stopped in the New Chapel and knelt at the altar. The pews and pulpit here were beautiful, ornate, and looked much older than they were. Though they were more Victorian aping of the antique, they were now venerable in their own right. They were not, however, the original pieces from the Old Chapel. Hudson wondered what had been done with those. He found that he didn't care. He was glad that *this* was the space devoted to worship now, and not the other room. He believed what he'd said to Meacham, but the cold spot still bothered him. It would until there was an explanation. On this front, he was Crawford's big backer. He wanted the rationalist explanation. He wanted the spooky loose end snipped, then shut up in a box. There was no point pretending he could pray in a chapel with that freezing distraction waiting for him to stumble back into it.

He shut his eyes and prayed. He prayed a lot for Gray. He very consciously did not wait for answers or inspirations. That kind of waiting wouldn't do his peace of mind any good. When he was done, he stood up and bowed to the cross on the altar. He turned to go, but the cross held his attention. It looked too cold and inert. He was struck by the emptiness of the chapel. It seemed as if its sanctity was as phony as the antiquity of the pulpits. All just for show. The cross was suddenly a widget in a useless shape.

He shook his head, trying to tear himself from suffocating cobwebs of doubt. He left the chapel, crossed another staircase landing, and entered the drawing room. This was one of the lighter spaces in the house. The furniture was more recent, submitting to the last century's demands for comfort. There were more Chinese vases here, small ones in alcoves of the ornate Jacobean mantelpieces. The wallpaper also was Chinese. Light streamed in north- and west-facing windows. Movement on the ceiling drew Hudson's eye. Reflections from the moat rippled over the plaster in a sinuous movement of shadow and light.

Gray was sitting in an armchair beside the west window. He was watching the reflections too. "Hypnotic," Hudson offered.

It took a moment for Gray to react and lower his eyes. It seemed to take another second before he registered who Hudson was. Then he nodded.

"I think you had a lot of fun with that press conference." Hudson took a seat facing Gray's at the window.

"I did."

"What are you up to?"

Gray smiled, animation coming back into his eyes. "What does it look like?"

"A cynical mind might say you're setting up teams to go at each other's throats."

"*Survivor: Haunted House*?"

"Very droll. I don't want to have a cynical mind."

"I'll admit that we'll probably see some entertaining shouting matches."

"That doesn't sound like you."

"Don't worry. This isn't just an elaborate practical joke. I'm not that bored with my own company already. I really do want to know what's happening here."

"What do *you* think is going on?"

A smile again, but tired, and maybe a bit frightened. "I think all of you are wrong."

Now the question he really wanted to ask. "What are you *hoping* for?"

Gray didn't answer. He turned to face the window again. He muttered a curse: "Hope." Above his head, the reflections twitched violently. Outside, the moat was mirror-placid.

chapter eleven

scene settings

They had dinner in the Great Hall. They sat at the monster table, in the evening light of spring, surrounded by the accumulated strata of history, and ate store-bought pizza. The meal was a sham. They were not eating together. They were consolidating alliances, probing for the weakness of enemies. The skeptics and the believers settled into their trenches. Each side made assumptions about the other and about their host. Gray watched the positioning, and it amused him, sometimes cutting through the tension that constricted his appetite. He made it through one slice of the pizza, but he couldn't stop thinking about the night. It was the time of year when days were growing noticeably longer, but night still arrived. With the dark, it seemed, came revelations. He feared sleep. He wanted to run from the house. He needed, with even more strength, to stay in his home. He said very little.

Pertwee said a lot. She was feeling defensive, so she went on the attack. She needled Crawford. She tried to use colleagues against him. But every Ph.D. she brought up was shot down as a discredited kook. Crawford never took any bait. He smiled a lot. He was polite. He drove her mad. He was exactly the sort of person she most wanted to have respect her and her research, and accept her as a peer. He was Nemesis. She finally said, "Can't you concede at least that you are predisposed not to believe in spiritual manifestations, and that this bias could be skewing your results? Because your mind is committed to one perspective, you might miss or ignore contradictory data."

His smile didn't falter. "Shouldn't you concede exactly the same thing?" he asked. And when she couldn't come up with the perfect response right away, he said, "Our experiments should complement each other nicely, then. Two closed minds attacking the same problem." He turned back to his pizza.

Pertwee knew she would find the perfect comeback sometime in the next eight hours, when trotting it out would be the worst kind of infantile irrelevance. She fumed. She didn't think about the house at all.

Corderman tried to be angrier on her behalf than he was, though he was ready to strike the moment he heard something really offensive. Getting his dander up might help with his nerves. It wasn't that his faith was faltering. That was the problem. He and Pertwee had never overnighted in one of their sites before. Ghost-hunting was the big and important adventure, and he believed completely in what they were doing, but the cool factor had kept the research at the level of a game. He had played Dungeons and Dragons in his teens, and more lately a couple of MMORPGs had taken more nights from him than he would own up to Pertwee. He knew what it was to play obsessively. He knew what it was when games had more depth and heft than real life. He'd participated in live role-playing too. Ghost-hunting was the real deal, he understood this, but the experience was part of the gaming continuum. But a man had died here. He knew what Pertwee believed about that. He was just as incensed about the slander the papers had levelled at Gethsemane Hall. But. He was here, now.

Night was coming, now. He'd seen his share of horror films, too. He was thinking quite a bit about the house.

Sturghill listened to the duel between Crawford and Pertwee, chuckled a few times, but kept her powder dry. She was going to bury this New Age flake. Hers was the kind of thinking that had taken Adams down. Sturghill wasn't going to reveal the stake up her sleeve before she plunged it into gullibility's heart.

Hudson tried to steer the conversation into lighter areas. He asked questions about families and interests. Everyone thought he was very nice. He wanted to know who these people were. He wanted to know if they were going to make things better or worse for his best friend. He was thinking about the house, but not about ghosts. The wrong combination of people could be just as poisonous.

Meacham asked questions, too. She established herself as a terrific listener. She lived up to her training. She did her job well. When she asked Pertwee about her work, she did so without sarcasm. When Pertwee answered briefly, cautiously, Meacham asked follow-up questions. It didn't take much before Pertwee was opening up and going on at length. This was where the training really made the difference. It would have been easy to glaze over. Meacham forced herself to listen, to absorb the information as if it weren't raving bullshit, because this wasn't a situation where it would be useful, yet, to have enemies. Come out of here with a debunking report from Crawford but Pertwee softened up? Sweet. Meacham had a few thoughts about the house during the meal. She was looking forward to exploring its age. The experiments might be fun, before she had to marshal her arguments. A bit of a holiday in luxury.

There were other thoughts in the Hall. They circled the diners. They calculated. They carried a gospel.

The meal ended. The diners parted. They retired to their rooms, to plan campaigns and to prepare for the night. Pertwee went for a stroll before bed. An evening constitutional. She wanted to walk the sacred grounds and be touched by them, be revitalized by them. She wanted to walk them alone, away from the siege of hostility inside, and away from Corderman's tense chivalry. Over dinner, he had been poised for the right provocation and the right dose of courage to rise up in righteous wrath. His cues hadn't come, thank God. Her credibility with this crowd was zero, as things stood. She would fight for better, and she would do so under whatever rules the opposing team imposed on her. What she didn't need was Corderman's puppy histrionics plunging her standing into the negative figures.

She breathed deeply, clearing her head, purging tension. She crunched across the gravel, walking away from the gatehouse tower. A small flight of stone steps lured her through an open iron gate and into a walled garden. The brickwork on the inside was overgrown with ivy and moss. The garden was laid out along rigid lines. The rectangular paving stones framed a rectangular pond with a clutch of reeds growing at each corner. A small marble Cupid pranced on a rock island in the centre of the pond. In the moonlight, Cupid had a pale glow. Wings and limbs, body and face, he was white and cold. Pertwee smiled at him. She felt the enclosure of the walls and was comforted. She spread her arms in a stretch that turned into a benediction. She smiled her thanks and greeting to the spirits of the Hall.

She noticed a darker rectangular patch in the far wall. At first she thought it was a shadow, but there was no source for it. She approached. In the corner, the walls did not meet. They gave way to hedge, and there was a narrow passage. Pertwee walked through and found herself in another walled garden. *I found a secret,* she thought and giggled. The stone walls here were almost bare, except in one corner where there was a luxuriance of peonies and valerian. There was a pond here, too. It was smaller, circular, and the water was pea-soup stagnant. Pertwee walked the perimeter of the garden, delighting in a storybook shiver. *No one else knows about this,* she thought. *This is something the Hall has given to me. Alone.*

The moon went out.

Cloud cover. She knew that had to be it. But the loss of light was so sudden. Flick of a switch, and she was in darkness. Alone. An afterimage of peonies shone on her retina, then faded. She didn't have a flashlight. She couldn't see. She looked up, expecting to see the moon as a faint smear behind clouds. The sky was black as isolation. Pertwee tried to laugh at the anxiety she felt rising. The sound came out as a choked gasp. *Wait it out,* she thought. *A minute or two, and we're off.* The minutes passed. The blackness remained pure. It was as if it were wrapped around her head, a snake-coil shroud.

She took a cautious step, reaching out with her hands. All she had to do was get to the wall, feel her way around it, reach the entrance to the secret garden. If she could do that, she felt against all reason, there would be light when she reached the other garden. *That's silly,* she tried to tell herself. She didn't listen. She hunted the wall. Her fingers brushed nothing but air. She took another step. The scuffing noise against the pavement was harsh. Another step. She couldn't be far from the wall. The garden wasn't more than ten yards across, and there was that pond in the middle. Still no wall. She moved her foot forward again, and as it came down, it touched emptiness. She almost lost her balance. She stepped back. *All right,* she thought. *You were moving toward the pond. Turn around.* She did. *Wall is this way.* She stepped, and her foot hit nothing again. She froze. She didn't see how she could have turned three-sixty and be facing the pond again. But she must have. Disorientation in the dark. She lowered herself to her knees. She reached forward. Her hand dropped below knee level, wanted to keep going into the void. *That's the pond,* she thought. She reached behind.

No paving stone here either. Only the drop. She toppled backward. She fell further than she should, and then she was embraced by liquid thick as muscle but ten times colder, and she knew she was *alone.* She paid the tribute and screamed.

Lights on. The moon was back. The peonies nodded from the passage of a breeze that had just left. Pertwee was sitting on stone, two arm's lengths from the pond. She stood and looked up. There were no clouds. The Milky Way, brighter than she'd ever seen it, shone its implacable age down.

So she'd made contact. She rubbed her arms. She'd never experienced anything that strong before. She'd never been frightened. She shouldn't have been, she decided. She hadn't been harmed. She had received a message. It was up to her to decipher it, to understand what was being asked of her. "Thank you." She said it like she meant it.

She made her way back to the Hall, building a high palisade of rationalizations. And then she, like all the others, went to bed. She lost her fear. The air was fresh in Roseminster, and she went to sleep quickly. She wasn't alone.

Fast and deep sleepers all. Except for Gray. He lay awake, waiting. He was in the master bedroom. It took up the southwest corner of the first floor and was almost as big as the entire bedroom suite on the other side of the house. The bed was a four-poster monolith, the frame three hundred years old, and the mattress didn't feel much more recent. Gray kept the bedside light on. He was pretending, for his own benefit, that he might want to read. The lamp cast a bright yellow aura around the bed. The shadows in the recesses of the room were darker for the contrast. Gray didn't look at them. He closed his eyes and wondered why he refused every impulse to leave. He wondered why he was frightened. His room was a long way from the Old Chapel and the crypt. He wasn't going near them, no fear. Gray turned over, facing into the lamp. Its light penetrated his lids, making him squint. There was still darkness leaking in. He didn't want to meet its gaze.

Gray did sleep. Like the rest, he did not wake until the morning. He did not wake rested. None of them did. Sleep came down that night like a judgment. Gethsemane Hall rolled its inhabitants over foam-capped waves. It had them struggling to break surface and breathe, but it always pushed their heads back under. Their lungs choked with thick, unconscious bile. They tangled sheets into sweat and knots. Their brows furrowed as their eyes shut tight against a greater darkness. The storm blasted the entire night, and it didn't calm with the morning. Instead, it built up a momentum roar of rage, a wind that piled the breakers into rogue mountains, and the dreamless black smashed down on the sleepers, swamping them, driving them so far down into the deeps that survival instincts screamed and woke them up. They came to, gasping, eyes blind for a moment, still oil-slicked by the dark that had come with the night. When their eyes cleared, and they saw it was morning, all of them, skeptics and faithful, near-sobbed with the relief of being awake, and the night being over. They lay in their beds, exhausted, needing rest, but when they felt as if they might drop back to sleep, they jerked with apprehension and jumped up. Those who shared rooms exchanged a look, but didn't ask, *You too?* because sometimes it is better to avoid confirmation.

And then the day began.

The equipment arrived after breakfast. They had foraged, bleary-eyed, in the kitchen for cereal and eggs. Gray gave Corderman some money and the keys to his car and sent him off to Tesco to lay in enough supplies for the duration. Corderman must have crossed the delivery truck coming in. As they began to unload the boxes, Crawford started to laugh. "Whose is whose?" he asked Pertwee.

"Why," she asked, "is it so surprising that I know a thing or two about science?"

Crawford refused to be drawn in. "At least we should have a redundancy of data."

Gray looked over the devices piling up in the outer hall. He shared Crawford's amusement. Identical means, opposite faiths. *There's a lesson aborning,* he thought. "What are these?" he asked. Most of the devices were handhelds of one sort or another. They didn't take up a lot of space on their own. It was the sheer number that filled the boxes, along with multiple tripods and a backup generator. The only differences between Crawford's equipment and Pertwee's were that it looked more expensive and there was a lot more duplication.

"This is the Trifield Natural EM Meter," Pertwee said. It looked simple enough: a knob on the lower half, and an analogue gauge with three scales. "It detects very small fluctuations in electric, magnetic, and radio and microwave fields. I have to be careful because it's sensitive enough to pick up fields generated by people or animals."

"It would be just awful to learn that positive findings are the result of mishandled equipment," Crawford deadpanned. He showed Gray his variations on Pertwee's theme. "These are the sensors," he said. There were six of them. "They have three axes. A magnetic field has static and dynamic components, and these measure both. The data is sent here." He tapped a laptop.

"What's the difference, besides expense?" Meacham asked.

"Ms. Pertwee's gadget will sound an alarm if it detects a change in the field. Am I right?" Pertwee nodded. "You put the meter down in the place that's supposed to be haunted, and then you wait. When the ghost walks by, the machine hollers." Pertwee made a face but didn't contradict. Crawford continued. "I'm interested in the mean strength of the field in different areas and the variances within those locations."

"Let's see if I follow," Gray said. "Say a fluctuation occurs. Anna's conclusion is that a presence caused the fluctuation. Yours is that the fluctuation caused the perception of a presence. Is that about right?"

They both nodded but were eyeing him warily.

"Isn't this chicken and egg?" he asked. "Couldn't a ghost cause the field to change, which makes someone experience another kind of ghost?" He raised his eyebrows in holy innocence. Meacham started laughing.

"It isn't that simple," Pertwee protested.

"She's right," Crawford said.

"Look what you've done." Sturghill was laughing too. "You made them agree. You," she stabbed a finger at Gray, "are bad."

He was. And he was having fun. When had he last been able to say that? "Tell me about the other toys," he said. Crawford and Pertwee didn't react. "I'll be good now," he promised.

They took him through the rest. Light level tricorder, air temperature and movement probes, motion sensors, sound recorders, microphones, cameras, camcorders. Then there was the helmet. "What," Meacham asked, "the hell is this?" She hefted it. It looked like a yellow motorcycle helmet with wires running out of the top and sides. It had a bulky black visor, from which dangled a USB cable.

"That," Crawford said, "is my ghost machine. Let me set it up." He grabbed his laptop and another machine Gray didn't recognize. It resembled a desktop computer's tower. Crawford led them all into the Great Hall. He hooked up the laptop and the helmet to the third machine. "This is a magnetic field generator," he said. "Sit down," he told Meacham. He placed the helmet on her head. "We'll do this the first time without the visuals."

"Should I close my eyes?"

"Up to you. It doesn't matter. Comfortable? Good." He turned on the generator, then tapped at the laptop. "Here we go. What I'm doing is bathing your brain with weak magnetic waves."

"How long before I develop a tumour?"

"It's harmless. Just relax. If I could have everyone else stay quiet, too? Thank you."

Meacham settled into her chair. Gray watched her stare into the middle distance. Her eyes began to glaze over. After a few minutes, she opened her mouth; Gray thought to say that she was bored and had had enough. Then her eyes snapped wide. She grunted, and jerked her head around to the right. She brushed at her shoulder as if fighting something. She jumped out of the chair and yanked the helmet off. "Jesus Electric *Fuck*!" she yelled.

Crawford retrieved the helmet from her. "I take it you experienced something."

"I'll say I did. Holy *Mother*." She had her arms wrapped tightly around herself. Her face was chalky. "You could have warned me."

"What happened?" Gray asked.

"Something came up behind me. I could feel its breath on my neck. Then it grabbed my shoulder." She shook her head. "It was *strong*."

Crawford was looking pleased. Gray asked him, "And this is normal?"

"The experience varies from person to person," he said. "Some subjects don't report much of anything, but the most common experience is a very convincing sensation of some kind of presence. The feeling of being touched or grabbed isn't unusual."

"How does it work?" Hudson asked.

Crawford hesitated. "Father," he began.

"I'm not ordained," Hudson corrected.

"Oh. Sorry. I was under the impression that —"

"A common mistake," Gray reassured him. "Patrick has that air, doesn't he?"

"Just so you understand," Crawford told Hudson, "that I'm not saying this as a specific attack on your faith."

"I don't follow."

"The helmet stimulates the temporal lobes. It creates an electrical event not unlike an epileptic seizure, but without the nastiness. The theory is that mystical experiences, visions of God or ghosts, and so forth, are actually the result of these events. A lot of seers and mystics were epileptic, so the correlation is there. In other words, the presence of an Other, a presence beyond the self, is entirely an invention of the brain."

"That's rather a bleak vision," Hudson commented.

Crawford shrugged then lifted the helmet with one hand. "Maybe. But it works."

"Let me try," Gray said. He sat down.

Crawford settled the helmet on his head and lowered the visor. "We'll try the other function, if you're interested."

"What is it?" Gray couldn't see a thing.

"Not every instance of haunting can be put down to magnetic field fluctuations," Crawford explained.

"Oh, so you admit that much," Pertwee said.

Crawford ignored her. "The mind is infinitely suggestible. When it encounters environments that tradition says are haunted, it will often *make* them haunted. When you step from a bright, sunny day to a dank, dark tomb, for instance, the contrast can predispose you toward certain experiences."

"In other words," Gray said, "it's all in our minds."

"Pretty much. Now, having told you all this, I've gone and sabotaged the effectiveness of the experiment. Magic isn't effective when you know how it works."

"Tell that to Penn and Teller," Sturghill said.

"What I'm going to do is trigger a virtual environment from the laptop. You're going to be moving through a setting that I control, with the idea of creating an effect along the lines of what Louise just experienced. Ready?"

"Go ahead."

He heard Crawford click away at his keys, and then other sounds took over. He heard a steady drip of water, each *ploc* echoing in a huge space. Wind was a sullen moan in the background. The helmet, he realized, had built-in speakers, and they were full surround. He felt the reality of the world before he could see it. The darkness gave way to gloom. He was in a great hall several orders of magnitude beyond the one at Gethsemane Hall. This one belonged to a fantasy version of a medieval castle. There were massive stone pillars rising immense heights to Gothic vaults. Torches in sconces along the walls created pools of brighter light, but the corners of the hall were a harsh black. The image filled his vision and didn't cut off at the periphery. Gray moved his head, and the perspective shifted. He looked up, and he was staring at the roof. The level of detail was very convincing, though the visuals were the hoariest clichés. "*Très* spooky," he said. If Crawford responded, Gray couldn't hear him. The torches began to go out. Still a cliché, and Gray had guessed that that would be the next event. But the dimming of the light was completely convincing. The shadows spread out from the corners, reaching for him. In spite of himself, he wanted to move away from the dark, and he found that he was. He hadn't been in the virtual castle for more than a minute, and it was already feeling like a real place. The wind picked up, walloping the outside walls with a huge gust, and he thought, just for a second, that he felt a draft on his arm.

The last of the torches winked out. Darkness rushed to meet him, and he recoiled. Then he saw a lighter patch to the right. It wasn't so much illumination as a splotch of grey. He rushed toward it, just to be able to see anything at all. It was a doorway opening onto a winding stone staircase. He could just make out the steps. He started down. He noticed now that he could hear the echoes of his heels. There was another blast of wind outside, and again, he thought he felt a draft, this time against his face. He saw humidity coating the walls. If he reached out, he thought he might feel the roughness and wetness of the stone. He didn't try. It seemed to him that the detail and reality of the environment were becoming more emphatic every second he was here.

He reached the bottom of the staircase. "Jesus," he whispered when he saw where he had arrived. He was standing at the entrance to the Gethsemane Hall crypt. The recreation was perfect. There was no detail missing, nothing that differed from the real thing, except that the source of the grey light was the southwest recess. He moved into the room. He had trouble speaking. "How ..." he began. He started over. "How did you do the modelling so quickly?" Still no answer from Crawford. He was alone. He stayed away from the centre of the crypt, but as he passed by, he felt the cold. Goddamn it, he *felt* it, an icy stab on his arm. He broke out in goose flesh. He looked down and noticed now that he could see himself, and that he was wearing the same clothes as in the real world. What kind of power was

Crawford packing in that equipment of his? He hadn't realized this kind of simulation was possible. Now that he had moved out of the hackneyed castle of the upper floor, there was no longer anything artificial about the world he was moving through.

The recess had changed. Its rear wall had collapsed, revealing a hole that plunged straight down. Its bottom was obscured by the light, which was a pulsing, twitching grey. He stared at the movement. He was mesmerized and revolted. His heart began to beat with the rhythm of the light. He'd had enough. He took a step backward. Hands of shivering mist shot out of the hole and grabbed his arms. He resisted. They tugged him. They ignored his struggles and hauled him towards the lip of the hole. He tried to shake them off, but they had him by the elbows, and all he could do was flap his hands. He moaned. He lost his balance and fell towards the grey. It grinned. He screamed.

Click. Blackout. And then the helmet was being removed from his head. He tumbled off the chair onto his hands and knees, gasping, his pulse an erratic snare drum. He was drenched in sweat. Hudson was at his side, trying to help him up. "Richard?" he asked. "My God, Richard, are you all right?"

Gray nodded, shook his head. He looked up at Crawford, who was holding the helmet and gazing at him with alarm. "Have you ever considered selling that to the film industry?" he croaked, desperate to reconnect with the mundane. "You would revolutionize horror movies. Make a mint, as long as there weren't too many strokes in the audience."

"Christ," Meacham said. "If he came up with something worse than what I could imagine, I'm glad he didn't run the movie for me."

"I'm terribly sorry," Crawford said. "I've never had a subject react as strongly as you did. If I'd know this would happen, I would never have —"

Gray waved off the apology. He staggered to his feet, leaning on Hudson's arm. "Just tell me this. How did you create the setting that fast? It was incredible."

Crawford looked puzzled. "I didn't create it just now. My programming colleagues and I have been working on it for ages. It's the kind of environment that is most suited to generating the effects we're looking for."

"I didn't mean the castle. I meant the crypt."

"The crypt?"

"The one here."

They stared at each other for a moment, neither processing what the other was saying. "What," Crawford asked, "exactly did you experience?"

Gray told him. He became aware of wide eyes around him. When he finished, he said, "I knew graphics were becoming incredibly realistic, but this ..."

Crawford said, "There is no simulation of the crypt in there."

Gray felt his breathing going funny again. "But I saw —"

"How could there be?" Crawford asked. "I'd never seen anything of the Hall before yesterday. I'm not a programmer, and even if I were, nobody's that fast, or that good."

"So what happened?" Meacham asked.

"Maybe nothing to do with the machine," Pertwee said. "Have you considered that?"

Gray was. His arms felt bruised from the grip of those hands. Pertwee sounded pleased and excited. He wondered if the event would seem so glamorous if she had been the one grabbed.

"I'm not one-hundred-per cent ready to make that conceptual leap yet," Crawford said dryly. "I'm just speculating," he told Gray, "but at a guess, I would say that your brain responded to the visual and aural stimulation in much the same way Lou's did to the magnetic waves. I provided the stereotypical image of a haunted castle. Your subconscious took over and built a simulacrum of the crypt."

"So I was in a dream state?"

"Or something very analogous. Yes, I think so. Has anything like this happened to you before?"

Gray thought about the dream in London. The chance of an empirical explanation hovered almost within reach. It was tantalizing. He distrusted it. He wanted it. He wanted to dismiss it. "Yes," he said.

Crawford nodded. "It may be that you're prone to the very condition the magnetic waves simulate."

"I'm not epileptic."

"Have you been tested?"

"No," Gray admitted.

"I'm not diagnosing you. I'm just pointing out a possibility. In any case, I don't think you should try the helmet again."

"No fear." Gray wouldn't go near the thing again, even if Crawford held a gun to his head.

"I wouldn't be too quick to dismiss the experience," Pertwee said. "It might be a mistake to shrug it off as a hallucination."

"Do you mean dangerous?" Gray asked her. He thought so, even if she didn't.

"Of course not." She was emphatic.

"The spirit world has never hurt anyone?"

She hesitated. "There's some disagreement in the community over that issue," she admitted. "But there's no way anything here could be harmful. This is not a tainted house." The hesitation had been momentary. She was vehement. "What I meant was that your vision might be important. It might have been a message."

Gray snorted. "If it was a message, it wasn't a friendly one. I don't fancy being dragged down to the abyss, thank you. I ..." He trailed off, wondering all at once if Pertwee weren't right. He thought about the recess in the crypt, an architectural loose end he had never been able to figure out. He thought about the cold spot that gathered strength with depth. He had been assuming that the crypt was the terminus, its force radiating up to the Old Chapel. He felt the force of those hands again. Their impulse was unambiguous. *Down.*

"What is it?" Hudson asked.

"Nothing." *Think this through.* Pertwee was watching him carefully. He could see the wheels turning in her head. *She knows,* he thought. She could smell victory. *Well, let her wait a bit longer. Let's do this carefully.* If he speculated aloud, she'd be calling in the bulldozers before the hour was up. "So," he looked at Crawford, then at Pertwee, "I realize my brain is very fascinating and all, but where do you begin the actual investigation?"

"The crypt," Pertwee said.

Crawford nodded. "I also want to take some readings elsewhere in the house. Try to establish a control, if possible. I want to know if the mean strength of the magnetic field in the crypt is different from the rest of the house."

Corderman returned half an hour later, and the set-up began. Gray, Meacham, and Hudson followed the teams of Pertwee and Corderman, Crawford and Sturghill, as they moved through the Hall. As he recovered from the helmet trip, Gray found his sense of irony returning. Crawford and Pertwee weren't simply using much of the same equipment for opposite ends, they were treating their devices in the same way. As they set up sensors and meters, cameras and recorders in the crypt, in the Great Hall, in the bedrooms, and in the drawing room, they treated the digital messengers with kid gloves. They placed them in rooms only after gridding the spaces and choosing spots with the care of fanatical Feng Shui consultants. They were priests and acolytes handling the Host, Gray thought. The disposition of the technology was along patterns as rigid and formal as any pentagram or mystic circle.

They were back in the crypt. Crawford directed Sturghill's placement of a sensor. Pertwee was setting up a camera with an infrared trigger. Corderman was moving back and forth in front of it, first closer, then farther away in stages, until he was standing in the recess. Pertwee had the camera covering a field of view that went diagonally through the cold spot to that corner. All four of them were speaking very quietly. Gray was standing beside Hudson at the entrance to the crypt. He heard Hudson mutter, "Likewise after supper he took the Cup; and, when he had given thanks, he gave it to them, saying, 'Drink ye all of this; for this is my Blood of the new Covenant.'" So he had picked up on the ceremonial atmosphere, too.

"Be nice," Gray whispered, surprised. "Show some respect."

"I am," Hudson answered. There was no sarcasm in his tone.

The ritual was complete by late evening. Gray braced himself for what might be summoned.

chapter twelve

the trace of anger

The scream jolted Meacham awake. She lay, eyes big-O wide against the dark, body vibrating with shock. *I dreamed it,* she thought. She had time to repeat this to herself, but not enough time for her heart to believe what she told it, before she heard the scream again. It tore itself out of the wall behind her bed, slammed into the window, bounced back and shrieked in her face, then rushed up through the ceiling. Silence slammed the echoes down. The room was taut, quivering. Meacham's hands had turned into claws around the sheets and blankets. Old instincts, forgotten but now revived, drew the covers over her face.

The scream erupted once more, too loud and mobile to be human. It rose from the floor, from under her bed where the monsters lived. It blasted up through her. It scraped her nerves like a metal claw over harp strings. It whirled around the room once, then blew through the door. Meacham half-expected the sound to shatter the wood. And the noise was here again, but now she realized there were two different screams, coming in pairs. The first was a howl of agony and fear. It was the despairing cry of prey being brought down. The second scream was sharper, more aggressive.

Meacham had always been a city girl, but when she was ten, the family had stayed with one of her father's drinking buddies out in the country, where the boys could bond and kill things. The first night in the Maine woods, she had heard a fox hunting. At first, she thought she was hearing a woman screaming, and she had come within a hair of wetting herself from the horror. But the cry had repeated at too steady a rhythm, each repetition identical to the last, the howl too short to be coming from a person's lungs. The scream she heard now made her think of that fox. It wasn't an animal's hunting cry (she should be so lucky), but it had that quality. The scream was rage and pursuit. It was predator. When it doubled back to roar in her face, it was making her a victim, not begging for her help. She disappeared under the blankets.

The screams, hunter and hunted, came back twice more, then stopped. The room lost its tension. Meacham stayed under the covers until she thought she was going to suffocate from the heat. She poked her head out, gasping. The bogeyman wasn't hovering overhead, waiting to grab her. She reached to her left and turned on the bedside lamp. It created a small island of light around the bed. That was just enough for her to jump out onto the floor and scramble for the wall switch. The ceiling light still left shadows in the corners, but they were a sullen brown, and weren't big or deep enough to hide anything dangerous. Meacham leaped back into the bed and curled up in the centre. She watched the walls. She waited for the horror.

She stayed like that for hours. She didn't feel silly at all. She was operating on an atavistic level. Shame and logic were irrelevant. Dawn finally came, the window turning from a black pane to grey. She began to relax. The grey grew lighter. The shadows diminished, retreating to bide their time until night would come again. Meacham allowed herself to lie down again. She was exhausted. Enough hours had gone by that she could almost kid herself into believing she'd had a nightmare. She tried the theory out. It wouldn't fly. She tried to close her eyes and sleep again. She couldn't. The idea of being woken again the same way kept her revved up and wide awake. *What was that?* she thought. *What the fuck was that?*

Then she thought, *Why are you alone?*

The corridors would be light enough, now. They should be clear of monsters. She threw on some clothes and went looking for company. She chose Sturghill and Crawford. She needed rationalism right now. She didn't want to hear about ghosts and their needs from Pertwee or Corderman. She wanted to hear that there were no ghosts.

Sturghill had the lights on too. She opened the door when Meacham knocked. "You heard it?" the magician asked. She was wearing an oversized Betty Boop T-shirt, and to Meacham, she suddenly looked about twelve years old. When Meacham nodded, Sturghill said, "Tell me what you heard. Precisely."

Meacham did. Sturghill began to smile as she spoke and was visibly more relaxed by the end. "What?" Meacham asked. She didn't see what was so goddamn reassuring about mobile screams.

"I heard exactly the same thing." Sturghill started to say more, but there was movement and the sound of low male voices coming from the next room. "It's okay, boys," she called out. "Come on in and join the slumber party."

The connecting door opened. Crawford and Hudson poked their heads around, looking sheepish. Crawford was in T-shirt and boxers, but Hudson had the whole pyjamas-and-dressing-gown thing happening. He was the only one in the room who fit with the decor.

"Let me guess," Sturghill said. "Screams that chased each other around your rooms." The two men nodded. Sturghill asked Crawford, "And your explanation is?"

"I'm not sure."

"Magnetic fields don't necessarily cover this, do they?"

"Well ..."

"I thought you were on the side of the skeptics," Meacham said.

"I am." She spoke to Crawford again. "Sorry, Jim. Just marking my territory a bit."

He waved off the apology. "Fix me up so I can go back to sleep, and all is forgiven."

"Would you mind explaining what you're talking about?" Hudson asked, and Meacham seconded the motion.

"We all experienced the same thing. Probably at the same time. That's the big mistake."

"Whose?" Meacham asked.

"I'm not positive, but my money's on Gray. He had the opportunity, even though I can't figure the motive. So look. Louise, if you were the only one who heard the screams, this might be a bit more convincing. A *bit*. A big, loud noise audible to only one person is plenty mysterious. But all of us? With the same movement of sound? Too easy." She paused.

Can't take the theatre out of the girl, Meacham thought. "So?" she prompted and waited for the climax.

"Speakers," Sturghill said. When Meacham looked around, she added, "In the walls, probably. Not that hard. I don't need to tell *you* that. Set up a halfway decent surround sound system in each room, connect them all to a computer, load up your FreakyScreams.mp3 and presto. Instant house of horrors. Now, if I were running the show, I would have had the scream migrate from one room to the other. Have us chasing the sounds like Scooby and the gang. That would have been classic. Maybe he ran out of time."

Hudson was shaking his head. "Richard was never one for practical jokes. Especially not recently. And when would he have had time to install the speakers? He would have had to do that before Pete Adams arrived, and Richard wouldn't have had any reason to pull that kind of a prank."

"I didn't say this was a joke," said Meacham. "This is too serious. Too involved. Way too much work." She thought of the scream Adams had recorded.

"So why would he do it?" Hudson was sounding more and more upset. When no one answered at first, he turned a pleading gaze on each face, one after the other, looking for an ally.

When Meacham's turn came, she said, "He's your friend. You know him best. You tell us."

Hudson shook his head, but Meacham thought there was uncertainty in his frown. "There's no good reason...." he began and trailed off miserably.

"His might not be good ones," Meacham said, prodding. Gray pulling some sort of crazy scare stunt was a messy explanation, and the papers would love it almost as much as real ghosts. But it was a kind of messy that would be short-lived and containable. She could work with it.

Hudson stared into the middle distance, thinking upsetting thoughts. He tried to rally. Meacham saluted him for his loyalty. "What about yesterday?" he demanded of Crawford. "What about what happened when he tried your helmet?"

Crawford's tone was quiet, free of judgment, and devastating. "We only have his word he saw what he did."

Hudson slumped down on the bed. "That wasn't what you suggested yesterday."

"I wasn't hearing screams in my bedroom last night." He looked at Sturghill. "Can you follow up on your theory?"

Sturghill was already off the bed and examining the walls. "Tricky. They're well hidden. I can't see any sign of recent work on this side."

"Plenty of picture frames," Meacham said.

"Yup. I'll find the gear, but it might take a while. I also don't need him breathing down my neck, suspecting what I'm up to. He could hide the evidence so I'll never find it."

Meacham nodded. "We'll make sure you have some alone time." She kept watching Hudson. He was looking more and more depressed, as if following a bleak but watertight logic. "What is it?" she asked him.

After a hesitation that went on so long Meacham didn't think he was going to answer, Hudson said, "He was very angry after his wife and daughter died." His voice was almost inaudible, the words so quiet they denied their own existence.

"That's not surprising," said Sturghill.

"Very angry with God," he continued as if she hadn't spoken. "He used to be a man of great faith."

"And he's lost that faith?" Meacham asked.

"Not in the sense of becoming atheist. I think, if anything, he might believe in God more than ever. But he hates Him now. He feels betrayed. He's been acting out on his anger. Pulling funding from our organization. He wants revenge. I think ... I think ... if he made me question my own faith, he might feel he'd achieved some form of revenge."

"What about the rest of us?" Sturghill asked.

"Anna has her own faith, and he's not open to optimistic world-views right now. Plus she's been on his case. You too," he said to Meacham. "So nobbling her and you might be something that would give him satisfaction."

"Which makes you and Kristine collateral damage," Meacham told Crawford.

The theory sat over them all in silence for a few minutes. Meacham stood up and walked over to Hudson. She put a hand on his shoulder. "I guess you don't really want to hear this," she said, "but I think you might be right."

Hudson didn't look convinced by his own argument. "But why would he do that to Adams? He wasn't angry then."

"You must have seen plenty in Darfur to shake a man's faith."

"He wasn't *angry* yet."

"Are you sure?"

Hudson didn't answer.

"Let us help you help him," Meacham lied. If Gray was working a con, she'd pin him to the wall and leave him wriggling there for the jackals. She knew she would have some sleepless nights, though not over Gray. Enemies that fell in combat weren't worthy of mourning. It was the desperation in Hudson's eyes that would, she knew right now, bother her. She was setting up a betrayal. It was part of the job. The trashing of the innocent shouldn't be, but Christ knew how often it was. And she would trash ten more of the guiltless if that shored up her explanation, dispelled the screams, and reaffirmed the world as it should be.

She decided she didn't want company anymore. She yawned. "Thanks for dispelling the bogeyman, ladies and gents. If we're going to flush him out in the morning, I need a bit more sleep." She headed for the door.

"I'll walk you back," Crawford said, and was at her side before she could decline offer. "Keep the monsters at bay," he joked.

"Thanks," Meacham said, dry as sticks.

When they were out of earshot of the others, Crawford said, voice low, "The night before we came here, did you have a nightmare? I mean a sleep-destroying monster."

"Why do you ask?" The dream was a void. The memory of its impact had lost some of its edge, but it could still draw blood.

"Kristine and I both did. I can't remember the details, but it was a doozy." Crawford's face had the pinched look of a man wrestling with new and unwelcome uncertainty.

Meacham needed him focused. She would hoard the doubts, let them eat at her peace of mind for the sake of the agenda. Work to be done, folks. Narratives to be tidied up. "No," she said. "Slept like a baby." Fluttering in her gut. The bogeyman wasn't so far away. The doubts went to work.

Pertwee had heard the screams. She and Corderman were up and had the lights on before the first cycle had finished. The next screams, hitting with the room lit, were worse, the monsters under the bed and in the closet not banished by the retreat of the dark. As the silence rang, they stared at each other from across the room. Corderman had been sleeping in the bed, Pertwee on a chesterfield. Corderman had wanted to be chivalrous, but Pertwee had insisted they flip a coin and take turns. Now she joined Corderman on the bed. His eyes were dancing around the room. He looked as if he wanted to be held as badly as she did.

"That wasn't good," Corderman whispered. "That was very, very not good." He turned to Pertwee, pleading for the explanation that would make everything right again. "Why were they screaming? That wasn't right."

No, it wasn't. Pertwee knew there were some tortured places in the world. She had studied some of them, though she hadn't visited them herself. But Gethsemane Hall wasn't of that number. It couldn't be. "This is probably not what it seemed," was what she came up with, and she knew how lame it sounded.

"*What?*" Corderman exploded. "What is it then? What's the good thing that makes walls scream?"

"That might have been a cry of mourning," she said, and oh, she was ad-libbing, she was bullshitting as fast as she could speak, there wasn't a single legitimate thought coming out of her mouth. "The spirits might be calling out to those who are alive and in pain, who are resisting the peace of the house." *Do you believe that?* she thought. *Do you believe the tiniest portion of that?* No, but Corderman calmed down just a bit. That was good enough. If he bought in to the point that he wasn't freaking out, then that would help her keep calm, too. Calm was the only way to examine the evidence, make a judgment. The screams couldn't be a sign of hostile or tormented spirits. That flew in the face of everything she knew about the Hall. So the screams meant something else, and she could find out what that was only by being a scientist, not a shivering cavewoman.

Corderman had his breathing under control. "Sorry," he said. "That scared the hell out of me."

"Me too," Pertwee admitted.

He looked at her. He wanted to be held. So did she. The impulse was natural, the need genuine. The problem was implications and consequences. She didn't know if Corderman would read anything into the act. It was the chance he might that made her hesitate. They weren't a couple. They couldn't be. The integrity of their research, she felt, wouldn't permit it. Not when credibility was such an elusive and rare fish. She didn't *want* to be a couple. But she thought that Corderman might. She caught the way he looked at her sometimes. At those moments, she usually found an excuse to take off on her own or send him on an errand. He didn't turn her crank.

(Who would, Anna? Maybe Jim Crawford, bullet-muscle body and heat-seeking logic? The god of credibility? Wouldn't you just love to suck some of that academic capital right off him?)

But right now, she and Corderman were together in a room that had screamed. Right now, daylight was a long way off. Right now, old instincts and fears were calling the shots. So she held out her arms, and they leaned back on the bed, and they held each other. Just for now. Just for right now.

Gray hadn't heard the screams. He didn't wake from his dream. It was a dream of sound and motion, but no images. He was in a darkness of muscle. It shifted with a slow giant's rhythm. He was caught in leviathan waves, and they ground him against an invisible shale of bones. They threw him down, dragged him out to sea, then smashed him again. His skin was being scoured off. So was his self. The undertow was an enormous force. It wasn't temptation, because there was no question of resistance, but it had its own dark attraction. He might have swum towards it, if he'd had a choice. He didn't. It pulled him, scraped him raw, and dragged him down, filling his lungs with the choking sweet taste of revenge.

Old man, you should be in bed, Roger Bellingham thought. *What do you think you're doing here? This is no place for an old man.*

Asleep is what you should be. At this time of the dawn, even old men, with their broken, reduced sleep, were resting. They were not standing in front of troubled gates. It was still full dark, the last moments of total despair before the horizon greyed with hope. He'd been standing at the gate of Gethsemane Hall for the last half-hour, since his too-old corpse had been dragged from bed and hauled down here by the tug. He heard footsteps behind him. He turned, saw John Porter. "And what brings you here?" he asked.

"Have to prepare the pub for the day ahead."

This early? "A likely story."

Porter shrugged an acknowledgement. "Do you have a better one?"

"Only the truth." He didn't elaborate. It wasn't the sort of truth either liked to speak.

"Is it locked?" Porter asked.

"Yes." He'd given the gate a good shake when he'd first arrived.

"Thank Christ."

"You could ring." Bellingham pointed to the call button. "He might let you in."

Porter shuddered. "Don't say things like that. For pity's sake." He stared at the button with horrified longing. "That wasn't funny." Bellingham could hear the cold sweat in his voice.

"No, it surely wasn't. I'm sorry." *That was a vicious bastard thing to do, old man, just because you went through the same struggle.* "Anyone else up and about?" he asked.

Porter nodded. "I saw plenty of lights on. Faces at the window. I think we're the only ones out on the street."

"We've had more to do with it. You were just there."

"What about you?"

"I've been fighting it longest. Been on my mind a lot lately."

After a minute, Porter said, "It's getting worse, isn't it?"

"It is." This wouldn't be their last vigil at the gate. They wouldn't be lonely much longer, either. The good people of Roseminster might be able to bar their doors to themselves for the moment. If the tug grew much stronger, the current would catch them up.

"Different, too," Porter said, and he sounded sick.

"Yes." The tug had nothing to do with desire anymore. It had shed its disguises of curiosity and affection. It was pure rip tide, now. It was strong enough that it didn't need to use their own impulses to draw them.

"Why?" Porter wondered. "Do you think it's something they're doing?"

The thought had occurred to Bellingham. The risk of making things worse was what had made him try to warn Pertwee off. But when he looked back, he realized that the strength had been growing before the ghost hunter had won her access to the Hall. "I doubt it."

Porter sighed. "I've been sleeping worse since he moved back."

"So have I." Gray's return was when Bellingham had felt the tug really pick up strength. But it had been building for a long time. Something about Gray might have sped things up, but they would be reaching this point sooner or later, whether the lord of the manor was present or not. The strength had been scary enough the night Pete Adams had died. High tide was coming.

"So what now?"

"We fight it as best we can for as long as we can."

"And then?"

"I don't know, John. I'd be happy to hear any suggestions." His grip on his stick was growing slippery.

Dread moved through Roseminster. It had been present before, but as a background nag in the chest. It had been something to be ignored, something to be dealt with later. Dread had been put off, forced to content itself as low-grade anxiety. Now it snickered, cocky in its approaching triumph. It travelled in shadows, broke in through dreams, and entered homes on reptile feet. It was a movement in the corner of the eye. It was a sound that became inaudible when the ear strained for it. Most of all, it was the tug. The people of Roseminster felt it, knew it for what it was, feared it. They were on the edge of the maelstrom, and the spin was just picking up. They were still far from the centre, where the ships of their lives would be smashed on the rocks, but they were still too close, and it was too late to escape. Denial had failed them. Things would not take care of themselves. There was nothing to do but wait, while dread walked in on reptile feet and tightened its grip.

They gathered in the Great Hall, breakfast ignored, eager as Christmas morning. Crawford and Pertwee rushed to their laptops, and they both looked as if they'd found coal in their stockings. "What is it?" Meacham asked Crawford.

"Nothing," he said, disgusted.

"I don't get it."

"Neither did the sensors. That's the problem." He and Pertwee raced each other to the crypt. Meacham and the others followed. Crawford picked up a sensor in the middle of the floor. He started to shake it, but kept his temper and pushed a button instead. A green light came on.

Sturghill and Corderman came down the stairs from the Old Chapel. They looked just as pissed and confused. "It's all screwed up," Sturghill said. "The sensor —"

"I know," Crawford interrupted. "Did you check the batteries?"

"They're fine."

"So are ours," Corderman said.

"Mind filling the rest of us in?" Meacham asked.

"Total waste of time," Crawford answered, disgusted. "Something must have gone wrong with the sensors. That or ..." He stopped himself.

"Or what?" Gray asked.

"I don't know." But he did know, Meacham realized. One sensor failing could happen. Two, that was odd. All of them? Sabotage. Could Gray be that obvious about it?

She decided not to push the issue yet. Give Sturghill a chance to dig around. She nudged Crawford onto a slightly different path. "The sensors didn't pick up anything at all? Did you forget to turn them on?"

"Oh, they were on, all right. But the readings are lunatic."

"Exaggerated magnetic field fluctuation?" Gray asked.

Crawford shook his head. "According to my equipment, there is no magnetic field here *at all*. Which is ridiculous. Also impossible."

"Same thing here," Pertwee said.

"Have you encountered something like that before?" Hudson asked her.

"Never."

"So you don't see a spiritual influence at work."

She hesitated. "No," she said at last. "I've never heard of any such thing. I agree with Dr. Crawford. This makes no sense." Meacham mentally saluted her for her rigour and honesty. The girl had some principles, after all. More than she could say for herself.

"Well, never mind magnetic fields for the moment," Hudson said. "What about all your other equipment?"

"It'll take me a few hours to review the video," Pertwee answered. "The audio should be faster." She had brought her laptop with her and plugged in the digital recorder. Meacham watched over her shoulder. Pertwee called up an audio editor and loaded the file. There were eight hours of sound, but she zoomed out until the entire track fit on the screen. There was a single big spike interrupting an otherwise flat line. Pertwee zoomed in on that segment, placed the cursor at a point just before the spike, and clicked on "play". There were a few seconds of ambient static and hissing. Then it came. At first, Meacham thought she was hearing a rumble of distant thunder, had time to wonder if she'd missed a storm last night before the quality of the rumble changed. It became a roar. It stormed out of the laptop's speaker like a runaway freight. The blow rocked Meacham back. Pertwee recoiled and tried to lower the volume. She was too late. The sound was out. It built even as she fumbled with the controls. The freight train derailed and smashed the room to flames with its anger. Meacham's breath was sucked away from her by the fury. Her knees buckled, and she grabbed at the table for support. She was buffeted by the wreckage of anger. She thought she might bleed. The throat that howled couldn't be human. It was too big, too powerful. But it held the memory of humanity in its teeth, and it bit down hard through the sinews of dreams and flesh of hopes, crunching bone and hammering the soul to dust. When the roar finally faded, its echoes covered the stones of the Hall like an oil slick, ready and waiting for the spark to burn again.

Meacham had her eyes closed, so she didn't know who was sobbing.

chapter thirteen

waiting stone

Hudson combed the Hall, looking for Gray. He had drifted away after they had taken Pertwee to her room, and an unspoken consensus had called a moratorium on the research for a little while. Hudson finally found him emerging from the former stables. He was pushing a wheelbarrow loaded with sledgehammer and pickaxe. "What are you planning to do with those?" Hudson asked.

"Confirm a suspicion," Gray answered. He began to move forward again.

Hudson blocked his way. "I thought we were taking a break."

"Go ahead. Take one. By the way, Patrick, tell me again what your role is in the investigation?"

"Very funny. But since you ask, to be a voice of sanity and reason."

"I thought that was Crawford and Sturghill's territory."

Hudson shook his head. "They have their own dogma. I think it might be just as dangerous as Pertwee's. Let's say I'm here for spiritual sanity."

"That would make you the lone voice in the wilderness, wouldn't it?" Gray was smiling, but it was still that sour smile. He no longer seemed capable of any other kind.

"I'm not kidding."

The smile vanished. "No," Gray said quietly. "I don't suppose you are."

"Don't you think this has gone far enough? Don't you think you should stop?" If Gray was working a hoax, it had crossed the line. They had all been upset, but Pertwee might have suffered some real psychological harm. If Sturghill was wrong, if Gray hadn't embedded speakers in the walls, if the manifestations were real, then all the more reason to pull out now, while the screams were still disembodied.

"Why?" Gray asked.

"*Why?* Didn't you hear that recording this morning?" *Or did you make it? And if you did, how? Whose voice was that?*

"I take it you don't want to know what's behind that sound."

"*No.*" He hadn't meant to put so much force into the word. He hadn't realized how desperately he wanted Gray to be a hoaxer and how little he believed in that possibility. Most of all, he hadn't realized how much he feared the answers Gray was seeking. Calling a halt was necessary for his own spiritual survival, too.

The emotions that flickered over Gray's face were hard to read. Hudson saw pain, gratitude, tenderness, anger. "I'm not being much of a friend to you," he said. "You really should go. For your own sake."

Gray was wrong about that. "I have to stay," Hudson told him, "for your sake and for mine." *Don't just listen to me*, he prayed. *Hear me.*

Gray didn't hear. Or perhaps, which was worse, he did. "You've had your warning, then."

"You say that as if you're making a threat."

"I don't mean to." He looked Hudson in the eye. His expression was a tug of war of concern and barely contained vengeance. "I don't want you to be hurt."

"Then you do think what's happening is dangerous."

"I know it is."

"Then why go on?"

Gray didn't answer for a moment. He seemed to be struggling to keep rage in check. "Because I'm on the verge of a big, hard, truth, and I want to know what it is." Some of the rage slipped out when he said *truth*. The word sounded like an awful thing. This truth would not set you free. It would stamp your face into the ground and break your spine. "Since you ask, no, I don't think the investigation has gone far enough. Not nearly far enough."

Gray had the crypt to himself. There was still some equipment lying around, and he moved it out of the way of the wheelbarrow. He approached the recess of the crypt. He ran his hands over the brickwork of the rear wall. He half expected it to crumble at his touch and reveal the hole that he had seen while wearing Crawford's helmet. It stayed firm, abrasive and faintly slick under his fingers. He took a step back and shone a flashlight over the recess. The difference was subtle, but he could see it now. The bricks of the rear wall were a shade lighter than those of the rest of the crypt. They were younger. He put the flashlight down and hefted the pickaxe. He paused, giving himself time to reconsider. He thought about the pulsing grey light of his vision, of the night screams and the harm and hostility he had already experienced. He let himself be afraid. He let himself be afraid, too, for the people in his home, and for his friend. Then he thought about God's laughter and let himself be angry. He waited, turning on the fulcrum. Once he brought the wall down, there might be no turning back. He let the battle run its course. Rage won. He felt the tug and answered it. He raised the pickaxe.

Meacham heard the noise. She knew what it meant even before she recognized it for the *chunnnggg* of metal against stone. It jabbed her nerves, a cold steel spike. *No*, she thought. *Stop*, she thought. Instinct ran fast, outstripped rationality. *Who?* she wondered, but only for a moment. Gray, she knew. She stood up from her chair and began to walk in the direction of the crypt. "Stop." She said the word aloud and was speaking to herself. *Keep it together. Do your job. Be who you are.* She rallied her skepticism and her cynicism, the pillars that had seen her through wind and gale. She had her breathing under control by the time she left the library. Her heart was less co-operative. It was enslaved by the rhythm of the blows. It jumped with each clash. Gethsemane Hall echoed with the tolling of a stone bell.

She was the first to reach the crypt. She couldn't see Gray right away. He was hidden in the recess. But the flashlight on the ground magnified his shadow and threw it up the height of the vault. It flailed with expressionist violence. The sound changed as Meacham approached. The ringing of the pickaxe became the deeper blow and sharper cracks of failing masonry. She moved forward until she could see Gray. He was drenched with sweat. His clothes clung to him like sodden rags. He was hammering at the wall with a rhythm as metronomic as it was manic. Chunks of stone flew from his attack. Shrapnel pinged off the walls. The bricks fell. Behind them was darkness. The black seeped into the crypt. The flashlight dimmed. So did the hurricane lamp that lay in the centre of the floor, its power cord an umbilical connection back to the light of the rest of the house, light that seemed now to Meacham to be conditional, an eccentricity allowed only at the sufferance of the Hall's true owner.

More bricks fell. More darkness crossed the growing threshold. "Lord Gray," she said, but her throat was dry, and her voice cracked. She tried again, called louder. Gray didn't respond. Momentum had taken him. He was an automaton constructed for this one motion. Meacham stepped forward, thinking of grabbing his shoulder. But the pickaxe swished the air with each savage backswing, its point inviting her flesh to step on up. She shouted Gray's name. She might as well have yelled at the Hall itself. More brick shattered. The hole became a maw. Soon it would be big enough for someone to fall through. It was already big enough for something bad to crawl out from. The blows became the pounding of a dark heart. Gray should have been exhausted, but he didn't slow. Instead, Meacham heard the heartbeat pick up speed. There was excitement to the pulse. Anticipation.

"*Stop*," she screamed. But the moment had arrived. The remains of the wall collapsed all at once. There was a rumbling crash that was almost swallowed up by another sound. It was a sigh, and Meacham felt herself being pushed back by a giant's palm. The darkness rushed in, and the lights went out. Black felt coated her eyes. There was no sound from Gray. The rumble faded, replaced by the ticking of pebbles against each other and the restless settling of dust. Then silence. Meacham strained her ears. They felt smothered. Old field training resurfaced, never once used during the length of her career. She was poised for a fight. But she couldn't see or hear. The enemy would snatch at her from the dark. Her enemy *was* the dark.

And then she realized she wasn't blind. She was seeing something. From the recess, on the other side of the threshold, there was a light. She could see the faint shape that was Gray's outline. He was slumping, motionless, his strings cut. There was light. It was grey. It pulsed. It was wrong. Her eyes widened.

Light flashed back on. She blinked. She breathed. She turned her head and saw Crawford stepping into the crypt. Pertwee was close behind him.

"What are you doing?" Crawford asked. "Why did you unplug the light?"

We didn't, Meacham thought. The cord was plugged into a socket in the outside corridor. *We didn't touch the light*, she tried to say, but she wasn't speaking yet. So she just shook her head.

Pertwee pushed past him, looked into the recess, and saw what Gray had done. "Oh," she said. There was a world of wonder in her single syllable. There was joy, too. *You should have been here,* Meacham thought. *A new light would have shone down on your optimism, oh you bet.*

The pickaxe slid out of Gray's hands. It clunked on the ground. Safe now, Meacham went up to him. "Are you okay?" she asked.

His skin was dust and sweat and pallor. His hair was soaked limp. His eyes were trained in the direction of the breach, and they were unfocused, twitching back and forth. When Meacham touched his shoulder, he jumped and turned his head to face her. After a moment, his eyes saw her again. He grunted. He looked at the collapsed wall, then back at her. He gave her a faint, despairing smile. "Well," he said and made a sound in his chest. A small, hurt laugh. "Well," he said again. "Here we are."

Gray went off to dig up two more flashlights and fresh batteries. The rest of the party gathered at the mouth of the hole, no one yet taking a step down the revealed staircase. Pertwee and Corderman crowded the front, eager as kids at Christmas to explore, only courtesy for their host holding them back. Meacham didn't appear to feel their hurry. She was sticking to the entrance of the crypt, close to the light of the rest of the house. Crawford peered into the depths. There wasn't much to see. A half-dozen steps dropping steeply into blackness. Vertigo entered his bloodstream. A dark invitation, it tried to make him topple forward. He backed out of the recess. He tore his eyes away from the void, forced them to look at the details of the breach, tried to analyze what he was seeing. This was rearguard action on behalf of rationality, and he knew it. He made the effort anyway. He wanted to see evidence of a hoax. He knew about as much about dating construction work as he did Swahili, but he still hoped, clutching at straws in the wind, that he would see traces of plaster and Styrofoam rocks. Nothing. He looked up and saw Meacham gesture him over. She had already corralled Sturghill. He joined them.

"Well?" Meacham asked.

"I wish I could say it looked fake."

"I could have told you it wasn't."

"What have I been telling everybody about believing the evidence of their eyes?" Sturghill said. She sounded annoyed. Crawford wondered how genuine her skepticism was. She might be fighting the same losing war as he.

Meacham seemed poised on the edge of unconditional surrender. "He didn't fake smashing down that wall," she told Sturghill.

"So it looks good. But consider the evidence. He puts on the helmet, says he sees things that the helmet couldn't possibly be showing him, claims he has a vision of a staircase behind the wall. He takes down the wall. Lo and behold, there it is. And in his own home, too. Now if *I* had had the vision, I might be a bit more convinced."

"Have you found any speakers in the walls?" Meacham asked.

"Not yet," Sturghill admitted.

"Any hard evidence of any kind to support the hoax theory?"

"No."

"Then how long can you pretend that thesis is viable?"

"Until I see hard evidence to the contrary. Lacking empirical evidence on either side, which is easier to believe: hoax or ghosts?"

"Occam's Razor," Meacham muttered.

"I was thinking more of David Hume and what he had to say about miracles. What's more likely: that the eyewitnesses are wrong, however many there are, and however much they may be in good faith, or that the laws of the universe have been violated? The miracle loses out every time." She cocked her head at Meacham. "You don't sound like you're fighting too hard for your own agenda. You're the one who wanted us here, remember."

Meacham nodded. "I also saw what I saw."

Sturghill smiled. "I don't think you'd see much of anything with the light unplugged. I can get freaked by sudden blackouts too."

"That wasn't the problem. I *did* see something."

"Well, it wasn't a ghost." Sturghill said. She left them to turn the magician's eye on the rubble.

"You're being quiet," Meacham said to Crawford.

He decided to be open with her — and with himself. It helped that she was voicing her own anxieties. "I don't like where this is heading," he said. "I've never experienced anything like this. And I haven't had a single reading on any instrument that makes the slightest bit of sense."

Meacham looked at the ground for a moment, then at him. "When you asked me if I had a dream the night before coming here," she said, "I lied."

"I thought maybe you had," he said.

Then Gray was back with the flashlights.

"Well?" their host asked.

Meacham still had her doubts. She doubted that heading down these stairs was in any way a good idea. She doubted that she was going to come out of this fiasco with anything that would satisfy Jim Korda and salvage her career. And though she suppressed the idea as soon as it rose, she was beginning to have concerns for her personal safety. Gray's behaviour was becoming erratic. People who wielded pickaxes while in a trance were to be approached with caution. That was the lost-cause rationalization she used to keep the anxiety from growing any worse. She didn't let herself ask *why* he was in a trance. She would hold off that question and its darkness just as long as she could. But oh, going down the stairs was a bad idea.

The light from the rest of the hall barely reached the recess. It died five steps down. The grey light was gone. Perhaps, now that the flies had been lured to the web, its job was done. There were three flashlight beams to light the way. They were strong enough, and even with their jouncing and the seizure dance of shadows, Meacham had no trouble with her footing. It wasn't the light's strength that she mistrusted. It was its permanence. It had already been taken away once in the last hour. She didn't want to lose it again down here.

The walls narrowed, and the staircase twisted, as if they were descending a Gothic cathedral's tower. Meacham reached out a hand to steady herself. The stairs were becoming thin wedges. If she moved too near the interior wall, there wouldn't be room to place her feet, and she would fall. The exterior wall was dank. She felt something slick and bristly crumble against her fingers. The brickwork here was very dark, as if soiled by centuries of candle smoke, or as if, given enough time, the darkness had seeped into the stone itself.

Gray's voice drifted up towards Meacham. He was at the front of the line, hidden from her by twists of the spiral. "The nitre!" he called out. "See, it increases. It hangs like moss upon the vaults."

Meacham looked back at Crawford. He was bringing up the rear with her and had one of the flashlights. His face, shadowed, twisted in distaste. "Poe," he said. "'The Cask of Amontillado.' He picks his time and place, doesn't he?"

"He's enjoying this," Meacham said.

"I do believe he is."

Hudson was just ahead of Meacham. His shoulders had slumped when Gray had spoken. "That's the first time I've heard him enjoy anything since his family died," he said.

"If he's having this much fun, maybe Kristine is right after all," Meacham offered. No one took her up on it. She didn't buy it, either. The words were thin, fragile. The dark snatched them, and they tore, parchment in wind.

The spiral tightened. The walls on both sides whispered against Meacham's shoulders. She fought against dizziness. They had to be near the bottom, she thought. If the staircase narrowed any further, it would become a dead end. They had to be closing in on the centre of the nautilus shell. But the walls did come closer, and now they weren't being subtle about it as they rubbed up against her. She heard exclamations coming from below, and braced herself for worse. It came. She had to turn sideways. The stairs became steeper, and she hugged the interior wall as she crab-walked down.

"This is insane," Crawford complained, and he was right. Meacham couldn't imagine the madness that would have such a thing built.

"This is wrong," Hudson moaned, and Meacham knew he was seeing a spiritual cancer. He was right, too.

She tried to keep her face away from the wall, but the space was too tight. Rough brick had turned slime-smooth. It smeared its kisses on her cheek. The stench of old mould and bad growth dug into her nostrils. Her eyes watered. They stung with grit and sweat, but it didn't matter that she was blind, because Crawford couldn't aim the flashlight anywhere but up as he scrabbled against the wall himself. There was nothing to see, but plenty to touch and smell as she was digested by the stone intestine. She closed her eyes, trying to squeeze out the dark.

Her right foot dangled over nothing. She gasped, tried to stop herself, but her balance was already gone. She went over, caught in the vertigo of the first moment of a plunge from a cliff. Her heart stammered, and then her foot landed heavily on the ground. She stumbled, windmilling, caught her balance and opened her eyes. The staircase had dropped them into a large, low-ceilinged space. There was no more brickwork. The walls were pure stone but had an odd, chipped look to them. Flashlight beams played over the black mouths of three tunnels.

"Did you know this was here?" Sturghill asked Gray.

He shook his head. Meacham thought there was still a hint of the manic in his eyes, but he seemed more cautious now. At least he wasn't joking.

Pertwee's face glowed. "We've found it," she whispered, rapt.

"'It'?" Meacham asked.

"Saint Rose lived on these grounds, but long before the Hall was built. No one has ever known where. There is no record of an earlier structure, and the Gray family has refused any request for a thorough archaeological search of the grounds." She shot an accusing glance at Gray. He shrugged. "But here. She must have lived here. I mean, listen." She held up a hand, and they were all quiet for a moment. The silence was vast. "This would be the perfect place for meditation."

Or for going quietly out of your mind, Meacham thought. "You think she died here?" she asked.

"Perhaps." Pertwee seemed excited by the idea. Meacham hadn't proposed it as a good thing.

Crawford was examining the cave walls. "This is an odd formation."

"I don't think it's a natural cave," Corderman said. "I think it's a mine."

They all looked at him. Meacham saw the other faces as startled as her own, Pertwee's most of all. She tried to think of another instance where Corderman had spoken with authority, couldn't come up with one.

"What makes you say that?" Crawford asked.

"The walls. These are tunnels that were chipped out of the ground. The floor's the same."

Meacham looked down. He was right. The floor was level in a way that was unlikely to be naturally occurring, but it had the same pockmarked texture. She could imagine centuries of pickaxes carving out the surface.

"How do you know this?" Sturghill asked.

Corderman blushed. "I do a lot of role-playing games at the Chislehurst Caves. This place looks the same."

"Let me guess. You play an elf."

Corderman's blush, even in the sallow illumination of the

flashlights, noticeably turned a deep crimson. "I'm a half-orc," he muttered.

"He's right," Hudson said, and for a lunatic moment, Meacham thought he was approving of Corderman's choice of fantasy race. "I've visited the Caves. This looks exactly the same."

"I've been there too," Crawford said. "I should have noticed the resemblance."

Gray approached Corderman. "Tell me about them," he said, softly.

"They've been used for all sorts of things," Corderman said, perking up. "They were a bomb shelter during the war, they —"

Gray cut him off. "No, no," he said. "Who made them? How old are they?"

"Oh. They're really old. The Druids and Saxons worked them. The Romans, too. They were flint and chalk mines. But people lived in them, too. Some sections became places of worship."

"Where there were sacrifices," Hudson added, pointedly. "Human ones."

"Yes, there were," Corderman admitted.

"There's no evidence for that," Crawford objected. "The earliest historical records only date back to 1250."

"There's no proof they aren't older than that," Corderman replied, offended. "There's no proof there weren't sacrifices." He didn't want his playground demythologized.

"So?" Pertwee asked. "That doesn't mean there were here. This is a place of peace," she insisted, and in the stridency of her claim, Meacham heard how brittle and desperate her faith had become. She looked at Pertwee's face, as grimed by sweat and wall muck as hers. She nodded to herself. *Coming down here bothered you as much as it did me. You won't admit it, especially not to yourself, but you're on the edge, girlfriend. The old certainties just aren't cutting it anymore. I sympathize. Believe me, I do.*

"Let's see what there is to see," Gray said. He wasn't being flip, but there was excitement in his tone. He was alive to the adventure, even as he took it seriously. Meacham glanced at Hudson, saw him staring at his friend in despair. *He wants the adventure to end,* she thought, *while he can still pray.*

"Which way?" Sturghill asked, while Crawford shone his light first down one tunnel, then the other.

"Be quiet for a minute," Gray said. He walked to each of the tunnels and listened. "This one," he said, standing at the left-hand entrance. "Seems most interesting."

Once they were all in the passageway, Meacham picked up on what had drawn Gray. There was a faint, cold breath blowing down the tunnel, and she could hear the distant drip of water. After the birth canal constriction of the staircase, the tunnel was spacious. There was room to walk three abreast here.

But the corridor was still a stone snake. Its coils were slow, gradual curves. The snake's movements were imperceptible. Meacham felt them, though. The same constriction attack as had happened in the staircase was going on here. It was slower, longer, bigger. The snake had all the time in the world as they ventured deeper down its length. Only its breath gave it away, that cold puff of breeze on Meacham's cheek. It wasn't constant; it came and went. It had a rhythm. Inhale, exhale, inhale, exhale. Meacham held her gait steady. She prevented her teeth from chattering. She thought, *How much of the spook show you're conjuring do you really believe?* Because she didn't know, she didn't answer, and she didn't scold herself. She was in new territory. For the first time in her life, she was faced with the prospect of actually believing in something. She was frightened.

The sound of dripping water grew louder. Each fall was a *plunk* amplified in an echo chamber. The tunnel dipped gradually, then opened out into a large cavern. Straight ahead was a body of water. It was a tangible darkness. When Gray shone his light over the water, the beam faded before it touched the other wall. No way to tell how big the room was and if the water was a pond or a lake. From somewhere beyond the lake came the drip of the water. Gray aimed his beam up. The cavern ceiling was very high, barely visible. Meacham had been too caught up in the nightmare spiral of the staircase to notice how far they had come down, but she thought the roof of this cave must be close to the surface.

"They can't have mined this," Meacham said.

"No," Gray agreed. "Looks natural."

Plunk went the water. A long pause, during which Meacham imagined the next drop falling from the great height, plunging through the lightless void. *Plunk.*

"So peaceful," Pertwee breathed. "Listen."

Meacham heard nothing but the toll of emptiness, the monotonous counting off of the centuries drop by endless, tedious, meaningless drop. The water wasn't peaceful. It was dead. She thought about drowning Pertwee and her optimism once and for all.

Crawford shone his light around and found an exit to the right of where they had come in. This tunnel too was angling downward. The slope was gradual, but it was still a slope. Meacham looked at it, wondered how far down into the snake she was willing to go. Gray had no qualms. He charged ahead. She read his face as he brushed past her. She saw the tension in the set of his jaw and the pinch of his brow. He was scared too, she realized. He wasn't blithely tripping off to adventure. But there was a desperate eagerness as well. He looked like a man frantic to know the worst and get it done. *He's dragging you down with him*, she thought. She could ask for one of the flashlights and head back with whoever else also wanted out. She could do that. She could show that leadership. Instead, she followed Gray. *You want to know, too,* said the voice of prosecution. *Yes,* she agreed. *I want to know.*

She didn't want to know the worst as badly as Gray. She was that much warier of it, so she didn't follow too closely. Pertwee was right on his heels, as desperate to believe in the best of all possible worlds and determined to see proof that she was right. She dragged Corderman in her wake. Hudson followed a few steps behind. Meacham noted that his attention never wavered from Gray. Crawford hung back with her. She squeezed his shoulder. "Sure you want to know?" she asked.

"No," he said. "But I do need to."

She nodded. "That's our curse," she said.

The sound of the water drops followed them down the tunnel. Somehow, the volume grew. The *plunk, plunk, plunk* turned into tick-tock torture, countdown and build-up. Each drop was a reminder of the lake, that huge, black, tangible *nothing*. The hollow echo rang in Meacham's head like a hammer on a steel drum. The overflow was coming.

Crawford began, "Do you think —" But there was one more *plunk*, and its echo was a cracking rumble, and as Meacham turned to face Crawford, he disappeared.

Meacham threw herself backward, away from the collapsing floor. Dust billowed in the second before Crawford's light went out and the hungry dark took her. "James!" she yelled. Then she was yelling for the others to come back, calling to them for their help and for their light.

He fell. There was a second of floating plunge. It couldn't have been longer, but his mind sped up to turn it into an infinity of dreadful anticipation. The landing didn't disappoint. Rock smashed him. He fell on stone, bounced on a corner that was sharp and punctured something important, fell on more stone, and stone fell on him. Underneath the roar he heard *crack*, and he heard *snap*, and he knew those sounds came from him. The pain was blocked by shock and didn't kick in right away. He was lying on his back and his back was bent farther than it should have been. His right leg was twisted beneath his body. He knew if he tried to move it, he would regret doing so. His head was stuffed with the darkness. It pressed in through his ears and eyes. It cut him off from the world. He tried to call, and the darkness came in through his mouth, too. He hacked dust but couldn't hear himself cough. He moaned. Gradually, the darkness in his ears faded, and he could hear the sound of his pain. He began to think about Hell. Then he heard another sound. It was Meacham, calling his name. "Yes!" he cried. "*Yes!*" The word was a spasm, an ecstasy of relief.

"Are you all right?"

Of course she would ask that. He would, too, if positions were reversed. But his reality was so at odds with her question that he started to laugh, even though that wracked pain down his spine. "No," he said, laughing now to hold off the despair. "I'm bloody well not all right."

"Anything broken?"

"My leg. My spine, too, I think."

He heard Meacham call for help. After a moment, she yelled down, "Hang on. They're coming back."

To do what? he wondered. No one had brought any rope. Still, it was a comfort to hear the sound of many voices. Then he saw a pinprick of light above him. It moved around uncertainly, winking in and out like a firefly. Was that a flashlight? Had he fallen that far?

"We can't see you," Meacham said. "Can you move around at all?"

He tried. His left arm wasn't screaming, and when he asked it to move, it did as it was told. "A bit," he answered. He picked up a rock, bashed it against another. He kept up the beat, and the firefly steadied.

"Jesus," said a male voice. Corderman's? He wasn't sure.

"What's that beside him?" That was Pertwee.

The firefly shifted. Gray called, "James, can you see what that is on your right?"

Crawford turned his head. He was surprised the distant flashlight was providing any illumination for him down here at all, but the darkness had receded slightly. A deep grey moved through the air, and he could make out some shapes. He saw the thing with the corner that had crippled him. It was a rectangular block of stone. Its lines were regular. It was a black shadow, void of detail. It shouted its name. "It's a tomb," he said softly.

"What?" Gray asked.

"A tomb!" he shouted. He wanted gone. "Get me out of here!"

He heard arguing, then Meacham spoke again. "The tunnel keeps going down," she said. "We're going to follow it and see if it leads to you."

"And if it doesn't?"

"We'll head back to the Hall for rope."

"Bugger that! Call an ambulance!"

"No one has a phone."

"So go back. Do it now."

"All right."

"Wait! Don't leave me alone."

More discussion. It became heated. Then Pertwee said, "Do you realize what you've found?"

"*Found?* I bloody well broke my back on it, you idiot!" Not in the mood for her bullshit. Just not in the mood. He wanted out.

"That must be the tomb of Saint Rose," Pertwee carried on. "You could hardly be in a more sacred place."

"Shut up!" Crawford yelled. His back and lungs screamed, but he shouted anyway. "Shut up shut up *shut up!* I don't give a fuck! Just *do* something!"

Scuffling. Raised voices. A barked order. Then Meacham again. "Patrick, Kristine, Anna, and I are going to try to find our way to you. Richard and Edgar are heading back up to call an ambulance. Okay?"

Pertwee was coming down. Of course she was. Thrilled to see the tomb of her heroine, he thought, his mood savage. Never mind the broken body beside it. Then fear swamped the anger. There would be no one at the hole, he realized. He would be alone while they searched for him. "Can't anyone stay at the hole?" he asked.

"There are only two flashlights," Meacham said with soft regret.

He closed his eyes for a moment, then opened them again. He didn't want to lose a second of what little light was allotted him. "Okay," he called, bracing himself. "Hurry," he added. "Hurry," he whispered.

The firefly disappeared.

The tunnel's slope was slow but steady. They were descending. The way began to curve. Enough of a turn, Meacham thought, and they would be heading toward the cavern where Crawford had fallen. That would be some luck. And then what? What could they do for him? *We can keep him company. He sounds scared. So am I.*

Words between Sturghill and Pertwee drew her attention. Sturghill must have been on the attack, because Pertwee was responding with outraged hurt. "I am not!" she was saying. "I'm as worried about him as you are."

"Couldn't wait to see your precious grave, though," Sturghill said.

"That has nothing to do with it. I want to help."

"Yeah, and you could hear how welcome your help is."

"Easy, you two," Meacham said.

Pertwee ignored her. "I just wanted to reassure him there's nothing to be afraid of. Why can't any of you see that?"

Because I can see plenty of things to fear, Meacham thought. *Christ, I'm scared.*

The snake twisted, taking them deep into the dark.

The light hadn't gone. Crawford could still see. That was no comfort. Light when there should be none was worse than total darkness. It was the light Meacham had described: grey and dead, pulsing with rot. It was brightest near the tomb. Unwilling, but lacking choice, Crawford turned his head to look at the stone slab.

He thought he saw a droplet of light gather at one corner and hang for a moment. He thought he saw that. Thought. Thought, thought, *thought*. *Remember who you are*, he told himself. *Remember your work. Remember what you know. Especially about susceptibility in suggestive environments. They don't get much more suggestive than this, and subjects don't come much more susceptible than you are right now. After all, you didn't see that drop of light fall to the ground, did you?* No, he hadn't.

The mental pep talk was a poor whistle in the dark, off-key and faltering. He wasn't imagining the light. He could see by it. And he could see it move. He could see the pulsing begin to acquire direction. Volition. *No*, he thought, *I am not seeing that. I'm hallucinating.* But more drops of light gathered at the lip of the tomb. He watched closely. They didn't fall down. They fell *up*. He watched them plummet toward the invisible roof of the cavern, and then he heard the familiar *plunk* of the water drops that had followed him from the underground lake. Implications and terrors gathered. He tried not to moan. He watched as another drop formed, noticed how the grey was turning black in the moment before the light took flight, and thought about that lake again, and how the surface had been so completely still. Of course it was still, he thought with rising hysteria, it was being fed from *below*.

The next thought was even worse. They had not touched the lake. They had only looked at its depth of physical darkness. They did not know if what they had been seeing was water.

It isn't water. He watched more droplets of light form, grey, turning black, and their rhythm beginning to build. *Oh Christ, I know what it is.* The irony would have made him laugh, if only he weren't so close to screaming. Ectoplasm. It wasn't the shimmering silver ooze of Victorian spirit photography. It was the fake phenomenon's dark cousin. Above him, an entire lake of ectoplasm had gathered and was waiting in its black contemplation. And here was the source. The drops gathered, flew up, building with the slow patience of cave formations. How long had the lake been gathering? What strength did it have coiled?

A drop formed, but this one didn't leave the tomb. It dangled on the corner, suspended by a prayer-thin strand. Another joined it. Then another. They fused, growing bigger. Each new drop added to the mass. Before too many seconds has passed, Crawford was staring at a blob floating in the air just above the tomb. It lengthened. The drops began to form quickly, as if the dam of the tomb were giving way, at long, long last. The shape grew longer yet. Now it was a worm. Soon it would be a snake. It pulsed with a bad substitute for life. The *plunk, plunk, plunk* of the drops was replaced by a steady, trickling, tearing sound. One end of the snake turned. It pointed down toward Crawford's face. It moved closer. Crawford began to scream.

The scream stopped them, when it should have made them move faster. It should have made them run. Meacham's heart froze as every bad thing was confirmed. She, Sturghill, Hudson, and Pertwee locked gazes for one panicked moment. Then they did run. Or they tried to. With one flashlight, the best they could do on the sloping, uneven floor was a jog. Meacham still had no idea if they would even find Crawford at the end of this tunnel, but it was still turning and still descending, and there was no other way to answer the screams except to plunge on down.

"James!" Sturghill called. "James! It's okay! We're coming!"

The screams were agonized. There was no pause for breath between them. They were one on top of the other, an overdub of terror and pain. They grew louder, then came in short, staccato bursts, as if each was interrupted by a fresh new horror. For an irrational moment, Meacham wished she had a gun. Pertwee was sobbing as she ran. Sturghill's face was taut and grim.

There was a hysterical, gurgling whine, and the screams stopped. Meacham kept moving. The snake took them down, and at last they reached its belly. The tunnel opened into the huge cavern. Sturghill shone her light forward. In the centre of the cave was the tomb. It was an unadorned sarcophagus, Stone Age in its simplicity. All about the monument was Crawford. His skin had been peeled off and wrapped around the slab.

chapter fourteen

the better part of valour

There were screams, then. And there was running. The devil was at their heels, and the only thing in life that mattered was to outrun him. In the first cave, they almost collided with Gray and Corderman, coming back down with more flashlights and rope. Meacham pushed them back up. The climb to the surface was worse than the descent. The claustrophobia was still present, but now there was danger, now there was something with bad desire in the dark beneath her, and the twisting staircase was too slow an exit. Spiral and spiral and spiral, breath rasping in her chest and legs aching from the run and the climb, and the staircase was a trap, it was never going to end, it was going to keep them in the twist until the darkness with teeth and claws caught up and had its way with them. Her pulse was the pounding of heavy artillery. She was frightened. She was terrified. She thought she had been scared earlier, but no. Not properly. Now she knew what terror pure and true was, for the first time in her life. It was bad. But it fuelled the drive to run, run, *run*, to stay alive for another extra second.

The staircase finally relented and spat her out into the crypt. She kept moving, and so did the others, and they didn't stop until they were in the relative illumination of the Great Hall. The electric lights were on. The windows were black. It was night already. She hadn't realized how long they'd been underground.

"What's happened?" Gray demanded. He and Corderman were gasping. They looked worried, but more puzzled than anything else. Sturghill, Pertwee, and Hudson were another story. Meacham imagined she must look like they did: eyes rabbit-wide with fright, skin white as the death that pursued them.

"He's dead," Hudson wheezed out and then described exactly how he was dead.

"We're getting out of here," Meacham said. "All of us. Right now." She put every ounce of authority she could muster into the command. She wanted no argument or delay. She wanted to be anywhere but here. She was a believer, now. She respected the object of her new faith.

There was no argument from those who had seen what was left of Crawford. They moved for the exit. Pertwee and Sturghill had identically anxious faces. A moment for history. Corderman said, "What about the equipment?"

"Leave it," Pertwee said. She didn't look back.

Outside, Meacham's breath steadied, if only a bit. The night was a giant's palm pressing down on her. Gethsemane Hall reached out for her, wanting her back. But at least she wasn't *inside*.

Gray said, "Are you sure that you saw —"

"*Yes*," Meacham snapped. She started up the drive. *Just leave.* She had fantasies of being on a transatlantic flight within the next twelve hours, flying home to the joyous everydayness of a shattered career. Maybe she would be lucky. Maybe, if she ran far and fast enough, the peeled-potato (with ketchup, thank you) corpse of James Crawford would be the worst thing she would ever see. And that would be a good thing, because, and here was another maybe, maybe, with enough time, she might reassemble something like her old understanding of how the world worked. But if she saw what had killed Crawford, then that would be the end of all things.

She didn't check to see who was following her, but she heard footsteps on gravel. She wasn't walking towards the embrace of the yew trees alone.

Gray's voice again. "What about the ambulance?"

She stopped and turned around. He hadn't moved. He was standing alone in the wide, parking area of the drive, facing the retreating troops. She couldn't make out his face. "It's too late for that," she said.

"It's still on its way."

"Then wait for it at the gate."

"And tell them what? 'Sorry, boys, the man's well dead. Needn't have bothered you. Off you go, then.'"

He was right. A corpse meant officials doing official things. For a moment, the prospect of authorities from the mundane world once again swarming all over Gethsemane Hall comforted her, tempted her to think that reality would reassert itself through sheer bureaucracy. She could almost be lured back. But then, *she* was one of those authorities. *She* was one of the officials. *She* was the bureaucracy. And *she* was running for her life. Right now, it was night. She knew better than to believe happy lies. "Fine," she said. "You want to greet them, you wait."

"You aren't leaving town, are you? You'll be wanted."

Shit. The first opportunity for escape receded. At least she'd be away from the Hall. "We'll be at the Nelson," she said and started up the drive again.

"Richard," she heard Hudson plead. He was right behind her.

"I can deal with this," was the response. Meacham admired his confidence. She wondered where it sprang from and if it was lethally foolish. "Why don't you stay and help?"

The question was cruel, whether Gray intended it to be or not. Hudson sighed so he would not stop, and kept walking. Up ahead, the night gathered strength as the drive rose into the woods. The darkness was thicker there. It was the fault of the yew trees. They gathered the black in their branches, hugged it close and squeezed out solid shadow. Hudson still had his flashlight, but the beam wasn't parting the dark, just pointing to it. Meacham slowed down a bit as she approached the trees, giving the rest of the group a chance to catch up. They bunched together. They were a turtle of defensive fear. Meacham remained at the front, leading a retreat as anxious as an over-the-trenches assault. She stepped first into the embrace of the yew trees. She was half-surprised when she didn't encounter a wall. She kept moving, waiting for the dark to gather substance and push back, slowing her down until its quicksand strength held her fast for the thing in the Hall to find. The retreat was slow. Hudson kept the flashlight trained on the ground so they could see to place their feet. The circle of illumination was weak magic. For Meacham, it was nothing more than a place to keep her eyes focused so they wouldn't look up and perhaps see something she didn't want to see.

The woods held the night but did not unleash it. Nothing reached out to touch Meacham. She walked a slow and steady pace, found a rhythm that moved her forward without risk of stumbling. She didn't want to fall. The others were in lock-step behind her. Footsteps crunched gravel in unison. *It's a forced march,* she thought. *We're abandoning Moscow.* Around them, the scorched earth waited.

At last, the woods relented. They loosened their grasp. The trees parted. Hudson's light stretched farther, as if pulling in air for the end of the race. There was the gate. Meacham had a panicked thought: that a combination would be needed to leave as well as to enter the grounds. She was wrong. On this side of the gate, there was only a button. She pushed it, and the gate opened.

She had thought, when the gate closed behind her, that she would breathe glorious new air. She had thought she would feel the exhilaration of release. She didn't. Instead, she felt a sharp tug of regret, and to her horror, she turned to look back down the drive, and she knew, even as the blood drained from her face, that the look she bore was one of longing. She knew this because Hudson, and Corderman, and Sturghill, and Pertwee wore identical expressions. They were all facing back.

The approaching flash of ambulance lights broke the spell. Meacham turned around to face the vehicle. As she did, she locked eyes with Sturghill. They shared the fear.

They'd left him. He was alone with the Hall for the first time since the investigation had begun. Surrounded by the night, he turned to face the house. It stared back at him, and it was not impassive. Its eyes, lit from within, were eager. So was he. He was charged up for a fight, could feel the tension thrum of victory, even if he didn't know why. He was winning a war.

The Hall tugged at him. *Come back inside*, it said. *In due course*, he told it. *Now*, it insisted. It reached out for him. Its tentacles were shadow and anger. They coiled around him. They squeezed. His confidence wavered. The nature of the war blurred. The fear, clamped down but only just by bravado, broke the surface. The reality of Crawford's death hit like a nitrogen-cooled spike to the base of his neck. He hadn't seen the body. He didn't have the visceral knowledge that Meacham and her group had. But he had seen the terror. He had seen Meacham, of all people, run from the place. The woman who believed in nothing believed in something now, and she was fleeing its pursuit. Crawford was dead. Whatever had killed him waited in the heartless depths of the Hall. For a moment, he tried to imagine a human killer, then dismissed the idea as dangerous. Clinging to rationality would be a lethal rigidity. He would be snapped in half.

And still, through the fear, through the growing sense that he was alone with something enormous, he could feel strange tickles, fragments of satisfaction, slaked anger, excited victory. He clenched his hands into fists. One to defend against the disturbing pleasures. The other to hold onto them.

He could hear the siren of the ambulance now. With an effort, he turned away from the house and looked up the drive. After a minute, the night began to pulse with red and blue glows. They grew brighter, turned into flashes, and the ambulance emerged from the woods, taking the last bend in the drive at speed.

"I hope you're up to a fair bit of climbing," he told the paramedics as they piled out.

He led them into the house. There was troubling relief in giving in to the tug and returning to the Hall's embrace. The paramedics were in a hurry. He told them Crawford was dead, and one of them called in for the police. Gray pointed the way, and they jogged ahead of him, humping a stretcher down the spiral of the staircase. Their halogen torches lit up the dark, turning the walls into a harsh-faced wasteland of edged shadows. "Don't fall," Gray said. "We're too late to be of any help." They didn't listen to him.

With more light, the cave itself looked even more like a maw, only this time Gray could see the jaws as they prepared to close. He tried to shrug off the sense of teeth descending when he wasn't looking and led the way down into the tunnels. When they reached the cave-in, one of the paramedics shone his light down into the hole. "Can't see anything," he said. "Too high up."

They continued the descent. As they went deeper and came closer to the cave where Crawford had fallen, Gray tensed, bracing himself for the bad sight. The tunnel bent. The cave opened up before them. Halogen lit it.

The paramedics stopped. One of them dropped his end of the stretcher and rounded on Gray. "You taking the piss?" he demanded, livid.

Gray blinked, ran his eyes over the cavern. There was nothing here. No Crawford. No body. No blood. "I was sure this was where they said he was," he said, confused. The man who had spoken lifted his lamp. The ceiling was distant and barely visible, but Gray could see the hole where Crawford had fallen. He shook his head. He looked down and saw the tomb. "This is the place," he said. He approached the tomb.

There was no mistaking it for anything else. It was a massive black slab, rough-hewn but rigorous in its lines. It appeared to be granite, a harsh intrusion amid the hard chalk walls. The stone would have had to have been hauled from a fair distance away and then wrestled down to the caverns. There were no inscriptions. Gray couched beside the stone, looking for a trace of Crawford. Nothing.

"So?" the other paramedic asked, sounding no more happy than his partner.

"He *was* here," Gray said.

They joined him and shone their lights over the ground, then up towards the roof of the cavern, and back down again. "You say he fell all this way," said one.

"Yes."

"Banged himself up good and proper," said the other.

"That's right. He broke his leg and his back."

One of the men lit a cigarette. "Bounced back pretty quick."

Gray tried to stare him down. "Do you take all your calls this seriously?"

The man returned his gaze steadily. "We do when they're hoaxes, *sir*." His "sir" had the warmth of dry ice.

"Listen —" Gray began.

"No, sir, I think you'd better listen. You say a man fell down here and died. And there's no corpse."

"I didn't actually see the body," Gray wavered.

"Pulled himself back together and crawled away, did he?"

"I didn't say —"

"But you said you saw him fall."

"I saw that he was down here, yes."

"Fell all that way, and now he's gone."

"You don't understand what's —"

"And I don't see any blood here. Do you?"

He didn't.

"Oi, Chris," the paramedic said to his partner. "Isn't there a legal consequence or two for this sort of thing?"

"Do believe you're right, Mike."

Mike drew on his cigarette, blew smoke at Gray. "We'll be off, then."

"But —"

"Save it for the police."

They left. Gray didn't follow them. He shone his own flashlight over the ground beside the tomb, then studied the slab again. He heard something drip. He almost called the paramedics back but thought better of it. He followed the sound and saw the liquid forming at the corner of the tomb. He watched the drop form. He saw it fall upward. He recognized the ectoplasm for what it was.

The instinct was to run. He believed what he'd been told. He knew that Crawford was dead. He knew that a great many things, all bad, were possible. He didn't run. He was frightened, but he also still felt the giddy exhilaration of imminent victory. He walked, steadily, without rushing, out of the cavern and started back up the tunnel. He made his way to the lake. He ran the light over its surface. He wondered how he could have ever thought this was water. It was far too taut. It was a huge muscle waiting to be flexed. He stepped closer and crouched at the edge of the shore. The lake was motionless. He wondered what made the muscle act. He reached out to touch it.

Rage took him.

The bottom fell out from Meacham's gut while she was on the phone to the local police. She hadn't been full of comfort and joy before. She'd seen the ambulance go by, had thought its hurry was a pointless irony. She'd led the retreat back to the Nelson, and there were plenty of rooms available, but they'd still doubled up. She was sharing with Sturghill. Hudson had gone on to the church rectory to bunker down with a brother in arms. She called the constabulary from her room, less than half an hour since the flight had begun. She was out of the grasp of the house. She was away from the layered age of Gethsemane Hall. The Nelson had been around a good hundred years, but it had been renovated and polished, its wood and brass a sanitized tourist fantasy of the antique. It was mundane in the purest, most life-affirming sense of the word. She could feel grief about Crawford, but she should feel safe.

She was talking to a Constable Walker. "You went down into where?" he was asking, and the alarm in his voice was distressing in and of itself, and then something hit. It rippled through Meacham, a shockwave of absence. It sank into her like the thinnest of stiletto blades, a hypodermic needle long and strong enough to pierce to her marrow and inject a concentrated lack of hope. The poison flashed through her system, and she remembered feeling this way before, in the wake of the lost dream the night before arriving at the Hall. She choked on her answer to Walker. She looked up and saw Sturghill clutch the comforter on her bed, saw her turn to look at Meacham with eyes that shone a new and deeper pain. But the worst thing wasn't anything she saw. The worst thing was what she heard. She heard Walker grunt as if he'd been punched in the stomach. Silence moved over the face of their waters. The silence was slick. It was contemptuous. It promised much.

Then the wave was over. It had been brief, but it did its damage. She heard Walker's breath catch and start again. "Oh, Lord," said the constable. He spoke with feeling. "What have you done?"

Gray crawled to the top of the stairs. His pants were torn, his knees bloody from the long climb on all fours. He didn't have the strength to walk. He did have the drive to make it back to the surface. It was the impulse of a prophet. He bore truth with him. It was a compound of anger, terror, and triumph.

The night passed with the suspense of a held breath. Meacham lay in her bed, eyes open, waiting for day. When she lay down, she had reached out to turn out the bedside lamp. Alarm arrested the gesture. Sturghill left hers on, too. "What happens in the morning?" the magician had asked.

"We leave."

"Can we?"

Meacham didn't know. She imagined every sort of tangle that might prevent her from completing her escape. As dawn finally broke, she wondered if Sturghill might have meant something else by her question. Could she, in good conscience, leave with something this bad going on, something she had played her own bit in triggering? *Girl, can you just take off? Watch me. Watch me fly.*

In the morning, her wings were clipped. Walker, following a chain of command that Meacham had to wonder if he really believed in, had called in reinforcements from outside Roseminster. The Detective Branch was back in town and looking more pissed than thrilled about it. They set up shop in the police station on Edgecomb Close, two blocks to the east of the church. The Gethsemane Hall party was summoned there just after breakfast. The station was squat and had flower boxes under its windows. It looked welcoming. DCI Kate Boulter did not. She was a couple of years older than Meacham. She was a stocky woman whose weight was muscle. She carried it like a club. She wore her brown hair very short, barely long enough to avoid making her look like a skinhead enforcer. Her eyes were lidded, fed up with a career-and-a-half of dealing with other people's bullshit. She glared at her subjects, had them wait in a station desk area barely big enough for three people to sit, let alone six, and hauled them one at a time behind the desk sergeant to an office that was, as far as Meacham could tell, the only other room in the building. "They don't speak to each other," Boulter told the sergeant. Hers was a voice that had reached the end of its patience tether twenty years ago.

"Yes'm." The man nodded. He looked like he hadn't slept well, if at all.

Gray was here, leaning against a wall while he waited for his turn. Meacham was half surprised to see him alive. She studied his face. It was even tighter than it had been, and she had never seen him relaxed. He met her gaze with a look that struck her hard with its determination. The man had a mission. *What happened last night?* she wanted to ask.

Meacham was the last to be summoned. The others had been banished from the station as the interviews were completed. Walker emerged from the rear office to invite her in. He looked exhausted, but also simultaneously nervous and resigned, as if he were going through ordained motions while waiting for a catastrophe. Meacham followed him into the room, where Boulter sat at Walker's desk. He took a plastic seat beside her, banished to the children's table at Christmas. Boulter had a digital recorder on the desk and was flipping through a notebook. Without looking up, she nodded for Meacham to sit. The chair before the desk was wooden and straight-backed. Meacham was ten years old again.

Boulter finished with her notes and looked up. "I hope you're enjoying being the pain in my arse," she said, "because one of us had better be getting something out of the day."

"I beg your pardon?"

Boulter sighed. "I have memos about you. Apparently, I'm to regard you as a colleague. Or something." *Something* translated as *scum*. "So how am I supposed to conduct my investigation?"

"Why don't you just ask me what you want to ask me," Meacham said, just as tired of the bull. The politics were irrelevant now. There was something nasty in the woodshed, and it was breaking down the door.

"Fine and thanks, then. Just so I can move on, would you mind telling me how your government's agenda is furthered through hoaxing?"

"What the hell are you talking about?"

Boulter was shaking her head. "You see, this is the sort of thing that disappoints me. I'm all for extending professional courtesy, but it should be a two-way street. James Crawford is not where you say he is, and there is no sign of anybody having been injured, so can we put a stop to this circus before it gets any worse?"

"I saw him dead."

Boulter picked up her digital recorder and turned it off. "Well, fuck you too, then," she said. "Just so you know, when the tabs come knocking on my door, I'm giving them your name and where to find you. If there's anything else I can do to make your life miserable, don't hesitate to ask."

"That's it?"

"Yes. Piss off."

Meacham stood up. She noticed Walker staring at the floor.

Boulter spoke again. "But don't piss off out of town." She smiled sweetly. "Before I'm done, sweetheart, I'm looking to charge you."

"Thanks," Meacham said and left.

The day went from strength to strength. The media had never really left, but their full contingent was back, and a much sunnier and more excited lot they were than the police. The CIA tracking ghosts was the best story of all, but the CIA hoaxing ghost encounters was still hard sexy. Boulter was true to her word, and Meacham spent most of the next several hours trying to counter the awful spin with nothing at all. Evening closed in, promising darkness, and she wasn't a step closer to leaving Roseminster. Worse yet, Korda called her before she could call him.

It was dinner time. Sturghill had gone downstairs to the Nelson's restaurant to try to eat and to bring food up to the room if the reporters were buzzing too thickly. The phone rang, catching Meacham as she was about to follow.

"You have a funny way of cleaning things up," Korda said. The man was browned, and then some.

"The situation is difficult," Meacham began, wondering why she was bothering.

"I'm not interested in hearing that. I'm interested in hearing that you're about to turn things around."

She went for the Hail Mary. "I need reinforcements," she said. She didn't know what good they would do, but she wanted them. Maybe sheer numbers of skeptics and game-players would shut the Hall down.

"You didn't just say that."

Desperate: "If you knew what's been going on —"

"I don't need to. I need to know that it's all going away."

She spoke her fear and the truth: "It won't. Things are going to get a lot worse."

"Do your job," Korda snapped. "Clean up the mess." He hung up.

She sat on the bed, his last words a sudden, unexpected call to duty. *Yes,* she thought. *You helped create the mess. Clean it up. Don't run. Fight.*

Determination. Purpose. She would fight. For the first time in her adult life, she felt the fortifying iron of belief. She would fight.

Come the morning. But right now, night was coming. Darkness was closing its fist around Roseminster.

chapter fifteen

the long arm of the night

Evensong was over. John Woodhead, the parish priest of St. Rose's Church since 1962, had retired to the rectory for the night. He'd had plenty of comforting words for his colleague, but he wasn't here now, as Roseminster lost the last of its light. Patrick Hudson knelt at the altar. He had his head bowed and his eyes closed. Shutting out the external world helped him to focus on his prayers. Keeping his eyes closed also meant, he hoped, that he wouldn't fixate on the altar and think about how much its shape resembled the tomb in the Gethsemane Hall caverns. Thoughts like that would lead to others that considered the way Crawford's secrets had been draped over stone and posed in exultant impossibility, and then he would start wondering if the monument was a tomb, after all. Maybe it was an altar. Or, worse, maybe it was both. So he kept his eyes closed and put all of his energy into a concentrated plea for strength. He needed the plea to be very, very big. He needed it to be so huge that it filled his own head and left no room for listening, in case he heard the absence of an answer.

"I thought I'd find you here."

Hudson opened his eyes and turned around. Gray was seated in the rearmost pew. He had his eyes on the altar's crucifix. His expression as he looked at the icon was a mixture of superiority and anger. Hudson stood up. His knees cracked. He walked down the aisle to Gray. "You would have been here, too, not so long ago," he said.

"That's true," Gray said. Implied: *I also once believed in the Easter Bunny.* He changed the subject. "Did the police speak to you?"

"Yes. They weren't pleased with me. What happened to Crawford's body?"

"I think it was consumed."

Hudson felt a wave of spiritual vertigo. *How can we be having this conversation?* he wondered. Its terms were perverse. Its ramifications were unspeakable.

Gray continued. "You left a job unfinished," he said.

"I was afraid for my life," Hudson replied. That was the simple truth.

"You were afraid in Sudan. You didn't run then."

That was true, too. "This is different." He hadn't feared spiritual harm in Africa. He'd had the backup of faith's strength. Now, his crutch was splintering badly.

"You should come back to the house," Gray said. His tone was quiet, almost casual, as if suggesting a grand day out.

"Why?" Hudson couldn't see what good that would do. He was with Meacham on this. He wanted to get as far away from Roseminster as he could, as fast as possible. Maybe, just maybe, once he was back in London, he might be able to start the healing of his spirituality. He might be able to hear the calling once more.

"There are things we should see. There is truth there."

"I doubt it." He was lying now. He was scared Gray was right.

"Come back with me," Gray insisted.

"When are you going?"

"Now."

At night? Hudson felt his bowels loosen. "Not now," he said. There was no debate. What Gray was asking was impossible and obscene.

Gray shrugged. He stood up. "I'll be there when you change your mind," he said. He headed for the exit. Hudson followed him onto the porch. The lights of Roseminster were weak embers in chilled coal. Gray took a couple of steps, then looked back over his shoulder. "Walk with me," he asked.

Hudson sensed it was the last thing his friend would ever ask of him. "No." He wasn't strong enough.

Gray turned away and moved into the night with the confidence of a man among friends.

Meacham said, "I need to know if you're with me."

Sturghill was sitting on her bed, back against the headboard. She drew her knees up to her chest, wrapped her arms around them She bumped her chin against her knees with a steady beat as she thought. "Can't see what good this is going to do," she muttered.

"We have a responsibility. We triggered something. We have to stop it."

"Since when are you so big on doing the right thing and acknowledging responsibility?"

"Since last night."

A trace of humour re-entered Sturghill's eye. "Ever hear of death-bed conversions?"

"Very funny."

Sturghill sighed, hugged herself more tightly. "I don't want to go."

"Neither do I."

"I'm scared."

"Me too."

"I'll go." And the thing that Meacham admired, and that pleased her, was that Sturghill didn't hesitate.

"Thank you," Meacham said.

Sturghill was the easy part. Pertwee was the challenge. Meacham found her pacing. Corderman was splitting his attention between watching her and the arrival of night outside. Meacham couldn't tell which made him more nervous. Pertwee flashed her a stricken glance as Meacham stepped into the room, and she paced even faster.

"Would you mind sitting still for a minute?" Meacham asked.

Pertwee glared but perched on the bed. She was taut enough to suspend a bridge. "What is it?" she snapped.

"I want to talk to you about the Hall."

"I don't want to talk to you about it."

"Why not?"

"Because something terrible has happened, and maybe rubbing my face in it and gloating about the collapse of my belief system will make you feel better, but I'm not going to help you out with that, I'm sorry." Pertwee stared straight ahead, through Meacham's chest and beyond the closed door of the room.

"That isn't what I'm here for." Meacham glanced up at Corderman. He wasn't positioning himself to act as Pertwee's guard dog, which was what she had expected. He hadn't moved from his station at the window and was keeping his back to the room now. The set of his shoulders read, *Keep me out of this.*

"Oh?" It was the first syllable Pertwee had uttered that wasn't spoiling for a fight.

"Of course not. If anything, you were closer to being right than the rest of us. You at least believed there *was* something active there. You believed in ghosts."

Pertwee nodded slowly. "I just never thought ..." she began, and trailed off.

"*Has* your faith collapsed?" Meacham asked.

Pertwee thought before answering. Her hesitation made Meacham respect the answer. "No," she said. "I never pretended that there weren't dark spirits out there. I'm not going to pretend that there was anything good in what happened. But I don't understand why it did. There can be dangers in these sorts of investigations, but why at Gethsemane Hall? Its reputation doesn't suggest *anything* like this."

"I was thinking about that," said Meacham. "When we talked about the reputation earlier, I reminded you that none of the stories about miracles and such were from first-hand sources."

"So?"

"So you felt pulled to the house, didn't you?"

"Yes. I've wanted to go there for years."

"I mean really pulled, like something was physically hauling you in."

Pertwee said it very slowly: "Yes."

"Too fucking right yes," Corderman said, sounding harsh and frightened. He didn't change his stance or turn his head.

"So did I," Meacham said. "I'm feeling it right now. Don't you? Don't you *need* to go back there, even though you don't want to?"

"Yes." Pertwee said it more quickly this time, as if relieved. "One of the locals spoke to me about this. I think he was very frightened of the house."

"Smart man. I'd like to meet him. So this is what I think. Many people over the years have felt that tug. If you're in the town, you're close enough to the house to be wary. But if you're not, and all you know is that you want to go there, then ..."

"'One feels drawn to a place one is convinced is holy,'" Pertwee quoted. "That's what Mr. Bellingham said."

"Exactly."

"So what do you want to do?"

"I'm not sure. But I think we stirred up a hornets' nest. We should try to make amends."

"You want to go back there."

"No, I don't. But I'm going to. I don't know how to fight this, but I want to try. How about you?"

"Yes," Pertwee said.

"*No!*" Corderman shouted at the same time.

Pertwee turned around to stare at Corderman. Meacham marked the moment. Open rebellion from the sidekick. The world was coming to an end.

"No," Corderman repeated, more softly, but more desperately. "We have to leave."

Meacham sympathized. "The police won't let us," she reminded him.

"Don't you believe we can help heal this place?" Pertwee asked.

"No," Corderman told her. "I thought you knew what you were doing. I believed in you. But you're just full of piss, Anna, and I don't want to risk my life for your theories."

"They're all we have now."

"Well that isn't very much, then, is it?" He shook his head, emphatic movements left and right. "I've been listening to you for years. Look where that got me. This time, no." The denial was absolute, irrevocable. He turned back to the window, conversation over.

Pertwee faced Meacham again. She looked miserable. "I'll do what I can," she said.

"Thank you. Any ideas?" She didn't trust Pertwee's notions, but she wanted to hear them. She hadn't progressed beyond *Clean up your mess* herself.

"I'll let you know tomorrow."

"Fair enough."

Meacham went back to the room. "Well?" Sturghill asked as Meacham closed the door behind her.

"She's in. Corderman's out."

"What about Patrick?"

"I'll speak to him."

"When?"

Meacham almost said, "Now." She almost stood up to head over to the rectory. But then she looked outside, at the night that coated the window, and didn't like the idea of walking outside, of touching the night itself. So she said, "In the morning."

Sturghill appeared satisfied, even relieved. "Mind if we sleep with the lights on?" she said.

"I was going to ask you the same thing."

Meacham lay back and stared at the ceiling. She glanced at her watch. Barely past ten. It was going to be a long countdown to dawn.

Pertwee came up behind Corderman. She touched his shoulder. It was rebar rigid. "I'd rather do this with you," she said.

"I'd rather live."

Give it up, she thought. She'd lost him. For years she'd taken him for granted, when he wasn't driving her crazy. She'd never been truly angry at him; that would have been too much like kicking a puppy. She'd never given him his due, either. She had wished for a different ally, one she could take seriously. She had thought that was what she wanted. But what if all she had really wanted was someone to lead around? What about that? Corderman had filled that bill quite nicely. And now, worse than mutiny, he was simply turning away. The loss was a big hurt. "Louise was right," she said, trying one more time. "We have a responsibility."

"Responsibility to do what? Walk in there and get mangled? You have no idea what to do."

"You're wrong."

"Am I? So what's the plan?"

"I'm going to ask the spirit world for help."

Corderman barked. It took Pertwee a moment to realize the sound was a laugh gone bad. He cleared his throat. "Good luck to you on that, then."

One last try. "I'd rather not do it alone."

"I don't blame you. But you're going to have to."

That was that, then. She left him at his post and walked to the door.

"You're trying something *tonight?*" he asked. He did turn around this time and moved to the side so he didn't have his back to the dark.

"Yes."

"You're going to die out there," he said. There was pain in his voice. He was terrified. He was furious. He still cared.

"I'll try not to," she said and waited a second to see if he would offer to come after all. He didn't, so she left.

Outside the hotel, she stepped into a night that pulsed with currents. Her neck tensed. *All right,* she thought as she worked to keep her breathing steady and her hair from standing on end, *you came out here to do something useful. Do it.* She'd been answering on the fly when she told Corderman she was going to the spirit world for help, but the idea made as much sense as anything else. No, it made a lot of sense. Whatever had killed Crawford wasn't going to be fought with recording equipment. Or arrest warrants, for that matter. *Where?* she asked herself. Where to go for the help she wanted? The answer occurred to her, and it made her nervous. She followed the logic through, though. She made her way to St. Rose's Church.

The streets were deserted. All sane people were in their homes and hiding under the covers. She wanted to be there, too. She didn't want to do this. She was scared. Corderman was right. She was probably going to die, and if she did, it would be knowing that her life had been constructed around a dangerous lie. But that might happen whether or not she tried to fight back. At least this way, she would also know that she had fallen with honour, attempting to do what was right. That counted for something, didn't it?

The night dripped down the walls of the buildings on either side of her. It watched her. It didn't answer.

She reached the church. It crossed her mind to go inside, see if Hudson was around. She decided not to. They would both be looking for help on a spiritual plane, but not the same one. She thought that his was even less likely to provide help than Meacham's material world. She crossed the green to the church, then walked around to the back of the building. The graveyard was a small one, and old. There were no tombstones more recent than the end of the nineteenth century. The slabs were dark grey with grime and green with moss, illegible in the daylight, crumbling bone and rotted tooth in the night. The light from the street was so diffuse in here that the graves seemed to be powered by their own glow.

Pertwee moved to the centre of the graveyard so she had markers on all sides of her. She knelt, closed her eyes, spread her arms, and listened. The silence was deep. She told herself it was peaceful. Her body had trouble believing her. It remained tense. *This is the home of the resting dead,* she thought. *This is a good place.* This is where you were taken when the struggles were finally done with, and you could sleep. If the spirits had any memories of — or connections to — this ground, they would be good ones. She tried to open herself up. She wasn't psychic, or at least no more than the average, but she didn't believe that mattered. If the spirits were strong enough or interested enough, they wouldn't need her to be a sensitive. They would make their influence felt. She had plenty of evidence of that. So did Crawford. "Help me," she whispered. The sound was harsh in the silence. It exposed her. "Help me," she said again, even more quietly. The words barely escaped her lips. "Help me help you and ..." She hesitated. She had been about to add "Saint Rose." But Meacham's theory was sticking with her. If Gethsemane Hall's reputation was a lie, a distorted response to its tidal pull, then Rose's sainthood might be part of that distortion. The thought shook her. The faith of many years took a crumbling hit as a shadow pooled under a heroine's feet.

Crawford's body, cat's cradle spread over the tomb. Blood everywhere. Bits of muscle and organ that she didn't recognize. And her last words to him: *You could hardly be in a more sacred place.* The worst lie of her life, only she hadn't realized it at the time. She knew the lie for what it was now, though, and she forced intercession for and from Saint Rose from her mind. She started again. "Help me. Speak to me. Tell me what we need to do."

She waited. *I am open,* she thought. The effort was physical. She stretched the skin of her forehead as if it would spread her mind wide. *Answer me, please,* she thought. *I need help so very badly.*

Time passed. Enough that she despaired of an answer. She was going to head back to the inn without a single useful idea. She would prove Corderman right. She would traipse off to the Hall tomorrow with Meacham and be a spectacular liability, bringing about the deaths of herself and everyone around her. She had time for all these thoughts. Her arms grew sore, and she lowered them. She became painfully aware of pebbles biting into her knees. She opened her eyes. *I give up,* she thought and began to stand.

The answer came. It wasn't directed at her, and it wasn't what she wanted. It was coming, though. The back of her head twitched. She clapped her hands over her ears. There was no sound, but her body was reacting to a rapid thrumming of wings. Fluttering overhead. Darkness huge and travelling. She fell back down to her knees. Stone cut through her jeans and drew blood. Deeper fluttering, thunder wings, leather and insect, muscle, and scream.

Her scream.

And others.

Gray was at the Hall. Metres from ground zero. He had felt a building of power and was standing at the entrance to the crypt, staring at the recess that, for all that he still felt a sense of victory, he didn't dare approach. He felt the movement, had just enough time to realize an ocean was moving when the force knocked him flat. He saw the ectoplasm rush from below, a black, unified geyser. Then he was out.

The gathered strength threw itself out of the Hall. It rode the sky. It swept over Roseminster. It was the deeper night. It was constrictor. It was severing edge. It was the hate.

Roger Bellingham tried to stay inside. The wind was up (though the trees were still). The night was worse than when Pete Adams had died. The pull was maelstrom-strong, and this time he could sense something approaching. He locked the doors of his house. He pulled all the curtains and blinds. He sat in his reading chair and gripped the arms, fighting the rip tide that was hauling him out to drown. A roar built in his mind, deafening him, greying out his peripheral vision. The strength of Gethsemane Hall yanked at him, and one moment he was sinking his fingernails into the leather upholstery, and the next he was watching his hands unlock, unchain, and open the front door. *No*, he thought. *Stop*, he ordered. *Please*, he begged. Nothing good replied, and he stepped out into dark. He looked up. High above, he saw something coiling.

The people were in their homes and hiding as the siege clamped down. Roseminster cowered from the night, but the night found its way in. It brought the whisper of dreams. It scratched at the mental doors. Roseminster moaned. Roseminster screamed.

Meacham felt it. There was a clawing at her consciousness, something trying to get in. It was an immanence of nightmare. Premonition of what visions might come terrified her. She shook her head, began to mutter "No." Agency training had included resistance to interrogation, and she was suddenly drawing on those lessons to distract her mind and keep out the enemy. She'd never had to use the skills against a human adversary. They were rusty, now that she needed them against something much stronger. She heard a whimper, looked up and saw Sturghill clutching her head. "One times one is one," Meacham gasped, reaching out. "One times two is two. One times three is three." She said it louder, then yelled "*Kristine*" into a raging gale (though the air was still). Sturghill looked at her. "One times four is four!" Meacham yelled, urging.

"One times five is five," Sturghill called it with her.

They chanted a spell of math and logic, their magic circle against the dream that wanted to speak with them.

The ectoplasm storm looked down. It found what it wanted.

Corderman stumbled away from the window. The room had a standalone wardrobe. He hid behind it.

Hudson clutched the altar. He pressed his head so hard against it that he drew blood.

Bellingham dropped his cane. He stumbled forward in a run that obliterated the cartilage of his knees. He wept his terror. He couldn't stop the run. Above, he saw the coil descend for him, a funnel cloud of anger.

Corderman howled. The window shattered. Something came into the room for him. Something with talons.

chapter sixteen

home again, home again, jiggety-jig

Corderman's screams cut through the multiplication tables. They sliced deep into Meacham's conscience. Sturghill's, too, to judge by the grief and guilt on her face. The women didn't move from their room. They didn't try to help. They stared at each other and recited arithmetic until they felt the winged dark retreat. In the morning, they opened their door and crossed the hallway to the other room. Meacham knocked, a futile gesture of useless hope. There was no answer. She tried the knob. The door was unlocked. She and Sturghill stepped inside. The room was empty. Curtains drooped over the broken window. Glass was spread across the floor. There were some shards embedded in the facing wall. The bed had been upended. The comforter was shredded. The wardrobe was in pieces. There was no blood. "Both of them?" Sturghill wondered. She sounded hardly less afraid than she had during the night.

Dragging footsteps on the staircase. Meacham ducked her head out the door, saw Pertwee staggering up. "Where were you?" she asked.

"Cemetery," Pertwee answered.

"Edgar wasn't with you, by any chance?" She didn't know why she was even trying. She'd heard the attack. She knew the answer to her question. But she entertained a brief fantasy of a terrified Corderman fleeing the hotel after the encounter in his room. Faint hope, no hope.

Pertwee shook her head, looked stricken, and shoved past Meacham. "Oh no," she whispered, taking in the wreckage.

Meacham thought for a moment. "Go look for Patrick at the church. I'll meet you there."

Sturghill and Pertwee headed out. Meacham stopped at the front desk. The day clerk had deep pouches under her eyes. "Bad night," Meacham commiserated. When the clerk nodded, Meacham felt an unspoken understanding, and she said, "We lost someone. Room 5."

The clerk nodded again, pain creasing her forehead. "Should I call the police?"

"If you would."

Hudson was sitting in a pew with Sturghill and Pertwee when Meacham reached St. Rose's. He had a large bandage on his forehead. He kept touching it gingerly. "What happened?" Meacham asked.

"An accident. I'm fine."

"All right. Then let's go." Now, while she had the momentum of first light. If they waited too long, she would run, no matter what might follow her.

Sturghill raised the problem. "What's the plan?"

Meacham took a few beats. Like she had any idea. She took a wild shot. "How are you with exorcisms?" she asked Hudson.

He grimaced. "It would help if I were ordained and Catholic."

"Anna?" she asked Pertwee. "Any ideas?"

"I tried last night." Terrible hurt in the ghost-hunter's voice. "There was no help. There was only that attack."

Meacham looked around the space of the church. If she were ever going to receive the touch of grace, now would be a good time.

There was no inspiration. There was vaulted stone and stained glass, sterile heights, and rigid figures, heavy testaments to humanity's need to construct monuments to the imaginary. There were forces out there, though. She knew that now. Might there not be others? She walked over to the altar, reached out to touch it. She felt the slick cold of marble and nothing else. She glanced down and saw a trace of blood on the side of the altar. She glanced back at Hudson's forehead. She felt a faint spiritual tickle, a faint seismic reading of darker revelation to come. She shut the premonition down, the same way she'd choked off her conscience during all her years with the Agency. She gathered her strength. Angst was an impediment to action. She turned back to Pertwee and said, "You told me last night that your faith in the spirit world hadn't collapsed. Has it now?"

"No." The response was immediate, but a bit too firm: Pertwee working to convince herself as much as the others.

"So what, from your angle, is standard procedure when you have bad juju going on?"

"I don't know. I've never heard of anything so huge."

"Forget the scale for a minute. What would you do if this were just an ordinary pissed-off ghost?"

"Look for patterns in behaviour," Pertwee answered. "Investigate the history of the location." Her voice gathered strength as she moved onto familiar ground. "If the spirit were invited in somehow, revoke the invitation. Look for evidence of unresolved trauma, try to bring closure to the spirit. Help it move on. Make it *want* to go. Lots of them don't know they're dead or are afraid to leave."

"I don't think this one's afraid of much," Sturghill muttered.

"It's very *strong*," Pertwee whispered, awe taking her down once more.

"Focus." Meacham snapped her fingers. "Pretend it isn't so big and bad and scary. Give me a diagnosis."

Pertwee bit her lip, concentrating. "It's growing stronger," she said. "A lot stronger, recently."

"Pete Adams," Sturghill suggested. "He stirred it up."

"Not as much as we did," Hudson put in.

"And we were doing the same kind of thing he was," Meacham summed up. "So investigating it unleashed it. How?"

Sturghill said, "The big events started when Richard opened the way to the caves."

"And we found the tomb," Hudson added.

Meacham nodded. "So we took the cork out of the bottle. What's happening now?"

"Negative spirits thrive on fear," Pertwee said. "They want to be noticed. The fear gives them strength."

"This one's doing a good job. But if I'm following you, all we need to do is find out why it's angry and make the problem go away."

"Assuming the ghost is human," Sturghill said.

Pertwee folded her arms. "I think it is. It's focused on the place and on that tomb. I don't think an inhuman spirit would be that specific."

"So that's where we start." Meacham felt her lips turn up in a sour smile at the cornball she was about to speak. "We look for the truth and use it to set the bad ghost free."

Hudson looked up. "That's what Richard said he wants. He's looking for truth."

Well? Meacham thought. That was good, wasn't it? No reason to feel a chill breeze at that idea. No reason for the gooseflesh on her arms. "Fine," she said. "So let's do it with him."

"That's what he asked me to do." Hudson sounded ashamed.

The gooseflesh wouldn't leave. She changed the subject. "Patrick, I asked Anna about her faith. What about yours?"

"What about it?"

She wondered if he was being evasive. "How is it holding up?"

"Why does it matter?"

Ah. Trading questions for questions, and so showing his hand. Not good. "Because we're going to need every conceivable weapon we can come up with to win this. Anna's going to use the strength of her belief. We need yours, too."

"I thought you didn't believe."

"I don't. At least, not in your God. I don't think so, anyway." The coldness of the marble. The emptiness of stone. "But I goddamn well have to accept the reality of something out there, don't I? So here's the deal. I don't know what, if anything, is going to work here. But you and Anna at least have a tradition behind you. Yes?"

Hudson nodded. "Yes."

"And what's the value of a faith that isn't tested?" *Dirty pool, girl. Yeah, but you fight the war any way you can. Boost the troop morale. Convince them they can do what they probably can't.*

More shame on Hudson's face. "It's been hard," he said.

She eased off. "I know."

Still, his spine seemed to straighten. "You're right, though." He looked at Pertwee. "What do you think? Maybe our systems are complementary."

She smiled. "Would be nice if we're both right, wouldn't it?"

As long as you're not both wrong, Meacham thought. She caught Sturghill's eye, saw her thinking the same thing, and warned her with a glance to keep it to herself.

Instead, Sturghill asked her, "So where does that leave us?"

"You can pray too, you know," Hudson said. "There's nothing to stop you."

"Except doubt and hypocrisy," Meacham replied.

"Doesn't answer my question," said Sturghill. "If anyone has turned out to be completely wrong about how things work, it's the two of us. What can we bring to the party?"

"You're a magician. You're a performer. You must have picked up some improv skills along the way. I know I have. So we stay on our toes." Meacham shrugged. "A certain pigheaded independence of mind might not hurt, either."

Sturghill actually laughed. "Do you have any idea how weak that sounds?"

"A pretty fair idea, yeah." Meacham faced the trio of sad sacks. *Here's your black bag team, honey, ready to open up a can of regime change on the nasty ghost.* She put her hands on her hips. "So now that we have that settled, shall we join the party?"

When they emerged from the church, Meacham saw Kate Boulter standing beside the war monument. She wondered how long the detective had been waiting there. Boulter approached. Meacham noticed the pouches under her eyes, the tautness of her lips. "You spent the night here, I take it," Meacham said.

"Yes." And not well, from the looks of it. Good. Nice to know others were being force-fed the gospel. The truth was spreading.

"Am I still the pain in your ass?"

"No. Where are you going?"

"Back to the Hall. We lost another friend."

"So did the town. One Roger Bellingham."

Pertwee looked like she'd been punched. "What happened?"

"You tell me," Boulter said, sounding old and scared and dead. "Many heard him scream. We found his stick. That's it."

Meacham said, "We're going to try to stop this thing."

Boulter's eyes flicked up to the cross at the top of the spire, then back to Meacham. "Anything I can do to help?"

Meacham heard her own exhausted sense of duty in Boulter's tone. "Yes," she said. "Run. Fast and far away."

It occurred to Meacham that they could call a taxi to drive them down to the Hall. They might have been able to beg a ride from someone, too. Maybe even Boulter. But she didn't suggest the idea. She didn't want to bring anyone else nearer the house than necessary. And she wasn't in a hurry to be there herself. So they walked, as they had before. The first time, she had thought she knew what she was heading into. Now, all she knew was bad trouble. She didn't want to go. For all her cheerleading, her most conscious desire was to flee the country. Going back, though, was easy.

When they reached the gate, they found it open, Gray or Gethsemane Hall welcoming them back. She had hoped she would feel a gravity-pull of reluctance as she crossed the threshold back into the Hall's domain. She was walking into a jungle with a very large predator loose. Her fight-or-flight instincts should be screaming holy hell. Instead, the return was an easy, comfortable slide down a chute, a surrender to the pull of the house. Her body was almost relaxed, relieved not to be fighting the current anymore. She noticed that she was starting to trot, her legs eager to be back. She forced herself to slow down, saw the others catch themselves. She feared her acceptance, wondered if she would ever again be able to leave of her own will. *It's laughing at us*, she thought.

Down the path and through the woods, out from under the guardian yews (their branches reaching out in hungry welcome), and there was Gethsemane Hall again, brooding over the strength that coiled within. As they approached, Pertwee asked, "Where do you think he is?"

"In the caves," Hudson answered, no hope in his voice.

He was wrong. They entered the open door and found Gray in the Great Hall. He was lying on the table. He raised his head when they entered, lifting a great weight. He blinked at them for a moment, then creaked upright, rubbing night from his eyes. "Were you attacked?" Meacham asked.

"Sideswiped." Meacham saw him do a headcount. "Where's Edgar?"

"Gone," she said. Meaning: *dead and eaten*. Like Crawford.

"And why are you back?"

"To stop this."

Gray nodded. He seemed detached, as if watching a philosophical debate that he found interesting but in which he had no investment. He cocked his head at Hudson. "Not here for the truth, Patrick?"

"That, too," Hudson said. "That's how we're going to stop this thing."

Gray thought that one over. "Good enough," he said and clambered off the table. He stretched. Joints cracked. Meacham noticed bruises on his arms and the side of his face. He saw her looking. "Fell hard," he told her. "So, fellow truth-seekers, where do we start?"

Meacham felt Hudson stiffen beside her. Gray's flippancy was weary, hard-earned, but it was still flippancy. His face, meanwhile, wasn't joking. It looked driven. It was the face of a man who *knew* a truth or two and wasn't planning on keeping it to himself. "The caves," Meacham said. She would parse Gray's attitude later.

"The tomb," Pertwee said, specifying.

Gray smiled. "Where else?"

They brought rope. They brought lamps. They brought nerves. *It's still early,* Meacham told herself. *It's still day.* No way to know that down in the caves. Noon or midnight, no difference there. She wondered if the anger in the Hall cared for the time of day.

They made their way slowly, Gray in front and testing the ground. He stopped when they reached the lake. He shone his light on the blackness. "Don't touch it," he warned. "Take a good look, though."

Meacham crouched at the shore, examined the liquid where Gray's light skimmed it. She saw the slow shifting movement, not so much tide or ripples as breath. She saw droplets that were still ink in the light. "What is it?" she asked.

"Ectoplasm," Gray said.

"*Black* ectoplasm?" Pertwee objected.

Gray shrugged. "Come up with a better name if you want to," he said.

Meacham backed away. The urge to plunge into the lake hit like a nightmare. Her heart stumbled as it sprinted. "Jesus," she muttered.

Gray moved on. When they reached the site of the cave-in, they tied themselves to the rope and skirted the hole one at a time. Meacham gave it as wide a berth as she could, clinging close to the wall. Once everyone had crossed, Gray made them pause again.

He shone his light so the beam passed horizontally over the hole. "Keep watching," he said. Then: "There. See that?"

Meacham had. Just. A drop of black liquid falling up toward the roof of the cave. She aimed her own light up, saw the reflected shine of dampness above. Her throat felt painfully dry.

Sturghill was looking up, too. "Why isn't the lake defying gravity?" she asked.

"Because it doesn't have to," Pertwee answered. "Sometimes you stand, sometimes you sit, sometimes you lie down. Nothing says you have to do one or the other."

"So it's conscious," Sturghill said. She was shielding her eyes, as if the droplets might come back down and target her. "Is it a ghost?"

"No. It's more like the residue of the ghost. It isn't conscious. It's a bridge between worlds. It's what gives the ghost material form."

Like an empty bag of skin, Meacham thought. Just waiting for the bones and the will to fill it up and move it around.

Sturghill was looking back in the direction of the lake. "Why is there so much of it? Are there many ghosts?"

"I don't know," Pertwee admitted.

"Things build up," Gray said simply and moved on.

Meacham thought about the lake at their back as she followed. They were putting the reservoir of hate and pain between them and the outside world. The strategy sucked. The strategy didn't matter. *Think hotel. Think Corderman.* If it wanted them, it would come to them. Location was irrelevant.

She felt better. She felt worse.

They descended. The stone throat twisted, happy to swallow them again. It took them along its ride to the destination. They reached the cave with the tomb. Meacham winced in anticipation as they entered. She was half-braced for the return of Crawford's mutilation. There was nothing. Only the steady drip from the slab in the centre of the space. They gathered around the tomb, shone lights on it, watched the drops form and fall up. The sound of the dripping was time's slow metronome.

"Build-up," Gray said. "Think about it. One drop of water with one grain of mineral. Given enough time, you get stalactites."

"No," Sturghill said. "That doesn't make sense."

"Why not?"

"We aren't below the lake. If this stuff has been dripping up out of this sarcophagus, or whatever the hell it is, for all this time, why isn't there a huge pool of ectoplasm above our heads? Why is the big deposit fifty metres to the side?"

Gray looked up, looked down, looked thoughtful. He didn't answer. He crouched over the tomb, ran a finger along the seal, careful not to touch any of the liquid.

"I don't care where this shit comes from," Meacham said. "I just want it gone. I don't suppose it's flammable? No? Well, worth the thought." She turned to Hudson and Pertwee. "Okay, you two. This is your show."

"It doesn't work that way," Pertwee objected.

"I'm not a priest," Hudson said, just as outraged.

"You're close enough," Meacham told him. "How does it work, then?" she asked Pertwee.

"We find the source of the problem, and we resolve the issue."

"And if the issue is a few hundred years old?"

"Usually, if the spirit realizes things are long in the past, that's enough, and it leaves."

"Usually." Meacham didn't have to put much sarcasm into the word. She spread her arms, reminding Pertwee of where they were and what had already happened.

"I didn't say it would be easy," Pertwee said

"No, you didn't," Meacham admitted. She looked at Hudson. "Any ideas on your side?"

He shrugged. "I'm not sure what to suggest. The original 1649 edition of the Book of Common Prayer had a form of exorcism as part of the ceremony of baptism, but —"

"Do you know it?" Meacham cut him off.

"More or less."

"Good enough for government work. What do you need to do this?"

"Nothing. Just my faith."

She didn't like the sound of that. "And how is that holding up?" she asked quietly.

"I'm not sure I'm up to the test."

She put a hand on his shoulder. "Your faith and Anna's are all we have," she told him.

"What about you and Kristine?"

"We were the rationalists, and we were wrong. We may admit that, but we don't have anything to fall back on. You do. After all, you're seeing proof that life, or something like it, keeps going." Over Hudson's shoulder, she saw Gray pause in his examination of the tomb and glance her way. She couldn't read his expression. "You or Anna must be right. Maybe you both are." Another look from Gray. His lips twitched, the movement so small it could have meant anything.

Hudson nodded. He turned around, and Meacham watched him face his friend. "What do you think, Richard?"

"I'm here for the truth. Do your thing." He moved away from the tomb and presented it to Hudson. Step right up.

Hudson approached the tomb. He knelt before it. He took his time and looked for strength. The others had backed off and were standing with their backs against the cave wall. He was aware of their eyes on him; he had locked gazes with each before he turned to the rock. Three of the looks were hopeful. Meacham's was also encouraging. The look that worried him was Gray's. It was noncommittal. It was unconcerned. But it was also interested and curious. He wanted to believe the man he had known for decades was still there. He wanted to believe there was still something more there than the many-coloured robe of anger. He wanted to believe. Instead, he doubted.

He tried to compartmentalize his doubts. They were about Gray. They weren't about God. Meacham was right: everything that had happened was proof of the spiritual. The precise dogma might be off, but that was all. He had said he didn't think he was up to the test. His wording was a giveaway he now clung to, a test. If he thought he was being tested, then his faith and belief went deeper than he had been crediting. He brought his hands together. *I'm here for You, Lord, he thought. Please be here for me.*

He began to speak. The words came easily. He remembered them because he had been struck by them. He had run across the prayer for deliverance while doing research during that period of his life when it had seemed he would take official orders, that he wasn't going to be too much of a rebel for the entrenched establishment of the Church of England. He could see why the passage had been removed from subsequent editions of the Book of Common Prayer. They were too harsh for a baptism. There was too great a presumption of evil. Or so he had thought then. Now, the words seemed timid. He spoke them slowly, feeling the meaning of each syllable, gathering strength from that meaning.

"I command thee, unclean spirit, in the name of the Father, of the Son, and of the Holy Ghost, that thou come out, and depart from ..." He hesitated. The next words were "these infants, whom our Lord Jesus Christ hath vouchsafed to call to His holy Baptism, to be made members of His body, and of His holy congregation." They hardly applied in this instance. *Make the substitution meaningful,* he told himself. Maintain the ritual's power. He regrouped. "Depart from this world," he said, "which our Lord Jesus Christ hath vouchsafed to call to His holy Baptism. Therefore, thou cursed spirit, remember thy sentence, remember thy judgment, remember the day to be at hand, wherein thou shalt burn in fire everlasting, prepared for thee and thy Angels." The prayer became momentum. He felt himself drawn into the strength of the words, of the iron faith they embodied. His old convictions and joys resurrected themselves. He *knew* he was not alone. "And presume not hereafter to exercise any tyranny toward this world, which Christ hath bought with his precious blood, and by this his holy Baptism calleth."

He opened his eyes. At first he thought that nothing had changed. Then he noticed that the droplets of ectoplasm emerging from the seam of the tomb were vibrating. "Go," he said. "You don't belong here. Your time is done. Go." He repeated the rite, revelling in its force. He kept his eyes open this time, watching the vibration, willing it to feel what he knew to be the truth. He thought he saw a recoil. Then he knew he did. A bit of black ectoplasm withdrew inside the seam of the stone lid. "Go!" he shouted. "GO!"

His ears popped as if the air pressure in the cave had just plunged. The droplets vanished inside the tomb. Their flight was so quick, Hudson thought he should have heard a sound like a cracking whip as they disappeared. He turned around to face his expectant audience. "The enemy," he said, smiling with the real first hope he'd felt in a long time, "is in retreat."

"To where?" Gray came over to see for himself.

"Inside the tomb."

The others approached more warily.

"Well," Gray said with cheerful cynicism, "that was easy."

"I said it was retreating, not that it was vanquished."

"What do you think?" Meacham asked Pertwee.

"Maybe," she conceded. She looked at Hudson, gave him a hopeful smile. "If the spirit hears the message that it's time for it to move on, maybe it will. And since the ghost is a Christian one, it might well have a strong response to that rite."

"Who says it's Christian?" Sturghill asked.

"It's Saint Rose," Pertwee said simply. She looked to Hudson for confirmation.

"Ah ..." he hesitated. "I don't know that it is." Pertwee was still clinging, he thought, to the Hall's mythology. Her insistence on the spiritual presence of Saint Rose bothered him. It struck him as dangerously dogmatic. She had believed in the benevolence of the Hall upon arriving here, and she'd been wrong. But instead of a full questioning of her assumptions, she was just revising slightly. She was granting that the presence here was a dangerous one, but only because it had been curdled by time. Saint Rose could be restored to her better self. The story was too neat. It had a narrative arc. Reality didn't. Tidiness was the sign of a lie, however generously believed. And there was this: he hadn't felt anything human as he reached out to strike with his prayer. He had seen black drops and felt a resistance that had all the personality of electricity. Saint Rose the Evangelist was not here. He didn't think she ever had been.

Gray said, "What if this isn't a tomb?"

A stymied silence. Hudson spoke first. "What else would it be?"

"Why make a stone sarcophagus and leave no sign of who is inside it? I've heard of unmarked graves, but not unmarked monuments."

"You didn't answer my question," Hudson persisted. "If not a grave, what then?" He wasn't sure why he wanted the thing to be a tomb. It shouldn't make any difference. If prayer worked, it worked. Perhaps the problem was a question of assumptions. If he were wrong about the nature of the stone, he might be wrong about other things. He looked at the slab. He worried. He saw something other than a tomb. He saw an altar. *I've been praying at that*, he thought. There was a squeeze in his chest.

Gray crouched beside the slab. He touched a point on the seam. "I was looking at this earlier," he said. He pushed. Hudson saw his finger disappear up to the knuckle. There was a click of stone unlatching. Gray stood up. "Most graves don't have mechanisms," he said.

Neither do altars, Hudson thought, feeling irrational relief.

Gray grasped the edges of the lid. "Anyone going to help me with this?" he asked.

Hudson took a step back on instinct. Meacham was eyeing the lid speculatively.

"Come on," Gray said to her. "Ye seeker after truth. Information is power. You of all people should know that."

"That's cheap," Meacham said, but she moved in to help anyway. They strained. The lid rotated. Stone scraped on stone. The sound was rough. The sound was hollow. The echo ran deep and straight down.

chapter seventeen

the cold spot

They shone their lights inside the stone box. They saw stairs. The descent looked long.

Meacham said, "I was wondering when we'd find the doorway to Hell." She tried to sound like she was joking. She wasn't able to. The steps were rough and steep. She couldn't see the bottom. She aimed her flashlight beam at the roof of the staircase, caught a glimpse of the ectoplasm as it pulled away from the light. *Are you retreating or luring?* she wondered.

Gray climbed up over the lip of the stone and started down.

"What are you doing?" Hudson asked, horrified.

"Don't be stupid," Gray said, and Meacham had to agree. Backing off in terrified self-preservation had ceased to be a useful option some time back. She followed, with Pertwee hard on her heels. Hudson would be there too, she knew. He wouldn't want to be left behind, alone. She knew she wouldn't.

The footing was treacherous. The steps were uneven, barely hewn from the stone. The rise of each step was different from the last, but all were high. Edges caught at Meacham's shoes, convex surfaces became concave with no warning. The walls were very close. There was nowhere to fall but straight ahead, onto stone that would smash bone with the bluntness of clubs and the tearing of flint knives. There was no curve to the descent, no slipknot twist like the stairs down from the crypt. This was a straight diagonal. Meacham sorted out her bearings. They were heading, she thought, to a point that would bring them beneath the ectoplasm lake. The stairs ended at last in a short, level corridor. Meacham looked back up and couldn't see the top of the steps. She wasn't surprised. She hadn't been able to see the bottom from the other end. So no, she wasn't surprised. She wasn't happy either.

Gray had walked forward a few steps and was reaching up to touch something on the wall. "What is it?" Meacham asked and caught up. It was a sconce, its iron deeply rusted.

"Should have brought torches," Gray said.

"I'm cold," Pertwee complained. No one answered, but she was right, Meacham thought. It was cold. The temperature had dropped at least ten degrees as they'd come down. The ectoplasm raced ahead, disappeared.

They moved on again, and the corridor dead-ended in a vast room. They shone their lights around. They took it all in. Gray didn't say anything. Neither did Meacham or Sturghill. Hudson breathed, "Oh, no." Pertwee began to cry.

The cave was almost as big as the one where Crawford had died. It was just as artificial as the rest of the network, but it still seemed out of place. The other tunnels and rooms had the shapes dictated by the contingencies of mining. There was no real planning, and the system *felt* natural. Here there was stonework on the walls. The stairs leading here were slap-dash efforts, but the room had had time, money, and attention. With its ribbed vault, it was a close sibling to the crypt, its fraternal if not its identical twin. And much, much larger. Plenty of room to strut its stuff.

Tapestries hung along the walls. They were a series. Meacham could see a progression to them, but she couldn't tell what was the beginning of the narrative, what was the end. Each tapestry spilled into the other in an Escher loop, the story growing worse with each spiral.

"Christ, Louise," Sturghill said. "You were right." She wasn't joking. Her voice cracked.

They'd found Hell. The tapestries were the arc of pain. They were faded, dank with humidity and time, muddy pinks and tarnished yellows. The souls of the damned were being tortured, broken, sundered. The screams of agony were frozen in medieval formality, flattened by the lack of perspective but as credible as photographs. They weren't being tortured by other human beings. As initial visceral recoil faded, Meacham frowned, puzzled by the iconography. She was as far out of her field as it was possible to be, but things still struck her as wrong. There were plenty of Christian images here. Christ showed up on the cross several times. But the crucifixion didn't come across as tragedy, as hope for redemption, as supreme act of love. And Christ was being hurt by more than nails, thorns, and spear. He was being twisted and shredded by the same teeth and claws as the other souls. He was no better off. If anything, the pain on his face was a despair that passed all understanding. His eyes were wide with terrible epiphany. The tapestry tore into him with enormous stylistic glee. There was fun to be had. Meacham frowned. The vibe was all wrong.

The teeth. The claws. More problems. If Meacham were looking at Hell, she should be seeing demons, she thought. There was monstrosity here, but not the right kind. Meacham looked for any trace of the old clichés: the horns, the hooves, the pitchforks, the wings. Nothing. She wasn't even sure if what was inflicting the pain was a single being or several. There were teeth, there were claws, there were scales. There was immensity. Meacham had the sense of fragments, of desperate representations pointing to something too huge to be contained by art. The sweep of the tapestries was a picture of sadistic, reptilian triumph. The hands that had crafted this work were humbled and exhilarated by the scale of what they were having to convey.

Meacham turned to Hudson. He was moving from one tapestry to the next, staring at the little details of torture, backing up to take in the whole blow, then circling round again. Meacham thought he should stop. She could feel the intensity of the narrative ramp up every time she turned around, and she didn't have a faith that was being assaulted. "Patrick," she called, trying to break the trance. He jumped, shook himself and joined her. His eyes were squinting from the pain. Meacham said, "I don't understand these. Have you ever seen anything like them?"

"No." He glanced at the tapestries, then away, as if they had stared back. "They aren't Christian by any measure I know of."

"What about the crucifixion imagery?"

"That's part of what I mean." He looked terrified. "This isn't even a repudiation."

"The triumph of the devil?"

"I don't think so. If there's a victor, there's a war. I don't see any sign of there having even been a contest here, do you?"

No, she didn't.

The rest of the room was, Meacham thought, what made Pertwee weep, even more than the tapestries. The metal on the machines was rusted, the leather rotted, but they still looked potent. Rack. Maiden. Wheel. Executioner's block. Heaped blades and hooks. Decomposed but still barbed whips. Dark stains on the stone floor, on stone blocks, on metal edges. On the other side of the cavern from the entrance, a metal throne sat on a rectangular dais. The ironwork of the chair was writhing muscle. It was sharp. If Meacham sat in it, she would bleed. There were manacles on the side. Pertwee had taken a few steps toward the chair but was standing still now, shivering. "There," she said. "It happened there. They killed her there."

They gathered beside Pertwee. The temperature plummeted. Meacham edged a bit closer to the chair. The cold bit into her face.

"They tied Saint Rose to that chair and tortured her to death," Pertwee whispered. She was creating a new mantra.

"No, they didn't," Sturghill said. She sounded definite.

"What?" And Pertwee sounded offended.

"Trust me, I'm a magician. I know from devices. Look at the placement of the manacles."

"I don't see it," Meacham said.

"Watch." Sturghill moved to the chair. She jumped just before reaching it. "God *damn* that is cold." She hugged herself for warmth and sat down, very carefully. Her teeth chattered. She shifted with discomfort, as if sitting on a bed of nails. "This is vicious sharp," she muttered.

"Of course it is," Pertwee said. "No one would sit there unless they were forced to."

"Or they were seriously fucked in the head," Sturghill countered. "Go on. Use the manacles. Chain me down here."

Meacham got it. The chains were too short, the clasps at the base and side of the chair. There was no way anyone sitting there could be held. "People were held *next* to the person sitting there," she said.

"Exactly." Sturghill stood up. "This is a throne." She danced away from the chair. "It's also bloody absolute zero right there."

Meacham walked over to the dais. The cold became more and more intense as she approached. When she reached the dais, the temperature turned into a scalpel. It sliced flesh and nicked bone. Meacham winced and forced herself to stand on the platform. She looked out at the cavern. From this position, every instrument in the space was visible. Fine perspective. Best seat in the house. She had a vision of the possessor of the chair, roaring joy and hatred at sadistic spectacle and masochistic pain. *And who, do you think, would be sitting here?* she wondered. She examined the back of the chair. "Check this out," she said. It was hard to speak. Her lips were numb. The others approached, shivering. There was an emblem in the iron. It was a black rose. Its petals were blades. Its stem was python twist of thorns. "What do you think of your saint now?" Meacham said to Pertwee.

Pertwee shook her head and backed away from the chair. They all did. The cold was too intense. But as she stepped away, Meacham's eyes dropped to the dais. There was another rose, in the same design, carved into the stone in bas-relief. She held back against the cold, hanging on for answers. The dais, she now saw, was not square. It was rectangular. If it hadn't been for the chair, she would have recognized the shape of the marble slab immediately. "Here," she said. "She's buried here. *This* is her tomb."

"That makes no sense," Pertwee said. There was a flash of hope in her objection, as if the logical problem might restore Rose to sainthood. "How could she have a throne on top of her own grave?"

Meacham was wondering the same thing. She was still on her hands and knees. She ran her flashlight and her fingers along the base of the slab. It was like touching dry ice. Her fingers burned. It was hard to feel anything other than the pain. She saw the indentation as she touched it. "There's a mechanism here, like the other one." The edges she touched felt jumbled, chaotic. She pulled her fingers away, peered at the tiny recess in the stone. "It's been smashed," she said. She could withdraw from the cold spot, now. She felt frostbite in her cheeks and the tip of her nose. But she stayed where she was, as if the ordeal granted her authority, her words the weight of truth.

"Meaning what?" Pertwee asked, stubborn.

"Meaning she had her tomb constructed before she died," Gray answered. "Meaning that she sat on her own grave as she watched others tortured and killed."

"I won't believe it," Pertwee pleaded.

"She's here," Meacham said and slapped the top of the marble.

Even through the deadening cold, she felt the vibration through her fingertips. She looked down at the grave. The vibration became a rumble. She threw herself backwards as the ectoplasm erupted from the centre of the rose emblem. It geysered up, hit the roof of the cavern, followed the curve of the vault. It flowed into the keystone. Meacham scrambled back, staring at the black flow. Here was the source. Here was what fed the lake that was directly above them now.

Hudson had his back against the wall. "Why?" he kept repeating. He finally choked out a sentence. "Why did it play possum?" Then another: "Why now?"

"To prove you wrong," Gray answered.

"To show I'm right," Meacham said, at the same moment. She spoke more quietly than Gray. His response had a sharp edge of triumph. The problem was, she thought he was correct. Hudson's faith had been teased in order to lure them all here. That thought led her to another *why?* There was sentience here, not mindless energy. It was playing a game. It had an agenda. Rose had not stopped her wanting with death.

"Can we leave?" Sturghill asked, eyes wide and breath short and fast. "Like *now?*" She didn't wait for an answer. She ran from the cavern. Meacham tore her eyes away from the pulsing stream of black. She began to run, too, conscious suddenly not of questions but of Crawford and of Corderman, and what the strength she saw could do to her. She was on the heels of Pertwee and Hudson. As she reached the staircase back up, she became aware of an absence at her back, and she looked over her shoulder. She had expected to see Gray right behind her. He wasn't. He was coming, but slowly, walking down the tunnel reluctantly, giving the cavern and its torture and the ectoplasm pillar-of-salt looks. He was mesmerized. Meacham ran back. "Come *on,*" she said and dragged him by the collar. He resisted at first, then seemed to shake himself awake and fell into step.

Up the staircase, the ascent more difficult and treacherous than the descent, each stone ledge finding its own uneven way of trying to make her fall and smash her face open. She stayed on her feet, made it out of the false tomb. And then they were still underground, deep underground, and there was more running through the rocky darkness, still the snake curl to navigate, still the black lake to run past, and it was choppy now, restless, vexed to nightmare, though it did not reach out for her. And after that, there was the spiral up to the crypt. And then at last they were on the ground floor of Gethsemane Hall, and there was air and space, but there was very little light, because time had slipped by and withered while they were in the caves, and night had come again, closing its stone roof over them once more.

They didn't regroup in the Great Hall. They stood in the courtyard. Gray stayed in the doorway to the outer hall, as if reluctant to step outside the house, away from what was *his*. Sturghill was eyeing the gatehouse tower. "Do you think we can still leave?" she asked Meacham. She looked as if she were expecting a portcullis to slam down, keeping them in for good and for all.

"Do you think we should?" Meacham countered. They'd accomplished nothing so far.

"You say that like we have a chance," said Sturghill.

Hudson looked broken. He took a half step in three different directions, seeking flight or faith, then rounded on Gray. "So?" he asked. "Are you happy now? Do you have your truth?"

"Getting there."

Avoiding Sturghill's contagious despair, Meacham asked Gray, "Why do you care so much about the truth?"

Gray said simply, "What's left?"

Point taken. All her old assumptions were smoking ruins. Comfortable beliefs and disbeliefs were having their bones picked over by the Hall and its tenant. She wasn't satisfied, though. "Is that it?" she asked. "You'll lie down and die as long as you understand why?"

"I'm not dead yet," said Gray. "Neither are you."

Smack upside the head. He was right. And though it raised a whole new batch of questions, there was her answer for Sturghill. "Kristine," she said. "Think about it. Why aren't we dead yet? Given what we know this thing can do, why hasn't it killed us?"

"Because it hasn't felt like it yet."

Too facile. Even under the new nightmare rules, the possibility didn't feel right. "So what's it doing in the meantime? Channel surfing? Does this thing strike you as the sort to be dangerous only periodically?"

"No," Sturghill said, sounding a bit more interested. Hudson and Pertwee were moving closer, moths to the candle flame of hope.

"It has a name," Gray said.

"No," Pertwee protested, but by rote, weakly.

"Yes," Meacham agreed. "Rose. Think about that setup down below. That wasn't a Sunday afternoon hobby, what she had going on down there."

"Her hatred must have been huge," Hudson said.

"So why would she let us off the hook?"

"That can't be Saint Rose," Pertwee whispered.

Meacham ignored her. "Unless she doesn't have a choice," she continued.

"Doesn't seem that weak to me," said Sturghill.

"I can still run pretty fast if I have to," Meacham pointed out. "I've been known to shift some heavy weights now and then. But not all the time. I get tired."

"The tide ebbs and flows," Gray said. He hadn't budged from the doorway.

"She isn't strong enough to hurt us all the time," Meacham concluded.

Hudson was engaged, but his hope was provisional. "She's growing stronger, though. People weren't dying here before."

"She's feeding, or being fed, somehow."

Sturghill said, "That's cool and all. But how does this help us?

We still have no idea how to avoid being killed when she's strong enough, and never mind hurting her back."

Meacham drew a blank. She looked at Gray. He smiled, shrugged, no more concerned than if they'd been discussing *Coronation Street* plot points. "She did retreat when you prayed," she said to Hudson, grasping for anything at all.

"You mean she pretended to and lured us to her torture chamber," he replied, not about to mount the breach a second time.

Another point worth thinking about. "Fair enough, but why? Why did she want us to see that?"

"Stop saying *she!*" Pertwee exploded. "This isn't Saint Rose. It can't be."

Meacham was about to ignore her, plunge on again. Nothing to be done in the face of such desperate belief. But Gray spoke first. "Why not?" he asked. He didn't sound dismissive.

"Because of what we know about her."

"The truth, you mean."

"Yes!" She was close to sobbing again.

"And what is that?" Gray's tone was still gentle, but to Meacham's ears, the probing was no less relentless.

"Her name just about says it all." Pertwee was regaining her composure as she moved into explanatory mode. "Saint Rose the Evangelist. She was a daughter of nobility. She was deeply committed to the dissemination of Christianity."

"To broadcasting the truth," Gray offered.

"If you like, yes. Spiritual truth as she understood it, anyway. She was revered for —"

Gray interrupted. "But she's also known for being something of a hermit, isn't she?"

"Well, yes."

"Isn't that a bit contradictory?"

"Richard," Hudson began. Meacham sensed a logic trap being drawn around Pertwee. But there was still nothing savage in the way Gray spoke, or in his eyes.

"No," Pertwee answered. "She did retreat from the world, but she invited the world to come here, to listen to her teaching, to heal. You should know all this."

Gray smiled. "The old family truths."

Meacham was startled. "You're a descendant?"

"Of her brother's. She didn't have children. The story has it that her brother and his wife were just as devoted to her ministry."

"It's more than a story," said Pertwee.

"But what is her reputation based on?" Gray asked.

"What are you talking about? Her teachings, her works, her —"

"Which are recorded where?"

"In everything that has ever been written about her."

"Including the works of her contemporaries?"

Pertwee hesitated.

Gray pushed on, unstoppable. "Like the traditions concerning this house? Rose lived over eight hundred years ago. She wasn't exactly introducing Christianity to England. It wasn't a minority faith. It was the law of the land. What was she evangelizing?"

"Stop it!"

"Did you look at the tapestries down there? Did you think about what their messages were? Did it occur to you that there *were* messages? I don't know about you, but I saw plenty of evangelizing down there." And his voice never stopped being gentle. It simply hit and hit and hit with the force of simple, unyielding truth.

"*No!*" Pertwee screamed. She pushed past him and ran inside, hands out to rescue her saint.

chapter eighteen
the night of faith

"What the hell do you think you're doing?" Hudson yelled at Gray.

"What I thought we were here for," Gray said. He hadn't set out to upset Pertwee, but he was having trouble sympathizing with her reaction. Reaching the truth was, he had thought, her goal, too. Things were long past the point of holding on to untenable illusions.

Hudson snorted in disgust and pushed past him, running after Pertwee. The other two were right behind. Meacham paused to give Gray a hard look. "Seriously," she said. "What do you *want?*"

"The truth. That's all."

"And what about stopping what's happening?"

"The truth shall make you free. Won't it?"

Meacham rolled her eyes and left him. He watched her go. He knew she thought he was sparring, and picking fine moments to do so. She was wrong. He meant what he said. Liberty could take dark forms, he knew. The truth will out, though. No more illusions. No more comforting lies.

Pertwee pounded through the Great Hall to the crypt. As she crossed the chapel's floor, she ran across the cold spot. It slapped her in the face, then in her core. It had none of the terminal chill it had in the depths of the caves, but it was still strong with scorn. She didn't let it stop her. Down the stairs, her flashlight beam bobbing in front of her. She could hear the others calling her above. She didn't answer. She ran faster, almost falling on the staircase. They would catch up soon enough, and she didn't want them with her. She wanted to be alone. She was aware of her stupidity and of the suicidal gesture she was making, but she didn't care. Pertwee had to keep this one belief. She had thought that her ghost hunting had been a quest to expand the horizons of science. Her dreams of credibility had been part of that desire. So she had thought. She'd been wrong. She rubbed tears from her eyes. The drive for credibility had been a mask, one designed to fool no one but herself. She didn't really need to be credible; she needed to be believed. She needed her own spiritual truth confirmed, and the benign ghost of Saint Rose casting afterlife blessings over Gethsemane Hall was the keystone of that belief. The keystone had been kicked out. The arch of her belief was collapsing. Beyond the ruins, there was nothing. Better to make one last stand, turn back the tsunami of dark truth before it swept even the ruins to oblivion. Hold off the epiphany that Gray had tried to force on her. He was wrong. He had to be. If he were right, despair would be too optimistic a response.

That there were spirits of ferocious darkness, she accepted. That one of those haunted the Hall, she accepted. That it was Rose the Evangelist, she tried not to accept. That it might be, she had to consider. She couldn't go any further down the road of Gray's truth than that.

She reached the caves. She ran faster — she flew. She could feel the wind of her movement against her face. Her hair was actually blowing.

It was the last stand of her belief: that Rose's spirit was trapped here, that centuries of imprisonment had blackened the soul. All Rose needed was release. Her freedom would cleanse Gethsemane Hall. It would purge Pertwee's mind of Gray's suggestions.

She was gasping from the effort of the run. Her chest was raw with hyperventilation and shouted denials. Her awareness shrank to the nails in her lungs and the lead in her legs. And still the epiphany came through. The worst thing seized her consciousness. The worst thing was the afterlife as logical extension of material life and its desires. The worst thing was the darkness as the ongoing ministry of the Evangelist. The torture chamber as lecture room, Rose bleeding from self-inflicted wounds on her throne of iron, shrieking the hatred and rage of her lessons, spreading agony in this world as a tiny, fragmented reflection of what waited and writhed in the other.

No, Pertwee thought. *No.* The denial drummed out with the rhythm of her running feet. A denial like the one she'd recorded in the home of Winnifred Tillingate. Was it the cry of a spirit experiencing the truth that Gray was pushing at her? *No, no, no, no, no.* She would prove Gray wrong. She would free Rose. She would wipe the reptilian darkness from her mind. She spread her arms wide, and though her light went wild, she kept her footing. She opened her mind. She had nothing but love. But even so, the truth stabbed its way through, and she gasped as she ran past the ectoplasm. The lake rose up.

The house shook. Meacham staggered. They had just reached the crypt, and she grabbed the doorway to hold herself up. The wood moved under her hand. It felt like a snake. She recoiled, banged into Sturghill, and they both fell. Hudson had been thrown down on his face. The floor squirmed. The walls seemed to expand away from Meacham, as if she were suddenly looking through a wide-angle lens. The house breathed. Its sigh was a subaural drone. Then floor and walls became solid again. Meacham's vision cleared.

Sturghill groaned. "Oh, fuck me. What did that stupid bitch do?"

Hudson had a tissue out and was holding it against his bleeding nose. "You think she went down there?"

Meacham gazed into the crypt's gloom. "Of course she did." So now what? Would she head back down into the darkness after that idiot? She hesitated at the entrance. Self-preservation fought with concern.

Gray came up behind them. "Wait here," he said. "I'll go down and fetch her." He looked completely calm, as if nothing had happened.

"We'll go with you," Meacham said.

He waved her offer away. "No point. My fault she's done this, anyway."

Meacham tried to repeat her offer. She tried to follow Gray. Nothing came out of her mouth. She didn't take a step forward. Neither did anyone else. They let him go.

Gray trotted down the stairs. It occurred to him that he was playing into a pattern of idiocy. Every person who had died had been alone. Here was one fool chasing after another. The idea didn't strike him as more than an idle speculation. He wasn't worried. The truth would come for him soon enough, whether he was alone or not.

"Anna!" he called when he reached the caves. His voice echoed down the stretch and curve of the tunnels. There was no answer. He started down the slope, moving his light from left to right across the floor. She'd been running. She might have tripped, might be unconscious. As he neared the bend that would take him to the lake, he saw a glow. He walked faster. He rounded the corner, saw Pertwee's flashlight on the ground. "Anna," he called again, expecting no answer and receiving none. He picked up the lamp, turned the beams on the lake.

It was gone.

He cast light over bare stone. The floor of the cave sloped gently here, shaped into the shallow bowl that had held the ectoplasm. Now there was nothing. He stepped down into the bowl, walked all the way to its centre. He turned around, casting light to the walls. There was nothing here at all.

He headed back to the main tunnel. He didn't call again. He knew his search was pointless. How far would Pertwee have gone without her flashlight? As far as the cave-in, and then fallen? He doubted she had gone any further than here. He kept going, though. When he reached the cave where Crawford had died, he looked for her body. Then he took the second staircase down. He went all the way back to the heart of the Evangelist's realm. Pertwee wasn't here, either. So that was definite, then. He confronted the cold and approached the throne. He reached out and touched it, then turned to look at the tapestries again. His head began to spin as he followed the loop. He found himself focusing on the thing that was meting out the agony and judgement. *What are you?* he wondered, sensing the answer would be the greatest truth yet. The tapestries were the theory, the torture instruments the practice that would drive the lesson home. The lesson was the nature of the thing with scales.

What are you? he thought again. He travelled the circle once more, then paused a long moment on the claws that dug into the forsaken Christ at his crucifixion.

They waited at the entrance to the crypt. They didn't step inside. They stayed out of the reach of the cold spot. Hudson thought of it as the physical touch of Rose's hatred, reaching up from the dark heart of her constructed Hell. He looked at his watch. "Richard's been gone quite a while," he said. *I should have gone, too,* he thought. *Coward,* he thought.

"We'll give him another few minutes," Meacham said. "Then we'll go look. All of us. No splitting up."

"No way. Unh-unh." Sturghill shook her head. "I'm not saying that to be a bitch or anything, but guys, just how suicidal do you want to be? I mean, Anna runs down, doesn't come back up. Richard goes down, same thing. So hey, let's do that too, why not?"

She was right. Hudson couldn't let that matter, though. There were still a few principles to believe in, and some were higher than pragmatic self-preservation. *We're probably going to die anyway,* he thought. *We can at least do so with clear consciences.* He thought this. But he didn't say it. He watched Meacham. Her hardness was showing again. He could see she was close to agreeing with Sturghill. Not out of cowardice but out of simple common sense. He tried to make himself plead against the sensible. There were higher values, the ones that made it worthwhile to be alive and to be human. He couldn't open his mouth. *But I will go,* he thought. *I can't make them do this. But I will go. In just another couple of minutes.*

He didn't have to. He wasn't put to the test. Those couple of minutes passed, and there was the sound of footsteps coming up the stairs. Gray emerged from the recess. He was alone. "I couldn't find her," he said. He raised one flashlight. "Just this." He paused for a moment. "Something else," he went on. "The ectoplasm is gone. No sign it was ever there."

Gone where? Hudson wondered. No point hoping Pertwee had performed the miracle he had tried, and freed Rose's spirit. The last time ectoplasm had disappeared, it had been a lure to something worse. This time? He stepped away from the walls.

"So now what?" Sturghill asked. When no one answered, she turned to Meacham. "Louise," she said, "I don't want to sound like a coward, and everything you said about coming back here to try to stop this thing is true, but I'm sorry. I'm scared. We don't stand a chance. Nothing we can do is going to work. I really, really don't want to die. So I don't know about you, but I'm out of here."

Meacham's shoulders were slumped. She didn't say anything, just nodded.

As Sturghill turned to go, Gray said, "You can take my car." He tossed Sturghill the keys.

"You're not coming?"

"No."

"For God's sake, *why not?*"

"I don't know the full truth yet."

"Your funeral." Sturghill headed for the exit. After a moment, Meacham followed.

"Are you going too?" Hudson asked.

"I'll let you know," she called back over her shoulder.

He was alone with Gray. He looked at his friend, at his calm.

"You could leave," Gray said.

"Not without you."

Gray smiled. "I'm fine."

"No, you're not. Especially if you think you are."

"I'm not afraid of dying, Patrick. I've already lost my reasons to stay alive. If the thing here kills me, well ..." He shrugged. *Que sera sera.*

"It's not your physical death that I'm worried about."

"So here we go. The concern for my spiritual well-being. You fear for my immortal soul." He didn't raise his voice, but he put a shade of extra emphasis on each word, turning the issue into ridiculous melodrama.

"That's right." Hudson refused to be embarrassed. "You can't pretend that what's happening is making you an atheist."

"No. No." Gray looked thoughtful. "You know that was never an issue. I never stopped believing. I started hating. Not the same thing."

"Then you're playing right into her hands. You see that, don't you?"

Gray cocked his head. "Maybe."

"*Maybe?*" Hudson sputtered.

"That doesn't matter." Hudson was about to explode, but Gray carried on, relentless. "What if there's a truth behind the hate? A real reason for it. Wouldn't that be worth knowing?"

Hudson took a step backward and raised his hands: *No.* Even now, even with what he had seen, even as he thought that Sturghill could try to run but would probably not get far, even with all of that, what Gray was suggesting was beyond the pale. "There is no truth here," he said.

"You should take another look at those tapestries."

"I refuse to regard Rose as an authority on divinity. Are you listening to what you're saying?" The debate was ludicrous. He wanted to beam the real truth, the *good* truth, directly into Gray's soul. He couldn't abandon him to damnation. This was the ground he refused to surrender. He'd been through his darkest night. He'd had his period of doubt. He was still terrified. He was still convinced he was helpless against the thing that walked Gethsemane Hall. He was sure he was going to die. But Meacham had been right when she said that all of this horror was proof of the numinous. There couldn't be one without the other. If there was a devil, there was a God.

Gray stared back at him, unmoved, unmovable.

Gray's car was still parked on the gravel drive. Sturghill had unlocked it and was climbing into the driver's seat when Meacham caught up to her and leaned into the window. "Any point in my trying to change your mind?" she asked.

"What do you think?"

Meacham shook her head.

"Come with me," Sturghill urged.

"I don't know." She spoke with huge exhaustion. She still felt that goddamned sense of duty. It made for a steel alliance with the undertow from the Hall. Hard to leave. How to fight, though, that was the problem. The closest thing she'd had to an idea had failed. She was trapped in *Now what?*

"We tried," Sturghill said. "We're too weak. Big surprise. What's the point in staying here to die?"

"None," Meacham admitted. She pictured herself on a flight back to the States. The pang of desire brought tears to her eyes.

"So get in."

Meacham took a step away from the car, as if it were playing an active role in her temptation. "Do you think you'll be able to leave?"

Sturghill nodded. "It won't be easy. Momentum's the key. As long as I don't stop, I think I can avoid being pulled back."

"Good luck."

"Last chance?"

"For whom?"

"Funny." Sturghill turned the key in the ignition. Nothing happened. Big funny, all right. She tried again. The click of the turn, otherwise dead silence. Sturghill placed both hands on the steering wheel. "Shiiiiiiiiit," she breathed. She pursed her lips, looking straight ahead and a thousand yards away.

"Kristine?" Meacham asked.

"Okay. Plan B." Sturghill got out of the car. She started up the drive.

"You're walking?"

"It worked before. See you."

"Hang on." Meacham trotted up and fell into step beside Sturghill. "I'll see you to the gate."

"Why?"

"If you don't come back, I want to be sure it's because you're actually safe and gone."

"No one walks alone."

"Absolutely."

"And what about you? If you don't come with me, you'll be walking back alone."

"I figure giving in and returning to the house is safe enough. Relatively speaking."

Up the drive again. At night again. Into the woods again. The act wasn't growing easier with practice. Each step was harder. The night was a thick coil around them, constricting, crushing ribs before it opened its jaws wide for the swallow. The flashlight beams were too narrow, too weak. Sturghill tripped. Her light showed a thick root snaking across the road. "Was this here before?" she asked. Her voice was very shaky.

The root was big enough to act as a speed bump. Meacham was sure she would have noticed. She traced the root back to its tree. It was one of the yews. The tree was massive, its trunk thick enough to be a castle turret. It was as old as it was huge, and Meacham was sure it was in the wrong place. The yews were the inner perimeter of the woods. She couldn't remember seeing any here, midway through the forest to the gate. "Keep going," she said.

They walked more slowly, careful of their footing, watching for more trees that might present threats. Meacham felt the back of her neck prickling, as if the yew were watching. She looked back at one point. The drive had curved, and she couldn't see the tree. The woods were a tangled mass of black. She could still sense it, though. It could see her. It was judging.

They reached the gate. Meacham tried to keep her pessimism at bay as Sturghill reached out to push the button. There wasn't even a click. The gate did not swing open. Sturghill began to shake. "Hang on," Meacham said. "Maybe Richard can trigger it from the Hall." She pulled her phone out. She half-expected it to be dead. It wasn't, but there was no service. "Battery's dead," she lied. She wanted to spare Sturghill what she was experiencing: the claustrophobic sense of total isolation from the outside world. "See if you can use the intercom."

Sturghill reached around the gatepost, felt up and down until she found the buzzer. Meacham saw her push. "Nothing," Sturghill said. She eyed the top of the gate and the wall. "Can you help me over?"

Meacham's flashlight caught the glint of broken glass embedded on the top of the wall, ten feet up. The gate was wrought-iron spikes, just as high, with no good crossbar footholds. "No. Not by myself. Not safely." Visions of Sturghill slashed and bleeding, Sturghill impaled, Sturghill dead. *Not by my hands.* "With the others helping, maybe," she said.

"That means going back."

"That's right."

Sturghill's shoulders slumped. "Oh, God," she whispered. Meacham thought she was going to start trembling. Instead, she straightened up and started back down the drive, her gait steady. "Just so you know," she said. "If that bitch of a ghost tries anything else to keep me from leaving, I'm torching the place."

chapter nineteen

from the walls

And the bitch heard what she said. There was a rumble behind them. Then the sound of metal twisting. Meacham looked back, saw nothing through the darkness of the forest. Her flashlight beam was useless. "You're not going over that gate," she said. "Not tonight, anyway." Sturghill opened her mouth to reply, but Meacham cut her off. "Shut up. Not another word. Don't make it any worse. Go. Just keep moving." They tried to walk faster. Heading back wasn't as easy as Meacham had expected. They were swimming with the current, but there was no simple pleasing of the Hall now. The darkness of the woods was growing thicker. There were more roots on the drive, roots that Meacham absolutely *knew* had not been there on the way up. More sounds in the night. They began as rustling in the underbrush. At first, Meacham thought she heard the rubbing of leaves on leaves, the foliage whisper of a light wind. Only the air was still. The rustling grew. It was the sound of a small animal moving along the forest floor. *Squirrel*, Meacham thought. *Bird*, she thought. *You wish*, she thought. The rustling became a slither. The slither grew in bulk. The thing that moved was huge. It multiplied. "*Run*," Meacham whispered.

Sturghill tried. So did Meacham. They couldn't do more than jog. Their lights couldn't show them more than the next immediate step. The roots were legion. They were big. They were knotted leg traps. Meacham's gait turned into panicked hopscotch. The slithering spread out on all sides. It was an embrace. Tentacles were stretching out to draw her in. She tripped and fell. Her left knee came down on a pebble the size of a golf ball. The pain was so white-flash intense she barely noticed the blow the bridge of her nose took against a root. Her flashlight smashed open, went out. Sturghill turned around, her light a smeared glare in Meacham's tearing eyes. "Keep going," Meacham croaked. Sturghill ignored her, grabbed her by the arm and helped her to her feet. The slithering was turning into something bigger yet. Immensity moved all around them. Meacham winced when she put weight on her knee. She limped forward, leaning on Sturghill as she tried to walk through the pain.

Down the drive. The darkness infinite. Meacham had no idea how far they had come. She had lost track of the curves and couldn't see the way out. The slithering was now a roar. The roar came from a throat of wood. So did the hiss, when it came. It bore down on top of them, pushing wind ahead of it, a subway train with jaws rushing through the tunnel of night. Meacham's back tensed for the impact. The sound was deafening. It blocked out the world. She fought the urge to close her eyes against the end.

The flashlight beam suddenly expanded. There were no trees ahead. They were out of the woods. She and Sturghill stumbled a few more steps, then collapsed on the gravel. They looked back at the woods. The noise had stopped. The trees were still. The darkness within the woods, starless and thick, lapped towards them but didn't pursue. Meacham eyed the line of yew trees, looking for a gap in the line-up where one had gone missing. The formation was solid. If anything, it was more of a wall than it had been before.

She stood up. Her knee spasmed, but it could support her. "Thanks," she said to Sturghill.

"Thanks for not letting me go in there alone," Sturghill answered. She took a step back, putting distance between her and the darker shadow of the woods. "I guess I'm not getting a second crack at that gate."

"Not tonight. Maybe in the morning."

"Think we'll make it that long?"

"I plan to." Which was no answer.

They headed back inside the house. They found Hudson and Gray in the Great Hall. They were seated at the table. Hudson looked exhausted, Gray reserved. Meacham had the impression of walking in on the aftermath of a struggle. Her money wasn't on Hudson.

He said, "I didn't hear the car."

"Not working." Sturghill tossed Gray's keys onto the table. He didn't reach for them. "Neither is the gate, and the woods are fucking dangerous. Where's your phone?" she asked Gray.

"Nearest one on this floor is in the library."

"Be right back." She left.

Meacham limped over to a chair and collapsed into it.

"What happened?" Hudson asked her.

Meacham filled him in. Sturghill came back just as she was wrapping up. "Phone's dead," the magician announced.

"So we're cut off." Hudson lost a bit more colour.

"Looks that way." Gray stood up.

"Where are you off to?" Sturghill asked.

"Bed," Gray said simply.

"Just like that?" Sturghill's eyes were shocked wide. "Anna's disappeared, probably dead, there are monsters in the woods, and we're trapped in this house. Well hell, that's quite the day. Better go sleep it off?"

"Do you have a plan of action that I'm interfering with?"

"No," she admitted.

Gray shrugged. Meacham said, "I don't think it's smart to be alone."

"Do you really think that makes any difference at all?" Gray asked. "If Rose wants to kill one of us, how would anyone interfere?"

"Why be alone if you don't have to be?"

"Because that's what I want. So if you'll excuse me ..."

He left, and they were three. "Ideas?" Meacham asked. There were none. "Patrick? Up for anything?"

"Right now, just staying alive."

"Okay. So. You two feel like a pyjama party?" Her words were flip. They were pathetic.

After a dinner of cold cuts, Gray was back in the old bedroom again. Close to the Old Chapel, close to the cold spot whose roots he now knew. He was here because he wasn't hiding. He sat on the edge of the bed, wondering why he wasn't afraid. He had been sent running from the Hall a few times already. He'd been spiritually assaulted. He had no reason to believe he was immune. Everything was escalating. His sleep in this room had a nice collection of nightmares and trauma. So here he was, ready to lie down and be hit again.

He wasn't worried. There was something building in his chest, but it wasn't anxiety. He was trying to hold it back, half-ashamed because he recognized it as a form of elation. He had never been so close to truth before. Gray was on the verge of absolute revelation, of knowledge that brooked no interpretation, no ambiguity, no contradiction. He was hungry for what would come next. The elation wasn't happiness, though. When Hudson had been pleading his case, Gray had had to bite down hard on anger. There had been an impulse to slap Hudson for his stupidity. There had been an even greater rage at the belief system Hudson was clinging to. He wanted to see that philosophy exploded. Truth was here. It was down in the torture vault. It would leave no room for an all-loving God and His self-sacrificing Son.

He lay down, fully clothed. He closed his eyes. He didn't expect to sleep. He was waiting for the next move. Each event pushed closer to an eruption of truth. He knew it would hurt. If he wasn't terrified now, he would be soon enough. That was fine. That was the price to be paid for revelation.

The bedrooms were not comforting. They couldn't be. The house was hostile down to the mortar. When, on the staircase to the upper floor, Meacham's shoulder brushed against the wall, she twitched. The wall didn't feel like it had when the house shook. It wasn't warm to the touch. It didn't give like flesh. But it radiated bad potential. It wasn't flesh, but it might be, should the spirit move it. Somewhere in the house, a spirit was moving, and it had them in its sights.

They settled on the room that Sturghill had shared with Crawford. There were two beds and an armchair that was old, but not so antique that it wasn't soft. Here, they could pretend they were going to sleep. Hudson insisted on taking the chair. Meacham and Sturghill sat on the beds, leaning against the wall. Neither lay down. Meacham didn't like the vulnerability of being horizontal. Sturghill hugged her knees to her chest, tight in a defensive ball. Meacham had the urge to hide under the covers. The laws of childhood stated that the monsters couldn't get you there. As a ritual, it made about as much sense as Hudson's prayers. She looked at him. He had his eyes closed, his head bowed, his hands clasped just below his mouth. He *was* praying, pulling his blanket over his head.

Sturghill said, "That isn't going to do any good, Patrick."

He paused, raised his head. "You don't know that."

"You weren't out in the woods. This is huge. We're not talking about a human scale here."

"God isn't on that scale, either." When Sturghill didn't respond, he continued. "I agree with you. We can't fight this. So I'm asking for help." He sounded almost calm.

"I wish there were someone there to hear you."

"With all that's happened, how can you doubt that there is?" He turned to Meacham. "You know better, now."

She was so tired. "I'm just not sure whoever is there is listening."

"He is," Hudson reassured. "He is." His voice was steady, but Meacham saw the vein throbbing in his forehead, the nervous-sweat rubbing of his hands. He was holding on hard to his faith. It wasn't coming easily. He wanted a convert. He wanted backup.

"I hope you're right," Meacham said. That was all she could give him.

It was enough. Hudson nodded, satisfied, and closed his eyes again. His lips moved as he prayed under his breath.

Meacham leaned back on her pillows. She had them bunched against the bed's headboard. She turned her face to the lamp on the side table. The 60-watt bulb was harsh on her exhaustion. It was also a thin flicker of comfort. No way she was turning it off. She didn't mind if it kept her awake. Sleep was dangerous and scary.

But Christ, she was tired.

She did sleep. She closed her eyes, thinking, *Just a short rest.* There was darkness that almost felt like a relief. She slept. She thought she did, anyway, because she began to dream. In the dream, she floated down through her bed and passed through the floor. She was swimming in air, and she was caught in a current. The current was pulling her down, toward the crypt. She knew she was going to be dragged to the caves. She didn't want to go. For the moment, all she felt was worry over what the dream might become. If she went underground, there would be no doubt: this would be a nightmare. She didn't want to have a nightmare, not here and now. The dream would be too awful. She whimpered softly and struggled against the current. It ignored her efforts. She didn't even slow her descent. She was sucked into the crypt.

She spiralled down the staircase, caught in a swirling drain. Her face passed close to the wall. It was no longer stone. It was a membrane. It pulsed. Beneath it, black blood coursed through runic veins. There was a rushing sound in her ears, loud as whitewater, hollow as an intaken breath. She fell faster. She spun. She was in a whirlpool. It was hauling her to the centre of the dark, to the room of tapestries and pain. The caves glowed with sentience. The walls of the tunnels had scales. She really was descending a serpent. She fell through the false tomb. She was rushed toward Rose's sanctum. She didn't want to see. She wasn't given a choice. She arrived in the room. The tapestries were neon bright. The chair was molten red and bleeding black. The figures in the tapestries were moving. They were screaming. The claws and teeth were rending flesh. Christ pulled an arm from the cross, trailing flesh and tendons caught by the nail, and reached *out*, into the room, pleading for help from her. The reptilian movement in the background gathered definition. Something was going to turn her way. Something was going to see her. If it saw her, it would drag her into the tapestry, and she would become part of the torture loop. And even worse than that was the thought that she might see the thing that would look at her. She tried to scream, but the dream-weakness was upon her, and her lungs could do nothing. Even her whimper came out as no more than expiring sigh. She wanted to close her eyes.

And she thought, *They are closed. I'm dreaming.*

And she thought, *Open your eyes and wake up.*

She opened her eyes. She was awake. She saw the bedroom.

But she was also in the caves. She still saw the tapestries. She was still floating in mid-air, trying to cover her eyes so she wouldn't see the reptilian arrival.

She was seeing double. The two scenes were superimposed over each other, first one, then the other becoming more solid, the unreality of the bedroom and the reality of the cave feeding her terror. *You're not awake yet*, she told herself. *You're still dreaming. Wake up, wake up, wake up.* She tried to scream again, and this time she did, an ear-shattering yell that hurt her throat, and the pain was too precise, her sense of her body too complete, and she knew she was awake, she was having a nightmare, but she *was* awake. She clawed at the air, trying to shred the images before her. She screamed again, saw Sturghill beside her, reaching out for her, but she wasn't real enough, the thing in the tapestries was closing in, its huge movement graceful with infinity, and she was going so *see* it.

There was another scream. Not her own. The dream ended, bleeding into a reality that was almost as bad.

Shrieks blew out of the walls, raced across the room, chased into the adjoining apartments, echoed in the hall and then howled back, deafening. The same pattern as before: hunter and hunted, the hunter's cry filled with rage and triumph, the prey's with agony and fear. Louder now. Huge force behind the sound. And the prey wasn't just one voice. There were many, a chorus of voices overlapping and overtaking each other in a race not to escape, because there was no escape, but to be the expression of the horror.

Meacham tumbled out of bed, she and Sturghill retreating on instinct to the centre of the room. Hudson was on the floor, on his knees, squeezing his eyes tight and his hands tighter. A scream shot out of the wall behind Meacham, knocking her forward. She ducked, crouched low, stayed near Hudson. Sturghill dropped down. The four corners of the room let loose an artillery barrage of howls. Meacham was able to make out individual voices now. The screamers were male and female. Some had the rasp of old age. There were other voices that made her cover her ears and yell, "*No!*" She tried to block their sound with her own cries. She didn't want to hear them. They were the voices whose gender she couldn't determine because they were too young. They were the vice-squeezed wails of tortured infants. She tried to banish the images the screams summoned. She tried not to think of the room of the tapestries. When she failed, she tried to tell herself that what she was hearing had been designed to beat her down. It wasn't necessarily the historical record.

Sturghill grabbed her shoulder. "I hear James," she shouted over the screams. Her face was stricken.

Unwilling, Meacham took her hands away from her ears. Listening for a specific male voice was almost a relief. The effort filtered out the other, more awful sounds. A little bit. *I'll never recognize him,* Meacham thought, but then, wasn't there something familiar in the timbre of that voice? The one that shot up through the floor, brushing past her face. Couldn't she suddenly picture Crawford's face, contorted in tendon-ripping pain? Yes, she could. And before she could conjure a denial, another scream ripped out from the wall to her left. She half-turned, caught the cry full in the face. It knocked her over. As she lifted her head, she saw the fresh horror in Hudson's expression. He had heard the same thing she had. His lips moved. They formed the word "Anna."

Gray dreamed of Christ again. He was back in St. Rose's church, facing the crucifix that had turned into the watching laugh. Christ wasn't laughing this time. Gray was vertical, floating about three feet off the floor. He sensed something at his back. It was too big for him to turn around and see. The fact of its presence was enough. The painted eyes of Christ were fixed on the thing behind him. The eyes were wide with horror and fear. Flecks of white and red fell from them as Gray watched. The figure seemed to struggle against the cross, trying to push away from what approached. Gray floated closer. He was suffused with truth. It came with power. He could reach out and dislocate arms, smash bones, sink his fingers deep into wooden flesh. There was only one way to teach.

"You dupe," Gray told Christ. "You stupid dupe. You only *wish* you'd been forsaken." He stretched out his arm. He opened his hand wide to wrap his fingers around the figure's throat. He was strong enough to throttle wood. Christ's mouth opened wide, wide, wider yet. Like the other dream, the mouth grew so huge and round it swallowed up the head. It became the entire figure. Gray waited for the sound, feeling satisfied, feeling vindicated, feeling sick. The sound came. Christ screamed.

The voice wasn't male. It was female. It was Anna Pertwee's. Gray jolted awake, the shriek still pouring down on him, pressing him into the mattress. The sound sat on his chest for a moment, a feral cat. It didn't want to suffer alone. Then it bounded away, pursued bloody by the hating yell. Gray stood up from the bed and followed. He opened the door, tracked the voices through the suite of bedrooms. He passed through the room where Hudson, Sturghill, and Meacham crouched on the floor. He didn't pause, said nothing. He was in a hurry. He felt the anticipation of ultimate revelation. Out in the hall, the voices bounced down the corridor, predator savaging prey and throwing it down, giving it time to start to flee and starting the judgment all over again. He stayed close behind the screams. He was surrounded by a cacophony of other voices, but the scream of rage and Pertwee's cry remained distinct. He had no trouble tracking them.

One of the yells was made of words. It was a moment before he realized the shout came from one of the living. Hudson was calling, running after him. A baby howled in Gray's right ear, drowning out Hudson. Gray ignored them both, followed the lure of Pertwee's pain. Hudson took his arm, tried to make him stop. Gray shook him off. Hudson tried again, still yelling something. *Not interested*, Gray thought. *Things to do. Things to learn.* Time for Hudson's nonsensical worldview to be firebombed. The philosophical duelling was over.

"*Please, Richard*," Hudson yelled. Gray heard that clearly enough. Hudson had wrapped both hands around Gray's upper arm and was digging his heels in.

Pertwee's screams dropped down the staircase, becoming distant. "Let go," he warned Hudson.

"No."

He didn't actually punch Hudson. He almost did. The anger was there. The hatred of stupidity. He pulled his arm back, at the last second opened his hand and turned the blow into a slap. Hudson dropped his arm and reeled back.

The screams stopped dead. Silence, hollow as the interior of a cathedral bell. One sound: Hudson's shocked breathing. In the corridor behind him, Meacham and Sturghill were still. Meacham looked like she was about to do something. Gray held a warning finger up for all three. He listened. No trace of the cries. They were gone. The certainty that he was being led to epiphany had evaporated. He'd lost his guide. He was cut loose. *No*, he thought. *No.* There was only one place the screams could have been leading. Perhaps, if he moved fast enough, he might arrive in time, be forgiven, be given the promised truth.

He ran.

Hudson leaned heavily against a wall. It must have felt wrong, because he shifted away again. He weaved, weak at the knees. He hadn't taken his hand away from his face. His eyes were glittering. Meacham went up to him, took his hand, forced it down. His cheek was a bright red. "He hit me," Hudson said, as if he weren't sure the blow had really happened.

"He isn't himself," Meacham said.

Hudson shook his head, agreeing. "He's in danger."

Meacham wasn't sure about that. If anyone had a chance of surviving the night, she thought it was Gray. But. "He might be dangerous," she amended.

"Will you help me stop him?"

"From doing what?"

Hudson didn't have an answer. He radiated desperation.

"All right," Meacham agreed. She had not gone after Gray or Pertwee earlier. The pragmatism still felt like cowardice. This time, she was less worried about Gray, more worried about what he might do. And the bigger issue was that Hudson was asking for help. They were all falling straight to Hell, so there was no more room to walk away.

"Where do you think he's going?" Sturghill asked.

"Only one place." *Here we go again,* she thought.

The silence was enormous. It prodded him to run faster. It felt like a pause, a balancing on a very fine point. It threatened to pull the truth away from him if the fall went the wrong way. He was being given one chance. He had the space between breaths. If he did not pass the test before the next exhalation, the truth would be lost to him.

He clattered down the stairs, raced to the crypt and to the caves. He might be being fooled; he knew he'd been manipulated from the start, but he didn't care. He didn't doubt. If he had to be twisted and broken before he could be brought to look the truth in the face, so be it. He ran faster. The air he pulled into his lungs was a lure, each breath yanking him further on. His footing was sure. He didn't stumble once on the steep stairs, or the uneven surface of the cavern floors. He didn't notice until he reached the false tomb that he hadn't brought a flashlight. He almost paused then, hundreds of feet below ground. There was no light source. He could see perfectly well. He was in Crawford's simulation again, the surroundings bypassing his eyes and presenting themselves directly to his brain. He recognized the danger of what was happening to him. That was why he *almost* paused. He saw the terrible impossibilities as part of the truth that at last was opening up to him. That was why he didn't pause.

He reached the torture chamber. Homecoming. He smiled. The tapestries stirred, breathing. Gray approached the throne. It was hard and real. He sat down on it. Its edges cut through his clothes and sank into his flesh. He felt the warmth of his blood flow down his back, pool around his thighs. He gripped the armrests, was slashed there too. The pain was that of a crocodile's jaw slowly biting down on him. He took a deep, shuddering breath. The tapestries billowed. Their figures began to move. Gray focused on them, letting the gestures pull his eyes from one panel to the other. He waited for revelation.

At first, the only movement came from the tortured. They pantomimed their pain. There was nothing new there. The screams started up again. Now, through his vision that seemed to grow clearer all the time until the cave was bright as cold sunlight, he could see which mouth produced which scream. He heard Pertwee's cry, and his gaze was riveted on the figure of a woman being pulled apart by giant talons. He looked at her face. It was distorted by agony, stylized in the manner of the tapestry's period, but it was recognizable. It was unmistakable. It was Pertwee. He was surprised he hadn't spotted the resemblance before. He squeezed the armrests more tightly. His fingers threatened to lose their grip as they became slippery with sweat and blood. He scanned the other tapestries for familiar faces. He found Corderman's hide stretched over an iron framework, his face recognizable even in its Silly Putty distortion. Crawford was trying to climb out of a boiling cauldron and being dragged back by a serpentine coil. They were here, all the victims of the house and its preaching inhabitant. He looked for his own face, for Meacham's, for anyone who was still alive. He found no one. Perhaps that was why he hadn't recognized the other figures before. They had only recently been added to the art. Who, he wondered now, were all the other characters? He didn't know those faces. Perhaps some were Rose's victims during her lifetime. Perhaps others were blank slots, holding patterns of medieval anonymity, waiting for new deaths to take on individuality.

Sharp, jerky movement in the corner of his eye, demanding attention. He looked. At first he thought one of the damned was waving. Her hand was shaking back and forth, but it was only through galvanic pain. The woman was being speared on four sides by enormous claws. She was his wife. She was Lillian. He stopped breathing, sick satisfaction stolen from him by a huge blow to his gut. He didn't want to look any further. He wasn't given the choice.

His eyes moved just to the left of Lillian and up. He was forced to see his daughter. Jill was cut in half. She was still twitching. She was still screaming. And there was her voice, and there was Lillian's, and had their cries always been there; had he simply been unable to bring himself to hear them? Had he been, for all his posturing, as resistant as Hudson to that crucial piece of the truth? He jerked his eyes away, gasping. He clutched the chair for support. His grip slipped with his blood, but the spikes caught him again. Pain was clarity's stiletto, and he continued to reason as he sobbed, his chest wracking hard and vicious. Lillian and Jill had not been killed by the house. They couldn't have been. They were too far away, they had no blood ties to the place, and he didn't think Rose's influence would have been strong enough to reach out that distance. Their deaths weren't mysterious. All of the deaths connected with Gethsemane Hall were. His family had died because of the uncaring stupidity of the universe. There was no other reason.

The reasoning moved forward, relentlessly, to the truth in all its scales. Perhaps he was seeing his wife and daughter not to learn about how they died, but about what came next. He had been staring at the floor, watching blood pool around his feet, but now he faced the tapestries again. He resisted the movement, the current that was trying to rush him back to his tragedy. He clung to the rock that was Pertwee's torment. The epiphany arrived, a slow, nuclear dawn. What was happening to Pertwee and all the others wasn't the real point. The torture was the iceberg tip of the real truth. What Rose had learned, and what she preached, was not that there was agony, but what *caused* the agony. Gray had been distracted by the damned as they screamed for mercy and called for a help he could not give. He should have paid attention to what was inflicting the torture. He should have looked more closely at the other movement, at the immensity that the tapestries could only hint at. He stared at one of the crucifixion scenes and tried to learn what he should about the being that was ripping Christ apart.

The pieces coalesced:

His family and the implacable sadism of the cosmos.

An afterlife of unending suffering, no exceptions.

(*We are not alone*, he thought with horror.)

The teeth.

The claws.

The scales.

The power.

The truth, when it arrived, was so simple. It boiled down to a single sentence.

chapter twenty

a cordial invitation

The screams had stopped. So had the sense of expectation. It seemed to Meacham as if the air itself had become brittle and snapped. The anticipation of the worst thing was over, now that the worst thing had happened, and the house was relaxing into aftermath. She felt better. She didn't know why. She distrusted the feeling. She was in the trough between shocks. Gethsemane Hall was simply pausing between dragon breaths.

She, Hudson, and Sturghill were in the caves. They were moving slowly, shining their beams left and right across the floor, covering the territory. When they had grabbed their flashlights from the table of research equipment that still stood, forgotten, in the crypt, they had noticed that none were missing. Gray had run down without one. They had expected to find his body, bones floppy with fractures, lying on the steps. Now they were wondering how far he had made it in the dark. They closed in on the site of the collapse. They knelt at the lip of the hole and aimed their lights down. Meacham said, "I don't see anything."

Sturghill puffed her cheeks. "No way he could have made it over this in the dark."

"Then he's gone?" Hudson asked. "Like the others?"

Meacham answered, "Maybe." She thought, *No.* There was something being woven around Gray. She didn't see his being tricked into a quick execution as a part of the whole pattern.

Then Gray proved her right and spoke. "What are you doing?" he said.

Meacham jumped. They all did. They all stood and caught him in the light as he walked up the tunnel toward them.

"Watch my eyes," he said and held up an arm to shield them. In the light, blood dripped. Meacham saw a grid of puncture wounds running from his hand to his shoulder.

"Jesus!" Sturghill said. "Are you okay?"

Gray glanced at his arm, dismissed it. "I'm fine." He stepped around the gap without even looking at it. As he reached them, Meacham saw the extent of his injuries. The back of his shirt was soaked and shining with blood. Flesh and clothing were torn from neck to ankles. "What happened to you?" she asked.

"I sat down."

The wounds made sense. "In that chair?"

He nodded, kept walking, forcing them to keep up.

"My God, Richard," Hudson began.

Gray cut him off with a short bark of a laugh, as if Hudson had said something very funny, but this wasn't the moment for Gray to indulge in a full guffaw. "I'm fine," he said, but he began to stagger.

"No, you're not," Meacham informed him. She and Hudson moved up to either side. Gray tried to shrug them off, but each step became more unsteady, as if the force that had held him up were leaking out. He was deflating. Five more steps, and he gave in and let them help him. They each took an arm. His weight became heavy very quickly.

The stairs were too narrow to go up any way other than single file. Gray went first, Hudson following with his hand on Gray's back to help keep him upright. The climb started off slow, grew worse. Gray had to pause and gather strength for each step. He leaned heavily against the wall, leaving smears of himself behind. Meacham couldn't avoid touching the wall. Her face become wet with Gray's blood.

When they reached the crypt, Gray turned around and gave them all a tight, knowing smile before he collapsed.

They carried him upstairs. They laid him face down on his bed and cleaned his wounds as best they could. Shreds of cotton from his clothing had been pushed into the holes in his skin. He was unconscious, but he winced every time they pulled out another blood-soaked strip of cloth.

"He needs a hospital," Sturghill said.

"If either one of you has a good idea about how to get him to one, I'm all ears," Meacham said.

Hudson buried his head in his hands. "So what do we do?"

"We stay together. Carry on as before. Make it through the rest of the night. See if we can't come up with something better during the day."

Sturghill said nothing. Hudson nodded and began to pray again. Meacham had long since given up on the idea that there was any point to his effort, but she admired his commitment. If there were a god, he had abandoned his servant, but the servant hadn't abandoned his god. Meacham wondered if holding firm to a belief made death any easier when it came. From the pallor of Hudson's face, she doubted it.

Gray twitched, drawing her attention. His eyes had snapped open. His head was turned to one side on the pillow, and he was looking at her. His expression was calm, cold. If he were experiencing pain, he didn't show it. "Please leave me," he said. "All of you."

"I don't think that's a good idea," she told him. "You're weak. You'd be very vulnerable if —"

"I'll be fine." He sounded absolutely certain.

Hudson said, "You can't know that."

Gray's eyes narrowed, glinting hostility. "Yes, I can. Now go."

Meacham stepped away from the bed. "The man says he wants to be alone, he wants to be alone."

Hudson caught up with her as she reached the doorway. "You can't be serious."

She jerked her head Gray's way. "His decision." To Gray, she said, "No more chasing after you, though. Clear?"

His smile was tight and showed no teeth. "I didn't ask you to the first time."

"You're welcome," she spat and turned away.

Hudson grabbed her arm. "He's not in his right mind."

"Sounds lucid enough to me."

"For God's sake, Louise."

She freed her elbow from his grip. "He says he'll be fine. You know what? I believe him." She didn't know what sort of understanding Gray had come to with the force in the house, but she sensed he had. Gray had no fear of harm, and though he was injured and bleeding, his conviction had the ring of truth. Nothing was going to touch him for now. She looked past Hudson's shoulder at Sturghill. "You had a good idea earlier," she said.

Sturghill frowned. "I did?"

"Yeah. Let's go talk about it. You too," she told Hudson. She took him by the collar and tugged him out of the room. "Don't make me pinch your ear," she said.

"Richard," he pleaded as she hauled him, stumbling, from the room.

Gray had closed his eyes again.

Back in the bedroom where they had begun the night, Sturghill asked, "What was my great idea?"

Meacham replied, "Later. Wait for daylight."

So they did. There were no more screams. Meacham found herself beginning to relax. There was no building tension in the atmosphere. Nothing was stretching taut. Rose was resting, or she was waiting, but she wasn't active. Towards dawn, Meacham slept.

She wasn't asleep long. Daylight entering the room was a call to flight. Meacham was up first, but the other two were right behind her. She ran downstairs, though the Great Hall, across the courtyard and out into the gardens. The sky was cloudless. The sun was squint-bright. Meacham inhaled air that tasted tantalizingly of freedom. It was the clean, living air of an English morning, fresh with evaporating dew. It was the breath of the lush green. In the daylight, the forest looked soothing, not hostile. At first glance. Looking again, Meacham saw that the woods were inviting only if one had never seen them before. "Kristine," she said. "Take a look at the trees. Notice anything?"

Sturghill caught it right off. "They're closer."

The advance guard of yews had constricted the perimeter of the lawn. The space was much less open than it had been when they had first arrived at the Hall. Meacham didn't think there were *more* yews than before, but they had tightened their ranks. Beneath their branches, the shadows still looked like night. Meacham asked, "Think we'd have any better luck?"

"Doubt it."

She nodded. She had hoped daylight would transform the woods, thinning them, pruning back the tentacles, chasing away the biggest shadows in which large, surreptitious movements could occur. Her hope was going the way of the dew, but she started walking towards the woods anyway. Perhaps the sense of darkness would be less absolute from closer.

"What was Kristine's idea?" Hudson wanted to know.

"I'd love to know that, too," Sturghill said.

"Tell you in a minute." Meacham was wary about speaking what she had in mind aloud. She didn't know what might be listening. She walked up the drive towards the woods. The other two kept pace. She stopped just shy of the trees. "Check it out," she said, amused, bitter, scared. The two nearest yews now had half the girth of their trunks on the left and right of the drive. Their roots joined in the centre. There was no longer any room for a vehicle to pass. A person could step over the roots, though. *Go on,* said the trees. *We dare you.* Meacham declined. Instead, she took another few steps forward, closing with the yew on the right. She stretched her hand out slowly, nervous. She touched the trunk. The tree did nothing. She felt the moist bark and moss under her hand. She reached up and rubbed the long, narrow leaves between her fingers. They were luxuriant. She folded one. It didn't break, sprang back to its shape when she let go. Not promising. "Right," she muttered and led the way back down the drive. She headed for the middle of the lawn, as far from both Hall and woods as she could be.

"So?" Sturghill asked.

Meacham kept her voice low. "Yesterday, you said if the house prevented you from leaving again, you'd burn it down."

Sturghill's response was slow. "... and?"

"I'm having thoughts of a cleansing fire too," she whispered.

"House or forest?" Hudson had the volume way down as well. The enemy had ears everywhere.

"You tell me. The power is centred in the house, but I don't know what effect a fire would have. The forest is what's physically preventing us from leaving, but there's so much moisture I don't know if we'd get much more than a bit of damp smoke."

"We might also seriously piss something off," Sturghill pointed out.

"There's that, too. But ask yourself: can you really get into any more trouble? I don't think I can."

Sturghill nodded. She turned her head towards the woods. "I vote for the trees. Quickest way out is through them. Anything will burn if you try hard enough."

"So plenty of fuel, and we do it during the day," Meacham said. "Agreed?" The other two nodded. "Next question: how do we get the party started?"

"Petrol in the car," Hudson suggested.

"Not your usual sort of holy water," Meacham said, grinning.

"You keep forgetting that I'm not a priest."

"I think you keep forgetting that you really are."

They headed back to the car. "Let's hope the gas tank hasn't been emptied," Sturghill said.

"Even if it hasn't, the petrol's not going to do us much good sitting in there. How do we get it out?" Hudson wanted to know.

Meacham said, "You've had far too nice an upbringing." A set of four stone steps and a narrow gravel path cut straight between the formal gardens to the half-timbered, connected cottages that stood apart from the main building. These were the former stables, half of which had been converted into staff quarters under Victoria. Meacham headed that way. "Glorified tool shed over here, yes?"

"Yes." Hudson followed. "What do you need?"

"Containers and tubing to start with."

"You sound sure you'll find everything."

"Are you saying that if I rummage through the equipment for maintaining an *English* garden, I won't find a hose?"

Hudson conceded the point.

The cottages were large enough to be a mansion in their own right. The wings had been turned over to vehicles and tool storage. The interior had been remodelled but still had a scent, present behind the odours of oil and fertilizer and paint, of well-mannered age. Wood and stone had matured like good wine. The west wing was the garage. Meacham was startled. She hadn't noticed an obvious way up here for cars, but when she opened one of the garage doors, she saw the drive had snaked its way here, looping out from the parking area in front of the Hall, entering more woods to the west of the formal gardens, before making its way discreetly here. The cars didn't look like Gray's.

They were vintage, but not in collectible condition. They were dusty, unused and untended to for a long time. They were the mechanical trace of Gray's ancestors, waiting in the darkness for their owners to return.

"What do you think?" Sturghill asked. "Any point in trying these?"

Meacham shrugged. "Can't hurt. We'll feel pretty stupid if we wind up dead because we passed on an easy out."

The keys were hanging on the walls of the former stalls. There were four cars: a Daimler, a Rolls, and two Saabs. Meacham and Sturghill tried them all. Click, click, click, click. Mechanisms cold with hostile silence. Meacham drummed her fingers on the steering wheel of the black Daimler. She tried not to feel disappointed. She hadn't expected anything. Still, there was a smug, petty sadism to the unresponsiveness of the cars. "Screw you," she muttered.

Thunk. The Daimler's left turn signal, an orange plastic rectangle, popped up above the driver's windshield. Meacham jumped. The leather seat was suddenly clammy. It was about to swallow her up. The car was a metal coffin. She fumbled at the door. She couldn't find the handle. The leather turned slick, viscous. Her hand grasped the handle and yanked it hard enough to make her shoulder scream. The metal dug into her palm, vicious. The door popped open and she tumbled out. She scrambled away. She looked back over her shoulder, saw the seatbelt flapping and squirming like a skewered snake. She ran and collided with Sturghill. They fell to the floor.

"You okay?" Sturghill asked as they picked themselves up.

"Think so." Another look back at the car. The belt was limp. The door hung open. The turn signal pointed like an idiot. The Daimler was inert. She brushed herself off, moderated her breathing. "Any luck?" she asked Sturghill, who shook her head. "Anything weird happen?"

"No. You?"

She nodded. "Let's go."

They cut across the cottages' front lawn to reach the east wing, where they'd left Hudson. Meacham told Sturghill about the Daimler. "I cursed it, and it retaliated."

"Think what'll happen when we start tossing Molotovs."

"That's my point. It hears us. I don't know how much it knows."

"We still doing this?"

"What do you think?"

"That there's nothing else to do."

"Too true." *Assume the worst,* she thought. *Assume Rose, or whatever it is at Gethsemane Hall, knows what you're up to. Don't give it a chance to counter. If you can. If.* Her lip curled. She'd never seen such pathetic grasping at straws.

The east wing was Handyman Central, special emphasis gardening. Wheelbarrows, hoes, rakes, spades, shears, rope, paint, stacks of wood that looked like a sampler from every fence in England. Workbenches invisible under pyramids of might-be-useful-someday junk. Rotting cardboard boxes of tools new and rusting surrounded by unidentifiable bits and bobs of metal. Jars of nails straight and bent. Scattered heaps of metallic and wooden objects that Meacham thought must have been breeding here on their own. They couldn't possibly have been made by the hand of man. They had no purpose.

Hudson had gathered four empty paint cans, a wine bottle grimed with dust, and three of the nail jars. "Is this what you had in mind?" he asked Meacham.

"None of them are perfect, but we'll make do. What about tubing?"

He pointed to a coil of garden hose. "Is that enough?"

Meacham laughed. "You *are* the innocent, aren't you?" She looked around, found a hacksaw. She knocked a pile of junk off a workbench, set the hose on top and cut a section a couple of feet long. "Bring the containers," she said and headed back outside, walking quickly back to Gray's car. She unscrewed the gas cap, slipped the hose into the tank, bent to one end, and began to suck. For a moment, she was worried that she would hit the perfect counter: no gas. But then her mouth flooded. She choked and gagged. She felt better than she had in days. She grabbed one of Hudson's paint cans and put the hose inside. Gas gushed into the can.

They filled the other containers. *The wine bottle might work all right,* Meacham thought. The jars, maybe. The paint cans were useless as cocktail shakers. But they could add fuel to the burn. Sturghill found a pile of cleaning rags and tore them into strips. Meacham looked at the arsenal when they were done. "We're not exactly going to start a revolution with this."

Sturghill said, "All we have to do is burn through one barricade."

"Are we ready to try this?" The sun was climbing fast. Time was zipping by with so much fun.

"What about Richard?" Hudson asked.

The temptation was to leave him. Meacham doubted he would agree to come. He might be worse than a liability. If this were still Geneva, she wouldn't hesitate. Hindmost to the devil. But those goddamned cancers of responsibility and duty were metastasizing in her gut. They were what had brought her back here to fight something that couldn't, she now accepted, be fought. At least not by her. She'd done her best, and now she was retreating. The best victory she could hope for now was an evacuation that brought everyone still alive to safety. Her conscience, she thought, would be able to live with that. "Let's get him," she said. "We should all be together, do this thing once. If it works, I'm not betting on a chance at a second strike or a long delay before retaliation."

"What if he refuses?" Hudson was watching her with that priest's eye, judging.

Screw you, Father. I know you're not a minister but screw you, anyway. "He will. And we'll drag him out. Satisfied?"

Hudson nodded. They left the bombs beside the car and headed back inside. Meacham paused in the outer hall. She thought she heard a voice. She held up a hand for silence, heard it again. It was Gray's. He was speaking to someone. Who? Pertwee, back and not dead after all? Pertwee, dead but back all the same? She exchanged a look with the other two and made for the Great Hall. Gray was there, sitting at the table. He was leaning forward, keeping his injured back from touching the rear of the chair. He was on a wireless phone. "I realize this is short notice," he was saying. "I appreciate your willingness to do this. I will, of course, be happy to pay for any additional expense the rush incurs." He looked up and waved a hand at Meacham. "Yes," he said into the phone. "That will be fine. Thank you." He turned the phone off. "Good morning," he said. He had changed his clothes, but his wounds hadn't finished scabbing over, and already the arms of his shirt were gathering red stains. He was sitting very gingerly. His greeting was cheerful, but his expression was flat, eyes half-lidded and unreadable.

"Were you on the *phone*?" Sturghill demanded.

"I rather thought I was."

"How the hell ..." she began but strode forward, grabbed the phone, turned it on and put it to her ear. The fierce hope on her face died. "Cute," she said to Gray. "You're a real asshole, you know that? Where do you get off playing games when we're in this kind of trouble?"

Gray frowned. "What are you on about?"

"It's dead," Sturghill told Meacham. "Bastard's talking to his imaginary friends."

"There is nothing wrong with that phone," Gray said. He snatched it from her hands, turned its speaker on. The Holy Grail sound of a dial tone filled the Hall. Sturghill's eyes bugged. She took the phone back. It went silent.

"Oh, funny," Sturghill said. "Humour. Rose," she called, "you're a hilarious bitch, and Hell's too good for you." She tossed the phone onto the table.

"Dead for us," Meacham commented.

"Yup."

Gray sighed, took the phone, turned it on again. Dial tone. "All right, then. I'll dial. Whom should I call?"

Good question, Meacham thought. The police? The Archbishop of Canterbury? Who had the best chance of hauling their sorry asses out of here? No one did. But the need for other people was there, the belief that sheer numbers would rescue them. Call for the cavalry. Call in the authorities. *Too bad you are the authorities, eh girl?* "The local police," she decided. "Ask for DCI Kate Boulter." *I'll explain the problem,* she thought. Boulter would believe, she was pretty sure. Have her bring in heavy artillery. Platoons of bulldozers to cut that forest down to size.

Gray punched buttons. The phone beeped at each press. He was halfway through the number when the beeps stopped. He hesitated, pushed the last digit a few more times, held the phone to his ear. "Dead," he said. "Sorry."

"There's a surprise," Sturghill muttered.

"I shouldn't worry," Gray told her. "I imagine DCI Boulter will be along sooner or later." He smiled.

"What do you mean?" Meacham asked, worried again by his cold cheerfulness.

"We're going to be having company," he said.

She should have been happy. That was what she wanted, wasn't it? Other people to be around. But not summoned by a Gray who was not as concerned as he should be, who didn't seem to be frightened at all, and whose sunny disposition was nothing more than a plastic turn of the lips. "Who was that you were talking to?" she asked.

At the same time, Hudson demanded, "What have you done?"

Gray answered him. "I've been sending out invitations. We're going to have a party."

In the distance, Meacham heard the growl of a diesel engine.

Art Gifford had never been on the grounds of Gethsemane Hall. His father had, in the early days of Gifford & Son Rentals, back when the "& Son" of the firm's name was an affectionate gesture towards a young boy many years yet from joining the family concern. This was decades ago, when the Gray family was still known to have a do from time to time. Hadn't happened once in Gifford the Younger's career, and he'd been at this over thirty years now. The name outside the shop still read Gifford & Son, but neither his own son, or, for that matter, his two daughters, had any interest in carrying on the business. The girls were in university, and more power to them. The boy was in a band, but not a proper rock band, thanks all the same. Oh no, he was in something called N-Street, which Gifford knew was referred to in the business as a boy band. Bloody hell. He was making money off screaming ten-year-old girls and coming across as a right ponce. *Thank you, Eurovision. Thank you ever so friggin' much.* The group's one single was everywhere. Gifford had done his best to avoid it, had failed. It was called "River of Love." Five high male voices harmonizing. The chorus went "Swing high, swing low / That's the way the river flows." Gifford did not pretend to be a poet or a man of refined musical ear, but he knew inane when he heard it. So did his mates. They made a point of playing it on the jukebox at the Stag as often as possible. The joke was evergreen, apparently. His cross to bear. And his partner in the business now was Freddie Sandiford. Hardly "& Son." Sandiford was three years older. No problems with Freddie as far as being the junior partner went, though. Good muscle, but the business sense of a gnat. He knew it, too.

No worries about Gifford's legacy this morning. The phone rang him out of bed. Crack of dawn, business not to open for hours yet, his answer had not been welcoming. He'd sharpened up when he heard Richard Gray's voice. The lord of the manor wanted his services, and sooner than now. Gifford lived above the shop. He'd stormed downstairs, calling Sandiford on his mobile. He was lucky: the lorry was already loaded with what he needed, and he didn't have to wait for Sandiford to be off and running. He was eager with the honour. He didn't think about how much his eagerness was simply the need to answer the lure of Gethsemane Hall. He'd lived with the tug a long time, had learned to be suspicious of it. But first thing in the morning, startled awake, big commission on offer, he'd forgotten to be suspicious.

Even now, he was feeling good as he manoeuvred the truck down the narrow drive. The gate had opened for him without his having to climb out of the cab and ring. Gray must have heard his vehicle's approach. Wasn't the quietest beast, truth be told. Nor the smallest. Negotiating the drive's descent was difficult. The forest pressed close and dark. Gifford had the odd impression of being a bubble moving through water, with the woods opening before him and closing again as he passed. Then he emerged from the woods and pulled into the gardens, and there were people running toward him. He recognized Gray's friend Patrick Hudson and two of those shit-disturbers from out of town. They were staring at his vehicle as if he'd mounted rocket launchers. The younger of the two women reached his door as he was coming to a stop. She didn't even let him open the door before she demanded, "How did you get in?"

"How'd you think?" Nutter.

The older woman was looking back up the drive. When she spoke, her voice was calmer, but she looked just as stricken as the other two. "More to the point," she said, "how are you planning on leaving again?"

When you encounter a nutcase, you don't give them the time of day. You certainly don't act on their suggestions. Gifford had ignored plenty of street loons in his day, gazing straight ahead and blanking out the raving. That was what he should have done here. Instead, like a fool, he looked in his rear-view mirror. And didn't the forest look like it had closed back over the road? Rubbish. He climbed down from his cab and walked around to the rear of the trailer.

"Why are you here?" the woman asked.

"I'm providing the tent and such, aren't I."

"Tent?" said Hudson.

Were they all raving? "For the party."

"Party," the older woman repeated, the word rasping like sandpaper in her throat. She'd turned a greyer pale.

Gifford was becoming lonely for sane company. The freaky three here hadn't managed to dissipate the elated relief he felt in finally being *here*, but they were working on it. And where was Sandiford? He couldn't unload and set up by himself, and he didn't trust these characters to help out in a useful way.

Sound of a car engine. Gifford looked up the drive hopefully. There it came: Sandiford's farting old Cortina. Gifford blinked. His eyes were being tricksy. It looked as if the forest had spat out the car, then closed up again.

Meacham watched the two men begin to set up tables and a marquee tent. Her heart sinking further every second (and she wondered how that was possible), she walked back into the Hall. Gray was still making calls. She stood in front of him until he put the phone down and gave her his full attention. "Why?" she asked.

"I want to share."

chapter twenty-one

rsvp

The call descended on Roseminster. It began with the phones. Then the virus mutated. The contagion spread through conversations, emails, text messages. By midday, flyers had appeared. They multiplied in mailboxes, on telephone poles and on lamp standards. Gethsemane Hall had been inviting the people of Roseminster in for a chat and a cuppa for centuries. For the first time, the request was made formal and flesh. The tug was irresistible. It had been growing very strong since the death of Pete Adams. Now Richard Gray had added his voice, insisting on the pleasure of everyone's company.

John Porter was thinking about wild horses. They couldn't keep him away from the glory of providing the catering at Gethsemane Hall. He wished they could. The part of him that was thinking of wild horses was detached, watching. The rest of John Porter was racing the clock and pushing his staff. That Porter was buzzing with the charge of the invitation and the tug. He was going. There was no choice. But the other Porter, the one who found a small corner

in which to think while running helter-skelter to the embrace
of the Hall, was frightened. He was frightened because of what
had happened to Roger Bellingham. He was frightened because
everyone else was. He was frightened because of the nightmares.
Last night, he had clawed his way out of the worst one yet, its
strands sticking to him like black treacle, its tendrils burning him.
He had gasped awake and seen that his wife was thrashing in the
same grip. He had reached out to wake her, but as he did so, he
thought he saw something in the corner of the room. He thought
he saw something move. It was hunched. It idiot-nodded. It
scraped across the floorboards. It had been in his dream, and it had
followed him out. He yelled. His wife woke. She struck out a hand
toward the bedside table and turned on the lamp. The nodding
thing was visible for a second more, then disappeared. Samantha
turned to him, her face haggard, and said the awful thing: "That
was in my dream."

In the morning, Richard Gray had called. Like a good vassal,
Porter had said yes, of course, very honoured. And had wanted to
scream. Now, rush rush rush, and oh how he wished he would slow
down. He couldn't. He could see the same strain in Samantha, in
the faces of his employees. They were all going. They were sliding
down the chute together. He cursed Gray. He'd been able to resist
the Hall until now, though standing his ground had become the
main work of each day. Gray's explicit request was the tipping
point. The Hall needed that one little bit of human agency. Gray
had reached out. He could not be refused.

The party was on.

None of the faces of the guests-to-be were ecstatic. Many
were curious, but not so curious that they could overcome the
dread. Even the media were having their doubts. The invitation
landed in their laps, a bonanza so unlikely it had not even been
asked for. Were they going? They were going. But not with the
enthusiasm they would have had when Gray's investigative party
had first been assembled.

"What do you think?" the reporter from the *Mirror* asked the photographer from the *Sun*. They were lounging outside the Nelson, waiting for nothing and hoping the daylight would burn away the slick of the night's dreams.

"Bugger me sideways," the photographer said.

Two steps away, a television crew was celebrating the morning with some heavy drinking.

DCI Kate Boulter wondered why she hadn't had the sense to shift her arse back to London before now. Last night, she still could have left. Now, an event horizon had closed around Roseminster, with her inside. She went through the motions of turning up at the station, as if she still had an investigation that made any kind of sense. Constable Keith Walker gave her an accusatory glare as she stepped inside. "Well," he said. "I guess you'll find out, now, won't you?"

"I guess I will."

Meacham watched them arrive. One after another, the forest spat the vehicles out into the domain of the Hall. Gifford first and his partner, then the others needed to make the day complete. Sturghill had asked them if they had any reason to head back into town for more equipment. They hadn't. They gave up on that possibility. John Porter showed up around noon, the most ashen-faced caterer she had ever seen. Meacham buttonholed him as he opened the rear doors of his van. "Did you bring everything you needed in one trip?" she asked.

"Pretty much," he said, not really paying attention. "My wife is heading up a convoy bringing the rest."

"That's a shame."

Now Porter looked at her. "Why do you say that?"

"I was hoping some necessity related to this evening's event would take you back to town." Porter waited for her to go on, and she said, "I thought perhaps my friends and I might catch a lift with you."

Comprehension and fear on the man's face. "You can't leave?"

She shook her head. "And we've tried. We're looking for any kind of loophole, now. Not to mention some way of derailing this insane party."

Porter pulled a cell phone out of his shirt pocket.

"I wouldn't bother," Meacham told him, but he checked it anyway, then folded it up again slowly, slid it away.

"My wife ..." he began

"Anything at all you might have forgotten?" Meacham pressed.

Thought creased his forehead. "We could always use another cooler for the drinks."

"Worth a shot." She waved an arm at Sturghill and Hudson, who climbed in the back with the food. Meacham rode shotgun. Porter turned the van around and headed back up the drive. He stopped at the treeline. The yews were blocking the way. Meacham sighed. "No surprise, but at least we tried."

Porter's forehead was shining with sweat as he reversed. "I didn't want to leave," he whispered.

"I know. I don't want to, either."

"But I know I have to."

"Welcome to the club, Mr. Porter."

"What's going to happen?"

"Nothing good." The man was looking for reassurance. She had none to give.

A few minutes later, Samantha Porter arrived, as frightened as her husband. Gray emerged from the Hall to welcome them. Meacham watched him closely. His manner was warm, sunny. He took the edge off the Porters' terror. He was smiles and calm words. He was weather talk. The act was very, very good. It almost fooled Meacham. The giveaways were subtle. Interrogation training had taught her to look for the telltales that the subject was lying. A recurring look to the right instead of into the eyes of the interrogator. A persistent clearing of the throat. Rubbing the nose. How does the subject inhale before answering the question? So many tells. Gray exhibited none of these. He looked the Porters straight in the eyes. There were no subconscious ticks. But he was off. It was as if there were a fraction of a second delay between his brain sending an impulse and his body reacting, as if he kept having to remind himself to interact in the here and now. His eyes met Porter's but did not see them. His smiles were thin shellac. He was an illusion.

Porter was working himself up to a question. "I don't mean to raise a fuss," he said, "but I just tried to head back to town to pick up some things I had forgotten, and couldn't. The forest, you see ..." *How very politely English,* Meacham thought. Hate to be a bother, but are you aware your home is cursed and that I'm afraid I might die? Still an honour to be here, though.

"It won't let you out," Gray said. He shook his head in commiseration, as if they were discussing potholes in the road on the way over. "I *am* sorry about that." He smiled as the Porters held hands, clutching hard. "I shouldn't worry, though. I have every reason to believe that come tonight, that will no longer be an issue." He clapped Porter on the shoulder. Chin up, there's a good chap. Meacham wished for a gun. "Must run," Gray said. "Things to do." He trotted off, back to the Hall.

Meacham followed. One thought: stop him.

Gray headed for the library to wait for Meacham. Might as well be comfortable. He had just chosen an armchair when she arrived. He gestured, inviting her to sit opposite him. She remained standing. "If you make one more phone call," she told him, "I'll kill you."

He believed her. "All right," he agreed. "No more."

She didn't relax. "Meaning you've already finished."

He shrugged. "What can I say?"

"You can tell me why you're trying to kill off the whole town."

"Is that what you think I'm doing?"

"You trick everyone and their monkey's uncle to come to a place you know they cannot leave. Yeah, I think you're trying to kill them."

Gray leaned forward. "So that means Roseminster is safe? That nothing bad happens there? That no one we know was killed there recently?" Meacham was silent. "I want to know, in all seriousness, if you think that what is happening here will leave the town unscathed come the endgame."

Meacham didn't answer right away, but not, Gray thought, because she didn't know what she believed. "No," she finally said, her admission grudging, grating. She was staring at a point above his head. After a moment, she dropped her gaze to his face again. "So what are you up to?"

"I already told you."

"Yeah. 'I want to share.' Cute. Cryptic. Coy. It's a great bad-guy aphorism and it tells me absolutely nothing."

Gray smiled. She was right. He'd been enjoying himself this morning, having real fun, and it had been a long time since that had happened. He sobered up. The fun was coming from a bad place. It was fuelled by anger. It was out of line. "I'm sorry," he said. "That was wrong of me. Listen. And sit down, please." She hesitated. "Please," he insisted. She sat. He leaned close. "We came here for the truth, didn't we? Isn't that what we all want?"

"No," she said. "I came here to kill bad publicity and, if necessary, inconvenient truths. You know what I do for a living. I'm not on a first-name basis with the truth."

"But *you* still want to know," he said, "even if you weren't going to reveal what really happened. If the Agency wants to spread disinformation, it first needs to know what the correct information is, doesn't it? Your profession is *intelligence*. Knowledge is power. Tell me I'm wrong."

"Is that what this is about? Power?"

He snorted. For a smart woman, she could make some stupid assumptions. "Of course not. I don't expect to leave this place alive any more than you do."

"I'm still planning to."

"I'm sure you are. But you don't expect to."

"So if this isn't about power or survival, what then?"

"It's about that truth," he said, quietly. "It affects all of us, and a real truth is universal. We're all entitled to it."

Comprehension dawned on her face. "You're spreading the word. You're evangelizing."

He hadn't considered the term before. It struck him as all too appropriate now. He chuckled. The sound in his ears was dry and hollow. "I guess I am," he said.

Meacham stood up. "I don't like true believers. They've done plenty of damage in my country."

"I could have sworn I saw you call on Patrick and Anna to use the power of their faith to beat back the forces of darkness."

"And we saw how well that turned out."

"Anyway, this isn't a question of belief. It's about seeing things as they really are."

"Spoken like the worst of the true believers."

He raised his hands in submission. "Whatever you say."

"No more calls?"

"Or else what?" When she didn't answer, he shrugged, letting the levity go. "No more calls," he agreed. "No need."

"I'd ask you to call into town and rescind the invitations...."

"... or issue dire warnings," he suggested. "I think I would find the telephone suddenly very uncooperative."

She nodded. "So you have your little party happening. What now?"

"I'm going to be the dutiful, attentive host."

"And what else?"

"Nothing." A lie. He would do what he said until it was time for the truth to come out.

The virus of the call spread. The town answered. The people

accepted the invitation, consciously or not. Those who had not lived in Roseminster for too many years, who did not know the tug as well as those born and bred in the town, were more likely to think, *Yes, this sounds wonderful. I can't wait to go.* It wasn't that they weren't frightened. They were having the dreams, too. They had heard the sounds and felt the threat in the air the night Bellingham and Corderman had been killed. But they could rationalize more easily. They took the sensation of being privileged to be invited at face value. The idea of a party at Gethsemane Hall was a good one. It was a welcome diversion from the darkness.

The older residents knew better. They looked at the invitation as a venomous snake. They knew the impulse to accept it was part of the problem. Many of them thought, *No. I will not go. There. I've made my decision.* Early in the day, that choice was easy. The people who made it felt strong. They had no reason to think they would change their minds. And they didn't. Even as, come seven o'clock in the evening, they closed up shop and locked up home and made their way towards the Hall. Even then, they hadn't changed their minds. They never planned to show up. They planned the reverse. They showed up all the same.

The party was all-ages. Even so, parents called on babysitters and made arrangements. Then they forgot to cancel as they took children in hand, gathered up babes in arms, and headed off for the big event. The babysitters didn't show up at empty homes. They were on their way to the Hall, too.

The people gathered in the gardens of Gethsemane Hall. The town poured itself into the black hole. The numbers became multitudes. The gardens contained them all.

There was still plenty of daylight left. The evening was slow in coming on. But the light had taken on the end-of-day sharpness. It was tired, brittle, and would soon retreat. The sun was moving down. Not long now, and it would drop behind the trees. Darkness wouldn't leap in just then. It would gather its strength a bit longer, send out recon forces of grey, leech out the colours, and undermine the foundations of hope. Then it would invade, cold and final.

Meacham watched the guests arrive. She had given up trying to stop them or make them turn back or take her out with them. Sturghill hadn't surrendered yet. Meacham could see her still running from one new arrival to another, to another, to another. She didn't think Sturghill had any more hope than she did. The magician simply couldn't stop going through the motions. Meacham couldn't see Hudson. He was inside, she assumed, in default mode: pleading with Gray. She didn't have to guess what he was saying. She knew. He wanted Gray to stop what had been set in motion. He wouldn't accept that it was too late. Or at least, like Sturghill, he was unable to stop engaging in futile gestures.

Meacham was standing in a small, circular garden across from the courtyard entrance to the hall. There was an elevation of four small steps above the drive that kept the greenery free of the gravel. The garden was twenty feet across and laid out in concentric circles. Low yew hedges marked the outer perimeter. A walkway of finely crushed stone was the next circle, followed by a ring of hedges trimmed into small, rounded pyramids about two feet high, separated by short rows of euphorbia. Then another walkway, and finally a small pond. At its centre was a fountain. It was a moss-covered stone pile, mirroring the shape of the hedges. Water spouted up about six inches. The gurgle was very peaceful.

Meacham blotted out the white noise of the crowd's conversations. She listened to the water. She looked away from assembled sheep and watched the water flow. She could almost believe in such a thing as peace. She knew, too, how easy it was to believe in comforting illusions. Over the course of her career, she had manufactured her fair share. The purpose of such illusions was to draw attention and energy away from effective action. They lulled. She could, she thought, let herself go. Be lulled. She could sit down here, stare at the water, listen to it murmur to itself, and wait for the end to come. That would be much easier than fighting. Wasn't the comforting illusion even more necessary, she thought, when there was no effective action to be taken? Sometimes, there really was no fighting to be done. Sometimes, the quiet lie of *there, there, it's all right* was necessary to see you more easily through your death.

What about it, then?

She sighed. No. Not in her nature. She was just as bad as Sturghill and Hudson. She would go through her own futile motions of struggle, different in kind but not in effect from theirs. She would tell herself that she would find a way out, even as she damned herself as a poor liar.

She looked away from the water and faced the broader prospect of the gardens again. She considered the options. They still had the petrol bombs. She should think of the townspeople not as fodder for Rose, but as possible allies. Some of them might be useful. Porter, maybe. The police. *Come on, then. Work to do.*

She found Kate Boulter in the tent. Porter and staff were dispensing tall glasses of Pimms with sprigs of mint. Gray's menu, it seemed. The drinks were being snatched up as quickly as they were poured. The gathering looked like a party. Sounded like a party. The faces, though, were all strained. Boulter was standing just inside the shade of the tent, looking around with an expression Meacham thought was the same as had been on her own face a few moments before: depressed speculation. "Welcome to the party," she said to Boulter.

The detective grimaced. "Couldn't have missed it," she said. Subtext: *though I tried.*

"Would you believe I was hoping the police might put a stop to this?"

Boulter chuckled. "I think I do believe you." She sighed, swept her gaze around. "What a piss-up."

"I'm looking for a few good pyromaniacs." When Boulter cocked an eyebrow, Meacham told her what she had in mind.

"What, now?"

Meacham shook her head. "We can't. Too many people still arriving."

"Nice to know the CIA has some concerns about collateral damage."

"Never said it did. I do. Fair enough?"

Boulter nodded, signing the peace treaty. "When, then?"

"Not much choice. Once everybody's here. Before full dark, I hope."

Boulter checked her watch, then looked at the steady stream of people still being emerging from the forest. "Good luck on that."

Meacham knew it. The ghost had blocked her move. The daylight grew more brittle, and still the late arrivals flowed in. Meacham pictured throwing the bottles, setting the forest on fire, burning families to death in her bid to run. She shook the image away. It was blood she would not have on her hands. She might not save anyone tonight. But she wouldn't kill anyone, either.

Gray moved away quickly. Hudson ran to catch up, then stopped. No point. At long last, time to admit that. He'd done his stuck record routine, and maybe now he could admit that there was no point in haranguing stone. That's what he might as well have been doing, for all the reaction he provoked in Gray. His friend had listened. Had smiled. Had spoken quietly, asking a few questions. Had not shown the slightest emotion. Hadn't even countered his arguments. Hudson had grown desperate for some kind of kind of response. He'd begun deliberately to stab at buttons, no longer really trying to win Gray over. He'd invoked God a lot. Even that had flatlined.

Now Gray moved into the crowd. Hudson stood at the courtyard entrance and watched his friend move from person to person. After a minute, Hudson lost sight of him. *Is he really still my friend?* he wondered. He wasn't asking himself whether Gray had had a change of heart. He was asking if Gray had gone away, leaving a shell animated by something else.

No. That was the easy answer. It was an easy out that would allow him to view Gray as an enemy, as a thing beyond help. It was also not true. Gray had changed. He was cold, closed. He was still Gray, though. He needed saving as much as Hudson did, if not more. If the worst happened, Hudson still had the comforting knowledge that death wasn't the end.

Oh, there were still doubts. He was only human. Absolute certainty wasn't possible. What he'd seen here was irrefutable proof of some form of afterlife, though. The tapestries in the cave disturbed him, but the fact that it was Christianity that was specifically targeted could be seen, he thought, as a sign that it was the threat to the evil in the house. A delusional belief could hardly be a worthy opponent, now could it? He didn't think it could be.

So, what now? He might have failed with Gray, but he hadn't given up on him. If Meacham was still set on burning her way out of here, he would drag Gray along by main force. For now, though, there were other people to think about. Before him was a large-scale garden party in mourning. People were well-dressed. They mingled. They carried drinks. They were scared. Hudson spotted John Woodhead. The Rector of St. Rose's had his arm around Melody Searwood's shoulder. She was clutching his other hand in a death grip. Woodhead was speaking quietly. Searwood was nodding as if taking comfort. She was crying, too. Hudson moved forward to help as he could.

Gray smiled, shook hands, welcomed. He chatted. He couldn't remember what he said from one second to the next. He wasn't listening to himself. He was taking in the scene of a gathered, concentrated Roseminster. *You have done this,* he thought. *All these people are here because you asked them to come.* Meacham's inquisition bounced around his mind, rattled uncomfortably now that it was too late to rescind the invitations. Why had he done this? The truth, that was why. So everybody could share in it. The answer didn't satisfy the way it had even a few minutes ago, when he had been speaking to Hudson. *The truth is coming whether they're here or not*, he thought. *Then what difference does it make?* The voice was small, accusatory, hurt. Why take an active hand in this? *Inaction isn't mercy*, he responded. *This way, maybe, just maybe, they'll understand. That would be a gift*, he thought. Given the scale of understanding, he didn't think it was a small one.

"Hello," he said to the next clump of guests. "Thank you for coming." They looked at him with frightened eyes. He smiled his smile, the one that said *all is normal, all is well, relax and enjoy yourselves*. He moved on, said hello again, said thanks again, and smiled the smile.

The daylight grew more brittle still. At last, it snapped. The sun dropped behind the trees. A few minutes later, it touched the hidden horizon. The sky bled. There had been thunderheads all day, but in the sunlight, they were bright and white, impressive but unthreatening. Now they picked up the glow of the sunset, radiated blinding crimson, then drew strength and darkened quickly. They became suspended anvils. The wind began to pick up. Before, it had been just enough to flap the tent's material. It had cooled the day. Now it was an insinuation. It wanted to be heard. It had things to say, to whisper in the ear. As the light retreated, the wind spoke louder. It blew in the face. It chilled. It commanded attention.

The garden party staggered on. All the guests had arrived now. Some, mostly those who had spoken to Sturghill, tried to leave. Word that they could not spread fast. Everyone else thought it best to preserve the illusion of normalcy and not try to escape. The guests of Gethsemane Hall herded together. They sought comfort and warmth. The spoke with Hudson and Woodhead.

Some wept. Some held each other. A few contemplated struggle. They were the ones who spoke to Meacham. They eyed the forest, looked at the sad little collection of incendiary devices, and tried hard to hold on to hope. Above them, the thunderheads turned into night and mockery.

Then there were the others. They were the majority. They drank, drank some more, and waited for the main event.

chapter twenty-two

one sentence

Meacham. Sturghill. Boulter. Porter. Keith Walker. They gathered the cocktails at the point where the drive was blocked by the yew trees. They knew no further guests were coming. None had arrived in the last fifteen minutes. Darkness had come thirty minutes before. Not the timetable Meacham preferred. She wasn't surprised. Time to go ahead. March into doom, probably, but fighting all the way.

Hudson joined them as she was picking up one of the jars. "Ready for this?" she asked him.

"Wait until I find Richard. I'm not leaving without him."

She shook her head. "First we get this started. Then you can drag him along. I don't trust him. He might try to stop us."

"Stop what?" It was Gray. He was a shadow coming up behind Hudson. The visibility in the gardens was very poor. There was no light from the windows of the Hall. The only illumination came from the tent. Art Gifford had brought along a generator and lighting. People were clustering like moths around the glow. The rest of the grounds were disappearing as the night pressed its weight down.

Meacham took Porter's lighter and lit it. Gray's features flickered into view. He looked at the jar she was holding, at the rag that hung down, waiting for the flame. Meacham held the lighter close to the rag, watched for sudden movement on Gray's part. If he lunged, a twitch was all she needed to light the fuse.

"Oh," Gray said, unconcerned. "I see."

"Is there a problem?" Meacham asked.

"Not at all. Feel free. Before you do, though," he said, and Meacham thought, *here it comes*, "could I borrow you and Patrick?"

"Why?"

"There's something I think you should see."

"Is it that important?"

"Yes." He didn't say anything else. He just waited.

She didn't have to look at Hudson to know that he was already willing to go along with whatever Gray wanted. Anything to win back the favour, and perhaps ultimately the soul, of his friend. She hesitated. Pointlessly. Goddamn her curiosity and need for information. If Gray wanted her to see something, she wanted to see it, too. Shit. "All right," she said. She handed the jar and lighter to Sturghill. Gray turned around and walked toward the Hall. Hudson followed.

Sturghill said, "How long should we wait?"

"Don't," Meacham answered. "As soon as we're out of sight, do it."

"What about you?"

"If I'm dumb enough to walk away now from a possible way out, I deserve whatever happens." She hurried to catch up with Hudson.

She hoped she would hear the shattering of glass and eruption of flames behind her. By the time she reached the courtyard, there had still been nothing.

Kate Boulter said, "So seriously, how long do we give them?"

"Ten minutes," Sturghill answered. "Agreed?"

Porter shifted uneasily. "Can you make it five? I don't mean to seem heartless, but ..."

"Five," Sturghill said.

They followed him. Gray didn't turn the lights on as they entered the Hall. He was walking the path of an internal radar. That, or his every step was predetermined, and not a one could go wrong. Meacham didn't have that luxury. She flicked on switches as they entered rooms and grabbed a flashlight from the equipment table when they reached the crypt. Hudson did, too. Gray walked on. He never paused. There was grace in his movements. He was a man, Meacham thought, who knew *exactly* where he was going and was satisfied at last to be going there.

Down again. *Let this be the last time,* Meacham thought. *One way or the other.* The route was not becoming comfortable through familiarity. The sense of dropping into a serpent's throat was stronger than ever. A slight breeze blew Meacham's hair forward as they descended. It was a bit stronger when they reached the caverns. It pushed down the tunnels, showing the way. Meacham thought of a huge intake of breath, very slow and steady, building to a dragon's exhalation.

At the cave-in, Meacham blinked. For a moment, she thought she had seen Gray walk right over the collapse. She shone her flashlight at his feet. He was walking on solid stone. He must have sidestepped the gap. She hoped he had.

Down. Into the throat. The air grew colder. It was more than the damp and dank of caves. It was the touch of the cold spot, spreading its influence, reaching into her bones this far up. Strength had been gathering. It was ready to pounce.

And down. Through the false tomb. The walls on either side of the stairs reached up to enclose her as she descended. She was being held in a stone fist, and it was closing tight. The wind was strong, now. It whistled rough and hollow over giant lungs. In the sanctum, it whirled around the periphery of the room, flapping the tapestries. The figures writhed. Their movements hurt Meacham's head. The figures weren't moving in synch with the tapestries themselves. They were mercury on plastic, unfixed, running and flowing to no other rhythm than that of pain.

"Why are we here?" Hudson asked.

Gray paused before the table on which were laid out the implements of creative surgery. He ran his fingers over the blades. "Because I want you to see," he said.

"See what?"

"The truth. Everyone will, but you should see it at its source." He moved away from the table, approached the throne.

"Richard ..." Hudson began.

"Patrick," Gray responded, quick and sharp.

"No," Hudson pleaded.

Gray smiled and sat down heavily in the chair. Meacham heard fabric tear. She heard a sound like teeth biting into raw steak. Gray didn't wince. His smile didn't falter. It became more savage. After a moment, blood began a steady drip onto the floor. It came from the arms of the chair and from behind Gray's legs.

"What are you doing?" Hudson moaned.

Meacham said nothing. She watched Gray closely. There was no flicker of pain on his face. There was something almost like relief in his expression, as a long-bottled emotion was finally set free. His features darkened with anger. The smile became a snarl. "What am I doing?" he hissed. "I'm putting an end to lies."

"Five minutes," Boulter said.

They might come back, Sturghill thought. *What if they come back and can't make it out because we abandoned them? What if nobody makes it out because we waited too long?* She lit the cloth. If the burn worked, Meacham and Hudson would be able to follow. Trail-blazing, wasn't that what it was called? No metaphor this time. "Stand back," she said. They each held a bomb. Porter had a paint can of gasoline in each hand. Splash damage would be major bad. Ten steps back, then. The rag flamed. Sturghill aimed at the network of roots and branches that blocked the path. She threw the jar. It traced a comet-tail arc in the night. It landed on the roots. Glass shattered. Flaming petrol bloomed. It spread slick and bright. The flames billowed high. The explosion was lovely. Sturghill grinned. The crowd stirred. She heard a noise that sounded like the birth of hope.

Boulter followed up with her jar. *Whoomp.* Fires overlapped. The light was blinding. Sturghill shouted, giddy with warrior blood. She was fighting back, goddamn it, for the first time since she'd arrived at the Hall. She roared her hate for the place, yelled the flames higher. The fire pooled. It dimmed.

"*No!*" Sturghill shouted. "Don't let it die!"

Porter ran forward with his cans. He put one on the ground, hefted the other like a water bucket and tossed the gas onto the flames. He stumbled back from the flare-up, arm up to shield his eyes from the glare. He grabbed the other can, added its fuel to the blaze. Sturghill quailed at how quickly they were burning through their ammunition. Maybe, if the fire caught properly, it would take on its own life. Burn the whole wretched forest to ash.

The flames receded even faster this time, disappearing like a wave withdrawing from sand. Sturghill grabbed the wine bottle. One more jar after this, and two paint cans. She felt like crying as she lit the fuse and tossed it, wouldn't give the trees that satisfaction. "*Fuuuuck,*" she muttered, teeth clenched tight as a vise clamp. She threw the bomb into the guttering remains of the fire. Porter had the last jar coming in right behind. Boulter and Walker ran forward with the paint cans. Double-impact and double reinforcement. The fire rasped in effort, and died. That was it. No more bombs.

"Make more." It was Gifford. He had joined them when Sturghill had thrown the first jar, and had cheered as loudly as anyone.

Porter said. "I have plenty of bottles."

"Lots of petrol in our vehicles," Gifford added.

"Hang on," Sturghill said. *Right*, she thought, *go through the same exercise in futility.* She approached the forest. Throat dry, she reached out to touch the trunk of a tree she had napalmed. The bark was still mossy, still damp. Like nothing had happened. She had dreamed an incendiary attack, but the tree hadn't shared the dream. She backed off. "I don't think more of the same is going to do any good."

"I'm not giving up," Boulter said.

"I didn't say I was." So much fuel, she thought, looking at Porter's van. Inspiration. She pointed at the vehicle. "*That's* our bottle," she said. She picked up a rag.

"What?" Porter asked.

She took him by the sleeve, pulled him toward the van. "Get it into position," she said. "Your van's going to be a big bomb." *See you shrug that off,* she told the trees. *My greatest and last trick. It'll blow your mind.*

Porter climbed into the cab and started the engine. He manoeuvred it onto the drive, aiming it at the forest. Sturghill unscrewed the gas cap, stuck the rag in. Gifford ran up with a toolbox. Porter put the stick in neutral, yanked the handbrake on, and wedged the toolbox on the accelerator. The van roared, anxious to be off. Kamikaze. He came around the back, rooted through the supplies until he found a case of beer. He took it up front and used it to jam to the clutch to the floor. He put the van into first. "Ready," he called.

Sturghill lit the rag. She jumped back. "Go!" she yelled.

Porter released the handbrake and knocked the case off the clutch. The van leaped forward, its engine screaming as it over-revved madly. It rumbled up the drive and slammed into the trees. It skewed to the side, wheels still turning as its way was blocked. The flames raced up the rag and into the tank. "Abracadabra," Sturghill muttered.

The explosion lifted the van off its wheels. It somersaulted against the trees. The fireball raced upwards in the triumph of freedom. Sturghill winced. The radiant heat was a sharp pain on her forehead. Something in the forest shouted in answer. Rage filled the shadows beyond the flames. *Now you're hurting*, Sturghill thought.

Metal screamed. The van didn't right itself. It stayed vertical. At first, Sturghill thought the wreckage had tangled itself in the trunks and branches. She waited to see trees topple. None did. The van seemed to shrink. It shook. More shrieks. The first dazzling brightness of the flames passed, and the forest became more than an indistinct black mass. In the fading light of the fire, Sturghill saw that the van wasn't tangled. It was held. Branches were wrapped around its middle. They squeezed. The van crumpled. The branches tightened, a fist around a soft drink can. Death cries from the vehicle. It shrank in on itself. The fire died with it. The forest stood, unbroken but angry now. Wood creaked. Big things rustled in the darkness. Sturghill looked at the barrier of yew trees. She saw branches begin to wave like Medusa snakes. She knew she'd lost. A huge sound, then. It was the sound of a vast movement, big enough to be an ocean in storm, bigger. It was a terrible uncoiling of strength. A wave was coming. A tsunami was coming. But the sound was not water. It was wood. Wood had never made that sound before. It had never been angered and strong with truth before.

"Run," Sturghill tried to say, and suddenly she was dreaming awake. She was trapped in nightmare paralysis. Her lips barely formed the word. Her lungs were weak and sluggish. She couldn't make any noise at all, much less one that might be heard over the sound of the forest. She didn't have to shout a warning. She was aware of the others running fast, as if from judgment. She hitched a chest-shaking sigh. She tried to say, "Run," again. She was speaking to herself, to her motionless body. The word came out as a lazy, drawn-out whisper, shamed by anaesthetized tongue and lips. She still couldn't move. "Help," she tried. The word was weaker than a tear. There was no one to hear.

The forest was upon her. The trees were size and rage. Their roots did not move, but they advanced all the same. They were strong with age and history. They had seen centuries and knew what that time had to hide. The smell of moss and bark filled Sturghill's nostrils. Her eardrums burst with the pressure of the noise. Branches swept towards her, a rigid writhing. She closed her eyes, but she was still dreaming, and so she still saw everything. Right up to the end, as the wood crushed her and filled her.

And after that, there was still more to see.

"What lies?" Meacham asked. She wanted to know. She wanted to stall. She didn't know what else to do.

Gray's snarl almost turned into a laugh. "That's nicely disingenuous, coming from you. All lies. Two lies in particular." He shook his head. "No. It doesn't matter which lies. It's their opposite that's important."

"If you're worried about a cover-up," Meacham began, knowing, even as she forged on, that this was the most trivial and stupid thing she would ever say in her life, "I can promise to —"

"Oh, shut up." Gray was rightly contemptuous.

"What lies?" Hudson asked. His voice was a pale tremble. In his tone, there was a terror of answers.

"Yours," Gray said softly. "And hers."

"I never lied to you." Hudson was shocked.

"You don't think you did, because you were telling yourself the same lie." Gray's eyes were shining anticipation. The moment was his, and he was stretching it. He was living the culmination of something that Meacham didn't understand. Gray pointed at her, but he never stopped looking at Hudson. "She said there was no God." The finger shifted. "You said there was an all-loving one."

"There is," Hudson whispered, a last-chance plea on his own behalf. Meacham heard a man who, desperate as he was to save his friend, was even more desperate to save his truth.

Gray sat back against the spikes of the chair. He grinned in the relief of gouging pain. "You're both going to be wrong." His right hand grew a claw in Meacham's flashlight beam. He had palmed a blade from the table. It was six inches long, hooked for gutting, saurian black iron. He raised it, as if it were the material evidence of his claim. Perhaps it was. Meacham couldn't move. Hudson moaned but stood still. Oncoming revelation was holding them fast. Gray's eyes focused on the tapestry behind Meacham's head. His face sagged. She didn't understand the expression she saw. The anger hadn't gone. Nor had the triumph. But they were fused with grief, a greater terror, and an even more terrible acceptance. Then he spoke. The revelation was a single sentence. Four words. "God is the Reptile."

He dragged the hooked blade across his throat. The movement was harsh, powerful, jagged. The knife was old. It had been dulled, perhaps deliberately, perhaps through use. Gray had to work hard. He dug the hook into the side of his neck and pulled, hacking through flesh and tendons. The blade went deep. Meacham heard the sound of gristle parting. Gray's head lolled back too far. Blood gouted. His arm didn't relax. It finished the act. *He's dead*, Meacham thought. *He's dead. He can stop now.* But the gesture was important, and it carried through to its end, the arm gathering energy as it hacked through the last of the throat. It flung out to the side, job done, and went limp. The fist didn't open. It held on to the knife. Gray's mouth moved. There was a gurgling sound, and then there was nothing but blood. It poured black from his mouth. It sprayed from the wound. Some of it hit Meacham and Hudson. Most of it poured down the front of Gray's body. It drenched him, clothed him in a red, shining robe. It flowed into the gutters around the iron throne. It pooled on the floor. It disappeared down drains, feeding something beneath.

Meacham had exactly one moment to think that the blood was what Rose wanted, that it was the key she needed to unlock absolute freedom, and then even that idea died, a comforting illusion. It wasn't the blood. It was the act. The willing sacrifice on the altar of truth.

Gray's corpse became harder to make out. The flashlights were failing. Meacham gasped and turned the light to look at the bulb. She was almost blinded. The batteries were fine. The lights weren't going out. It was the darkness that was gathering. Ectoplasmic mist formed around Gray. It grew dense. Meacham grabbed Hudson's sleeve and yanked him after her. They ran. As they left the chamber, Meacham caught a glimpse of a tapestry. One of the damned had Gray's face.

John Porter saw what the trees had done to Sturghill. He looked back over his shoulder as he ran. He saw them line up and advance. Fully mature yew trees, giant with age, were tangled together, a monolithic hedge. They had become a tightening noose around the grounds of Gethsemane Hall. No way through them. Nowhere to run except towards the Hall. Porter felt like a pheasant, flushed by the beaters towards the hunter's guns in the house.

The party was over. Screaming everywhere. The treeline reached the marquee tent. Branches coiled around it, lifted it up and shredded the canvas. Roots tangled and crushed tables. Not everyone was running fast enough. Porter saw an older woman stumble, fall. The roots wrapped around her. The sound of bones cracking to shards travelled across the lawn.

Then the worst thing happened. Porter didn't know what it was, only that it had taken place, and the last of hope had suddenly died. Something spread itself over the Hall and the grounds in a rush. His vision began to swim. His flight slowed. He tried to run faster, but he couldn't. He could barely move at all. He was still moving as if he were running, his legs working in slow motion, but it took endless seconds for each step to happen. He realized he was dreaming and tried to laugh with crazy relief. There was only weakness in his chest, and the laugh was a half-wheeze. A nightmare. He was at home. In a moment, the monster would come for him, the big fear would arrive, and he would wake. His foot finally finished its descent. It hit the ground with an impact that ran up his spine. He could feel the burn in his lungs from running. The night breathed against his skin, a cold wind growing to chill his sweat. He was awake. He was dreaming. His nightmare was leaking out into the conscious world and becoming flesh. His pre-scream breath was long and slow in building. His shriek was silent, as all nightmare cries are. His right foot caught itself up in the left, as it would have to. He fell through air thick as dough. It took a long time to hit the ground. He landed on his side and saw the trees marching forward. Were they dreaming, too? Perhaps this was their dream: to move and grind the mammals that had shaped them, trimmed them, mutilated them, ruled their fates. Now they were nothing but motion and vengeance.

The dreams spread. He tried to rise, but the weight of the air was now on him, a palm pressing him hard into the earth. Everyone he saw was stumbling, clawing at things in front of their eyes, falling.

The ground beneath him squirmed.

They were climbing the spiral staircase to the crypt when the nightmares began. Strength had gathered behind them in the tapestry chamber and then leapt through and ahead of them, engulfing the world of Gethsemane Hall. Hudson felt the nature of things change. At first, he and Meacham were left alone. He hoped they were being ignored, beneath notice. Then, on the stairs, he saw Meacham gasp and bang against the wall. He opened his mouth to ask what was wrong, and then he was dreaming too. The staircase doubled. Overlaid on the real one was another, running slick with blood. The walls began to flake black chunks. A smell dug into his nostrils, pungent and eye-watering in its awful identity. The stone of the walls had become burning flesh. He struggled to retain his footing. He tried to see through the blood and flesh to the real. He put his foot down, and it slipped in blood. He reached out to steady himself. The wall beneath his hand gave and trembled. It was hot. Its pulse was very, very fast. The lesson Gray had begun to teach sank in further. The nightmare hadn't infected and disguised reality. The illusion of the comforting mundane was being scorched away, revealing the nightmare at the heart. The nightmare *was* the real. He took another step, prepared to sink ankle-deep in gore, and his balance steadied. "Accept it," he called to Meacham. He was preaching Gray's word, Rose's word. He cursed the world. "Don't try to fight what you're seeing. It isn't you. It's really there."

Meacham found her footing. They splashed up the rest of the way, against the current, trying not to touch the agonized walls. Hudson's vision stabilized. The ordinary staircase faded away, its illusion dying. When they reached the crypt, Hudson almost fell again. For a moment, the double-vision returned, two identical visions of Gethsemane Hall dancing over each other. The house as he had known it, and as it really was, were the same. He and Meacham paused, catching their breath. The sense of oasis was false, and he knew it, but he took it anyway. He looked around. "Why?" he asked. Why hadn't it changed?

Meacham grunted. "Because it was the lure," she said.

Hudson pictured it. The house as an extrusion of the real, calling and seducing, powerful because it wasn't disguised, effective because it appeared to belong. It was a monster that could hide in plain sight.

Screams outside. Bigger sounds, too. Huge movement. "Where do we go?" Hudson asked.

He was speaking to himself, putting his fear into words, but Meacham answered. "Outside. Like we said we would."

"They're dead."

"Probably." She started moving again anyway, leaving the crypt, heading for what waited beyond the walls.

"And if they are?" Hudson asked.

Meacham said nothing, walked briskly.

Hudson caught up. "What are we going to do?" he insisted.

Meacham said, "How well can you die?"

Hudson wondered about that as they walked through the Great Hall. Each echo of their footsteps felt different now. The sounds did not belong to them. They were another creation of the real, a planned element of Gethsemane Hall's bait. They were as much a piece of the house as the timbers and masonry.

Could he die well? He wanted to. In Darfur, he could have. There, he'd been surrounded by the savage worthlessness of man, but he'd had God. There had been faith and its promises. He could have fallen there. He wished he had. He would have been happy in his last moment, ignorant of what really waited on the other side. That ignorance had been stolen from him now. He still wanted to believe. More than ever, he needed his faith. But Gray had killed it.

God is the Reptile.

What was left was human dignity? Die well. Don't bow your head to the worship of agony. Make that futile gesture as a gift to yourself. And try not to think about what comes next. *I can do this*, he thought. *I can do this.*

The outer hall. The courtyard. The main gate. They were at the exit. They crossed the moat. They saw what was outside.

Hudson tried to utter the word *no.* He couldn't. The denial that filled him was too huge. It couldn't come out. It filled his chest to bursting. And it was also too small. In the face of what he saw, denial was senseless.

They were back in the cave. The tapestries had followed them here. There was nothing but the tapestries. The gardens had become the depictions of Hell. There were cauldrons. There were crucifixes. There were flames. There were the damned. The yew trees were the borders, containing the art and celebrating it with storming, writhing branches. The wind was the sound of the screams.

There were the coils.

Immensity moved through the gardens. It governed the atrocities. It looked upon its good works. It made them happen. It was too big for Hudson to make out a shape. He saw scales. They said *god*. They said *dragon*. They hurt his eyes. He was too small to look at the lord of the dance. So his gaze went to the suffering. He had recognized faces in the tapestries. Here he *saw* the faces. There were no representations. That really was John Porter on a crucifix, only it was a crucifix *in* John Porter. The vertical beam plunged between his legs and emerged from his mouth. The cross-beam shot out of his wrists. His head was split wide open, his jaw into four hanging pieces. He was dead. He still screamed. His body still pulsed and twitched against the wood. So did those of every other person on the grounds. In their thousands. The town of Roseminster was dead and shrieking in Hudson's face. Hudson saw what his faith was worth, and he shrieked back.

Consequences. Connections. Viral infection. Spread.

In London, the good news editors of the print and visual media were working phones, digitally circling the black hole into which their staff had fallen. They knew their people had been off to a big do at Gethsemane Hall. Some had even been in contact as they approached the gate to the grounds. And then nothing. The silence stretched long. The editors told themselves they were angry at derelictions of duty, at failures of responsibility. They wondered why their palms were so sweaty, why their hearts were sick and pounding.

In his office in the MI-5 building, Gerald Fretwell was ploughing through files that had nothing to do with Pete Adams and Gethsemane Hall. But suddenly he was thinking of the scream recording, and he was hearing the sound of the shriek in his head, not cut off this time, but going on and on, building in pain and horror, and he was trying very hard not to scream himself.

In Washington, DC, it was late afternoon. Jim Korda was working hard and sweating worse. The Geneva shitstorm had birthed a new one. The designated scapegoat was fighting back. Things were hitting too close to home. His position was not secure. He was having to move beyond aggressive damage control and into pre-emptive strikes. His mind wasn't on Meacham's mission. That scandal was a mosquito annoyance. He was worrying about exploding hornets' nests. So was President Sam Reed. Korda had him on the horn. Reed asked a question. Korda opened his mouth to answer.

"Jim?" Reed asked into the silence.

Korda heard the president. He couldn't answer. He was having a nightmare, and he couldn't punch through it back to waking reality. Claws sharpened on fear sank into his gut. In the dream, he was dying. The world had gone a searing flash-white. It was filled with a sound so loud it destroyed his hearing, and Reed's voice disappeared along with everything else. He was burning. His flesh was evaporating from his bones. His bones were disintegrating. He knew his death was done in an instant, but it took a very long time. It was eternity. His dead tongue found its voice in the dream.

In the White House, Sam Reed jerked away from the phone and the howl.

Meacham retreated a step from the phantasmagoria of the gardens. Hudson had fallen to his knees. She looked away from the torture and the coiling. She kept her eyes on the ground. It was bad enough. The gravel looked like skin. It heaved with slow, lizard movements. Its texture was familiar in all the wrong ways. She reached out and grabbed Hudson by the collar. He didn't respond, wouldn't stop screaming. "Patrick!" she yelled, and yanked. "Get away from there." Hudson fell over. His face went slack. The screams moved into his eyes. Meacham looked closely. Her breath caught. Hudson's pupils had expanded, swallowing up the whites. Their darkness didn't reflect Meacham's face. They were the torture garden in miniature, updated in real-time. Meacham backed away from him. Hudson's agony was working on him from the inside out. As she stepped backwards into the courtyard, Hudson's body began to jerk as the pain made its way out. Something that looked like a mouth formed in the ground just outside the Hall's entrance. It was a tube lined with teeth. It grabbed Hudson's ankle and sucked him off the bridge. He raised his head, and Meacham knew he was dead now. He turned to face her. There was pleading on his face as he was dragged into Hell.

Meacham ran back inside the house. In the Great Hall, she hesitated. She had run out of actions. She wanted to burn the house down. She knew the attempt would be pointless. Reality was waiting for her outside. If it grew bored, it would take her in the house. The Hall wasn't a refuge. It was an antechamber.

Nothing left to do. And yet her mind was working the details of what she had seen outside as if there were something that didn't fit. False dawn hope, she thought, dismissive of her own efforts.

Come for me, then. She wouldn't go rushing for the end. She might yet pull off that good death, like that was worth anything. She made her way to the library. The howls of the wind and the damned were more muted here. She kept her face turned away from the window. She approached an armchair. She almost didn't sit down, in case it decided to eat her. But then, there was nothing preventing the floor from doing the same thing. She sat. The upholstery didn't feel any different. *All right,* she thought. *Let's get this over with.* She waited.

Night deepened. She didn't know if that was because time was passing or not. She didn't think she'd been sitting there long before the shape formed in the centre of the room. The black ectoplasm gathered consistency and definition. It became the silhouette of a woman. The silhouette took on pale colouring. It grew a face. It was a bone-white, angular, iceberg woman. Rose looked at Meacham steadily. *Special treatment for the last in line*, Meacham thought. Rose glided forward.

The wrong details clicked into place. Gray's phrasing: "You're both *going to be* wrong." And there had been another texture overlying the vistas outside. She glanced away from the ghost, let herself go cross-eyed and saw the twinned versions of the Hall again, and saw that they weren't identical. One of them had the same quality as the gardens. The texture was a grid, a weave, *textile*. A tapestry. She looked back at the ghost. Rose had seen the real and was bringing her message to the rest of the world, but she hadn't really opened up the portal. The world that had swallowed Meacham's reality was another simulacrum, closer yet to the truth, but still an interpretation. It was Rose's testament, her evangel. It took power from its accuracy, but it was still a shadow on Plato's wall. It was a prophecy. It was a real yet to come, a truth so terrible that the power of its mere arrival echoed down to the present and past and made all other truths lies because they would end.

If only Hudson had known. The coming truth was even worse than what had killed him.

(God is the Reptile.)

"Wait," Meacham said, and perhaps because she wasn't pleading, merely asking to finish her thought, the ghost paused. Her mind sped. She was back in Intelligence again. She had never left. The arc of her career had been aimed at this point. Her working life had been tied to the control of information, its spread, its distortion, its suppression. Its release. She made compromises. She brokered deals. She had sold her soul a hundred times over. She could do it again. Anything to hold onto life a little bit longer, to stave off the inevitable. "I can help you," she said.

There was no expression on the ghost's face. Its angles deepened slightly, as if amused.

"What are you going to do after me?" Meacham asked. She was making a pitch. "Stay here like a spider, waiting for the next flies? That's no way to spread the truth."

The ghost was motionless, waiting.

Meacham was sweating. How much time was she buying with each word? *I want years,* she thought. *Many years. I can't face that eternity.* "When this is over," she said, "people are going to wonder what happened. If there's no one left, how will anyone learn the truth?" *Use the words that will resonate.* "How will anyone hear your gospel? How will anyone know the prophecy? You need an apostle."

I swear I'll be that apostle, she thought. She didn't need to speak.

Rose cocked her head. She floated towards Meacham again. A hand, white as the face, emerged from the ectoplasm. It stretched out a finger. Meacham waited for it touch her, but the finger paused, having covered only half the distance between them. The ghost waited. Meacham swallowed, and reached out with her right hand. She extended her index finger and touched the ghost's.

The last layer was stripped away. The tapestry was pulled back, and Meacham *saw.*

chapter twenty-three

catch and release

Meacham walked up the drive from Gethsemane Hall. The web was ready once again. The gardens were quiet, their grooming perfect. There were no bodies. There was no trace of the party. The air was fresh with morning. Meacham heard birds. The woods were well-behaved and did not block her path. They held shadows. The smell of moss was the reminder of darkness.

She reached the gate. It was open. She marched along the road to the ghost town. She would wait at the train station. If the authorities arrived first, she would deal with them and answer their questions. If the train came first, she would board it and head for London. She had a lot of travel ahead.

She would keep her word. She would spread Rose's virus. The contagion of future reality would eat away at the foundations of the illusion she had bargained to live in for a bit longer. She didn't care for it as much as she thought she did. Not now. She understood Rose's contempt for the lie.

Meacham had touched the truth of the coming god.

More Fiction from Dundurn

Blind Luck
by Scott Carter
978-1926607009
$18.95

Dave Bolden's life feels like it's on repeat. He works his eight hours at an accounting firm, goes home, gets drunk, and wakes up the next day to go back to work with a hangover. But his life changes when a truck crashes through the front windows of his workplace, killing everyone but him. Shortly after the accident, he is approached by an eccentric businessman, Mr. Thorrin, who interprets Dave's survival as luck and sets out to exploit what he perceives as a gift. Thorrin wants Dave to participate in gambling, stock manipulation, and extreme betting, all based on this belief.

Complicating Dave's life further is his strained relationship with his father, a lifelong compulsive gambler. The more he interacts with his father, the more he realizes a series of events from his childhood supports the theory that he is unusually lucky. What follows is a series of extreme tests of luck, orchestrated by the very mysterious Mr. Thorrin. As the stakes rise both financially and personally, Dave is left to decide whether his run of good fortune is a gift or a curse.

The Sixth Extinction
by d leonard freeston
978-1554889037
$22.99

Jason Conrad, a man with the wealth of Bill Gates, decides to preserve for posterity the seeds of as many animal and plant species as possible in a vast and remote underground facility, taking the world's legitimate seed banks and "frozen zoos" to a whole new level. Conrad's secret doomsday complex, though, is staffed by a combination of environmental experts and mercenaries who will stop at nothing to achieve their once-noble ambitions.

After a fellow police officer is murdered and his award-winning German shepherd disappears, Montreal Sergeant-Detective Irina Drach and her young partner, Sergeant-Detective Hudson, connect the crime with a seed bank raid in Ardingly, England, and the kidnapping of a Triple Crown Thoroughbred named Zarathustra. Soon it becomes apparent that highly organized, ruthless abduction teams are raiding seed banks around the world, as well as scooping up the finest animal specimens from zoos, nature preserves, and the wild. Despite the global implications and ballooning media interest, however, Irina never forgets that her foremost aim is to solve the murder of a friend and fellow officer.

Available at your favourite bookseller.

DUNDURN
www.dundurn.com

What did you think of this book?
Visit www.dundurn.com for reviews, videos, updates, and more!